ERIN HAWKINS

UNEXPECTEDLY IN LOVE SERIES BOOK ONE

Reluctantly Yours

Edited by Chelly Peeler inkitoutediting.com

Cover Design by Cover Ever After covereverafter.com

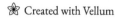 Created with Vellum

CHAPTER 1
Barrett

The clinking of spoons against champagne glasses rises to an ear-splitting level around me. I use the deafening sound as an excuse to extract myself from another tedious conversation with members of New York City's upper crust.

"Another whiskey, neat, please." I set my empty glass on the bar.

Behind me, the sharp sound dissipates indicating that the bride and groom have given in to the obnoxious tradition and kissed.

The bartender makes quick work of filling my glass, a large square ice cube and two fingers of Macallan, but not quick enough to allow me to escape my mother, who is quickly approaching. She's wearing a beaded gown, likely one of hundreds she owns, her makeup is professionally done for the occasion and her short, white hair is curled and styled to perfection.

"There you are, Barrett. I haven't seen you since the cock-tail hour." She looks pointedly at the amber liquid in my glass. "It appears you're still there."

"Good evening, Mother." I lean down far enough so she

can access my cheek. I may be avoiding her but now that she's found me, there's no reason to be an asshole.

"It was a lovely wedding, wasn't it?" she asks while waving to a couple across the room.

JoAnna St. Clair is in her element. A social butterfly regaling in the love that two people have found with each other. She's a romantic and jumps at any chance to celebrate love. Or to try and convince me I'm missing out by being alone.

She's the head of publishing at St. Clair Press, the publishing house she and my father started. St. Clair Press is housed under the parent company St. Clair Media, known in the industry as SCM.

I nod. "Sure."

What I mean is I'm guessing it was. I had been checking work emails in the pew during the ceremony.

"Did you speak with Mark and Amber?" she asks.

I nod solemnly.

"Yes, I gave them my condolences," I cough, "I mean best wishes for a long and happy marriage."

I raise my glass in the air in a mock toast.

I find weddings and love in general to be a waste of my time.

I give her my best smile, which the alcohol has made a bit lazy. She glances around the room, a brilliant smile plastered to her face. Only I can see the tightness in her jaw.

"It wouldn't kill you to at least talk to her."

"Who would that be, Mother? The woman you set me up with tonight unwillingly, or her mother that is already picking out names for our non-existent children?" I take another sip. I love the burning sensation the whiskey creates in my stomach. It overpowers the headache that my mother's meddling in my personal life always creates.

"You're being ridiculous. It was just an idea that Estelle and I had. We thought you two might hit it off."

Estelle being my mother's tennis partner at the club. I'm sure this plan was hatched post victory over dirty martinis with the vision of chubby-cheeked grandbabies dancing in their heads.

"Because we have so much in common?" I practically snort.

My second drink of the evening was the only thing that got me through listening to Kristin, Krista, or was it Kristy's sorority house drama. Kristy, I'm seventy-five percent sure. Something about her best friend's boyfriend dating another girl behind her back, and they were all roommates, I think. Shit, I give myself props for listening that long.

Estelle's daughter is the latest in a long line of set ups my mother has attempted. Kristy is a twenty-two-year-old socialite who just graduated college and is looking to find a husband and become a housewife. Good luck to her, because I'm not that guy.

I don't have time for personal exploits. The sole reason for accepting today's invitation is for business purposes. Not so my mother can play matchmaker.

I would think my mother would be running out of female relatives of her friends and acquaintances, but being the warm and friendly extrovert that she is, she will likely never run out of fresh-faced females to dangle in front of me. No disrespect, the women are nice, I'm sure. They would make another man happy and content, but that is not the focus of my life right now.

Closing a deal with Voltaire Telecom is my sole focus. Why can't my mother see that my attention needs to be on the company my father started? The company that after my father's death, my Uncle Leo, a delightfully charming man with no business sense, slowly ran into the ground in my late teens and early twenties. A company that she still holds the majority stock in and has entrusted me to run.

My mother side-eyes me. I can tell she's waiting for me to cave on this. To be the obedient son she raised. That's the thing. I have always conceded and done what I was supposed to. I've gotten good grades, gone to the right schools, taken over the family business. But I'll be damned if I'm going to let my mother interfere with my personal life. I'm thirty-two years old and I have no intention of settling down. Especially not for someone my mother handpicked for me.

"It's wedding season, Barrett."

It's her way of telling me that she's got three months' worth of events to ambush me with more of her future daughter-in-law candidates. It's my mother's version of a threat. She doesn't come right out and tell me she's going to drive me insane over the next few months trying to set me up with a date at every social event we attend, but I know her and she doesn't give up that easily.

"There's an actual season for dry cake and misery?" I ask, deadpan, then take another sip of my whiskey.

She ignores my jab.

"I know you're working on Voltaire Telecom and the importance of that acquisition is not lost on me, but you need to find balance. Besides, it might do you some good to have a woman on your arm at business dinners. I sat alongside your father for thirty-five years, so trust me, I know how it works."

I hum around a sip of my whiskey. I know she's right in some respects, but I refuse to give her any encouragement.

"Tessa Green. She's thirty and a lawyer with Cooper Stanley Williams. She's smart and beautiful. The least you can do is meet her for lunch. I'll have Chloe set it up."

At the mention of my mother's assistant, the muscles in my shoulders tense. It's an automatic response. Chloe Anderson tests my limits with every encounter. She's been my mother's assistant for two years, and though I rarely see her, my mind easily conjures her image. Her fiery red hair always pulled up into a knot on her head, allowing access to her slender neck. Those crystal blue eyes, which I find on most occasions pinning me with a disapproving glare, are other worldly. For every inch her petite frame is lacking, she makes up for it in snark and bite. She's a pint-sized human carrying out my mother's agenda, which on occasion, like setting up blind dates, only makes my life more difficult.

The fact that my mother would request for her to set up a reservation for a lunch date that I have no interest in going on only fuels my dislike for her. It's unwarranted, but none-theless, it's my only defense mechanism at this point.

"I'm sure Tessa is a nice woman, but I'm not taking her to lunch. My calendar is already full with business meetings."

She hums her disapproval. It's a trait we share, apparently.

"Have it your way, Barrett."

It's a parting shot. A warning that this discussion and her plan to set me up with every fertile woman she runs into isn't over.

She smiles sweetly before leaning in to kiss me on the cheek. I watch as her retreating back is swallowed into the crowd of gowns and tuxedos.

With my mother off my back for now, I scan the crowd until my gaze lands on the large, bald head of Fred Hinkle, President and CEO of Voltaire Telecom. The shine bouncing off his head is like a North Star guiding me home. My feet immediately start moving, my eyes scanning the periphery to avoid being trapped into another conversation with Kristy.

Fred Hinkle and the acquisition of his company, Voltaire Telecom, will secure SCM's place at the top of the media industry. To the company it was when my father was running it. It's the only goal I've had for the past seven years. Every meeting, every deal I've made, every acquisition I've completed has been in pursuit of restoring SCM's legacy. Now, I'm so close. There's no way I can take my eyes off the ball now.

The shiny, gleaming ball that is Fred Hinkle's scalp.

"Fred." I place a hand on his suit-clad shoulder. He turns from the group he's talking to, his jovial smile dropping when his eyes recognize me.

Fred doesn't like me. He thinks I'm an arrogant businessman buying and gutting other businesses at the expense of the hard-working people who have made them what they are.

It would be hearsay but he told me that himself when I tried to book a meeting with him.

'A vulture preying on the weak' is what he likened me to.

He'd be right. I have had to make decisions along the way that cost workers' jobs but it wasn't personal, it was business. Decisions that were right for my company in the long run.

He also does not want to sell Voltaire Telecom voluntarily. His company is in trouble. Banks are calling on their loans, investors want payouts and his stock is plummeting. He's desperate for a cash injection. A takeover is inevitable, and I've put SCM in the perfect position to do it. Fred has a crumbling empire, but he's got enough time and wherewithal to be able to choose who is going to pick up the pieces. I need him to choose me.

But there are plenty of other companies that are jockeying for the same position.

The man talking to Fred is Ryan Shaw.

If I'm a vulture, then Ryan is a leech.

His company, Shaw & Graham, is SCM's biggest competitor. Competition is healthy. That's not my issue with him. But, whenever I'm at the table with a company for a deal or merger, he's on my heels trying to beat me to it. The man doesn't have an original idea. He waits for me to make my intentions known, then tosses his hat into the ring.

"Mr. St. Clair." Fred's use of formality is his way of

keeping me aware of the situation. He's in his sixties, and that generation always had their own way of doing things. Like the fact that he won't take a meeting with me so I've reduced myself to stalking him at an event I knew he would be at. While it is questionable if he will be at the gala or fundraiser of the week, I knew he wouldn't miss his daughter's wedding.

"St. Clair." Ryan gives me a nod and a smirk.

"Shaw." I respond with my own nod, but I keep my attention on Fred.

"Mr. Hinkle, it was a beautiful wedding. Amber looked stunning. I'm sure you're a proud father tonight." Amber and I went to prep school together, and our mothers are friends. That's the only reason I was invited to this wedding. That and I'm sure with a million more important things to do, Fred didn't bother to monitor the guest list.

Fred's face softens with the mention of his daughter.

"I'm a very proud father."

A faraway look takes over his face, his smile returns and his eyes go misty. Fred looks like he's moments away from becoming a blubbering mess. My collar feels tight, suffocating. Maybe this is what I get for trying to talk to a man who just gave away his little girl. Fuck.

For a moment I think he's going to turn back toward the group he was talking with and leave it at that, but something over my shoulder catches his eye.

"Are you missing your date?"

"What?"

I turn to find Kristy bouncing on her heels to scan over the crowd. Before she spots me, I turn back to Fred.

"No." I shake my head. "No date."

The corners of Fred's lips turn down, the frown lines near his mouth are set deep, indicating his innate preference for displeasure.

I was hoping to take full advantage of his jovial mood, and

possibly the fact that like me, Fred's had a few drinks tonight. My mind is searching for what went wrong. Fred was talking about his daughter, family and love. He was happy. He asked if I had a date, I said no and then he frowned. If there's one thing I've excelled at in business, it's reading people and being able to appeal to their emotions. While I never like to mix emotions with business, I don't mind playing on someone else's to get what I want.

I'm trying to find my angle when a woman approaches Fred from behind. Her manicured nails, which are a good three inches long, scrape along the fabric at the shoulder of his suit jacket before she places her glossy pink lips onto his cheek.

"There you are, baby," she coos.

Fred lights up at this woman's affection. Fred and Helen have been divorced for a few years now, but I wasn't aware that Fred had a new woman in his life. She's young, closer to my age, at least twenty years younger than Fred. In her high heels, she towers over his hairless head, her long blonde hair straight and shiny, nearly draping over his shoulder. She moves to Fred's side to reveal a curvy body encased in a dark blue satin gown, her large breasts barely held in by thin spaghetti straps.

"Hi there." The woman turns her attention on me. "I'm Frankie."

She smiles and extends a hand out to me.

"Barrett St. Clair."

I shake her hand, a surprisingly awkward task with her long nails. I turn her hand to examine said nails.

"Those are quite the nails."

It wasn't exactly a compliment but Frankie takes it as such.

"Oh my God, thank you. They're part of the nail line I'm launching." She wiggles her fingers with excitement. I take a step back to avoid an eyebrow gash. "Frankie's Faux Nails. That's what we've come up with so far, right, baby?"

We both turn toward Fred, while Frankie seems oblivious, I can see that Fred's eyes are narrowed. And directed at me.

Uh oh. I know what that look is and it's not '*hey, man, can I buy you a beer and discuss your takeover of my company?*'

It's territorial. My mind goes back to Fred's displeasure of me not having a date. Now having met Frankie, I can see why Fred would want to keep her away from any age appropriate, successful, single men. That being me.

While I have no interest in Frankie, Fred doesn't know that.

"That's wonderful. I bet my girlfriend would love them." The words tumble out before I can fully realize the consequences of what I'm about to say.

"Girlfriend?" Fred asks, surprised. "You said you didn't have a date."

"She's out of town. Visiting her family," I lie.

Fred's frown lines smooth as his mouth ticks up a quarter of an inch.

"So, there is a heart beneath that tuxedo jacket."

"You bet." I smile, knowing I've made some kind of crack in Fred's impenetrable exterior. And because I'm on a roll, and want to assure him I have no interest in his girlfriend, I continue, "She's the love of my life."

"Ahh." Frankie sighs, clutching a hand to her chest. Her nails press into her breasts, indenting the skin there.

"Good," Fred affirms, his animosity gone. "I'm glad you're not just tolling away in your ivory tower. That you've found something, *someone* that is more important than business."

"Of course not. What is life without love? I wouldn't be the successful man I am today without it. *Her*, I mean. She's great. It's a shame that she wasn't able to make it tonight. I would have loved for you to meet her. Both of you." I nod to Frankie. "I think you two would get along great."

At this point, I don't know what is coming out of my

mouth, but Fred's newfound willingness to talk with me makes it impossible to stop.

"We totally would." Frankie nods, even though I have given zero information about my supposed girlfriend.

Fred stares at me a moment longer than feels comfortable. His blank stare makes me think that maybe I went too far, that he knows I'm full of shit and he's going to call me out on it. But Frankie shrieks with excitement.

"Oh my God, you guys. We should totally do a double date." Frankie bounces next to Fred, stroking his chest with her Wolverine-like nails.

The universe must be on my side because Fred breaks into a huge grin.

"Let's do that." Fred nods. "A week from Saturday."

"Sounds great," I say with all the confidence of a man who has a girlfriend.

Apparently, I've found an in with Fred Hinkle. The only problem now is I have a week to find this so called 'love of my life.'

CHAPTER 2

Chloe

"You fell asleep with a book on your face again, didn't you?" Jules, my friend and co-worker at St. Clair Press, points at the crease lines that must still be prominent on my face.

While she places her coffee order, I scrub at my cheek. I'd hoped they'd have softened by now.

We're at the coffee shop down the street from our office building.

"Please tell me you didn't ditch me this weekend to read manuscripts," she says.

I smile sheepishly.

"Would you feel better if that wasn't the only reason?" I ask.

Yes, I was reading, but most of my Saturday afternoon was spent gathering supplies for my childhood best friend's bachelorette party. Lauren, her mom and aunt, along with her friends and co-workers will be descending on New York City Friday afternoon. The thought makes the mocha latte I just consumed swirl in my belly.

"All right, you get a pass." Jules grabs her coffee off the counter. "How's everything going for Lauren's party?"

"I think I'm all set." I shrug, following her out the door. "I've never thrown a bachelorette party before."

"That's because who gets married at twenty-five anymore? At our age, how can you commit to one dick and know you're making the right decision?" She waves to the bustling streets around us. "I mean this city alone has a sea of dicks just waiting to be explored."

A man walking by gives Jules a concerned look, but she walks on, oblivious.

Two years ago, Jules and I started on the same day at St. Clair Press, one of the top publishing companies in the country. She's a marketing assistant and I'm the editorial assistant for JoAnna St. Clair, the founder and publisher of St. Clair Press. We're completely different, but I think that's what makes our friendship work.

"I don't know. Love, I guess?" I wouldn't know much about either, love or committing to one dick. In this city of apparent endless dicks—according to Jules—I've yet to explore even one. The last dick I encountered was in college three years ago. It seems like a lifetime. Would I even know what to do? Is it like riding a bicycle, you just remember how?

Maybe that's why I'm nervous about this weekend. I want everything to go smoothly, as anyone throwing a party for a major milestone in their childhood best friend's life would want, but after being in New York for two years, it feels like I should have more glamour and excitement in my life. Lauren thinks I do. That was her reason for wanting to celebrate her impending nuptials in the city that never sleeps. Little does she know, I'm usually passed out by ten o'clock. The only reason I'm up past midnight is if I can't put down the book I'm reading.

I'll give myself some credit. I did move to New York City on my own, without knowing anyone. I found my apartment in East Harlem. It's a shoebox, but it's all mine. No roommates or pesky younger siblings rummaging through my stuff and stealing my dad's hand-me-down vintage concert t-shirts. As the oldest of five kids, I earned those.

And, out of a large and highly-qualified pool of candidates, JoAnna St. Clair selected me as her editorial assistant. So maybe the pressure of living up to her expectations has put my love life, aka dick exploration, on pause. Like Jules said, we're only twenty-five, there's plenty of time for that.

"We were at Bounce on Saturday. It was such a vibe. Oh! And I met a guy." She takes a sip of her iced caramel macchiato. "For you."

"For me?"

"Yes! He's handsome and successful. A finance guy or something. The music was really loud. I didn't get the details, but I showed him a picture of you and he said he was interested."

"I don't love blind dates. You know I'm not the best at going in blind. I need talking points. Areas of common interest."

"How about you're both attractive people that are interested in sex at the end of the night?"

"Jules." I level her with a stare.

"What? It works for me." She tosses her empty coffee in a nearby trash can before she follows me into our building. "And I already set it up. So you could go and see what you think. No pressure."

I sigh. "When?"

"Next week. Wednesday. For dinner."

"Fine," I say, punching the elevator button.

"This will be good for you. You'll see."

A minute later, the elevator opens to reception at St. Clair Press. Jules waves as she takes the hallway toward marketing and I go left toward the executive area where my and JoAnna's offices are located.

There's something about the office that's buzzing today. I'm not sure what it is exactly but there's something in the air that has me crackling with excitement.

Lindy, one of the romance editors, passes me in the hallway.

"Lacey had her baby early." She's gathering signatures on a congratulatory card and offers it to me to sign.

"That's great." I smile, feeling happy for Lacey, but also wondering what that means for her position during maternity leave.

I have been subtle—and not so subtle—about wanting the job whenever JoAnna brings it up. This has got to be it and it's what I've come to New York for.

JoAnna summons me from her office with a quick email that reads *"Come see me, please."* I quickly stop by the kitchen to grab her a coffee with two hazelnut creamers, the way she likes it, and a black coffee for me—definitely not the way I like it. But today I feel like being like those book editors I've always read about, drinking black coffee and smoking cigarettes. I refuse to smoke but I'll try the coffee.

"So, I'm sure you've heard that Lacey had her baby early," JoAnna says as I place both coffees on the desk.

"Yes. I saw Lindy in the hallway. That's exciting!" I grin at her. I take a sip of the warm black liquid, trying not to grimace. Black coffee is gross.

JoAnna pauses—probably from the look on my face—but doesn't say anything. She continues, "I had hoped for more of a transition period, but babies are unpredictable. I have decided that you will be taking over for Lacey while she's on maternity leave."

"Yes!" I say a bit too loud and JoAnna looks at me with an amused smirk. *Come on, Chloe, keep it together.* "I mean, thank you!"

"This won't be easy. You'll still be performing all your

editorial assistant tasks on top of filling in for Lacey, as well as helping me with the upcoming Books 4 Kids event."

I should be intimidated by the workload. She's right, it won't be easy, but being an assistant editor is my goal, and if I don't take this chance now, I don't know when I will get another opportunity.

"Speaking of which, where are we on the Books 4 Kids event?" she asks.

I smile and grab my tablet. My hands still shaking with excitement from JoAnna's news.

And while I had been slightly intimidated by JoAnna initially, beneath her sophisticated demeanor and flawless appearance, she's got a heart of gold and is fairly easygoing, unless you're incompetent. She really has zero tolerance for that.

"Everything is on track. We've got all the major sponsor tables accounted for. I just need to collect sponsor checks from a few." I glance down at the list.

SCM, the event's main sponsor, and St. Clair Press's parent company, is one of them.

In an ideal world, the check would magically appear in my inbox.

If it sounds like I'm dreading the trek to SCM to retrieve the fundraiser check, you'd be correct. In the same two years I've enjoyed working for JoAnna at St. Clair Press, I've not had the same pleasure when it comes to interacting with her son, Barrett, the Executive Vice President and CEO of SCM.

While JoAnna is warm and personable, Barrett is a robot in a suit. His cold, dismissive eyes could refreeze the melting polar ice caps. With one glance, he could put an end to global warming. He's obnoxiously handsome, which maybe isn't his fault. Barrett is a spitting image of his father, but where I've seen pictures of the elder St. Clair with a devilishly handsome smile, Barrett's media shots are in the running for "Most Expressionless, Yet Devastatingly Handsome Man" category.

"Anything I can help with?" JoAnna asks.

Asking JoAnna to get the check from Barrett would be the easy way out, but I don't want her to think that I can't handle an easy task like collecting a check. She's just offered me a shot at my dream job with far more demanding duties, I don't want her to think I'm not capable of something so simple. Barrett won't likely be the one I need to talk to anyways. He's much too busy and important for that kind of thing. He'll have his assistant, Bea, help me out.

"No," I shake my head. "I've got it handled."

"Perfect." JoAnna smiles. "One more thing I need you to handle. Would you please make a reservation for two at Sea Fire Grill for twelve thirty on Thursday?"

"Of course. Under St. Clair?"

"Yes." She nods.

"I'll add it to your calendar once it's confirmed."

"No need. It's for Barrett and Tessa Green. A lunch date."

"Oh," I say, a little shocked that JoAnna is having me arrange lunch dates for her son now, but it's also completely understandable. With his icy demeanor and brooding attitude, I'm sure she's determined she has to resort to matchmaking if she ever wants grandchildren. They'd likely be half-robot, but I hope for JoAnna's sake, that skips a generation. "Should I forward the details to Bea?"

"Yes. Thank you." She nods.

I continue through the week's calendar, highlighting appointments and important meetings. JoAnna has me block off time in her schedule for a Pilates class.

"Your flight on Friday to LA is at seven. I've arranged a car to pick you up at four thirty."

She nods. "What are your plans for the weekend?"

"It's my childhood friend's bachelorette party."

16

"That's right. You mentioned you were hosting them. That sounds like a fun girls' weekend."

"I'm hosting the party at Le Pavillon."

"That will be a treat for your guests."

If all goes according to plan, it should be a fabulous weekend.

"Make an appointment with Lindy to go over where Lacey left things. She'll get you squared away."

"Of course."

The promotion, however temporary it may be, was just what I needed to boost my confidence about this weekend.

SCM is located in the Helmsley Building near East 46th Street and Park Avenue. The building is gorgeous, built over Park Avenue, two arches were constructed to allow each one-way street to pass through. A large clock is situated between the Greek god Mercury and a goddess with vines and wheat on the other side. The large glass-windowed front of the building is trimmed in black with the lobby made of marble floors and bronze fixtures.

It's one of my favorite buildings in New York. It's unfortunate all this beauty is tainted by the reason I have to come here.

Maybe my dislike for Barrett is rooted in the fact that from our very first encounter, *he* didn't like *me.* JoAnna introduced us at a luncheon she hosted two years ago, when I had first started working for her. He took one look at me, those hazel eyes of his briefly tracking over my body before he gave a curt nod and brushed past me.

I could overlook that. Further interaction has proven that is just how Barrett is. Cold and assessing. But, overhearing him question JoAnna, telling her he didn't think I was a good fit as her assistant was how I found issue with him. He barely looked at me, let alone tried to learn anything about me. How would he know about my qualifications? What an asshole.

The mature adult that I am felt it was only fair to meet him halfway—full contempt.

I pull the door open and make my way to the elevator. My heels click against the Italian marble. I'm not a tall person. Five foot two if it's an eighties themed party and I've got an inch of teased hair. While heels aren't practical for running errands around the city, they're a must when entering enemy camp. I'll need full height today. It's important to stand tall and appear larger so I don't look like prey.

While preparation is key, I'm confident I won't see Barrett. He's rarely spotted in the wild, he prefers to hole up in board rooms day after day. And, I already placed a call to his assistant, Bea. She's aware I will be stopping by.

I step out on the thirteenth floor, the large SCM logo greeting me upon my exit. The main receptionist, Maggie, directs me down the hall toward Bea's desk.

There's a buzz of productivity as I pass by people's offices; phones ringing, keys clicking on keyboards.

Bea is on the phone when I arrive, but she motions to one of the guest chairs sitting across from her desk. They're against the wall of the enclave that is her office outside of Barrett's door. It very nearly feels like I'm waiting for the principal to see me and Bea is the kind secretary here to offer words of encouragement. Again, I've done nothing wrong and won't be intimidated.

My eyes move around the space, trying to decide if anything looks different. I've been here a few times before. Accompanying JoAnna to an SCM board meeting, or dropping off contracts that needed to be reviewed by SCM lawyers. The fact is I try to come here as little as possible. That's what couriers are for.

My attention falls on the far wall where the SCM logo is

surrounded by a large number of smaller logos. St. Clair Press is among them.

With SCM being the parent company to St. Clair Press, I should be familiar with their business, but I honestly don't know much about the media giant. JoAnna's late husband started the company back in the 80s and Barrett is now the CEO. Under his direction SCM has been buying up smaller companies in advertising, broadcasting, print publication, digital media and motion pictures. As evidenced by the wall of logos.

"Chloe," Bea says when she hangs up the phone. "It's good to see you."

I stand and offer her the box of chocolate chip cookies I picked up from Levain Bakery on the way.

"These are my favorite," she says.

"I know." I smile, relishing in one of my favorite feelings in the world—giving someone something you know they will enjoy.

"You are so sweet."

"Not as sweet as the cookies, though." I laugh.

She snaps her fingers as if just remembering something. "The Books 4 Kids donation check. Sorry. It slipped my mind. It's been a hectic day here."

"I can only imagine." Having a raging asshole for a boss would be hectic. I keep that to myself. Working with Barrett, I imagine Bea's job is stressful every day. I smile sympathetically.

"I apologize. I haven't had a chance to get the check filled out yet." She shuffles a few papers around.

In contrast to the way I feel inside, I plaster on an easy breezy smile.

"No problem," I say, though my plan to quickly get in and get out is crumbling like the cookie I ate on the way here.

"Thank you." Bea sits down to type at her computer while I sit down again.

My eyes are pulled in the direction of the open door leading into Barrett's office. I can see a black leather sofa—the color of Barrett's soul—and a glass-topped desk with a high-back chair. But more than the cold furniture, it's void of any personal effects. My gaze moves back to Bea's desk. A warm mahogany piece that barely has enough space for her computer, it's covered in framed photos and knick knacks, tiny potted succulents sit along her file cabinet with a handful of scribbled crayon drawings tacked to a bulletin board. At least Barrett doesn't impart his robotic tendencies onto his employees.

"How's everything going over there?" I ask when another minute ticks by.

"It'll be just another minute."

"Promise?" My laugh comes out awkward.

Bea smiles, completely oblivious to my desire to move this process along. I'm Tom Cruise suspended from the ceiling trying to go undetected in a room full of sensors.

True to her word, a minute later she stands to grab something from her printer. "We'll just wait for Mr. St. Clair to finish with his meeting so he can sign it and you'll be good to go."

My hopes of picking up the check undetected are dashed.

"Oh, is that necessary?" I ask, checking my watch to indicate a time constraint. I've been here for five minutes; it feels like a lifetime.

"Mr. St. Clair is the only one who can sign the check." She shows me the blank signature line with Barrett St. Clair, President and CEO underneath.

"I'm sure you've had to sign his name a time or two, yeah?" I wink. Because what's a little forgery for a good cause? The money is for the kids, but the good cause is me not having to see Barrett. I could probably sign it myself. Just draw two horns and a pitchfork.

Bea leans into me, conspiratorially. "I did have to sign his name for the company holiday card once when he was out of town and the cards had to make it to the printers that afternoon."

See? Maybe I can convince Bea to use her power for good. Hope blooms in my chest, but before I can press her further, my phone buzzes in my purse. My phone never rang, but it appears I have a voicemail.

"Would you excuse me a moment?" I ask Bea, then turn away from her desk.

I click play to hear it.

"This message is for Chloe, this is Angelica calling from Le Pavillon to confirm the private party room for your sixteen guests on Friday..."

I'm listening to the message when the hairs on the back of my neck stand at attention. The sound of size twelve wing tips striding toward us ratchets up my pulse. Even on carpet, his footfalls echo ominously. And because every villain has a theme song, somewhere an imaginary speaker system pipes in Foreigner's "Cold As Ice."

The instinct to not leave my back exposed has me dropping my phone into my purse and turning around.

Barrett's approach feels like it's in slow motion. His dark hair is thick and wavy, the kind of hair your hands could get lost in. It's styled meticulously, not a hair out of place. I doubt he ever has bed head because robots don't sleep. His hazel eyes, the same as JoAnna's, are framed by long, dark lashes. Lashes that any woman would kill for and are completely wasted on a man. Perfect nose, square jaw—you know the type.

While I'm aware of his facial features, I try to keep the details of Barrett's body out of my mind. He's not just a floating head, so I know he has one. It's been covered in a suit every time I've seen him. A suit that fits over broad shoulders and a trim waist. There's no need to go into details about the fit of his pants over his muscular thighs or the way they hug his firm ass. We won't even discuss the slight bulge at the front of his pants that I most definitely do not ever squint to see better.

He's the kind of man that you could stare at for hours imagining all the filthy things he might say to you, but when he opens his mouth to speak, he inevitably ruins everything.

"What are you doing here?" Barrett asks, barely stopping before we're toe to toe.

I silence the call and drop my phone into my purse.

"Ms. Anderson came by to collect the check for the Books 4 Kids fundraising event," Bea volunteers, lifting said check in Barrett's direction.

I'm still as a statue, a tight smile plastered to my face. *Just sign the check,* I want to say through my teeth. Barrett glances at the check, then back to me. While his hazel eyes bore into me, his expression is unreadable.

Without a word, he takes the check from Bea and walks into his office.

"Mr. St. Clair will see you now." Bea nods encouragingly, then ushers me toward his office door.

I don't want to be *seen.* I want to collect the check and skedaddle. Barrett could have signed the check and carried on without a word. But, that's not his style. He likes silence, but only as a form of torture. To make the other person squirm. My defense tactic is to talk enough for the both of us.

"Wow, I really like what you've done with the place," I announce, as I take in the entirety of his office. Empty shelves, blank walls. It looks like he's been here seven minutes, not seven years.

"It's minimalist," he says with an edge to his tone as he takes a seat behind his desk. His elbows rest casually on the chair arms, his long fingers intertwine and hang in the space between him and the desk. He looks like he's in no hurry. Yay for me.

"I actually think you went a step beyond that, this is more like nothingness."

"I like to keep things tidy. It doesn't appear that is one of your attributes." Barrett's eyes drop to my blouse. For a moment, I think he's checking out my boobs until I look down to discover there's a smudge of chocolate on my camisole from the warm, gooey cookie I ate on the way here. I couldn't not get a cookie for myself. That's disrespectful to the cookie gods. I pull my pink cardigan farther over to cover the chocolate stain.

I pick up the single pen that is on his desk, the only thing besides his computer and phone, and offer it to him.

He doesn't take the pen so now I'm awkwardly holding it out and it weighs more than any writing utensil should. It's got to be encased in gold or lead or something.

"Pitch it to me," he says, crossing his arms over his chest in a power pose that is both arrogant and sexy at the same time.

"What do you mean?" I say, my eyes narrowing.

"The reason I should donate my hard-earned money to Books 4 Kids."

A choked laugh escapes me.

"You already pledged the money for the sponsorship." I can feel myself getting worked up. If Barrett thinks he's going to mess with me by withdrawing his sponsorship, he's ridiculous. Books 4 Kids is JoAnna's pet project. He'll have to explain to her why he withdrew SCM's donation. Although, if I come back without a check, I'll have to explain that, too.

"I want to hear where my money is going. Why I'm donating a million dollars to your cause."

"That's a good question. Why are you only donating a million dollars? You're a gajillionaire. You could afford to donate more."

He smirks, but doesn't say anything. Again, silence is his weapon of choice.

"It's not my cause. It's a charity organization that your mother created and sits on the board for. She asked you to pledge the money."

His reaction is a nonreaction. I realize I'm not going anywhere with that check unless I comply with his request. A frivolous demand that only makes me realize how much of an ass he really is.

"Fine," I say. I can barely refrain from slamming the pen down on the glass tabletop. "Books 4 Kids NYC is an organization that donates millions of books to children each year, and provides literacy programs that reach at-risk and lower income families throughout the city. Funding from grants and donations like yours will allow Books 4 Kids to introduce a new online platform that will reach more children and help promote early literacy." I pause. While the stats are great, I sound like an infomercial. I take a breath in, and ignore Barrett's silent disapproval. "Do you remember the power that learning to read gave you? The independence that reading a book on your own allowed? The places that reading could transport you on a rainy day when it was too wet to play outside? I would devour book after book. That's the excitement that we want to give to kids. The ability to read and having resources that provide kids with books isn't frivolous, it's a lifeline." I turn to find Barrett's hazel eyes intently staring at me. "So, are you going to sign the check or not?"

He clears his throat, his gaze lingering another moment before he slowly reaches for the pen. Feeling like a badass now that I've put him in his place, sort of, I decide to press my luck.

"We need a few more celebrity readers for the story time slots."

His eyes flick up to mine, his hand gripping the pen holding steady over the signature line.

"And you're telling me this because?" he asks.

"I'm asking if you'll fill one of those slots. It's for a great cause, which I just explained. Not to mention it would be supportive of your mother and the signage will have SCM written all over it. It would be good publicity and it's not that hard."

"No." He drops his gaze and finishes signing the check.

"It's only fifteen minutes," I press. "You can pick the book. I'm sure your deep baritone would lend itself nicely to *There's a Monster Under My Bed* or *Creepy Underwear*." Or hot phone sex but that wouldn't be appropriate for a children's story time.

"I'm busy. Have Bea help you pick someone from the executive team. That should suffice."

"I think it would mean more if you were there yourself." I don't want Barrett there anymore than he wants to be there, but the idea of Barrett reading a book to children is so out of his norm that I can't help but want to see it.

Barrett hands me the check, his signature lining the bottom in black ink.

"Find someone else," he says with finality before he turns toward his computer. Apparently, I've been dismissed.

I'm halfway to the door when I remember the note in my pocket. The lunch reservation that JoAnna had me make for Barrett and his date. I'd intended to pass it along to Bea, but with my anxiety about running into Barrett, I'd forgotten. I pull it out and march back toward Barrett's desk. With a thud, I smack the note down onto the glass then leave.

CHAPTER 3

Barrett

The familiar sounds of tennis shoes squeaking against the waxed wood floor, and the smack of the rubber ball against the wall take me back to the countless number of times I would come to the racquet club with my dad. Carl, a friend and in-house counsel at St. Clair Media, banks a shot off the right wall and I scramble to make contact before the ball flies past me.

"Jesus, St. Clair, where the fuck is your head at today?" Carl taunts. "That ball couldn't have been an easier hit if I put it in a box and shipped it directly to you."

Ignoring his prodding, I make my way over to the side of the court with my water and towel. I let my racquet clatter against the wood floor before sliding the protective eyeglasses to the top of my head to towel the sweat off my brow.

It's Friday morning. It's been nearly a week since Fred invited me to dinner with our girlfriends and I am no closer to having one today than I was last week. That doesn't mean I haven't tried. Leaning into my mother's desire to play match-maker, I let her arrange a lunch with Tessa Green. Tessa, an accomplished lawyer and activist, and I had some things in common, mostly our summers spent in the Hamptons and our busy work schedules, yet I spent the majority of our one-hour lunch date thinking about another woman. The one who had delivered the news of the date via post-it note on my desk.

When Tessa started talking about her two-year plan for marriage and babies, I knew there was no need to reveal my two-day plan to find a fake girlfriend for a business meeting. After lunch, we parted ways, both knowing nothing would come of it.

This dinner with Fred Hinkle is imperative to my business, I can't ask any random woman off the street. I need discretion. If Fred found out that I lied, not only would any hope of a business deal with him be ruined, but my reputation could be tarnished. The walls of the corner I've backed myself into are closing in.

Carl is a mediocre racquetball player, he's even worse at tennis. He does more shit talking than actual playing, so the fact that my shirt is drenched from my efforts is a telling sign to us both. He wanders over to where I'm standing and uncaps his water bottle.

"I've never seen you suck this bad." He takes a swig of his water, while I run the towel behind my neck. "Normally when a guy's game is off, I'd say there's a woman involved, but since you live like a monk, it's got to be about business."

"I don't live like a monk. Unlike some people, I prefer to keep my personal life off Page Six."

"Man, you must forget who you are. If there was anything to report, you'd be front and center with the rest of us."

I've known Carl since our days at Hawthorne Prep. After undergrad at Columbia, I got my MBA from Wharton while Carl went to Harvard for his law degree. When I took over SCM from my uncle, Carl was an easy choice for in-house counsel. I trust him and he's a far better lawyer than a racquet-ball player.

I hesitate to tell Carl about my predicament. I pride myself on being a problem solver. In the seven years since I took over running SCM, there's never been an issue I couldn't resolve. I love a good challenge. The fact that I've put myself in a position with Fred Hinkle that I'm not clear on the path forward has kept me up the past two nights.

"It is about a woman," I grumble, before taking a drink of my water.

Carl's eyebrows shoot up.

"Or lack thereof."

"Oh, shit. You can't get laid?"

"I'm fine," I practically growl, not because I need to get laid but because I need Carl to not think with his dick for a moment. "That's not what it's about. You know I'm determined to land the deal with Voltaire Telecom, but Fred Hinkle is prideful."

"That's the pot calling the kettle black."

I pin him with a look. "Not the point. I couldn't get him to take a meeting, so I tracked him down at Amber's wedding. He's got a new girlfriend."

"Did you hit on her?" Carl's eyes go wide.

"No. I told him I have a girlfriend."

"Why the hell did you do that?"

"He looked like he wanted to murder me when I was talking to his girlfriend. I wasn't trying to flirt with her. I gave her one compliment about her nails to be nice and Fred did not like it. So, I made up a girlfriend so he'd relax and not think I was flirting with his."

"So, it was a little white lie. What's the issue?" Carl asks.

"Frankie, Fred's girlfriend, was excited and said we should do a double date. We're going to Gallagher's tomorrow night." I take another sip of water, trying to wash down the doubt that is building up again. The nagging feeling that I've pushed it too far this time.

I've taken some risks over the years. I've found that in business, that's how you get ahead. Jumping out of the plane and hoping that the parachute opens. When it does, the fools who weren't brave enough to jump wish they'd had the guts. Telling Fred I had a girlfriend, setting up a date with him and Frankie, was a huge gamble. One that at this point I'm uncertain how I can make work. I need someone who I can be honest with about the situation, but all the women I've seen recently want a serious relationship. I can't be sure that they'll play along and if they decide not to, I'm fucked.

Carl's mouth gapes open, "Fuck, dude, what are you going to do?"

"I'm going to find a girlfriend in the next thirty-six hours."

I sent Marcus home early, opting to walk home from the club, hoping it will give me time to think.

I'm determined to find a solution to my lack of girlfriend issue. I have to show up with someone to the double date tomorrow night, or tell Fred I'm a liar. The latter is not an option. If Fred finds out I lied about having a girlfriend, I'm in a worse position than I was a week ago when he wouldn't give me the time of day.

Maybe I could cancel. Tell Fred my girlfriend is ill. Buy myself more time. But there's no guarantee I'd get the opportunity again.

I've thought about hiring an escort and demanding she sign an NDA, but there's the risk that we'd be seen and it would end up on every one of the city's gossip sites by morning that I, Barrett St. Clair, had to hire a date. My teeth clench. This shouldn't be this hard, but the problem is that

I've found most women want to be my actual girlfriend, not a fake one.

It's Friday evening and the streets are already filled with couples strolling hand in hand, laughing and talking.

I'm not jealous. If I didn't need a girlfriend for dinner with Fred tomorrow night, I couldn't care less about my singledom. It's preferred. No one to answer to, no one to inevitably disappoint when I need to choose business dinners over date nights.

I keep walking, willing my brain to come up with a solution.

I could call up Heather—or was it Haley? The girl that I dated for a month about four years ago. I stroke my chin, thinking of a way how I could possibly propose this idea to her. It would never work. She'd been too interested in a committed relationship, which is why it lasted a mere four weeks.

That had been a setup by my mother, back before I refused to entertain them.

I'd nearly stood Tessa up strictly based on my need to deny the pint-sized woman who delivered the message the smugness of knowing that my mother was setting me up on dates.

Thinking of Chloe's full, pink lips twitching with amusement makes my jaw ache with the pressure my molars are applying to each other.

I need to forget about Chloe. I won't let myself wonder if she's somewhere in the city with her own date tonight.

While I don't appreciate my mother meddling in my personal life, I've found her to be the person I turn to when I'm facing uncertainty. It doesn't happen often, my father's death and then my first year running SCM being the most difficult times in my life. She's a calming presence. And I could use that right now, even if I don't plan to share with her my current predicament.

I send her a quick text and ask if she has the books I asked her for as samples from a publisher in Beijing we might be partnering with at her apartment. She takes a minute to reply.

JSC: In LA to meet with the film producers for the thriller we purchased. Books are in the study. You can pop by to grab them if you need xo

It's Friday and my mother doesn't even question why I'd be looking for those books now. She knows that when it comes to a personal life, mine is all business.

The books aren't a pressing issue, but I've got no other plans but to work tonight. That, and come up with a solution to my girlfriend issue.

CHAPTER 4

Chloe

My phone buzzes again. Another message on the group text. Lauren and Claire are getting ready and sending me pics of their outfits. They arrived a few hours ago, along with the thirteen other women attending this party, most of whom I haven't met, checked into their hotel and are already tossing back the champagne I had sent up to their room.

I look up from my phone.

"Could you check again?" I ask politely and smile, hoping this will give the hostess time to realize her mistake. That she does have a reservation under my name. It's for the large party room in the back. A party room that is necessary to host Lauren's bachelorette party, due to the inexplicably tiny size of my apartment.

"I made it a month ago," I add, in case the timing aids in her locating it. "Lauren's bachelorette party, party of sixteen." I adjust the forty-pound tote on my shoulder that contains all the party supplies. Sashes, tiaras, party games, even those obnoxious penis straws, I couldn't help myself.

This shouldn't be that difficult, but I don't want to be rude, so I wait patiently while she scrolls and taps on the tablet's screen. I force myself to take a step back from the stand, afraid I might circle around the side and offer to find it for her.

"I found it," she announces a moment later.

"Oh, good." I breathe a sigh of relief, and prepare to wave off the apologies she is sure to offer after that heart-stopping moment when she made me think I didn't have a reservation for the party tonight.

"It was cancelled," she says unapologetically.

"What do you mean it was *cancelled*?" I try to keep my voice calm, but it rises two octaves in panic.

Even though Lauren's bachelorette party doesn't start for another hour, I'm here early to make sure every small detail is taken care of. Now, I'm finding that one very large issue has arisen. I take a breath, glad that I'm dealing with this now, so that it will be long forgotten by the time everyone else arrives.

Even while I'm reassuring myself this is a silly misunderstanding, my brain is working overtime trying to recall the moment when I confirmed the reservation. I've confirmed dozens of reservations recently. Surely this was one of them. It's been a busy week. The usual meetings and errands, and helping JoAnna prep for her trip, all while working on the Books 4 Kids fundraiser and late nights putting together the finishing touches for this party.

The hostess taps on her screen. "It says here, a message was left on Tuesday to confirm the reservation but it was never confirmed."

I want to laugh. Look around for the cameras, it's obvious I'm being set up for some kind of prank here. I didn't confirm the reservation for my childhood best friend's bachelorette party for which she has flown all the way from Colorado to attend this weekend? That has to be a joke. I've never failed to confirm an appointment or reservation in my life. I've even called the dentist to check on my appointment when they failed to send a confirmation email two days prior. They had been backed up with reschedules due to the doctor being out sick and thanked me for my diligence. Where's that reservation karma when you need it?

"That's not possible." I shake my head, only to realize a second later that it is in fact possible.

Shit. I know she's right. I remember the voicemail now. I had missed the call that afternoon and had been checking my voicemail while I waited for the fundraiser check at Barrett's office. I got distracted when he showed up and then forgot about calling the restaurant back to confirm. I have an over-whelming urge to scream. That wouldn't help the situation at all, but it would relieve the rising anger I'm feeling toward Barrett right now. Logically, it's not his fault, but the stress of the situation is taking over my brain. Whether it's his fault or not, I have the desire to lump this misunderstanding in with all the other grievances I have with him. Like why does he look so good in a suit? How can his hazel eyes look both green and gold at the same time? It's obnoxious really.

Forget about Barrett, I need to focus on the task at hand. There's got to be a way out of this. It's like getting a speeding ticket for the first time, they have to let you off with a warning, right? I've never had a speeding ticket, but I would hope that a clean record would allow me a pass for the first offense. I pause to put on my friendliest smile.

"I apologize for not confirming, but I'm here early to set up so if you could just add me back to the reservation that would be great."

Without lifting her head, the hostess flicks her eyes up to me.

"I'm sorry, there was a waitlist for the space. We've already confirmed the next party on the list."

"What?" I drop my gaze to the ground, where it feels like the floor has dropped out from underneath me. "You're saying the space I reserved for the bachelorette party I'm throwing for my childhood friend, which starts in one hour and includes sixteen attendees, most of whom flew in specifically for this event, is no longer available?!"

"Sorry." Her tone is bored and she caps it off with a shrug. I swear I can hear her mentally add 'not sorry.' It's no big deal to her that my reservation was stolen from me on a technicality. The action makes me want to reach across the stand and strangle her with the ribbons of the twenty balloons I'm clutching. Instead, I try a new tactic.

"Listen, I'm JoAnna St. Clair's assistant, is there anything you can do?"

"Who?" She looks at me confused.

"JoAnna St. Clair," I say slower, as if that will trigger her understanding. "She's the publisher at St. Clair Press."

Her blank stare makes me shift on my feet.

I realize that while JoAnna is a household name in the book and publishing world, this twenty-something hostess has no idea who she is. Even if JoAnna's name were to have influence here, I feel bad that I'm using it. She's at the airport right now. She'll be on a plane to LA in less than thirty minutes. That's a reservation I did confirm this week. I shake my head.

"Oh, wait!" She snaps her fingers and I feel a glimmer of hope. "I know that name. She's got a son. He's gorgeous and rich. One of the youngest billionaires in the world. Barrett, right?"

I cluck my tongue. "Right."

"Is he going to be here?" she asks.

"At my friend's bachelorette party?" I ask.

She nods excitedly.

It's Friday night, yet I imagine Barrett is holed up in his barren office, performing his nightly ritual of counting his gold coins by lamp light. A modern-day Ebenezer Scrooge.

Except he's not exactly stingy with his money. He did

donate a million dollars to the Books 4 Kids campaign. And I'm aware of all the other philanthropy he and SCM participates in, but that doesn't mean he's pleasant to be around. All that money and generosity can't make up for his abysmal personality. His ever-present scowl and contemptuous attitude.

But, who knows? Maybe he and Tessa Green hit it off yesterday and are having a romantic second date tonight. Either way, he's not making an appearance.

"No," I say.

Her smile drops. "We're completely booked. You could try the bar; it's standing room only."

I glance over at the bar area. It's got a fun atmosphere, but there's no way the party would fit in the space even if there were no other patrons. My stomach drops. I'm normally organized, details are my jam. This can't be happening.

I take a breath. I've never missed a confirmation, whether it be for a travel itinerary, an important meeting or a dinner reservation. I'm here now, shouldn't that count for something? I'm about to argue this point when the hostess speaks again.

"I need you to move your cake." She purses her lips as she drops her eyes to the white cake box with a clear window resting on her stand before pulling two menus from underneath. Before I can cling to her leg and beg her to help me, she's leaving, guiding the couple behind me, who are in their sixties and have been staring wide-eyed at said cake, toward their table.

The cake is in the shape of a man's chest, his pecs and abs are chiseled to buttercream perfection while a fondant penis juts upward to his belly button, a clear creamy substance spills from the crown and spells out 'Here cums the bride' across his abdominals.

I thought it was hilarious when I picked it out. It's not my fault that this massive man cake is too large for the bakery's traditional cake boxes, leaving this clear box the only option. They should have warned me when I ordered it. Maybe suggested they shave a few inches off of the giant cock so that it could fit in a proper box. One that didn't display its contents to everyone within a five-foot viewing radius.

In my hurry to get to the restaurant, I didn't have time to tape a piece of paper over it. I figured once I got it here and set up in the private room that the cake would be a non-issue. Now, the massive penis on the cake I'm holding is the least of my problems.

I maneuver the bag of party supplies in my right hand so I can move the cake box off of the host stand, then set everything down on the deep-set windowsill. I need to think. There has to be a solution here. Then, I remember all the effort it took to find a location and make the reservation. The reasons that I booked the restaurant in the first place.

My apartment is tiny with a capital T. It would be against fire code to have that many people in it at once. That and we wouldn't be able to move if we happened to cram all of us inside. Lauren and Claire's hotel room is bigger than my apartment. I could show up there and tell Lauren what happened. That she flew to New York City for her bachelorette party and I forgot to confirm the restaurant reservation. This trendy, upscale and completely unaccommodating restaurant was one of the only places I could find that didn't have a room fee. A rare gem in this expensive city.

My phone buzzes, and while I expect it to be from my friends, I look down to see it's JoAnna calling me.

"Hello?"

"Oh, Chloe, I'm glad I got hold of you. Are you busy?"

I want to laugh. I need to find a new location for my friend's bachelorette party of sixteen women on a Friday night in New York. Nothing too pressing.

"Um, no," I lie, "what do you need?"

"The review copies of *Take Me Down* got delivered to my building today instead of the office on Monday."

"Oh, no." My brain starts cranking, wondering if I made that mistake. The way this day is going, anything is possible.

"Paul's assistant put the wrong address, so now there are twenty boxes of books in the lobby at the Pierre. Would you go over and let Orlando into my place?"

This is the last thing I need, another item on my growing to-do list.

"I don't want them sitting there all weekend," she adds.

"Of course. I'll take care of it," I say, fighting back the panic that's telling me this detour is only going to eat into the time I have to figure out the bachelorette party location situation. I need JoAnna to know that I've got everything under control.

JoAnna isn't an egotistical, demanding boss. If she's calling me on a Friday evening, she legitimately needs my help.

"Please have him put them in the guest bedroom next to my office."

"Okay. I'm on my way now."

On the bright side, JoAnna's penthouse apartment is only a few blocks away from the restaurant so I gather my things—balloons, party tote and obscene man cake—with the hope that the short walk will give me time to brainstorm a new plan for the night's festivities.

JoAnna's apartment is the entire top floor of the Pierre Hotel, across from Central Park. The doorman, Hank, opens the palatial gold door for me, offering to help me carry the items I'm loaded down with. I wave him off, though. It's one of those situations that if I try to hand off anything I'm going to end up dropping it all. Also, there's no way I want this sweet, white-haired man seeing this cake.

If Hank notices the cake, he doesn't say anything.

Orlando at the concierge desk greets me with a smile.

"Good evening, Chloe. You're here for the delivery, I presume?"

"Yes." Looking at all the boxes, my eyes go wide. How long is this going to take?

He must read my panic.

"Don't worry, I've got a dolly and I'll do the heavy lifting."

"Oh, great." I'm relieved. I didn't come for heavy lifting in my heels and sequined party dress.

I use the key card JoAnna gave me months ago to let myself into the elevator and Orlando follows with the loaded dolly, up to the top floor. When I exit the elevator into her apartment, I'm greeted by the scent of the large floral bouquet on the entryway table.

The arrangement that is refreshed weekly is currently packed with roses, ranunculus, mums, carnations and thistle. JoAnna's penthouse apartment's décor is bright pops of color mixed with neutrals that give perfect balance. It's JoAnna's style, polished and elegant, with a hint of sass and flair.

"Let me know where I can put these and I'll go get another load," Orlando tells me.

I set the cake and tote on the foyer table, and let the balloons drift freely, then I show Orlando to the guest bedroom by JoAnna's office and indicate where he can stack the boxes.

I give him the key card to get back up, and while he goes downstairs for another load, I take a moment to drop onto the overstuffed sofa to think. Scrolling through my phone, I hope to find someone's name that could help me. A favor that I could call in to get me out of this bind. The party starts in less than an hour, I have to figure something out. I scroll to Jules's name and hit the call button.

Jules barely answers before I blurt out, "I've got a huge problem."

"Is this about the cake? Because I don't think huge can ever be a problem in that regard. Whether it's of the flesh or baked good variety, huge dicks are never a problem."

"No. It's not about the cake, though I did get a few odd looks on the subway. The private room reservation was cancelled."

"Oh, no. Why?" Jules asks.

"Okay, not necessarily cancelled," I sigh. "I forgot to confirm the reservation and the restaurant gave it to the next party on the waitlist. I'm so screwed! Where am I going to find a place that will fit sixteen people with such short notice? I'm going to have to cancel the party. Lauren's mom and aunt and sister flew into New York this afternoon just for the party. Not to mention her co-workers and friends. Friends that I haven't met yet, but will soon learn that I'm an incompetent bridesmaid for messing this up. She's going to be devastated."

"Okay. Time out. Just breathe. Where are you now?" she asks.

"I'm at JoAnna's apartment. There was an issue with a review copy order and she needed me to stop by. She flew to Los Angeles this afternoon. Maybe I can try calling Vance at The Magnolia. JoAnna's done so many events there. Maybe he can cram us into one of the conference rooms. Or—"

"Wait. So, you're in JoAnna's penthouse and she's gone for the weekend?"

"Yes!" I exclaim. "Sorry, I don't mean to snap at you, but I'm under a lot of pressure here and you keep asking where I am, but it's not where I am that's important, it's where I need to be...finding a location for Lauren's party."

"That's where I think you're wrong." I can hear her smiling through the phone.

"Listen, Jules, I know you love a good brain teaser, but the clock is running down on me here, so I need straightforward responses."

"It's the simplest answer. You should have the party at JoAnna's."

I take another shot because hosting your friend's bachelorette party in your boss's penthouse apartment without her permission is super stressful. When Jules originally suggested it, my gut reaction was *hell, no* but then Lauren texted me how excited she was for the party and with no other options this late in the game, I caved, sending a mass text with the updated address.

The thing is I couldn't even ask JoAnna for permission even if I wanted to. Her flight would land at LAX long after Lauren's party was scheduled to start. And what if she said no? JoAnna has been nothing but kind to me, even motherly as I navigate this city on my own, but using her apartment for a personal gathering is definitely crossing into inappropriate territory. I scratch at my neck. Either the sequins on this rented dress are irritating my skin or breaking the rules is giving me hives.

In addition to giving me the idea to host the party at JoAnna's, Jules called a caterer friend of hers that was able to make extra hors d'oeuvres last minute. She didn't have time or ingredients for me to make personal selections so I was at the mercy of what Jamie and Greg picked for their Hawaiian luau themed wedding reception. So, Luau Thai chicken and sweet and sour meatballs it is!

While the rest of the ladies are out in JoAnna's living

room, snacking and sipping on drinks, thanks to an alcohol delivery service, I pull my custom-made pin the junk on the hunk game out of my tote. That's right, Etsy, I made it myself and saved fifty bucks. Although the guy at Kinkos gave me a funny look when it came off the machine.

Ryan Gosling smiles back at me, the over-muscled body double I used for the lower half is disproportionate to the size of his head. The empty spot between his legs the intended target for my printed and hand-cut paper dicks.

"Chloe!" I can hear my friend Claire yelling for me down the hall.

Claire, Lauren and I were three peas in a pod growing up. Claire lives in Seattle now and while we haven't been the best at keeping in touch, when she arrived an hour ago, we easily picked back up where we left off in high school.

"The dicks are coming!" I shout as I pull the paper dicks out of the bag, but she's already there in the doorway, and I hold up the poster so she can check out Ryan Gosling on steroids. I wave the paper dicks around, then I explode with the giggles at my little joke. "Get it? They're coming?"

"Hilarious," she deadpans before waving me out toward the hallway.

I'm still laughing as she waves her hands, urgently motioning me out of the guest room where I've stashed all the party supplies. I didn't think pin the junk on the hunk would garner such enthusiasm.

"Where should we hang it?" I ask.

"Forget the game. The stripper is here. And he's gorgeous. Not like a Jersey Shore beef cake, fake tan kind of stripper, but a sexy businessman stripper. Where did you find him? Wall-StreetStrippers.com?"

Ooh la la. A stripper sounds fun. Even better than pin the dick on the prick or whatever this game is called. But I gather the game up and bring it anyways because I did put a lot of effort into it.

As I start to follow Claire back into the living room, her words finally penetrate the vodka-induced fog clouding my brain. I really should have been keeping track of how many shots I've taken.

"Wait." I stop short, nearly dropping the paper dicks on the floor. "I didn't hire a stripper."

There's only one man that would have access to JoAnna's apartment without needing to be buzzed in. My stomach clenches with anxiety. Oh God.

"Really?" Claire's eyes turn to saucers. "So, who's the stud in the suit?"

My eyes scan the sea of scantily-clad women until I find him. There, across the room, looking like sex on a stick in a navy suit, with his thick, dark hair, perfect nose and chiseled jaw, being hounded by all the bachelorette party attendees is Barrett.

My heart stops. This is a scenario that I never in a million years considered. And why would I? Why would Barrett stop by JoAnna's on a Friday night? When she's out of town? Doesn't he have better things to do? Like take candy from babies and suck people's souls from their bodies dementor-style?

He sees me then, and when our eyes connect, everything stops. It's what I imagine a deer feels when its body is lit up by the high beams of an oncoming vehicle. Frozen, stunned, unable to do anything but wait for impact.

His hazel gaze holds mine, intense and challenging, before his full lips slide into a devilish smirk.

"Chloe Anderson," he shakes his head, "you've been a bad girl."

CHAPTER 5

Chloe

I'm having an out-of-body experience. When I made the decision to host Lauren's bachelorette party in JoAnna's living room, never in a million years did I imagine this scenario. If I thought I was stressed out before, no amount of vodka is going to fix this. Barrett's cold, assessing eyes skim the length of me. His gaze is a chilly fifty-five degrees, and I visibly shiver. I'm stunned speechless, unable to say or do anything but watch this nightmare unfold.

One of Lauren's co-workers, Molly, a tall blonde in a red strapless dress, moves toward Barrett. "Oh, Chloe isn't the bride." She grabs Lauren by the hand and pulls her out of the group of women. "Lauren is."

I'm dead. Dead and fired. There is likely nothing Barrett would like more than to see me fired. I don't know why, but it seems like something that would give him satisfaction. That and making babies cry.

My mind flashes to the image of the plethora of editorial assistant candidates that JoAnna had to choose from two years ago. There may be even more of them now. Just last week the news reported a population increase due to young professionals moving to the city. I'll be replaced instantly. JoAnna is Beyonce and I'm her cheating boyfriend, she can have another me by tomorrow. I'm not irreplaceable.

Worse than losing my job with St. Clair Press, with one word, JoAnna could banish me from the entire publishing industry in New York if she wanted to. That's the power that she has. I've rarely seen it wielded for anything other than the benefit of her clients, but I wouldn't want to find out.

There would be no associate editor job in my future. No job at all. I'd have to move home and work at The Book Nook —the local bookstore I worked at for five years before I left for college—for the rest of my life.

Or I might be able to find some corner of the world where JoAnna St. Clair's influence in the publishing industry can't reach. Like Antarctica.

"It's Lauren. Lauren has been a very bad girl," Molly says, winking at Barrett.

Lauren, in her white sparkly romper and bride-to-be sash, bounces in her heels.

While I'm watching my life and career in New York City flash before my eyes, Lauren laughs and covers her mouth with both hands. "Oh my God, this is so fun!" She turns to find me across the room. "Chloe, I can't believe you got a stripper. And he's so hot!"

After three drinks, her tiara is crooked and her cheeks are rosy. She's also oblivious to the stress Barrett's arrival has caused me.

I think I'm having a heart attack. Finally, my feet get the message to move my body and I close the ten feet between me and Barrett. Around me, the conversation about Barrett's performance kicks into high gear.

"Where's your boom box?" Lana, Lauren's cousin, asks. "Wouldn't that be so nineties if he had a boom box?"

"Are you taking requests?" Lauren's aunt, Clara, chimes in, her mouth practically salivating.

"Chloe, I think he needs a music hook up," another co-worker of Lauren's shouts excitedly.

"Um, can I talk to you for a minute?" I blurt out, before grabbing Barrett's arm and pulling him toward the kitchen. My only goal right now is to get Barrett away from the women and to not have him tell them I'm technically trespassing.

He could call the cops. Have me thrown out or worse, arrested. In this dress and heels, I'd be mistaken for a hooker. My vivid imagination is working overtime thinking of all the worst-case scenarios.

I'm thankful Barrett follows me easily. That he doesn't protest a relocation and demand he humiliate me in front of everyone.

I've never touched Barrett before. There's been no reason to. Our interactions are few and brief, but laced with enough hostility to know that he's more foe than friend. That being said, I didn't expect the warmth of his body. I expected his body to mirror that of his icy stare. Cold and rigid. That there must also be cold blood running through his veins, either that or wires to connect to his hard drive. It's nice to feel the heat of his skin and muscle through the fabric of his suit. I immediately drop his arm and reach for the pantry door.

Once he's inside, I close the door behind us. In the small space, I can smell his cologne. It's highly distracting. Has he always smelled like that? Intoxicating and decadent? His scent makes me wish we were in this pantry for another reason. Oh, no, did I just think about kissing Barrett? The vodka must be lowering my defenses. I need to focus.

Barrett has taken a firm stance on the opposite side of the pantry. One hand in his pocket, the other propped on a shelf next to JoAnna's array of herb and supplement bottles.

I cross my arms over my chest, and swear for a nano second

Barrett's eyes drop below my face. My eyes drop to find my breasts pushed up higher on my chest, giving Barrett a full view of my cleavage. There's no way Barrett is staring at my chest. That would require feeling something and he's dead inside, but I drop my arms anyway.

"Okay, listen," I say, now fidgeting with my hands. "This is not what it looks like."

"What does it look like, Chloe?" Barrett asks casually.

"That I'm having a party at your mother's apartment."

"I'm imagining all those women in the living room? Women that think I'm a male stripper here to perform?"

I can't help the nervous laughter that escapes.

"No, that's all true. But, I didn't plan this. I wasn't intending to have the party here. There was a mix up at the restaurant."

"What kind of mix up?" he asks and I hate that I can't tell what he's thinking. What he's going to do with this knowledge.

"I forgot to confirm the reservation so they canceled it and gave it to someone else. The party is for my childhood friend, Lauren." I motion back toward the living room. "She's getting married in a few months. Everyone flew out to New York for the party. I mean everyone. Even her Aunt Clara. She's the one who asked if you were taking requests. And we all know that Aunt Clara doesn't travel. She's probably still wasted from all the vodka it took to get her on the plane. There's no way I could cancel.

"Maybe I should have told them the truth, but everyone was so excited to come to New York. They think it's so amazing that I live this glamorous life here." I don't mention my hole-in-the-wall apartment or the lack of dating that I've done during my short time living in New York. The only thing giving me any credit at all is my job at St. Clair Press. "Your mother called me to have boxes of books brought up. I came over to do that and then I just stayed."

I hate how it sounds.

"We weren't going to stay here all night. Just for food and drinks and some party games. A strip tease from a man off the street." I wave my hand in his direction, but he doesn't even crack a smile. "We're going to Bounce later. Not like we're going to bounce," I make an awkward movement with my body, "but the nightclub, Bounce."

I'd ask if he was familiar with that dance club but Barrett doesn't seem like the kind of guy who would be caught dead anywhere named Bounce.

"I see." That's all Barrett says. For a moment, I have a glimmer of hope that he'll understand my dilemma and turn a blind eye to this evening. Am I too hopeful to think that living underneath that designer suit might be a beating heart that could understand my predicament?

"Are you going to tell JoAnna?" I ask, my lower lip getting the brunt of my teeth while I wait on pins and needles for his reply.

"No." He shakes his head, and relief immediately floods my body, only to be replaced by panic a second later when he continues. "You're going to tell her."

"Shit. You're right. I have to tell her. It's the right thing to do." I nod, knowing it's right but still hating it, knowing it will undoubtedly change my life.

Barrett is the last person I want to be vulnerable with, but he knows his mom best and will likely be able to predict my fate.

"Do you think she's going to fire me?" I ask.

Barrett's mouth opens, ready to deliver his answer like a guillotine, swift and sharp, but it closes without response. I watch as his fingertips trace over the shelf absently. He lifts them again, rubbing his fingers together, as if there could be a speck of dust on JoAnna's pantry shelves.

Waiting for his answer, I'm imagining the worst.

"It's highly likely," he finally responds.

"Yeah." I sigh, expecting that response, but wishing it were different all the same.

"Okay." I nod, certain of my fate. An image of me on my knees begging Barrett to not tell JoAnna, to keep this indiscretion between the two of us emerges, but I quickly cast it aside. There's no way he would grant me that favor, so I might as well save myself the embarrassment. "Can you please not mention it to the group and give me an hour to clear everything out?"

He doesn't respond for a minute. I sigh.

"Did you hear—"

"I heard you." He runs his hand through his hair, an action I've never seen him do before. His dark, perfectly-styled mane never has a hair out of place. I was starting to wonder if it was a wig he took off at night and returned to his titanium skull every morning. It's too perfect. I want to push my hands into it and mess it up. Leave the ends tangled and askew. Barrett St. Clair with bed head, that would be a sight to behold.

"I've got a business proposition for you."

"What is it?" I ask with a glimmer of hope that we can settle this just between us.

"I need a date for a business dinner tomorrow evening."

"You can't get a date?" The moment I say it, I realize analyzing Barrett's personal life should not be at the forefront of my thoughts right now, but I'm intrigued. While I know JoAnna has arranged dates for him on occasion, the latest being the lunch with Tessa Green this week, and Barrett is part-robot, it has been determined that many women are willing to overlook his reptilian disposition in order to snag a billionaire. And he is gorgeous, I'll admit it begrudgingly, so really any woman could be ensnared in his web as long as he doesn't do a lot of talking.

He ignores my question.

"I'm having dinner with a business associate. I need a companion for the evening."

"I'm not sleeping with you."

Barrett's eyebrows shoot to his hairline. Oh, shit. Did I say that out loud?

"I mean, why me?" I ask.

"You're tolerable."

"Geez, catch me before I swoon."

"It's a business arrangement. I will ignore what I've seen here tonight and you will attend dinner tomorrow night with me."

"Tomorrow night?" I wince. "That's bad timing. I've got guests in town. They don't leave until Sunday."

Barrett's eyebrows lift again and I realize how silly that sounded. He's giving me an out. A way to make my misstep disappear and I need to make whatever he's asking me to do work. Lauren will have to understand.

"Are we in agreement?" he asks.

"Fine," I say, albeit reluctantly because going on a date with Barrett sounds like a nightmare. "What should I wear?" I ask.

"Not that." His eyes do that thing again where I think he's so appalled by my outfit but it's like a train wreck he can't look away from so he's forced to examine every inch. His eyes eventually land back on mine, his lips a flat line when he moves past me and out of the pantry.

It takes me a few minutes—twenty—to console the ladies about the loss of our assumed male exotic dancer. My pin the junk on the hunk game doesn't go over as well as I thought it would after a real-life hunk of a man had been in our midst. I assured the ladies that they wouldn't have wanted to see under his suit anyway. Titanium isn't that thrilling.

During a titillating drinking game of Never Have I Ever, which I was thankful I didn't have to participate in because of my limited sexual experience, I packed up all the party stuff, placed the remnants of the man cake in the refrigerator and took out the trash. I'll return tomorrow to gather the cake and take care of any cleaning, thankful that I will be able to put a fresh set of eyes on the apartment before JoAnna will return Sunday evening.

An hour later, we've said goodbye to Lauren's mom and Aunt Clara, and managed to pile into two Uber XLs headed to Bounce.

"Tell us more about the hottie in the suit." Lauren nudges me in the back seat.

"Like I said, he's my boss's son and he was just making sure we had everything we needed."

I want to be chill about the evening and the fact that I now have to be Barrett's date at a business dinner, but the stress of throwing a party at JoAnna's apartment has now been transferred into being Barrett's date. It's not a real date, just business, but that doesn't make it any less disturbing that I have to sit next to Barrett and pretend that we like each other enough to go on a date. That's distressing.

Lana plugs her phone into the sound system and we annoy the driver the rest of the way to the club with our off-key singing to Taylor Swift. Then, we file out of the vehicles and into the growing line in front of Bounce.

"I knew there would be a line, but this is crazy," Lauren says, stumbling in her heels. I reach out to steady her and wave the rest of the group to the end of the line. "Is it always like this?"

"This is pretty normal," I say, glancing down the line of club-goers.

I've been here zero times. I leaned on Jules for a recommendation. Also, an internet search for 'Best Night Clubs for twenty-five-year-olds in NYC' gave this one the best reviews, so here we are.

"I have to pee so bad," Lauren says.

Claire sighs. "You should have gone at the apartment."

"I did go at the apartment," Lauren whines. "I broke the seal."

I make a mental note to clean the main bathroom, too.

"Let me see what I can do." Being an editorial assistant doesn't translate to having any connections at a night club, but I am a girl and I'm in a flashy dress, so I hope for the best.

At the front door, there's a man in an all-black suit checking IDs and a woman at a tiny stand with a tablet. My luck with hostesses and tablets is not great tonight, but I'm hoping she'll understand Lauren's predicament and let her pop in for a minute to use the restroom.

"Hi there, we're at the back of the line and I was wondering if my friend could go in to use the restroom really quick. It won't take a minute, she's fast. We're here for her bachelorette party and I'd hate for her to pee her pants. Well, it's a romper, so the pee would probably just run down her leg, but you know what I mean."

She stares at me a moment. "Hold on."

I have nothing to do but hold on so I wait while she presses her hand to an earpiece and talks into her headset.

"Are you Chloe? Party of sixteen?" She taps on her tablet.

"Um, there are fourteen of us, but only one has to pee. At least that was the current status before I came up here."

"Grab your party and stand over there." She points next to the roped-off line by one of the entrance doors.

I do as she says, ushering the ladies up to the front, and ignoring the glares we get from the other patrons in line.

"Okay, Lance will check your IDs then Veronica will meet you inside."

"Are we all going to the bathroom?" Molly asks. "I have to pee, too!"

"Apparently," I say, handing my ID over to Lance. Once we're all checked in, we walk in the front door to find Veronica, who is going to lead us to the restroom. It's a service they offer, I guess, either that or they're afraid we'll go rogue and hit the dance floor when we've only been admitted to the restroom. Now that we're inside, it's going to be hard to go back out and wait in line. Crap. I should have asked if we could save our spots. We're going to be at the back of the line again. Not that we moved up much in the two minutes we stood there.

Veronica leads us through the club and then upstairs. I'm confused when she stops in front of a low table surrounded by three plush loveseats.

"Where's the restroom?" Lauren asks, her eyeballs floating.

"Down the hallway on the right," Veronica responds. "Make yourselves comfortable, I'll be right back."

She's back quickly, and now carrying a tray with bottles of champagne and flute glasses.

"I'm sorry, what is this?" I ask.

"Champagne service." She smiles and pops the cork on one of the bottles.

I'm not sure how much a bottle of champagne costs here, let alone how much multiple bottles will cost.

"We just needed to pee," I shout over the music, but Veronica continues to pour and hand out the glasses.

"This is so cool, Chloe." Molly beams, looking around at the busy club.

"Wow, Chloe," Claire gushes. "This is impressive."

I smile, because it is impressive, though I have no idea where it came from. Maybe it's those good karma reservation confirmation vibes righting themselves after my mishap with the restaurant. Whatever it is, it gives me the boost of confidence that the women are enjoying themselves and while this is nothing like my typical Friday night in NYC, it's exactly what I wanted them to experience.

I'm on cloud nine until Veronica finishes filling the champagne glasses, and hands me a small card.

Be safe – B

The only person who knew I was coming here tonight besides Jules was Barrett. He must have arranged this. It doesn't make sense. Why would he do that? So I'm indebted to him further? My stomach sinks. That's the only reason I can think of.

Claire squeezes my arm with excitement. "Lauren is having the best time. We're all having so much fun."

Lauren returns from the bathroom.

"Oh my God, are we staying? How'd you arrange this?" she asks.

"It's fun, right?" I smile brilliantly, not wanting to give away my unease.

As the women sip champagne and dance around our private space, I glance back down at the card Veronica had given to me. I think I might have sold my soul to the devil.

CHAPTER 6
Barrett

This is not my style. I hate not having all the details planned out, but I got myself into this mess and the only way out is through it. A date night with Fred and Frankie with Chloe by my side.

I'm waiting down the street from the restaurant when my driver, Marcus, pulls up. My office is a few blocks away and since I was working there all afternoon, I directed him to pick Chloe up and meet me a short distance away from the restaurant. I want it to appear that Chloe and I arrived together.

He gets out to open the door to the back seat, but the door opens on its own. A set of legs, from ankle to mid-thigh, come into view. I recognize them instantly. I tell myself it's because I know Chloe is in the car, not because I have the shape of her legs memorized.

It rained earlier, the warm June day giving way to a cooler evening. At my desk, I'd watched the rain drops fall on the city and briefly wondered what Chloe and her friends visiting the city were up to. But I refused to feel guilty about taking her away from them for the evening. There was no way I was going to change plans with Fred.

She slides out of the vehicle with a helping hand from Marcus. My jaw drops at the sight of her. Chloe has no jacket on her bare arms. That's not the only thing that is bare. Her dress is black, short and tight.

"What the hell are you wearing?" My eyes scan her up and down. It's a feast, and the delicacy is Chloe's smooth, creamy skin.

Finding Chloe at my mother's apartment had been a surprise, but seeing Chloe across the room, looking like a fucking dream in a short, sparkly dress that accentuated her toned legs, curvy hips and full breasts, her hair in loose waves around her bare shoulders. She looked nothing like the cardigan-wearing, bun-sporting Chloe I've seen before.

Her in that dress was all I thought about last night when I lay in bed, one hand around my cock, and now here she is dressed like a bombshell, scattering my brain when I need to focus on Fred.

"A dress." She motions to the length of said dress.

"Where's the rest of it?" I growl.

"This is all there is."

"Bea sent over a dress, why didn't you wear it?"

"This is the dress Bea sent over," she argues.

"You're kidding." I press the pads of my fingers into my temples. What the hell was Bea thinking?

"Yeah, you're right. I thought to myself, why not wear something outrageously uncomfortable and revealing to dinner just for laughs. I thought you wanted me to wear this. I thought maybe it was some form of punishment."

"Not just for you," I mutter under my breath.

She motions to her chest. "I can barely breathe and I spent twenty minutes adjusting my boobs in this damn thing!"

My eyes immediately drop to Chloe's chest. The top of her dress is tight which pushes her breasts up, exposing generous cleavage. Her hair is pulled back away from her face, creating an unobstructed view. She looks hot. There's no point in denying that, but her outfit would do better at a night club, not a dinner at an upscale restaurant. It's incredibly short which is wild because Chloe is so petite. Bea must be out of practice. There haven't been many women in my life to pick clothing out for.

I'm regretting not picking her up at her apartment. There's no way to change her outfit now, so we have to go with it. Chloe pulls on the dress hem for the fifth time.

"Stop fidgeting. You look fine," I assure her, stealing another glance. More than fine. She looks fucking delectable. And distracting. Which makes me second guess this whole arrangement. But, there's no backing out now, we're minutes away from walking into the restaurant.

"I hope you didn't strain yourself giving me that compliment," she says.

I reach for her hand and start walking toward the entrance of the restaurant.

"What's with the hand holding?" she asks, rushing to keep up with my longer stride.

"It's so you don't run away."

Chloe hums in disapproval, but doesn't fight me on it.

"Thank you for the champagne last night," she says softly.

"It was nothing," I say.

"It was something."

I don't respond. There's nothing to say. Hell, I don't know why I did it. When I reached the car and directed Marcus home, I found myself pulling out my phone and making the call. I don't want to analyze it.

"Who are we having dinner with?" she asks.

"A business associate, Fred Hinkle, and his girlfriend, Frankie."

"Frankie's a girl? I thought it would be two old guys and

I'd be the little lady to keep all your gentlemanly manners intact."

"This isn't a regency novel. It's two business associates having dinner with their girlfriends."

Chloe halts suddenly, our arms pull taut, but my forward momentum causes her heels to skitter against the concrete.

"Girlfriend? You said it was *a* date."

I continue walking, and with a stutter step, she falls back into stride beside me.

"Pretend it's one of many that we've been on."

Chloe stops again. "No, no, no. I thought I was just here for decoration. Now I'm supposed to be pretending to be your *girlfriend*?"

"Why is that a problem?" I ask.

"A little background would have been nice. How did we meet? How long have we been together? Things that could have been discussed if you actually picked me up."

"I was busy with work."

"On a Saturday?" she asks.

"I work every day," I reply.

"You must really love your job."

"Love has nothing to do with it. I work hard because people depend on me. SCM is the top media company in the country and I intend to keep it that way. This dinner is important. I need it to go well. I've got a business deal in the works with Fred. His company is up for sale, or will be soon, and I need him to like me in order to be the one to purchase it when it does."

"And he doesn't like you now?" Her lack of surprise is evident. The way her lips quirk to one side and her eyes widen with feigned shock.

I shrug. "He doesn't know me. This dinner will help him get to know me better."

"Yeah, I can definitely see how bringing a fake girlfriend to dinner will strengthen your bond. It's all making sense now."

"I need you to appeal to his girlfriend, Frankie. Keep her engaged so I can talk with Fred."

"Are you calling me charming?" She smirks.

"It's a stretch, but I'm sure you'll figure it out."

I place my hand on Chloe's back as we walk through the door and to the host stand. I shouldn't be surprised that my hand nearly spans the width of her. I lower down so my mouth is near her ear. "I know how much you value *your* job, so I know you'll figure it out."

My hand detects a quiver moving down Chloe's spine, but she keeps her gaze ahead.

I check in with the hostess and she motions for us to follow her.

Fred and Frankie are already seated at the table when we arrive. They stand up and I make the introductions. I do a double take when I see Frankie's dress. It appears to be the exact same dress as Chloe's, except in a bright fuchsia color. Frankie is a good six inches taller than Chloe so what was short on Chloe is barely covering Frankie's assets. I suck in a breath, wondering how this is going to go. Experience has taught me that women don't like it when they are dressed similarly.

"Girl, I love your dress!" Frankie beams. "Is Balmain not the best designer ever? Fits like a glove. Fred could barely keep his hands off me in the car."

I guess in Frankie's case, she enjoys not being the only one half-dressed for dinner.

"I'm sure you had the same problem, Barrett." She winks at me while waving her nails playfully. Her nails are just as long as they were last week when I met her at the wedding, but they have a new design. Pink, orange and yellow layered. They look like a blinding sunset.

"This was a gift from Barrett." Chloe smiles sweetly. "We

ERIN HAWKINS

actually didn't ride together. Barrett was working, so we met here."

"He's got fabulous taste," Frankie replies.

"Working on a Saturday?" Fred admonishes.

"Chloe had some friends in town so I made myself scarce." It's a half truth.

Fred nods. "Ah. Well, it's important to find balance."

"We were in bed most of the day," Frankie winks again, her exceptionally long lashes sticking for a moment before retracting, "but we didn't rest, if you know what I mean."

I know what she means, and it's the last thing I want to think about before I eat dinner.

I move for the seat next to Fred, but when I pull out the chair, Chloe drops into it. Now any conversation I try to have with him will be crossing through the table.

"Let's get some drinks." Fred motions for the waiter.

When the waiter arrives, Fred orders a Manhattan for himself and a sex on the beach for Frankie.

"He knows what I like." Frankie places a kiss on Fred's cheek. "It also happens to be my favorite drink."

Chloe's eyes nearly bulge out of her head. It's hard to tell if she's overwhelmed by Frankie's directness or the drink menu.

"Do you want me to order for you?" I ask her.

"Yes, please." She sighs, placing the menu back on the table.

"You should try a sex on the beach. They're delicious."

"Okay," Chloe agrees.

When our drinks arrive, Chloe takes a sip of her drink and winces.

"Isn't it fabulous?" Frankie asks, raising her cocktail glass toward Chloe.

"Absolutely." But I can hear Chloe stifling a cough as she extends her glass to Frankie.

"First sip is always a little spicy. These remind me of Florida. I grew up there."

Chloe takes another sip.

"Did you live by the water?" she asks Frankie.

"Daytona Beach."

"I bet that was nice. I'm from Colorado. Buena Vista. It's a small town."

"Oh, is it near Aspen? Fred has a place in Aspen." Frankie leans closer, pressing her breasts into Fred's arm.

Chloe nods. "It's close by."

"Have you skied Aspen?" Frankie asks.

"We weren't skiers growing up. With the equipment, lift tickets and all the other gear, ski days were too expensive with five kids."

"Five kids?" The question falls out of my mouth before I realize this is surely something I would know about Chloe if we were really dating.

Everyone's eyes shift toward me.

"Five kids! It's still a shock even after all this time," I reply while internally chastising myself for making this mistake.

"How long have you been dating?" Fred asks.

"Six months," I reply as Chloe responds, "Three months."

"Oh. I guess it's been six." Chloe nods before burying her face in the menu.

"Time flies when you're having fun." Fred kisses Frankie on the cheek.

"What about you two?" I ask, trying desperately to steer the conversation away from Chloe and me. "How long has it been?"

"Six weeks on Tuesday," Fred announces. "I asked her to move in with me on our second date."

"Oh wow." Chloe's smile is tight. I can tell she thinks that's insane. It is, but we're not here to judge Fred and

Frankie's relationship. I'm here to help Fred see that I'm the man he needs to sell his company to.

"I just knew when I saw her." Fred gazes adoringly at Frankie. "She was playing tennis at The Racquet Club. Her ball kept landing in my court. She was pretty bad, so I offered to give her a lesson."

"Then I reciprocated." Frankie purses her lips, a devilish look on her face.

Chloe is mid-drink and starts sputtering. She coughs repeatedly so I place my hand on her back to offer her comfort. The second my hand makes contact with her body, she jolts upright in her seat, the top knee of her crossed legs banging into the underside of the table. The liquid in our glasses sways with the aftershocks.

I withdraw my hand. "You okay?" I ask.

Chloe pats her chest. "Yes. Sorry about that."

She smiles, seemingly recovered.

"Barrett and I play tennis frequently, too," Chloe announces.

"That's great." Fred smiles, his eyes moving between us.

"Sometimes I even let Barrett win." Chloe laughs.

"You must be pretty good. Barrett has been the club's singles champion eight years in a row."

Chloe pauses for a moment but then smiles and says, "I'm a three-time high school state champion, so we challenge each other."

Fred nods. "We'll all have to play sometime."

"Definitely." Chloe smiles warmly at Fred, but when she catches me staring at her, the corner of her lips drop.

The waiter arrives to take our order. Fred orders for Frankie and then himself. Since Chloe had been unsure about her drink, I figure ordering her dinner would be the boyfriend thing to do.

"She'll have the veal filet—" I start, but Chloe cuts me off.

"Actually, I'll take the chicken primavera."

"Right," I say, then order the veal filet for myself.

While Frankie and Fred converse with Chloe, I finish my drink and order another. As I listen, hearing about Chloe's family, where she grew up, how she saved up money to move to New York and her career aspirations, I almost forget why we're here. That I'm supposed to be focused on Fred and getting him talking about business.

Chloe must feel my eyes on the side of her face. She turns to meet my gaze.

"Look at you two." Frankie giggles. "I'm a sucker for romance. Tell us how you fell in love."

"Oh." Chloe sets her drink back on the table. "It's pretty boring really."

"I'd love to hear." Fred nods enthusiastically.

"How did we meet, Barrett?" Chloe turns toward me. "Do you want to tell the story? Or should I?" What she's really saying is 'I have no idea what to tell them.'

I reach for my water.

"It's not much of a story. My mother introduced us. Chloe is my mother's assistant at St. Clair Press."

"I'm an editorial assistant, but I've recently taken on some assistant editor duties while a co-worker is on maternity leave. That's what I'd love to do full-time."

"A workplace romance?" Frankie sighs dreamily. "Love it."

"Not really. I don't work at St. Clair Press," I add.

"Barrett is the CEO of SCM," Fred offers.

"Was it love at first sight like with me and Fred?" Frankie asks, then slides one hand affectionately over Fred's shoulder.

"Yes," I answer as Chloe responds, "No."

"What Chloe means is that she was not a big fan of me but I was quite taken with her."

I casually drape my arm over the back of Chloe's chair and she lunges forward, knocking her water glass over.

"Oh, gosh! I'm so sorry."

"No harm done," Fred says easily. Our waiter quickly swoops in to clear the ice off the table and replace Chloe's glass.

"Frankie, I like your nails," Chloe says, obviously trying to change the subject.

"Thanks, doll. They're part of my new line, Frankie's Faux Nails."

"So, you're an entrepreneur? That's great."

Frankie runs her hand and said nails over the back of Fred's head. "He's making all my dreams come true."

"You're the one with all the ideas, baby."

As Frankie and Fred look adoringly at each other, an awkward silence falls over the table. Or maybe it's only on mine and Chloe's side.

"I'm going to use the ladies' room," Chloe announces, grabbing her clutch, before turning to me.

I stand. "I'll show you where it is," I say, then I'm hot on Chloe's heels as we approach the alcove where the restrooms are located.

I'm not sure what Chloe is thinking, but we need to regroup. I'm regretting not telling her about the girlfriend thing earlier, but I thought it would be easier if it wasn't staged, more natural. Chloe is not a natural.

"What is happening out there?" I ask when we've cleared the main dining room.

"What do you mean?" she asks.

"We're not on the same page at all."

"I'm sorry. If you wanted a solid relationship back story, I need more than three minutes' notice."

"I thought it would be more natural if we winged it. Less pressure to perform."

"That sounds like your insecurity, not mine," she fires back.

"I've never had any complaints." I smirk.

Chloe's eyes find the ceiling and I feel my lips tug upwards. I could go back and forth with her all night, but that's not why we're here.

"You're practically on the other side of the table."

"And?"

"I need you to touch me," I say.

Chloe's eyes go wide.

"I thought you said this wasn't that kind of favor."

"Like we're together. Make it believable."

"You want me to make out with you at the table?"

"God, no." I have to pinch the bridge of my nose, and take a moment to gather myself. When I find Chloe less infuriating, I open my eyes again. "Fred and Frankie are an affectionate couple. Try to match their energy. Act like you've touched me before. Like we're familiar with each other. Can you do that?"

"I think so." She nods slowly, mulling it over. "I don't have much experience in this department."

For the first time tonight, I look at her. It was impossible to miss the dress, that scrap of material hit me over the head the moment she stepped out of the car. Now, my eyes rake over Chloe's face. Her big blue eyes, her pouty lower lip that is caught between her teeth. Her long, red hair has been straightened. It's glossy and thick, but I prefer the wild waves she had last night. The delicate gold chain around her neck dips into the hollow where her clavicles meet.

I don't even want to chance looking down at her body. Fuck, too late. With our height difference, my eyes fall straight into her cleavage. Chloe is petite in stature, but she's got curves. Those curves are accentuated in this dress. Full breasts, trim waist, soft hips. My hand itches to reach out and trace the outline of her hip. To press my fingers into the forgiving flesh there, move along her side body to feel the contrast between her rib cage and the softness of her breasts before settling them in the indented space above her hip. I shouldn't be looking at her like this. I should be focused on how the hell we're going to make it through this dinner.

"Sex?" I ask, not remembering what we were talking about but more what I was imagining.

"What?" she asks, clearly confused. Her brain is obviously not being controlled by her nether regions. "No. I'm saying I've never had to pretend to like a guy before. This," she motions between us, "is new to me."

Right. "That's normal. I've never had to pretend to be interested in a woman either." Except, whether I want to admit it or not, I am attracted to Chloe. Based on my reaction to Chloe in her dress, or the fact that I couldn't get the image of her in that sparkly dress she was in last night out of my head, I won't have to pretend. She doesn't need to know that.

Chloe doesn't leave the conversation there. "I guess maybe it's hard for you, too, right? I'm not exactly your favorite person." She laughs, more at ease now that she thinks this is challenging for me as well.

"Definitely," I say, looking away from her, glad to be done with the conversation. Something will be hard and it won't be pretending to be close with Chloe.

I reach for Chloe's hand. "Okay, show time."

"I actually have to pee." She smiles sheepishly.

"Right. I'll meet you out there."

I watch Chloe disappear into the ladies' room then move to make my way back to the table. I need to get my head on straight, remember the goal of tonight. Show Fred Hinkle that I'm exactly the kind of guy he can entrust his company to. I need to forget about the slight attraction I have to Chloe. Or better yet, use it to make our relationship believable.

I glance back toward the restrooms and find that Chloe is making her way over to the table.

It's impossible for my eyes to not lower to where the material of her dress inches up with every stride. She's far from runway model height, yet in her high heels she looks like she's making her way down a catwalk.

"Look at this guy." Fred draws my attention back to the table. "He can't take his eyes off her."

"Just like you, Freddy boo. Your eyes are always on me. Your hands, too."

Chloe takes her seat beside me and looks around the table. "Sorry about that. What did I miss?"

"We're talking about how Barrett can't take his eyes off you."

"Oh." A blush spreads over Chloe's cheeks. She reaches for her drink and I'm concerned that she's retreating, our pep talk long forgotten. She surprises me by scooting her chair closer to mine. When she leans in to grab a piece of bread from the basket, she places her free hand on my thigh, and now I'm the one nearly jumping out of his skin.

She keeps it there. Her fingers featherlight over the inside of my pant leg, yet the heat of it feels like I'm being branded. Now I'm imagining what it would be like to have Chloe's hand wrapped around my shaft, that red-polished thumb circling around the tip.

I clear my throat and move Chloe's hand lower, toward my knee.

Chloe turns to find me staring at her.

"What?" she mouths, eyebrows raised.

"Nothing," I whisper, trying not to scowl. Then, I attempt to discreetly adjust myself.

Our food is delivered and over the course of the meal I make several attempts to engage Fred in business conversation, but he's too busy gushing over Frankie or asking Chloe questions about growing up in Colorado.

"Are we boring you?" Chloe squeezes my arm. "He's heard all these stories a million times."

Her once tentative fingers now easily slide behind my neck. Her touch is more relaxed now. A response to finishing off her drink. Her touch is soft at first, almost a tickle, before she applies more pressure. The pads of her fingers sink into my neck, gently kneading the tension there. It feels so fucking good, but I'm not going to be able to stand up from this table if she keeps doing that.

"Chloe, if you like Balmain dresses, you're going to love their new line of crop tops and leggings." Frankie manages to put down her drink for a second to clap her hands. "Oh my God, we should go shopping together. We obviously have similar tastes. It would be so fun."

"That would be nice," Chloe responds as her fingers continue to tease along my collar. I can't imagine Chloe and Frankie shopping together. Other than their coincidentally matching dresses tonight courtesy of Bea, they have very different styles.

After paying the bill, a 50/50 split between Fred and myself, we exit the restaurant.

"Very nice to meet you, Chloe." Fred pats Chloe on the forearm before extending his hand to me. "Barrett, it was a nice time."

I nod. It's the only thing I can manage with Chloe's body tucked into my side. One hand pressed into my stomach while the other has snaked under my suit jacket behind my back.

With a hand on my shoulder and one on Chloe's, Frankie air kisses us both before Fred ushers her into their car.

Once they're down the street, Chloe pulls away from my side.

"I think that went well," she says.

The frustration I've been feeling all night with the lack of opportunity to talk with Fred comes to a head. Not to mention the fact that Chloe was an unwelcome distraction. While that may not be her fault, it's maddening as hell.

"Are you kidding? That was a disaster. I made no head way with Fred because you and Frankie talked the entire time."

"Oh, I'm sorry. I was unaware I was supposed to help you in your business dealings." Chloe's arms spread wide and I'm momentarily distracted by her cleavage. "That makes perfect sense because I was unaware about anything for this 'date.' Next time you blackmail someone into being your date, maybe fill them in on the details. It would be helpful."

Having summoned him earlier, Marcus pulls up at the curb.

"Forget it." I yank the car door open. "I'll take you home."

She wraps her bare arms around her mid-section. "No thanks. I'll order a ride share."

"I can take you home," I repeat.

"It's fine." She doesn't bother to look at me while she types on her phone.

I blow out an exasperated breath. This woman frustrates the hell out of me, while also managing to make my dick as hard as stone. It's a paradox I want nothing to do with, but I can't let her shiver on the sidewalk. I remove my jacket and drape it over her shoulders.

"I'm fine. Really. I don't need your jacket."

She tries to shake it off, but I move out of her reach.

"Goodnight, Chloe," I say as I climb into my car.

"All set, Mr. St. Clair?" Marcus asks.

"Please wait until Ms. Anderson's car arrives," I run my hand through my hair in frustration, "then we can go."

"Yes, sir."

As we idle there on the curb, I reflect on the evening again.

Chloe's right. It wasn't her fault that she was ill prepared, but the frustration of making no progress with Fred made me lash out. That and the fact that I'd been distracted by all the touching she'd been doing, with my encouragement, no less. Fuck. All I can hope is that we made a good impression with Fred and that he'll be in contact. Hope is not a business strategy, but it's where I'm at right now. As for the raging hard on I now have, I'll have to take care of that later, and try not to think about the woman who caused it.

CHAPTER 7

Chloe

Monday morning my stomach is in knots. At the coffee shop, it's a debate between decaf and regular. My hands don't need anything else making them jittery, yet the caffeine would come in handy for the fact that I haven't slept well the past three nights.

I've seemingly checked all the boxes on the how to keep your boss from finding out that you hosted a bachelorette party at her apartment. I only served clear alcohol. Cleaned her apartment top to bottom. Fulfilled Barrett's business dinner requirement to keep him silent on the matter. But I'm still beyond terrified that JoAnna knows and her first order of business this morning will be to fire me.

When I wasn't thinking of a contingency plan for when JoAnna fires me, I was having dirty—I mean disturbing—thoughts about Barrett. Unwanted thoughts. I've chalked it up to our close proximity during dinner with Fred and Frankie. I used to have nightmares about snakes after a day at the zoo. It's practically the same thing.

I've heard nothing from Barrett since I left the restaurant Saturday night. I didn't expect to. Our arrangement is finished. The only reminder of the evening being the suit jacket he draped around my shoulders hanging on my clothing rack. Its large, dark silhouette looming over my much smaller, and more colorful wardrobe. I'll have it couriered over to his office. It won't be cheap, but it'll be worth not having to see him again.

The elevator doors part and I breeze through the reception at St. Clair Press, waving to Lydia at the front desk as I walk by. I make my way down the hall, toward JoAnna's office. The coffee tray in my hand starts shaking and I have to remind myself to breathe or I'm going to be wearing this coffee.

After another deep breath, I put on a confident smile and stride into her office. I really hope that JoAnna won't be able to see the guilt on my face.

She's there behind her desk with her attention focused on her computer.

"Good morning." My voice comes out a bit squeaky, so I clear my throat in an effort to correct its high pitch. I set the coffee on her desk and step back.

She turns to look at me. "Good morning, Chloe. Thank you for the coffee."

"Of course." I nod. "How was your trip?"

"Productive. I don't particularly enjoy LA but there's only so much you can do with a phone call."

"Totally. Okay, well, I'm going to—" I motion to leave, but she turns from her computer, settling her full attention on me.

"How was your weekend?" she asks.

That question doesn't usually cause so much anxiety. The extent of my time away from work is spent reading or perusing bookstores throughout the city. Sometimes my neighbor, Todd, and I drink wine and play cards. Or the rare occasion Jules can convince me to go out with her.

"Um, you know, it was good." I can feel my face heating.

"Is there anything you wish to tell me?" JoAnna asks, setting her coffee aside. This must be serious, JoAnna lives for that first sip of her coffee every morning. Alarm bells are going off in my head. She knows. My thoughts immediately jump to Barrett. Did he tell her anyway? Even after I fulfilled my part of our deal? What a no good, double crossing—the sound of footsteps in the hallway distracts me from cursing Barrett in my head. A moment later said double crosser walks through the door. When his hazel gaze meets mine, my heart starts galloping in my chest. His pressed charcoal suit fits every inch of him. In contrast to the bags I feel weighing down my face, he looks well rested and that only serves to annoy me more.

"What is it that couldn't wait, Mother?" Barrett asks, detaching his eyes from mine and putting his focus on JoAnna.

"I wanted to talk to both of you." She laces her fingers together in her lap before lifting her gaze. Her eyes move between me and Barrett, before settling back on me. "I received a phone call this morning."

Oh, God. She knows.

"JoAnna, I'm so sorry," I say, trying to fight back tears. "I know it's not okay, but I can explain."

"There's nothing to explain," she says simply. "I know everything."

That's it? She doesn't even want to hear what I have to say?

"I won't say I'm not surprised, but these things happen." She shrugs, then her lips drop into a thin line. "However, I did not like hearing about this from Eileen. She's already been impossible to live with since she took over the ladies' tennis club chair position so this only made her ego even bigger."

I have so many questions. How would JoAnna's friend, Eileen Minton, know anything about this? It was supposed to be between me and Barrett.

Barrett and I exchange a glance. If he's as confused as I am, he doesn't show it.

"What are you talking about, Mother? What does Eileen have to do with anything?"

"She was the one to tell me that you two are dating."

"What?!" I exclaim, but Barrett remains stoic, unphased. I give him my best wide-eyed, what the hell is going on, you should say something to fix this look, but he turns his attention back to JoAnna without acknowledging my plea.

"Oh, yes. She was all too happy to deliver that news. I suspect she's still sore from you not taking a liking to Kristy when we tried to set you up. This," she motions between Barrett and I, "is obviously the reason you've been so resistant to my efforts to find you dates."

Barrett sighs. "How did Eileen find out?"

"Marjorie Green's stylist, Dolce, was at Gallagher's Saturday night when you were having dinner with Fred Hinkle and his new girlfriend, Francesca. She's a handful. Not the most elegant woman Fred could have stepped out with after he and Helen split." Barrett clears his throat impatiently, something I would never do to one of my parents, but only receives a stern gaze from JoAnna, "That's another story." She waves it off with her hand, "Dolce told Marjorie who told Melinda who told Eileen who told me." JoAnna scoffs. "I leave town for the weekend and return to hear through the Upper East Side's gossip chain that you two are dating?"

I'm speechless. This is not what I envisioned happening. I've been so worried that JoAnna would find out about the party that I didn't even take a moment to think that our very public date would get back to her. That never crossed my mind. I turn to find Barrett watching me and I swear the corner of his mouth twitches. Son of a—

"Is it true?" she asks.

She looks at me, but I'm unable to form words before Barrett opens his mouth.

"Yes, Mother." Barrett nods, confirming my worst nightmare.

"And you two acting like the other one barely exists, that was an effort to conceal your relationship?"

"I—" I have yet to find the words to respond. My brain is a chaotic mess of tangled thoughts. Barrett, on the other hand, has all the words.

"Our relationship is our business."

Our relationship? My mind is still swirling. I'm listening to the conversation between Barrett and JoAnna, but unable to clear my mind enough to contribute anything helpful. If we tell her we're not really together, she'll want to know why we were on a date. We can't tell her that Barrett demanded that I attend his business dinner date in exchange for his silence about the party. But, maybe I could say I was filling in. That we are not together but I was doing Barrett a favor. He was alone and desperate for a date. I like the sound of that. He didn't want to be the third wheel, so he asked me to go. That could work.

"Chloe and I are together," Barrett confirms solemnly. He looks like he's identifying a dead body. "Now, if you'll excuse me, I've got to get back to work."

I'm too stunned to speak. Barrett and JoAnna haven't even noticed. Barrett turns to leave.

"Aren't you forgetting something?" JoAnna asks.

"What?" Barrett asks, his tone sharp.

"Now that the cat is out of the bag, you can kiss Chloe goodbye." She smiles. "I don't mind."

"We're not into public displays of affection," he says. This conversation is surreal. No one's even noticed that I've yet to say anything.

"That's not what Marjorie's stylist said." JoAnna lifts her brows.

I think about all the affection I gave Barrett Saturday night based on following Frankie's lead. The firmness of his thigh under my palm, the way his bicep flexed when I squeezed his arm, and how my hand smelled like his body wash after I rubbed the back of his neck.

"Besides, this isn't public. It's always proper form to kiss your special someone when you leave the room." JoAnna's voice is stern.

I'm standing very still, my hands clasped in front of my body. My legs are shaky, I'm barely holding it together here. I missed that last part. What's proper form?

Barrett walks back the five feet to stand next to me. With one large hand on my lower back, he leans down to press his lips to my cheek. His lips are warm, but they're a ghost of a touch against my skin.

"For goodness' sake. Kiss her."

Barrett grumbles under his breath, obviously displeased by the notion of placing his lips on mine. Which is completely fine, because that's the last thing I want to do either. I get it, buddy, I'm right there with you.

But Barrett doesn't back down from JoAnna's prodding. Apparently, he's not going to let something like his dislike for me stand in the way of playing out this farce. With one hand on my hip, his other hand reaches up to cradle my face. The pads of his fingers caress the shell of my ear and it causes a shiver to run through me. The air in my lungs escapes with a whoosh and before I can take another breath in, Barrett's lips are on mine. It's a soft, firm press, nothing more. That's fine. It's not real anyways.

But then something unexpected happens. Barrett's thumb grazes the globe of my cheek bone, and his hand on my hip tightens.

I'm waiting for the kiss to end, for Barrett to retract his warm, firm lips so I can breathe. But Barrett's lips dive in further, his fingertips applying firm pressure, causing me to lean into the kiss.

Time stops, but my need to breathe doesn't. On a sharp inhale, I open my mouth.

It's an invitation for air, but I get more than that. I get tongue. And what's worse is I like it. Barrett's tongue teases the seam of my mouth and I tease right back.

I don't know how long it lasts, five seconds or five minutes, but when his lips retreat, I feel dizzy.

When my eyes open, Barrett's face is right there. His hazel eyes, green with flecks of gold that I never noticed, studying me.

"I should go," he says, his voice like gravel.

"Yup," is all I can manage.

He releases me abruptly and I nearly fall backwards.

"Mother." He nods in JoAnna's direction before leaving me standing in the middle of her office.

When I turn to JoAnna, she's smiling brilliantly.

"You two make an attractive couple. You always seemed to be at each other's throats. Chemistry, I suppose it is."

Her words flick on a light switch in my brain. There's light now whereas before I was stumbling around in the dark trying to make sense of this situation. We're a couple now. Wait a minute...

"JoAnna, will you excuse me a moment?"

"Of course." She puts her glasses on and turns back to her computer, as if everything is settled and life can go on as usual.

While I arrived to work on nervous, shaky legs, now I feel like I could run a marathon. Adrenaline is flowing through my body. I tell myself it has nothing to do with Barrett's kiss and everything to do with the situation he's created.

The elevator ride to the building lobby is slow, but when

the doors open, I manage to skitter out just in time to see Barrett exiting the front doors.

~

Barrett

"Barrett! Wait!" I hear behind me.

I turn from the open car door to find a bright flash of color barreling toward me. Chloe's pink skirt sways around her hips with every heeled step she takes.

When she stops in front of me, she's out of breath. One hand on her rapidly rising chest, the other smoothing down wild hairs at her temple. She squints in the morning sun to look up at me.

"You have to fix this."

"What are you talking about?"

"The fact that your mother thinks we're dating." She bites her lip. I remember how those soft pink lips were pressed to mine only minutes ago. "And we're not."

"I figured you didn't want me telling her the real reason you were next to me at Gallagher's Saturday night."

"Yeah, but there are surely better explanations than that. I get it. You were caught off guard. I was, too. We weren't prepared for this. But you have to tell her it was a mistake. That I was doing you a favor by filling in as your date for a last-minute business dinner. I don't know. Make something up. Anything."

Chloe's right. I was caught off guard. I shouldn't have been. I should have known that someone would see us and the news would get back to my mother. I've been so focused on getting face time with Fred that I've let details like this slip through the cracks. But my mother finding out about our date couldn't be better. If I want to keep the charade up that I'm in a serious relationship for the sake of my business dealings with Fred, then I need Chloe on board.

"No," I say simply.

Chloe's face scrunches in confusion.

"What do you mean? I fulfilled my part of the bargain. I attended the business dinner with you. I rubbed your thigh, Barrett! That is like a thousand favors right there. You can't go back on your word. You promised once I pretended to be your girlfriend at your business dinner that was it."

"I made no such promise."

"It was a favor for a favor. We're even. Done," she argues, again.

"That's not how it works," I say.

"What do you mean? That's exactly how it works."

"In order for me to keep my silence about the party you threw at my mother's apartment, I requested you attend my business dinner as my girlfriend."

"I know. That's what I'm saying." She looks at me like I'm insane.

"I never specified the terms of that agreement. Your assistance is still required until I can close my business deal with Fred Hinkle."

Chloe scoffs. "Um, no."

"A piece of business advice...put everything in writing."

"You're saying I should have made you sign some document saying you were only eligible for one date?"

"I'm saying without a contract, nothing is concrete."

"Well, I can't be your fake girlfriend. I have a date on Wednesday."

The thought of Chloe going on a date shouldn't bother me, but it does.

"Cancel it."

Her lips part in outrage.

"You can't force me to keep playing along. Besides, there's

no evidence. Wouldn't it be your word against mine?" She crosses her arms in front of her chest. I ignore the desire to drop my gaze there.

Instead, I pull my phone out of my pocket, and pull up the video I saved from my mother's apartment cameras Friday night. It was insurance. Now I'm glad I did it.

I move to stand behind Chloe, keeping my phone screen in front of us.

"I've deleted the feed from the hard drive. This is the only copy," I say. "So no, Chloe, it wouldn't be my word against yours. It would be hours of video footage documenting everything that happened Friday night."

"God, you're an asshole." I can hear the tightening of her throat and the emotion behind her words. I close the video and drop the phone back into my pocket. Standing this close to Chloe, I can smell her hair. It's sweet and floral and reminds me of the kiss we shared minutes ago. Part of the ruse to convince my mother we're together, yet when my mouth covered hers, I felt the electricity between us. The need to press further and take more, but I managed to control myself not only because my mother was present, but because this is business. Nothing more.

When she spins around to face me, her eyes are glassy and I can see the lump in her throat she tries to swallow past. I can't let it affect me. I need her and even if I have to muddy the water to get this deal done, I'm going to do it. It's worth that to me. But, fuck if her big blue eyes looking at me like I'm a monster don't make me want to do better. There's a pinch in my chest that makes me decide I don't want to be the asshole she thinks I am. While I need her to continue playing her role, I could offer her something in return.

"I'll offer you a deal."

Chloe searches my face, and for a moment I see hope in her eyes. Hope that I'm not the kind of guy that would blackmail her into pretending to be my girlfriend so I can close a business deal.

"You'll continue to pretend to be my girlfriend for the sake of business dealings, and as far as my mother is concerned, we are together, but you can come up with something you want in return."

Her face falls, and anger pinches her delicate features. "And what would I want from you?"

I shrug. "Think about it."

I'm shocked to find my body leaning in toward hers again. As if kissing goodbye is what we do now. How easily that one kiss with Chloe upstairs has reset its programming.

She takes a wide step around me to avoid our arms touching and moves toward the door.

"And, Chloe?"

"What?" she snaps, not bothering to turn around.

"Put it in writing," I call.

The meeting with my mother and Chloe has given me a late start to the day. When I get to my office door, Bea is waiting there with a cup of coffee in her hands.

"Thank you." I accept the coffee, grateful that I can always count on Bea to get an early start. She's snoozing in her chair by four, but she walks through the door at seven o'clock sharp every morning.

"A meeting with my mother has me running behind this morning."

Bea smiles politely, like she's minding her own business, but also patiently waiting to find out every detail. She's like my mother that way.

Moving into my office with Bea on my heels, I set the

coffee cup on my desk, then drop my wallet and cell phone into my drawer.

"I've got the list you requested of upcoming events where Mr. Hinkle will likely be in attendance. The Top Dog Gala is this Saturday. Would you like me to RSVP for you?"

I drop into my seat and shake my mouse to wake up my computer.

"Yes, and Chloe Anderson will be attending with me."

There's silence for long enough that it pulls my attention away from the computer screen and back to Bea.

"Miss Chloe?" Bea's eyes sparkle with interest.

"Yes. We're dating." The words are foreign in my mouth and come out curt. Before she can ask any questions, I add, "I need you to find out who's handling seating arrangements for this event. Find out where Fred is sitting. If Voltaire doesn't have their own table, make sure he's sitting at mine."

"Of course." Bea nods, writing down notes.

"Chloe will need a dress." I narrow my eyes at Bea. "An appropriate dress."

"Was there something wrong with the dress I picked out on Saturday?" she asks innocently.

"Yes, half of it was missing."

"Well, I did my research. It was a designer and style that Fred's girlfriend prefers. I saw it on the gram."

"You mean Instagram?"

"Yes, my granddaughter showed me how. I thought it would be a talking point for the group."

"It was thoroughly discussed." I think of Frankie's domination of the evening's conversation and my inability to speak at all with Fred about business. "While that may have turned out in our favor, I'm not a fan of surprises."

"I don't mean to pry," she says.

"Then don't."

She carries on without hesitation. "But I always thought

there was something between you and Miss Chloe." She smiles. "I had a feeling about it. Now I know I was right."

"Sure." I nod. There's no way I'm going to tell Bea that I'm using Chloe to help me get into good graces with Fred and secure a deal to purchase Voltaire Telecom. She'd have a heart attack, then that would be on my conscience. Blackmailing Chloe to pretend to be my girlfriend is all I can handle right now.

CHAPTER 8
Chloe

After the shock of Monday morning's events wears off, I realize while Barrett has the upper hand with that video, I still have a say in all this. Will I lose my job if Barrett shows JoAnna that video? The odds are high. But if I choose to tell her about the party and end this charade, Barrett's business deal could go up in smoke. For as much as JoAnna would be disappointed in me for not telling her the truth, I imagine Fred Hinkle won't appreciate Barrett lying to him about having a girlfriend, using me to play to Fred's soft heart and pretending to be someone he is not.

Because Barrett is not boyfriend material. He's the last guy I would want to date. Dismissive, demanding, only cares about himself.

Even the fact that he set up a table and champagne for Lauren's bachelorette at the club was self-serving. I wanted to think that he was being nice, but he wanted my guard down. And the way he wasn't the least bit surprised when JoAnna called us out on our 'date' yesterday means he knew that would happen. He knew it wouldn't just be one date and then we were even. Now, I'm stuck playing his fake girlfriend role for the next six weeks, the time Barrett estimated it would take to seal his deal with Fred.

We're having lunch today. We're going to sit down and eat a meal together. Alone. No Frankie and Fred to distract from the fact that we despise each other. This is not where I saw my life going.

While I wait for Barrett to arrive, I catch up on work emails. Now that I'm filling in for Lacey, I've got her workload as well as my usual tasks for JoAnna, along with helping coordinate the Books 4 Kids event.

With the busy weekend I had, I didn't get much reading in and I've needed every spare minute the last two days to get caught up. I know that JoAnna is giving me this opportunity to prove to her that I can handle being promoted to an assistant editor. It's all that I want, all that I've been working toward.

Career goals aside, I haven't had a moment to think about what I want from Barrett in return for me agreeing to be his fake girlfriend. Not that I agreed. But, if he's offering something in return, I want to take full advantage of it.

That's when it hits me. I pull out my notebook and jot down the only thing I've been able to think of.

"Have you been waiting long?" His deep voice pulls my attention upward. There's suddenly a chill in the air. You could argue that the restaurant kicked on the air conditioning, but I'm seated on the patio, so it's likely the chilly visage of my lunch companion.

Besides his text to meet him here for lunch today, we haven't talked since JoAnna's office on Monday morning. It's perfectly normal, that's more communication than we've had in the last two years, but the fact that my thoughts have been wandering to him at least a thousand times since Monday morning is highly problematic.

"Do you care if I've been waiting long or does your upbringing require you to ask?"

My snark rolls right off Barrett's Italian designer suit. Meaning he ignores my dig and stands silent, yet confident until I respond in the manner he deems appropriate. I hate that I know him that well.

"No, I was working."

"I prefer to sit inside," he says, still standing.

"Said no one ever on a beautiful afternoon in June."

Now it's his turn to ignore me.

He nods to my list. Before I can shove it back in my bag, Barrett has it in his hands.

"You want me to attend the Books 4 Kids event," he reads, dropping into the chair across from me. "That's all? An appearance at a children's charity book event? Easy. Done."

I snatch the paper back, hating that my only request was so easily fulfilled.

"No, that's not all," I say defiantly, hoping I can come up with something else in the next five seconds. My mind goes blank. "Okay. That's all I could think of off the top of my head. That's because I don't even know what my options are. It's like going to an ice cream shop and they have the glass cases covered. I can pick chocolate because every ice cream shop has chocolate but I might be missing out on raspberry chocolate chunk cheesecake because I didn't even know it was a possibility."

"Raspberry chocolate chunk cheesecake," he repeats. "Is that your favorite ice cream flavor?"

"No, I made it up. Or maybe it does exist, but I wouldn't select it out of the case if it were there. It's a metaphor for something more elaborate than basic chocolate. I'm more of a cookie dough fan."

He wrinkles his nose.

"You hate cookie dough ice cream?" I ask.

"Never had it."

"What?" I can't even with this guy. But then again, am I really surprised? "You're missing out."

"Not likely."

"Let me guess, you're a vanilla kind of guy?"

"I don't eat ice cream," he responds. I nearly fall out of my seat with this discovery, but then again, maybe it makes sense.

"I think that's worse than being vanilla guy. At least vanilla guy is in the game."

"What game is that?" he asks.

"The ice cream eating game. Your ice cream flavor says a lot about your personality. Vanilla guy is classic, and confident in what he likes. Sometimes he adds sprinkles if he's feeling wild, but mostly enjoys his ice cream in a cone because he likes to keep things simple."

Barrett smirks. "Sounds like you know this vanilla guy pretty well."

I don't need to tell Barrett about any guys that I do or do not know. Vanilla or not. We're in a fake relationship so my sex life, or lack thereof, is not of his concern.

I busy myself with putting my laptop away, but now it's just me and Barrett, staring at each other from across the table. Barrett's doing that thing again where he's obnoxiously quiet, yet completely comfortable. It makes me want to jump out of my chair. Where is that waiter?

"So, you want me to uncover the cases?" he says, finally.

"Yes." I nod, pleased that my ice cream analogy was well received. "Pull back the paper and get out the tasting spoons."

Barrett eyes me for a minute, a hint of a smile playing at the corner of his lips. "I've got an idea."

He reaches for the paper which I continue to hold tight to. Barrett lifts his brows.

"Please?" He extends his hand.

Manners. What a treat. I finally hand it over.

Barrett uncaps his pen, then places the cap on the end. Why that simple movement makes my legs start to shake is unexplainable. Or completely obvious. It's the same reaction I had when he signed the fundraiser check in his office last week.

Apparently, I'm horny for Barrett's hands. They are sexy. They're large, yet elegant. Can hands be elegant? Maybe it's his long fingers or the way they look so fucking capable, and capable of fucking. Oh, shit. Do not think that. He might also be a mind reader. That could be why he's silent a lot. He's keeping the pathway open to be able to read other people's thoughts. My cheeks heat and I wish I had my paper back so I could fold it into a fan. The accordion style you'd make at summer camp in arts and crafts.

I'm so distracted with calming myself down that when Barrett hands me back the paper I'm confused at what I'm looking at.

Barrett has added some language at the top that reads like a contract. It states that I will continue to pretend to be his girlfriend for business purposes until his deal with Fred is signed or for six weeks, whichever comes first, and in return he will grant me six conditions that can be added at any time. Below, there are six lines that Barrett has drawn on the page.

"Six weeks," I say, noting the timeline. "Do you really think you'll be able to close a deal with Fred in that time frame?"

"That's not your concern, but yes. I know what I want and I know how to get it."

"They can be anything?" I ask.

"No conditions on your conditions, with the exception of getting rid of the contract that requires you to be my girlfriend for business purposes. Other than that, it is up to you, but there are only six, so use them wisely."

"You sound like a genie in a lamp." I pause to think for a moment. "Why six?"

"One per week. Or you can use them as you choose."

The waiter returns to take our order, but I'm confused when he sets down a bag on the table.

"Here is that order for you, sir." The waiter turns to me, "Miss, what can I get for you?"

"What is that?" I ask.

Barrett stands, his chair scraping loudly on the cement patio.

"I can't stay. I've got a meeting downtown." He turns to the waiter, "Put her meal on my card." Barrett hands him a fifty-dollar bill, then slides his gaze back to me to add, "I'll be in touch."

The waiter is excited about his tip, but when he reads my annoyance, his face turns guilty.

"Your boyfriend is super-hot," he smiles, obviously thinking the compliment about Barrett's looks will make me feel better about being ditched at lunch, then tucks the bill into his apron, "and generous."

The playfulness I felt for a half second between us vanishes with Barrett's abrupt departure. I need to remind myself of the situation. Barrett and I have a contract for me to be his fake girlfriend. He's in it for himself. The very fact that he couldn't take thirty minutes to eat a meal with me is evidence of that. Next time I start ogling his hands, I'll need to remember that.

"He's something all right," I respond, before placing my order.

Thursday afternoon I'm finishing up notes on a manuscript that I pulled from the slush pile. It's got real potential and I'm going to pitch it to JoAnna at our next editorial meeting. My phone vibrates from its place on my desk.

Barrett: I need your girlfriend services. Marcus will be picking you up in ten minutes.

I glance at the clock. It's three thirty in the afternoon. What the hell? I can't just leave work.

I type out my response.

Me: I'm working.

His response is quick.

Barrett: Your job depends on it.

Ugh. God, I hate that he has this over my head. I could tell JoAnna and blow up his business deal. That would show him. But that would blow up my life, too.

My stomach churns at Barrett's reminder that I'd be jobless, possibly ousted from the entire industry if every publishing house knew I was fired from St. Clair Press. I glance down at the manuscript I've been reading and I instantly know I'll have to go along with his demands.

I text back a thumbs up, which is really a giant fuck you, but I doubt Barrett knows that, then start gathering my things.

On my way out, I stop by JoAnna's office to let her know that I'm leaving. Fake relationship with her son aside, ever since the party at her apartment, I'm determined to be on my best behavior. After this deal with Barrett ends, the slate will be wiped clean and I don't want to give her any other reason to fire me. It's only honesty from here on out.

I've never left work early before. While I do tend to work from home in the evenings, reading manuscripts and checking emails, I hate that I'm cutting out early.

With my heart pounding in my chest, I knock on the doorframe to JoAnna's office.

"Chloe," she says, looking up from her computer. "Come on in."

"Oh, actually I didn't need anything, I was just letting you know I'm on my way out for the day."

"Okay, sure."

"I know it's early, but I'll be working later, at home." I motion to my tote bag full of manuscripts.

"Sounds good."

"I've got a thing with Barrett," I continue, feeling the need to explain the situation without confessing everything. "I'm meeting him to, you know, um…"

JoAnna holds up a hand.

"Chloe, I don't need the details."

Oh my God. I realize now that she thinks I'm skipping out on work to have sex with Barrett. Her *son*. Eww. Not the sex part, because let's be honest, I like a good science fiction romance with hot robot/human sex, but to talk to JoAnna about it is just wrong.

Now, it's occurring to me that people think that Barrett and I are having sex. That's what you do in most adult romantic relationships. That's what you do when your boyfriend looks like Barrett. You consummate like bunnies, everywhere and at all hours of the day.

JoAnna is staring at me.

"I'm not leaving early to have sex with Barrett," I announce, a little too loudly.

"Okay, Chloe. I'll see you tomorrow."

JoAnna's smile is tight before she puts her glasses back on and turns to her computer.

Shit. I made it worse.

I've been dismissed and I'd be an idiot to stand there and try to explain what I meant. I decide to leave it at awkward and not aim for wildly inappropriate.

Like Barrett indicated, Marcus is waiting downstairs for me. He opens the door to help me into the car.

"Hi, Marcus. How are you?"

"Good afternoon, Miss Anderson. I'm well." He's so

formal. Takes his job seriously. I don't imagine he ever thought of hosting a party at Barrett's apartment.

"Are you going to tell me where we're going?" I ask.

"It's a short drive. Only about a half mile."

"I could have walked."

"Mr. St. Clair wanted me to drive you."

Of course, he did. He probably doesn't trust me to make it there on my own. Which is silly because he doesn't even know about the time I rode the subway for three hours because I was reading a book and missed my stop.

It's only a half mile, but it takes twelve minutes to get there. Each minute that ticks by only gets me more worked up. Not because of traffic, but because it gives me more time to think about the mortifying conversation I just had with my boss. What she must think.

JoAnna had been surprised to hear about me and Barrett but happy.

When Barrett and I break up will she be devastated? When he moves on will she continue to talk about me, haunt him with stories from the past? The one that got away? God, I hope so.

It would drive him crazy. It puts a small smile on my face in my otherwise annoyed state.

Barrett has made it crystal clear that nothing can get in the way of his business deal, but not to the detriment of my job. My career. That's the entire reason I'm going along with this.

When Marcus pulls up to our destination, any thoughts of my embarrassing conversation with JoAnna vanishes.

Marcus opens the door and in front of me stands the NYC Racquet Club.

I can see Barrett waiting in front of the large wooden doors. It looks more like a cathedral than a health club. Barrett strides over to meet me. He looks impeccable in his navy suit, crisp white shirt and designer shades. His lips in a firm, straight line like a brooding model. I glance around for the photographer who's shooting this Gucci ad campaign.

We stand there for a moment, toe to toe, neither of us sure of the proper protocol for greeting your fake significant other. Add it to the list of things we haven't discussed about this farce of a relationship.

Until Barrett wraps a hand around each of my upper arms and leans down to kiss me on the cheek. It's quick, a whisper of a kiss against my skin, yet his proximity, the scent of his cologne has my lady parts fluttering with excitement.

Jesus, if that's all it takes, I really need to resolve to date more when this is over.

"I'll be back at five o'clock, sir," Marcus announces from behind us.

Barrett pulls away and acknowledges his driver with a nod.

When Marcus retreats into the car, I finally remember that before I laid eyes on his gorgeous face, I was mad at him.

"It's not okay how you summoned me from my job. I can't just leave work anytime you have a whim. I'm not your beck and call girl. When this charade is over, I still need to have a job, remember?" I take a breath, then glance toward the wooden doors. "What is it? What is so important? Did you seriously call me out of work to sit and watch you play?"

"We're playing tennis with Fred and Frankie," he says.

"What?" I ask, the octave of my voice rising with panic as I recall the lies that I told at dinner with Fred and Frankie about my tennis abilities.

He shrugs. "Fred called and I didn't want to miss the opportunity to connect."

He moves to open the door.

"Barrett," I whisper-hiss. "I can't play tennis."

"Don't worry, they have loner racquets and a pro shop where you can get an outfit."

"No. It's not that. I was lying when I said that I was state champ in high school. I thought I was helping you out. Giving you more in common with Fred and Frankie. I never realized we'd actually be playing tennis with them."

"You've got to be kidding me." I can hear his molars grinding.

My mouth pinches together at his exasperated tone. "It was supposed to be one date, remember?"

"We're not backing out now. We'll figure it out. Tell them you're injured. A minor injury that allows you to play but not very well."

"Ah, yes, more lies."

"It's harmless. Besides, I was planning to let them win anyways, so your handicap will make it more believable."

I stare at Barrett. I don't know whether to be horrified or impressed by the lengths that he's going to for this business deal. I've heard he's an impressive businessman, but also that he can be ruthless, calculating and self-serving. A vulture that preys on the weak.

I make a mental note not to let him get his claws into me anymore than he already has.

"Fine," I say sharply, motioning for him to lead the way.

The building is three stories high, with large arches above the plated glass windows. Plush navy carpet with an intricate design in burgundy and gold flows down the hallway as far as I can see. The air feels cool and smells like rich, old men. A faint cigar smell lingers in the air. An odd scent for a gym.

Inside we are greeted by a woman with short black hair dressed in all white standing at an ornate looking reception desk. She smiles and I'm blinded, her white teeth a perfect match for her crisp white polo.

"Good afternoon, Mr. St. Clair," she says cheerfully. "I see you have court seven reserved."

"Yes." Barrett nods, then places his hand on my lower

back, giving me a little push forward. "This is my girlfriend, Chloe Anderson."

"Nice to meet you, Miss Anderson, I'm Alana."

"Hi." I smile back, but her brilliance is unmatched.

"Chloe is going to need a tennis outfit and shoes."

"Of course." She nods like people show up to a racquet club every day completely unprepared to play tennis.

"Before I send her over to the pro shop for a fitting, let me get your racket, Mr. St. Clair."

Alana disappears through the door, only to come back a moment later with a racket bag.

"David did a wonderful job restringing your racket. It's good as new."

"Thank you," Barrett says, then takes the racket bag from her.

"Do you have a preference for racket brand and style, Miss Anderson?"

I look to Barrett.

"She'll do a Babolat Pure Aero. Right-handed."

My brows lift at how fancy that sounded. "What happened to Prince and Wilson?"

"They're still around." He shrugs.

Alana hands me the racket Barrett requested, then offers to walk me to the pro shop.

"I'll take her." Barrett motions for me to follow.

We pass through a great room that is large enough to be a tennis court, but it's decorated with high-back reading chairs, side tables and lamps. The lamps cast a warm glow, the perfect reading light. I'm jealous of the man reading his paper in peace.

A thought comes to mind.

"As your girlfriend, do I have access to the racket club?"

"Court reservations may only be made by members, but

you have access to the other amenities, whirlpool, sauna, lounge and reading room."

Forget tennis. Sign me up for the reading room.

"I've added you to my guest list."

"So, when we break up, am I going to be removed?" I ask.

From the sign on the door that says Pro Shop, I can see our destination ahead.

"I hadn't thought about it," he says.

"The racquet club or the breakup?"

"Either."

"Wait." My footsteps slow and our joined hands pull taut. Barrett turns back toward me. "How are we going to break up?"

"I don't know. I hadn't given it much thought."

"We are going to break up. Six weeks or as soon as your deal with Fred is done, whichever comes first. It's what you wrote," I remind him. I marked the day on my calendar. It's a week before Lauren's wedding. I remember the relief I felt when I realized I wouldn't have to explain any of this to my parents. My fake relationship with Barrett will be in the rearview mirror before I'm back in Colorado.

"I'm going to vote for a conscious uncoupling that leaves me unlimited access to that reading room," I offer.

Barrett's lips quirk. He finds my arrangement amusing.

"What do I get?" he asks.

His eyes scan over my face.

"What do you want?" I ask earnestly because apparently negotiating is our thing.

Barrett's eyes drop lower on my body. I swear I can feel the heat of his gaze all the way down to my toes. It happens so quickly, or maybe not even at all. I probably imagined it. Maybe he's eyeing a mole on my neck. Yeah, that's probably it.

His brow furrows in concentration. He's trying to

remember the name of the dermatologist he's going to refer me to.

But then, there are those long fingers reaching up toward his mouth. I'm not imagining *those*. Two fingers slide across his bottom lip, tugging the flesh sideways. My eyes follow their path. It's a slow seduction of my pupils. Is that a thing?

With that one movement, all the air gets sucked out of my lungs. Suddenly the two-thousand-square-foot space around us feels stifling.

Barrett's lips haven't touched mine in three days and suddenly that feels like an eternity. If his kiss on the cheek outside affected my lady bits, now they're fully alert. And wet.

It makes no sense, but that's what happens when he taunts me with his kissable lips and capable fingers. I'll give up the reading room right now if he would just bend down and kiss me, press those skilled digits into my hair.

No, that's not right.

I need to get my priorities straight. Minutes earlier I was telling myself not to be affected by Barrett's appeal. There's no heart behind those pouty lips and perfect smile. How have I forgotten so quickly?

The door to the pro shop swings open giving me a much-needed breeze of fresh air. And to remind me why we're here.

"There you are!" Frankie exclaims when she sees us. "Is this skirt not the cutest thing you've ever seen? I just love tennis."

And by cute, she means tiny.

If I felt overwhelmed by Barrett a moment ago, that's nothing compared to the sensory overload that Frankie provides. From her perfume to her jewelry and makeup. It doesn't matter that Frankie is in the requisite white skirt and tennis tank, the rest of her drowns out the boring tennis outfit.

Her fuchsia nails graze my back when she pulls me into a hug.

"Barrett." She kisses him on the cheek. "Fred is in the men's locker room getting changed."

Barrett nods. "Chloe needs to get outfitted."

"Didn't realize we were playing today so I left my stuff at home," I say.

Alana from the front desk appears. "Miss Anderson, sorry to interrupt, here is your guest key card," she says cheerfully, handing me the plastic card. "Welcome to the NYC Racquet Club."

Barrett clears his throat. He does that a lot around me. I've yet to decipher if he's annoyed or amused.

"Ha ha, thanks, Alana." I take the card and Alana floats away. "She's funny. I forgot my card." I motion to the card in my hands. "Isn't she nice?"

Frankie smiles, oblivious to the fact that Alana is treating me like a new guest when I've supposedly been here many times.

"I'll help Chloe pick out clothes and meet you out there."

Frankie grabs my hand and pulls me into the pro shop. I follow along like a good fake girlfriend would and do my best to forget about Barrett's lips.

CHAPTER 9

Barrett

A court attendant is feeding balls into the machine for Fred and me to warm up. Fred's agility is impressive for a middle-aged, overweight man.

"Nice backhand," I comment as we switch positions and I get ready to receive the next ball.

"I've been playing tennis every day," Fred says. "It's what keeps me fit. Frankie thinks I've recently lost weight."

He pats his thick mid-section and I struggle to come up with a response that isn't a bold-faced lie.

I didn't like the way Chloe looked at me downstairs when she learned I would be lying to Fred and Frankie. Yes, sometimes I manipulate the truth in my business dealings. There is a gray area where the truth is not always necessary. Things that aren't important, like whether my fake girlfriend is good at tennis or not.

"That's great."

"You're not so bad yourself." Fred nods to the corner where I returned the ball on the line. "Your father was a great player as well."

"I learned from the best," I say, disregarding the nostalgia that Fred's mention of my father causes. It was a lifetime ago that he was across the court from me.

"Shoot it to me straight, kid. I know you're after Voltaire. You haven't said it as plainly, but I know it's your intention. I don't blame you. If I were in your position, I'd want it, too. But, in my situation, I have to make sure that the company I sell to, the person at the helm is the right kind of person. That they have their priorities straight."

Fred pauses to return the next ball, then turns back to me.

"I like you. I didn't think I did, but then you surprised me at dinner with Chloe. I'm never surprised. I always know what's coming. I can read people, their intentions. I thought you were a savage businessman with no heart, but now I realize there's no way a woman like Chloe would be interested in a guy like that. And Frankie adores Chloe. They really hit it off."

"I appreciate that, Fred, and Chloe feels the same." It's not exactly a lie, I know Chloe doesn't have a lot of friends in the city so it could be true. "I want to start by giving you an idea of where SCM could go once we acquire Voltaire."

"Hold that thought, kid." Fred holds up a hand to silence me, his attention drawn across the tennis courts to where Frankie and Chloe are walking out onto the court. Fred's jaw goes slack at the sight of Frankie in her tiny skirt and low plunging top. "Now I don't want to say this is the only reason I've been playing tennis every day but it sure is a perk."

Fred chuckles, his additional comments not even registering as I take in the sight of Chloe in a short white tennis skirt outfit. I don't know how it's possible but this tennis outfit manages to make the dress Bea picked out for dinner look like a tent. I can see nearly every inch of her toned legs. The tiny built-in shorts peek out from underneath the skirt that barely covers her ass and her breasts are exploding out of the zipper of the low V-neck top. Her bun has been replaced by a ponytail that swings with every step as they approach.

Fuck. I can feel the crotch of my starched tennis shorts tightening.

I'd be annoyed at Fred's short attention span but I couldn't form a coherent business thought right now if I tried.

"Ladies, you look lovely." Fred wraps an arm around Frankie's mid-section and pulls her in for a kiss.

When Chloe stops in front of me, obviously waiting for a response, I lift my hand and pat her on the head.

She swats me away like I'm a gnat.

"What are you doing?"

I have no idea why I did that. It was the only place on Chloe's body I felt safe to touch. I shake my head because there are no thoughts there anymore. All the blood my brain needs to function has headed south.

"What are you wearing?" I ask.

"The regular sizes were too big and there was no petite section, so I'm tween Chloe, your tennis partner with her ass and boobs hanging out." She groans.

"Your ass isn't hanging out."

"But my boobs are?" she exclaims.

"Nothing is hanging out," I emphasize.

"Why do tennis clothes have to be so fitted?" She scans her body then looks over to mine.

Normally, I don't have issues with getting spontaneous boners in public. That was before I started hanging out with Chloe. It's like my dick knows she's looking and wants to say hi. Fucking idiot.

Now I'm watching her look at my crotch and I'm begging my body not to respond. It's an impossible feat. Her gaze only makes it harder. The way her mouth parts in surprise. Her eyes widen and her tongue slips out to wet her lips.

"You two ready?" Frankie calls from the other side of the

net. The attendant has cleared the ball machine and Frankie is bouncing a ball at the serving line.

"Just a minute," I call. I grab the white club pullover from my bag on the bench and pull it over Chloe's head. The hem matches the length of her skirt.

"What's this for?" she asks while I adjust the collar, then roll the sleeves up on both sides.

"This is so I can focus on the game," I say, pulling the quarter zip up to Chloe's neck.

"I thought we were going to let them win?" She rolls her eyes at me.

"Not by much," I reply, knowing the competitor in me will have a hard time throwing the game.

I coach Chloe on the basics and what she can do to appear knowledgeable before we explain to Fred that she's still recovering from a recent wrist injury.

I instruct Chloe where to stand, the opposite side of where Frankie will be serving the ball. She stays close to the net, bouncing on her toes like she's jogging in place. The action makes her ass bounce and nearly distracts me from returning the serve.

Chloe does her best to return serves and play up at the net, but in the end I'm a single playing a doubles game. After two games, my shirt is drenched.

We take a water break. I towel off and get water while Chloe takes off my pullover.

"It's too hot to wear that." She fans her face then reaches for my water bottle.

She takes my hesitation for rejection.

"Seriously? You can stick your tongue in my mouth, but not share your water?"

"I didn't stick my tongue in your mouth."

"There was definitely tongue. I remember tongue."

"I'm sure you've been recounting every detail so you're probably right. I barely recall."

Her fair cheeks are rosy now. Partially from playing tennis, but they darken when I tease her about the kiss. They're the same color they were when I kissed her goodbye in my mother's office on Monday. I'm teasing her about it, but I'd be lying if I said that kiss hasn't been on my mind all week. It had surprised me how perfectly her lips felt against mine. How sweet she tasted. Now, I can't stare at her lips without triggering the memory.

She narrows her gaze at me, then yanks the bottle out of my hands to take a drink.

She lifts the bottle to her lips. I watch a bead of sweat roll along her collar bone, then down between her breasts.

"It's like a million degrees up here." She fans her face.

That just made it warmer, I think.

"I want to try to return the serve," Chloe says, determined. She seems to be getting into the game.

"Are you sure that's a good idea with your wrist injury?" I ask.

Chloe pinches her lips together, annoyed. I'm annoyed, too, that I can't stop staring at her mouth.

"Yes. It's not like she's Serena Williams. I'm tired of bouncing over here while you play most of the returns."

"I'm tired of you bouncing over there, too." The sight of Chloe's perky ass in that tiny tennis skirt is going to haunt my dreams.

I relent, and switch Chloe's position while Frankie gets ready to serve.

The ball flies over the net, Chloe attacks it like I showed her and returns it. Frankie is startled at first but manages to return it back to Chloe. Chloe reaches for the ball before it goes out of bounds and returns it. Chloe is excitedly jumping up and down, and it occurs to me that she doesn't realize that the play is still going.

"I did it!" She jumps with enthusiasm. Fred returns the ball and still in celebration mode, with little to no reaction time, it smacks Chloe in the forehead.

I watch helplessly as her body falls backwards, and her racket rattles on the ground next to her.

Shit.

"Chloe?" I drop to the ground to examine her. A moment later, her eyelashes flutter and her eyes open.

"Did we win?" she asks, her eyes searching my face with a dazed expression.

Gently, I brush the loose hairs that have escaped from her ponytail to the side so I can get a better look. There's a red mark, the size of the ball, that is growing in height before my eyes.

"The award for largest goose egg on your head? Yes," I say.

Chloe's brows knit together in confusion, but the movement causes her to wince and one hand to shoot up to her forehead.

"Oh God, Chloe!!" Frankie screams as she drops to Chloe's side. "Are you okay? Fred, I can't believe you hit her in the head."

"I'm sorry, Chloe." Fred looks sheepish. "Next time wait to celebrate when the ball is dead."

I help Chloe up. Her white skirt is dirty and instinctively I dust it off, grazing her ass. Chloe doesn't saw my hand off with a machete so she must be pretty out of it. Fred apologizes again, and Frankie pulls Chloe into a bear hug that makes her wince, then we're taking the elevators down to the lobby.

"Let's go get you checked out."

～

As instructed by Dr. Patel, I'm keeping a close eye on Chloe, and escorting her home. She gives Marcus the address and I'm thankful that she's still got her memory. I'd hate for her to forget that she despises me, and ruin all the fun.

"How does it look?" Chloe removes the ice pack from her forehead. Her fair complexion is no aid in disguising the red mark on her skin, though I do think the ice is helping with the swelling. I should be staring at her face, but my gaze drops to her chest. The spot where her quarter-zip tennis dress is displaying her cleavage.

She catches me looking.

"They didn't have a sports bra in my size so I had to wear my regular bra. If Fred didn't nail me in the head with the ball, I probably would have knocked myself out with one of these bouncing around." She pats her chest. "Seriously, why are tennis clothes so snug? You know what I'm talking about. Those shorts aren't hiding anything."

Chloe finds my lap out of the corner of her eye.

"Did I say that out loud?" She clamps a hand over her mouth.

"Yes." I hold back a chuckle, because the only thing more entertaining than angry Chloe is nervous, rambling Chloe.

"It looks fine." I point to her head. "Your head, that is. I'm not going to comment on your breasts."

"That's fair. I won't comment on your dick either." She gasps. "Is having no filter a symptom of a concussion?"

"No," I say, feeling my shorts grow tighter with Chloe's innocent, yet effective dirty talk. At that moment, I'm grateful that Marcus pulls up to Chloe's building.

Chloe moves to get out of the car.

"I'll see you in," I say.

"No, it's fine. I'm good."

"I want to make sure you get into your apartment okay."

Whether it's because I don't want her to pass out in her hallway or because I'm plain curious, I'm not sure.

Chloe grabs the bag with her work clothes in it and proceeds to an orange door nestled between a pawn shop and a business advertising money orders and jail bonds. I glance down the street. My attention in the car had been on Chloe. I don't even know where we are. I haven't seen the inside and I already hate it.

Inside the small entryway, there are four mailboxes on the wall, and a steep set of stairs leading upward.

"No doorman, I take it?"

Chloe narrows her eyes at me. She coughs and I swear I hear the word 'snob' under her breath. Trying to keep an open mind, I follow Chloe's lead, up another flight of stairs, to the third floor.

After inserting the key, she jiggles the handle twice before cranking it to the right.

"That doesn't seem safe," I say.

"You have to know just how to jiggle it or it doesn't work. It's more effective than if the key worked normally. Trust me, I've been locked out several times. It's the equivalent of a randomly selected password online. You know the ones where you're never going to remember them because they're like twenty characters long and have no relevance to you whatsoever so you immediately change it to Bobcatpretzel1997?"

What is she even talking about right now? Maybe I shouldn't let her stay alone.

These thoughts immediately invade my brain, but I don't voice them.

"What significance is that?" I ask.

"I had a cat named Bob, he liked to lick pretzels and I was born in 1997. I probably shouldn't be telling you that. I use that password for everything." She sighs, obviously disgruntled that she's going to have to change her password now. "Okay, I made it. Thanks for seeing me home."

Ignoring her attempt to leave me on the outside of the door, I quickly move past her. I'm only two strides in and nearly run into a brick wall. I look around. Chloe's apartment is the smallest I've ever seen. I don't know if it could technically be called an apartment, but more so a room.

"What the hell, Chloe?" I motion to the space around me. The twelve-by-eighteen room that appears to be Chloe's home.

She closes the door and turns toward me. We're practically on top of each other.

"I didn't move the wall. It's always been there." She points to the brick wall I nearly crashed into. We would have both had facial injuries if I hadn't stopped short. "You act like I did some kind of voodoo magic to make the walls close in on themselves. Don't worry, your perfect nose didn't get crushed." She heels off her tennis shoes, then mumbles, but not quietly at all, "Maybe if you weren't so tall and broad shouldered, you'd fit better."

"Right, because my stature is the issue here."

I glance around, finally able to take in the rest of her place now that I know this is all of it. A twin bed with a pink comforter with tiny flowers on it. A six-drawer dresser that also serves as a nightstand and a desk with her laptop, lamp and books on it. A folding camp chair tucked in the corner is the only seating other than her bed. On the wall opposite her bed there's a two-foot-wide counter with a sink and one upper and lower cabinet. There's a hot plate taking up the remainder of the counter, its cord hanging precariously close to the sink.

I move toward the kitchen area.

"This is where you live?" I ask, examining the hot plate, before opening the cabinet above the counter. A variety of brightly colored mugs and a mismatch of plates and bowls are on one side, while a few box dinners and miscellaneous pantry items are on the other.

"Would you like a tour?" Chloe can't help but laugh at her own joke. "It's supposed to be funny, because you don't need a tour to see all of my stuff. It's all within arm's reach."

I don't find this funny at all.

"I can tell you're excited. You're thinking 'wow, look at all the deeply personal items I can peruse through to get to know my fake girlfriend better.'"

I look around again. There is a stack of books by her bed. Instead of a closet, there's a clothing rack affixed to the wall with garment bags on hangers.

I push one aside to see the label on the front.

"What's Threads?"

"It's a wardrobe service. You pay a monthly fee and they send you outfits for the week. You return them when you're done and they send more. I figured since I don't have much room for clothes or a budget it made the most sense. Also, it's eco-friendly. I feel better about not purchasing so many clothes and they have really cute designer stuff that I wouldn't be able to afford anyway. I've been telling everyone about it. I think if we all did something like this it would really help cut down on fashion waste in our landfills."

It occurs to me; I haven't seen Chloe in the same outfit twice. It's a shame that pink skirt she wore on Monday isn't hers. I've been thinking about it all week. My hands fisting the bubblegum pink material to push it up around her hips and explore what's underneath.

I shake the thought loose.

"All your clothes are from this service?"

"Not my underwear or pajamas." She moves to the dresser and pulls open a drawer. "See?"

I'll admit I'm interested in Chloe's underwear, but now isn't the time.

"Where's the bathroom?" I ask.

"Down the hall, to the right." She makes a face. "Oh, technically Todd has it booked for shower time from five to six, he's a nightshift worker, but if you need to use it you could probably just slip in quick. Todd's super nice. He's my neighbor. Doesn't get out much so sometimes when our schedules align, we have wine night in the hallway and play gin rummy."

I'm completely caught off guard by the bathroom situation, I can't even rib her for her lackluster social life.

"You share a bathroom? With a guy?" I have a hard time keeping the irritation out of my voice.

"Yeah." Chloe lets out an exasperated sigh. "It's not like we're in there at the same time. And we've established ground rules. Like no peeing in the shower or other bodily substances," she makes a jerking off hand gesture, "I'm sure you're familiar. And I do my best to not get hair in the sink. Todd had a huge problem with the man that lived here before me. I guess he would brush his wigs over the sink and the whole sewer system backed up." She pauses to take a breath. "Anyway, it's nothing compared to sharing with three younger sisters. That was a horrific experience."

The bulb flickers above our heads.

"What was that?" I ask.

"Nothing." Chloe feigns innocence, but I know that can't be the first time that's happened.

I take another look around. Even if I had the door fixed, added in a security panel for the building downstairs, and hired someone to deep clean the bathroom weekly, none of that would give me peace of mind.

"You can't stay here," I say.

"What do you mean? I live here. I've been living here for two years."

"Because I didn't know," I mutter, checking out the loose wire coming from the corner of the ceiling.

"I appreciate your concern but I'm good here. It fits my budget."

A door slams above us and tiny pieces of loose brick from the wall sprinkle onto Chloe's hardwood floor. My eyes take in the tiny chips of brick and then my gaze lifts to hers. She grabs her hand broom and dustpan to quickly clean up the debris.

"It doesn't feel safe. You couldn't even get out that window if there was a fire. And that's saying something."

"Ah, small person jokes. You're hilarious."

"I like that you're small," I say without thinking.

"What?" Her head jerks in my direction.

"Nothing." I clear my throat, bringing focus back to the point that I need to make. "My girlfriend would not live *here*."

"You shouldn't be so judgy," Chloe says, standing from where she was crouched cleaning up the rubble. "I'm sure your closet is bigger than my apartment but this apartment has charm. Character. It's not some cookie cutter fancy schmancy penthouse in Gramercy. And I'm on a budget."

"My girlfriend doesn't need to be on a budget."

"I'm your fake girlfriend and we are going to last for like five seconds. No one will know where I live. It's not like we're going to invite Fred and Frankie over here for dinner. Which is a relief, because I've only got the one chair."

I sigh, then drop down onto her twin bed. The thing nearly collapses under my weight. It may work for a small person like Chloe, but there's no way this bed could hold much more weight. That thought makes me happier than it should. When she bends over to empty the dustpan into the trash under the sink, I argue that I would look away from her perfect ass if there was anywhere else to look.

I finally divert my gaze from Chloe's ass and catch a glimpse of something small, gray and furry run past my shoes.

"Chloe?"

"Hang on. I'm trying to figure out what that sound is."

"Chloe."

"What, Barrett?"

She finally turns around. I point to the rodent on the floor.

It moves again and Chloe yelps.

My gaze darts to hers.

"Do you have a pet?" I ask like it's a legitimate question. At this point, I wouldn't be surprised if instead of calling her landlord about a rodent problem, she befriended it.

"Oh, yeah, that's just Ralph," she says nonchalantly, while also backing herself up against the wall.

Suddenly the mouse darts across the room and Chloe runs for the door screaming.

CHAPTER 10

Chloe

An hour later, Marcus pulls up to a brownstone on 71st Street. Not because it took me that long to pack my meager personal items but because I spent half of that time arguing with Barrett about staying at his place.

I laid out a perfectly plausible plan to catch Ralph in a live trap and keep him as a pet. I'd feel much better about the situation if I knew his whereabouts. Barrett argued that where there is one, there are many. I counterargued that as a collective they could probably make me a dress while I was sleeping. Barrett said it was only a matter of time before they used my rental designer wardrobe for their nests. Or started chewing up my books.

That got me packing faster than you can say Colleen Hoover.

Ultimately, I agreed to move into Barrett's place temporarily while the mouse and maintenance issues in my apartment are being resolved. It was a tough decision, living with small possibly disease-ridden rodents or Barrett.

But my new living arrangement with Barrett will be as temporary as our fake relationship, even shorter if the sobs of my landlord through Barrett's phone are any indication. She'll have that place in tiptop shape in no time.

I do a double take out the car window. The brownstone is white stucco with black-framed windows and an archway door to match. Plant baskets with tidy green shrubs line all ten windows from which warm yellow light flows.

The windows are like porn. I imagine a decorated Christmas tree filling the large one on the main floor. Yes, it's June, but a girl can dream.

A black wrought iron gate and railing leading up to the stoop.

This place is quintessential New York City. Or at least the New York City I had envisioned before I found my two-hundred-square-foot budget apartment in East Harlem.

"I'm covered in dirt and sweat. You can't expect me to meet the governor looking like this."

Barrett reaches across me to open the door.

"This is where I live."

"No. That's not possible." I shake my head. "Your home is perched on top of a building, overlooking the mere mortals that dare to breathe your same air." I glance forlornly at the beautiful exterior of the home I imagine Barrett has ruined the inside of. He's likely outfitted it with some modern concrete and glass décor a la his minimalist office. Turned it into some cold gray box with square lights and chairs that look like they belong in a dentist office. Ugh. "Where are the gargoyles?"

"Now who's being judgy?" His brows lift and his lips twitch with amusement.

He's too close again. Close enough I can smell him. And what's up with Barrett not smelling after playing tennis in the heat? His cologne is faint now, mixed with potent pheromones and an intoxicating musk. He should bottle his scent, call it Sweaty Guy. It would sell millions.

It's the racquet club all over again only now there's one

thousand nine hundred and ninety-five square feet less surrounding us. His eyes, those lips, that lickable jaw. I need to find something on his face that doesn't make me want to spontaneously combust when I look at it.

"You have great eyebrows. Do you get them waxed?" I ask.

"Do I look like a man who gets his eyebrows waxed?" He furrows them now, really showing off their range.

"No. You look like a man whose hair is genetically programed to grow in the exact right spot."

He studies me for a moment.

"Anything else, Chloe?"

"I just really like your eyebrows. They're probably my favorite thing about you," I lie. "No one's ever asked, but I want to be prepared with an answer."

"Is that what you would say, if asked?"

"It's not the girlfriend answer I would give."

"What is the girlfriend answer you would give?"

My eyes betray me, landing squarely in Barrett's lap. When I glance back up to meet his gaze, he's practically laughing at me. It's a rare sight to behold. So much so that I almost manage to forget that I was just staring at his crotch.

"Your charming personality," I choke out.

Barrett leans in closer, his face barely visible in my periphery.

"Do you know what I'd say?" he asks.

"Hmm?"

"The way your eyes light up when they spot the outline of my dick in tennis shorts."

My jaw drops to the floor of the car.

"That's not—" I begin to argue.

"My boyfriend answer is your smile."

Barrett retreats from the side of my head and exits out the other door. Marcus has already unloaded most of my items. He's set my suitcase and laptop bag on the quaint stoop I was admiring minutes ago. Back before Barrett's deep, full-bodied voice whispered the word dick into my ear. That must have been in another life because I'm dead now.

I think he said something about my smile. I can't be sure, he lost me at dick. I've also had a head injury today so I'm not sure if he didn't just say to make myself at home.

I have two options. Stay in this car and live here until my apartment is rodent-free or manage to get my highly aroused body out of the car and climb the stairs to Barrett's stoop with wobbly legs. I opt for option two because option one will inevitably have me coming face to face with Barrett at some point, since this is his car, and I'd like to put more than two feet between us. So, I discreetly fan my flushed cheeks for half a minute then meet him on the sidewalk.

Gripping the handrail, I manage to make it up the stairs without any more head trauma.

"I love that you have a stoop. It's so quaint." I turn to look back to the street from my temporary residence. "I'm sure there's some interesting history behind it."

"It was so the parlor floor was a level above the horse manure." Barrett's lips twitch.

"Thanks for ruining the magic for me," I pout.

"Anytime."

Marcus returns from inside, the entirety of my possessions now inside Barrett's home.

"Thank you, Marcus. We'll see you tomorrow."

"Goodnight, Mr. St. Clair." He nods in my direction. "Miss Anderson."

I feel better knowing Marcus knows I'm here. That way if Barrett decides to strangle me with his giant hands in my sleep Marcus will alert the authorities. Unless Barrett pays him off. I'll have to tell someone else I'm here. Unfortunately, 'temporarily moved in with my fake boyfriend because my apartment has a mice infestation, among other issues' isn't the call

I want to make to my parents, so I fire off a quick text to Jules.

ME: I'm moving in with Barrett. I'll fill you in later, but in the meantime if I go missing...it was him.

JULES: WHAAAATTTTT???!!!!!!!!!!!!!!!

I don't have time to respond to her because Barrett is talking to me.

"Are you planning to live inside or just out here on the stoop?" Barrett unlocks the mailbox beside the door and takes out a handful of mail.

"I thought you'd have people to do that for you."

"Check my mail?" he asks.

I shrug, then follow him inside.

"I've got an assistant, a driver, a housekeeper, and a chef who makes all my meals for the week. I can get my own mail."

"Look at you doing hard things." I toe off my tennis shoes at the door—it's definitely a shoes off kind of home—and glance around.

I'm in shock. Natural wood floors and staircase, original crown molding.

Barrett drops the mail on the table by the door.

"Would you like a tour?" he asks.

"Um, yes, please," I say, practically sprinting past him, deeper into the lion's den I go.

He follows behind me, pointing out the rooms as I peek into them. Sitting room, dining room, kitchen, powder bath. It's one surprise after another as I realize Barrett's home isn't a mausoleum made of stone and tile. It's got color and warmth and oh my god...

I open the door to another room and my heart pitter patters with delight at what I find.

I don't know where to look first. The walls of bookshelves filled from floor to ceiling. A gold chandelier that offsets the dark navy walls. Cognac leather couches arranged around a fireplace. Did I mention the bookshelves? And there's a ladder, too. There's an honest to God ladder so you can reach the books on the top shelf because the ceiling is at least twelve feet tall.

The wall across from the bookcases is an art collector's dream. Various paintings are set into the wainscoting panels behind a large and very sturdy looking desk.

"This is my study," Barrett says sternly. In contrast to his icy tone, his warm breath makes the loose hairs from my pony-tail tickle my neck. "You won't need to be in here."

He reaches for the door to pull it closed, nearly smacking me in the nose, but my hand lifts, stopping the door's movement.

"Chloe." He tries to shut the door again, but I ignore his denial.

I step forward, still fascinated by what I have found in Barrett's home.

"Okay, where's the sixty-year-old poet who collects obscure Renaissance era art and writes sonnets of his world travels stashed?" I turn to Barrett. "Is he tied up naked in a closet? You really should be kinder to your elders."

"This is my personal space, so if you wouldn't mind..." he sweeps his arm toward the open door.

"I don't mind," I ignore him and continue my perusal. "This is not what I expected."

I can hear Barrett let out a puff of air from ten feet away, but I think his frustration has dimmed to curiosity.

"What did you expect?" he asks.

I decide to keep the vampire coffin slash mausoleum thoughts to myself. My hand reaches out to touch the books, my fingers caressing their spines.

"Not this," I finally answer, my eyes hungrily consuming the titles. There's a wide array of book genres. Classics, history, non-fiction, memoirs, biographies. "I thought I had you figured out. I thought it would be cold and impersonal like," Barrett's brows raise in anticipation of my response, "your office." I was going to say like him, but now the idea of who I thought he was has muddied in my brain.

"Does that work?" I motion to the fireplace.

Barrett walks over and flips a switch. It immediately roars to life and I think I spontaneously orgasm. I don't need a bedroom; I'll just live in here.

A collection of photos and frames sit along the back wall below the windows. I see family photos, pictures with JoAnna and his dad. A diploma from Columbia for a degree in art history.

"Did you buy this on eBay?" I ask.

He takes the frame from my hand and sets it back into place. Wanting order and control, now that is something that still rings true for Barrett.

"No, that is my undergraduate degree."

"Then you got an MBA at Wharton?" I ask, noting the other, larger framed diploma.

"Yes, when I realized my father was sick. It was his request and I fulfilled it."

"So, what did you want to do with your degree?"

"I don't know. I was young and rebelling against my parents."

"Ivy league grad. With honors," I note. "You're such a rebel."

"I don't regret it. It was the best time of my life. Visiting Paris and Milan to travel and study. I still like to collect, as you can see."

"Oh God, I'd love to visit Paris."

Barrett motions toward the door again, this time I follow his lead.

"Are you going to be like the Beast and allow me access to any book in your library?"

"What beast?"

"Like in the Disney movie *Beauty and the Beast* where he holds her captive and she loves to read so he lets her use his library."

"I'm not holding you captive."

"Blackmail is a form of captivity."

"And you're Beauty in this instance?"

"Belle. Her name is Belle. And, no. If I were a Disney princess, I'd be Ariel," I motion to my red tresses, "which sucks because I'm not the best swimmer, but if I had a mermaid tail, I guess that would be helpful."

Barrett stares at me blankly. Clearly, I lost him at Ariel.

"Oh, I know!" I raise a finger into the air as the lightbulb moment hits me. "I'll add it to the list."

"Add what?" he asks.

"Using your study. For reading and such. I could make a whole afternoon of sitting on that comfy looking chair and staring into the fireplace."

"It's June," he says grumpily.

"You saw my apartment. Don't make it a thing."

He sighs, pushing a hand through his hair. "Fine. Add it to the list. But my desk is off limits."

My eyes return to the solid wood structure that is Barrett's desk. Similar to his office, it is clean except for a lamp and a laptop computer. If Barrett was to have sex on his desk, a passionate sweep of all its contents wouldn't even be necessary. He probably has a specific spot marked for a woman's ass, maybe a couple of 'place hand here' signs if he's bending her over it. Now I'm thinking about Barrett having sex at his desk. I want to pretend it would be mechanical but something tells me his art history degree isn't the only surprise in this room.

"I'll show you to your room."

"Right," I say, flustered those dirty thoughts about Barrett have again entered my brain.

On the way upstairs, Barrett walks us through the kitchen, informing me that Rose, his housekeeper, is here every day from seven to five. She oversees shopping, cleaning and other errands for the house. The pantry alone is larger than my apartment.

"Where is the food?"

"Dimitri prepares my meals and portions them out." Barrett opens the refrigerator to reveal neatly stacked foil tins each labeled for the day and meal. I glance over the options. Mostly protein and a vegetable.

"No cheat day, huh?" I say, then reach for the freezer handle.

It's empty.

"Do you even realize how much ice cream you could fit in here?" I ask.

Barrett's response is to roll his eyes and start walking. I think I'm rubbing off on him.

I follow him up the natural wood staircase, stopping as we go to admire the art collection on the wall.

"Marcus will pick us up for work at eight o'clock sharp. Be ready."

"I like to walk, especially now that I'm this close to my office."

He nods, clearly indifferent about how I get to work.

"You can stay in this room." He opens the door to the first room on the right.

Inside there's a gray wood canopy bed with soft, white bedding. At the foot of the bed, a turquoise sofa sits under a white pearl chandelier. A coordinating oriental rug in teal, ivory and mossy green peeks out from under the bed and sofa.

"It's perfect!" I exclaim as if Barrett hand chose everything in it for me, which he did not. He didn't even know I'd be seeing his home until an hour ago. I take my response down a notch. "It's nice. Thank you."

I turn to find Barrett staring at me from the doorway. His once perfectly styled hair is now perfectly messy from the humidity and sweat that it endured. And his hands. They've been working through his tresses ever since I walked through the front door.

"Do you want to take a shower?"

"Yes. That would be great. Just point me in the right direction." I glance down the hallway. "Unless you wanted to go first."

I don't even let my mind entertain the idea of Barrett naked in the shower.

"Unlike your apartment, there are multiple bathrooms here and none of them require a reservation system."

"You're hilarious," I say, my tone devoid of humor.

Barrett moves to open the door on the left side of the room and it appears I have my own bathroom now. I think I might actually start to cry.

I've never had my own bathroom. Not growing up when I shared a bathroom with my two sisters, not when I went to college and used communal bathrooms, and definitely not at my current apartment.

There's a huge soaking tub *and* a separate shower stall. A double vanity with *two* sinks. I guess that's what double means, but how the heck am I going to choose which one to use? I've never had access to two sinks that at least two to four other people haven't been clamoring to get to. Maybe I'll use one for morning and one for night. That makes the most sense.

There are white fluffy towels stacked on a shelf next to the shower. They're so fluffy, only two can fit on the shelf. If I were a gymnast, I could do an entire floor routine in this room.

"Will this do?" Barrett asks from the doorway.

"I suppose it will have to." I sigh. Barrett shakes his head, then pushes off the door frame to leave.

"Dinner will be in twenty minutes," he calls as he exits.

"Uh huh," is my only response. I'm too busy turning the bathtub on and stripping out of my clothes.

Holy freaking bananas. I might get fired from my job because I never leave this tub. That would be ironic.

I sink into the warm water and let it soothe my tired muscles. It's been a day.

I pop in my earbuds, turn on some relaxing music on my phone, and let my mind wander. The goal is to zone out, meditate, become one with this tub, but instead my brain automatically draws up the image of Barrett on the tennis court. It must be my head injury that has me recalling every detail. Sweat-soaked shirt clinging to his muscular frame. Forearm muscles bunching with every swing. And my favorite, those long fingers of his gripping his racquet handle.

The thought of Barrett has caused an ache between my thighs. If I'm being honest, it's been there since I saw him standing outside the racquet club.

I bite my lip and trace a finger along the surface of the water, fighting the urge to give into temptation. When I close my eyes again, he's there. Standing outside the pro shop door, those tantalizing fingers sliding over his jaw.

The water ripples as I move a hand between my legs.

After the busy day, I thought I'd be up for relaxation, but in the end dirty thoughts of Barrett win out.

CHAPTER 11

Barrett

I glance at the clock again. It's nearly eight o'clock. Fifteen minutes past when I told Chloe to meet me for dinner.

I've showered, dressed and heated up the meal Dimitri left for this evening. With an unexpected guest, the portions were light so I threw together a spinach, strawberry and walnut salad from the refrigerator. I've watched the clock on the kitchen counter tick off the minutes, my frustration growing with every minute that goes by.

I don't wait on people, especially in my own home.

I push back my chair and head for the stairs. With each step, my irritation is building.

It doesn't matter that forty minutes ago I was in the shower with my dick in my hand thinking about Chloe's perfect ass and full lips. Any calm I felt from that release has left my body and now I can feel every muscle start to ratchet down tight again.

Outside Chloe's door, I knock.

It's quiet, and there's no response.

This time, I bang on it. Still nothing. I push the door open to find an empty room. Chloe's suitcase is still at the foot of the bed, her bags of books sitting on the sofa untouched. No evidence that she's attempted to unpack.

That's when I hear a sound. It's faint. I move to put my ear to the bathroom door.

The door is solid, not giving me any feedback, but I swear I hear it again.

For a moment, my anger subsides as it occurs to me that she could be hurt. Fred's shot nailed her in the head pretty hard. Maybe she felt dizzy in the shower and collapsed. Or lost consciousness in the bathtub. I knock on the bathroom door and yell her name. No answer.

"Chloe!" I try again.

Panic grips my chest. I try the handle. It's unlocked, so I throw the door open.

My eyes immediately find her. She's lying in the tub, eyes closed. I scan her body head to toe to determine if she's hurt. My observations tell me she's okay. I know she's conscious because her head is tilted back, and she's got her bottom lip pinned between her teeth. And her hand is moving between her legs. I can see it clear as day. With the exception of a few ripples her movement is making, the water is like glass.

The sound registers. It's Chloe's soft moan while her hand vigorously rubs her clit. Oh, fuck.

I should leave. Turn around and close the door. But my legs aren't functioning. My eyes are in control of my body and they are taking in everything. The way Chloe's hard, pink nipples break the surface of the water. Her wet hair floating over her shoulders, her neck exposed as she arches up toward the ceiling, her forehead wrinkling in focused concentration bordering on pleasure. The red polish on the toes that are curling around the edge of the tub. Fuck. There's no way I'll be able to get this image out of my brain. I'll play it over and over again until I can close my eyes and sketch it in detail.

My conscience wakes up at the same time Chloe's eyes fly open. We stare at each other.

"Barrett! What are you doing?!" she screams, water splashing everywhere as she flails about. She pulls an earbud from her ear, then scrambles to sit and hug her legs to her chest, her cheeks flushing with embarrassment. "Don't you knock?"

"Yes. Multiple times. You didn't answer and I was worried you were hurt." I clear my parched throat. "I thought with your head you got dizzy or something."

"Oh." Her voice is small. "Sorry. I lost track of time. I was listening to music."

Among other things.

Now that I know she's okay, my irritation is back.

"You're late for dinner."

"Okay. I'm coming." I didn't think it was possible for Chloe's blush to get any deeper, but the realization of her words turns her skin crimson. "I mean, I'll be there. Soon."

My legs finally get the signal to move, so I leave, pulling the door shut behind me.

Three minutes later, Chloe appears in the kitchen in a bathrobe. It's the robe Rose puts in all the guest bathrooms. It's one size fits all and it swallows Chloe up. She looks like a giant marshmallow. Good. I think I'll lose my mind if I have to see any of her soft, creamy skin right now. I'm sure the bath water has made it warm and pliable.

She takes the seat where I've put a place setting for her and sets the napkin in her lap.

"Sorry about that. I didn't realize you were waiting for me to come," she says.

"I didn't either." I pick up my fork and start eating.

Chloe's mouth opens wide with surprise, but then her eyes shift to her plate and she fills it with a bite of food. Those lips closing around her fork threaten to make my dick hard again. This is going to be a problem.

I usually like to taste my food. Enjoy what Dimitri has prepared, but tonight I shovel everything down in two minutes and excuse myself. I grab my laptop from my desk and head for my bedroom. With Chloe adding it to her list, the study is no longer a safe space, and with the way I'm feeling tonight, I need to be alone.

In my bedroom, I drop into the chair by the window and open my computer. But work is not enough of a distraction and eventually my mind wanders back to Chloe.

I wonder how I'm going to navigate this new living situation, how I'm going to keep things professional with Chloe—keep my hands to myself—but most of all, I wonder if Chloe finished.

The next morning, I don't expect to see Chloe. She was adamant that she would be walking to work, and I was glad to hear it. I like the routine of checking emails and going over my daily schedule on the drive to the office. I don't need Chloe's presence distracting me from my morning routine.

Marcus is about to pull away from the curb when Chloe comes running down the steps.

"Wait!" I hear her call.

I have half a mind to pretend I don't hear her, but Marcus is much nicer and hits the brakes.

Chloe flings open the door.

"Hi. Sorry," she says, out of breath. "I'm running late."

The ivory lace bra peeking through the buttons on her blouse catches my attention. So late apparently that she forgot to button her blouse.

With a clenched jaw, I pull my gaze away from Chloe's cleavage. "You missed a button."

"Oh. Thanks." She looks down, a blush coloring her fair cheeks before she scrambles into the car. The height of the SUV gives her momentary pause before she uses the handle by the door to lift herself up.

Along with the white blouse, she's wearing a fitted red skirt that hugs her hips and nude heels. Her thick, red hair is pinned up on her head in a messy bun, and her lips are the color of her skirt. Deep red. My brain automatically wonders what those red lips would look like wrapped around my cock.

She sets her purse and her travel coffee thermos on the seat next to her and when Marcus hits the gas, her thermos tips over and sloshes its contents onto my pant leg.

"Shit!" I exclaim, my blood reaching a temperature close to that of her liquid caffeine.

I upright the mug and place it next to mine in the cup holder in the middle console by our feet. Where coffee thermoses are intended to go.

"Oh God." Chloe leans toward me, using a tissue from her purse to dab at the wet spot on my thigh. "I'm sorry."

I grab her wrist, probably harder than I mean to, but her actions are not helping this situation.

"Please stop."

"Sorry, again. I'm having an off morning. I didn't sleep well."

"The luxury Egyptian cotton sheets were too comfortable?" I ask, trying not to take offense to Chloe's lack of rest.

"Oh, it wasn't the sheets. Those are amazing. Very soft and pleasing to the touch. Just first night in a new place. You know when you wake up in a strange bed and forget how you got there. That kind of thing."

I want to ask her how often she's woken up in a strange bed but I choose a safer topic.

"How's your head?" I ask.

"Good. It hurts less than yesterday. How does it look?"

I study her face. Those big blue eyes surrounded by long, dark lashes and her petite nose. If she has makeup on, it's hard to tell with the light smattering of freckles still visible across her nose and cheeks. There's one prominent freckle near her lips. It's always pulled my attention there. Lush, pink lips that taunt me. Because they're red today, I'm even more entranced.

Finally, I lift my gaze to her forehead. The ice took care of most of the swelling, but there is definitely a bruise. My chest tightens with regret. I hate that she got hurt.

"Better," I reply.

"Good." She gently touches the spot before reaching for her purse. "How'd you sleep?"

I know she's making conversation but her question provokes the reason for my curtness this morning. I slept like shit. Like Chloe, it wasn't due to lack of comfort. Knowing Chloe was down the hall set my body on high alert. Then there was the hour I spent wondering what she sleeps in, and my mind replayed the scene with her in the bathtub over and over until I had to take matters into my own hands for the second time that day. By the time I drifted off to sleep, it wasn't long before my alarm clock was going off.

"Good," I say. No one really wants to know how you're feeling or how well you slept. Chloe is the rare person who offers up nuanced details when people ask her questions, and even when they don't.

"Thanks for the coffee. Even though I spilled it on you. It was nice to have it ready to go this morning."

"That was Rose."

"Oh, well then I'll have to thank her."

She takes the thermos from the cup holder and takes a sip. That seems to calm her erratic behavior, which I appreciate because all I want to do is sit in peace and work.

A few minutes later, she's staring at her phone and I think the rest of the drive will be in peace until she starts talking again.

"Oh, this one is hard," she announces. I turn to find her bruised forehead wrinkled in concentration.

"Excuse me?"

"The WordIt today." She waves her phone at me. A grid with letters is on display. "Do you play?"

"I have no idea what you're talking about." I realize I should have simply said no to avoid her explanation.

"It's a word game. Online. You guess a five-letter word and it tells you if the letters you guess are in the correct place or if they're in the word, but not in the correct place. You get six tries to guess the word. It's fun."

"I don't have time for games."

I look back down at my phone.

"We're going to an event tomorrow night," I say.

"Oh. What kind of event?" she asks.

"The Top Dog Gala benefitting the Animal Medical Center."

"Really?" Chloe lights up. "That sounds like fun."

"It's not fun, it's work. Bea will have a dress sent over, and you'll have a hair and makeup team to get ready."

Chloe shrugs. "It kind of sounds fun to me." She's quiet a moment before adding, "I didn't know you were an animal lover."

"I'm not. Fred and Frankie will be there. He's got two Bassett Hounds that have received hip replacements at AMC. It's another opportunity to bring up business."

"We didn't have pets growing up. You'd think with that many people to take care of an animal it would have been a no brainer, but my mom's allergic to pet dander. What about you? Have you ever had a dog?"

"No. Dogs are messy and require training, and most of all time that I don't have."

"They are also adorable and snuggly and lovable."

"Pass."

There's silence for a minute, and I think I'll have some peace, but then Chloe exclaims, "I got it!"

She turns her phone in my direction.

"The word was MOIST. Isn't that funny? So many people hate the word moist."

I glance from her phone with the game grid to her beaming face, then back down to my phone. I don't want to encourage talking during my morning commute. I prefer silence and solitude. Out of the corner of my eye, I can see her tucking her phone into her purse.

The car pulls over and I glance up to find we've arrived at my office. I slip my phone into my pocket and reach for the door.

I'm on the curb when Chloe leans toward my side of the car, the action causing the material of her blouse to hang from her body and give me a glimpse down her shirt.

"Aren't you forgetting something?" she asks.

My eyes feast upon the swells of her breasts resting above her lace bra. I can't remember anything at the moment.

It takes me a second to hear her question. I'm not sure what she thinks I'm forgetting. My eyes dart toward the front of the car where Marcus is sitting in the driver's seat. It occurs to me that Chloe might think we need to keep up appearances for our fake relationship in front of my staff. She's leaning onto my side of the car, her face looking up at me expectantly.

I lean down, meeting her where she sits.

Instinctively, my hand moves to her face, my fingers grazing the shell of her ear. I place my lips firmly on hers. Fuck. I've forgotten how soft her lips are. I mean for it to be a chaste kiss, but I linger there, not wanting to break the contact.

Chloe pulls back. When my eyes open, she's staring at me, confused. Her fingers tracing the curve of her lower lip.

"That's not...I didn't mean...um...your coffee." She reaches forward, my travel thermos in her hand.

"Right." I nod, taking the coffee from her. Her cheeks are flushed, likely with embarrassment about my misunderstanding. For me or for her, I'm not certain. "It won't happen again," I reassure her.

"Have a good day." She recovers from the mortification of my kiss just as I slam the door shut.

"That was cozy." I find Carl waiting for me in front of the building. I pull the door open and head for the elevators.

When I don't respond he continues.

"How did tennis with Fred go?"

I don't bother to answer but punch the button for the elevator.

"You're chatty this morning. You've got a little something..." He motions to his lips and I lift my hand to wipe at my mouth.

"Chloe moved into my place."

"That's rather quick for a fake relationship."

We step onto the open elevator.

"She got hit in the head with the ball at tennis, so I took her home and found out her apartment is a disaster. It needs work. It's not safe, so I moved her into my place."

"That's why you're a surly son of a bitch this morning?" My glare is met with Carl's hands in the air. "No offense to JoAnna. I love your mother."

"I'll be able to control the situation better with Chloe at my place. It looks more believable than my girlfriend holed up in a dilapidated apartment."

"It looks believable all right." Carl shakes his head and we move back in the elevator so a woman can step on. "So, are you two," he lifts his brows.

131

Two floors up, the door opens and the woman gets off, so I continue my conversation with Carl.

"No. It's strictly business between Chloe and me. Everything is for the benefit of showing Fred I'm a settled man who he should sell his company to."

The elevator doors open again and we step out onto our floor.

"I never doubt you; you've always got a plan."

I nod. Carl's right, I'm always in control. This thing with Chloe will be no exception. While I didn't originally plan for her to move in, it's better this way. That's what I'm telling myself anyway.

We push through the glass doors, then walk down the hallway toward the executive office wing.

"Have you heard of WordIt? It's some kind of word game app."

"Oh, yeah. Everyone is playing it. Lindsay loves it. It's the first thing she does when she wakes up. She broke her streak the other day and she was not pleasant to be around."

"Find the developer. Draw up an offer."

"You want to buy the app?" Carl is surprised by my request. Hell, I am, too, but I don't let it show.

"If it's as popular as you say it is, it shouldn't come as a shock. It's in our wheelhouse and it'll be an advertising goldmine."

"You're the boss."

I nod. "Let me know what you come up with."

"Sure thing." Carl peels off toward his office and I continue on to mine.

Bea greets me with a smile.

"Good morning, sir. Your eight thirty meeting is already set up in the conference room on twelve. I moved your lunch meeting to twelve thirty because your call with Qwest Corp was moved to eleven. And I sent you an email of optional dresses for Chloe for tomorrow evening's event."

I drop into my desk chair and wake up my computer. Ignoring the people waiting for my eight thirty meeting, I open Bea's email to find three dress options for Chloe.

Bea looks over my shoulder as I scan through the options.

"I'm a fan of the green one," she comments.

The neckline would expose Chloe's breasts. It's a charity event for dogs, I don't want to be the one drooling over her all night.

I click through to find a blue dress. The sapphire color would look great on Chloe, but unlike the green one, it has a higher neckline.

"The blue one," I confirm.

"Of course. I'll have it ordered and sent over to Chloe's apartment."

"You can send it to my address," I say.

"Oh." Bea's eyebrows lift to her hairline. I can tell she's dying to ask, but I give her a stern look and she withdraws. "My pleasure."

After Bea leaves my office, I walk to the small closet on the far side and select one of the spare suits I have hanging there. The coffee stain on my pant leg is dry but has left a brown ring. Then, I move on with my day, doing my best to get back into my routine and to not think about Chloe.

CHAPTER 12

Chloe

I've barely sat down at my desk, when Jules barges into my office.

"What the hell is going on? You sent that text last night and then nothing. You can't leave me hanging like that." She pauses her ramblings, and does a double take. "Oh my God. Did he knock you over the head and drag you to his lair? Should I call the police? Blink twice if you need help."

"Jules. Relax. I've got everything under control."

"The angry bruise on your forehead does not convey that."

"It's a tennis injury. I got hit in the head yesterday when Barrett and I played with Fred and Frankie."

"Ah. For a moment I thought maybe you and Barrett were banging and things got a little wild." She wiggles her eyebrows. "I imagine that's how it would be with him. Those cold eyes boring into you. His lips in a frown, all moody and pissed. A good stern fucking."

"Jules!" I glance toward my door, knowing that JoAnna's office is a mere ten feet down the hall. And Jules' voice carries at least double that distance.

"I think you should at least have some fun with this fake relationship. No reason to make it miserable."

"I'm just trying to make it through this without losing my mind. Now that JoAnna has given me a real shot at assistant editor, I don't want to mess it up."

"I know," Jules says, nodding sympathetically. "You deserve that promotion. You've been kicking ass with selecting submissions."

"Thanks." I give her a small smile. "I have to focus on work and do my best to play along with Barrett, then I'll put this fake relationship behind me."

Jules nods. I can tell she wants there to be more to it than that. There isn't, not with Barrett. He's got his own agenda, and I'm just a pawn in his game. At least I'm aware of it. But, now that I'm not dying of mortification anymore, I can tell her about last night.

"Barrett walked in on me in the bathtub last night."

"WHATT??!!" she shrieks.

I sigh. "Volume."

"Sorry."

"I was, you know." I make a circular motion toward my lower half.

Her mouth drops open.

"What did he do?"

"He stared, then told me I was late for dinner."

The image of Barrett standing in the bathroom doorway pops into my head. His hard expression never wavered from its usual frown. I could have been trimming my toenails for how uninterested he appeared to be in what he saw.

"Shut up."

I cover my face with my hands, the embarrassment of the moment creeping back in. I shouldn't let it bother me; Barrett obviously wasn't fazed by it.

"Damn." She fans herself. "I knew you were holding out on me."

I laugh. "There's nothing to it but an embarrassing story and a reminder to lock the bathroom door."

Jules' lips quirk. "I don't know. I think there's more to it."

I shake my head and Jules rises from the chair.

She pauses in the doorway. "Some gals from admin and marketing are getting drinks tomorrow night. Want to join?"

"Can't. Barrett and I are going to a charity gala."

"Fancy. I can't wait to hear how that goes." She exits with a smirk and a wave. "Ta ta for now."

I glance back at my computer screen, and try to recall what I was doing before Jules walked in. I was going over JoAnna's editorial calendar to send out reminders.

I open up my email, but my mind skips back to this morning in the car when Barrett kissed me. How he must have thought I meant for him to give me a goodbye kiss. The same way he had done in JoAnna's office on Monday, except today his lips lingered longer. I could feel the tip of his tongue teasing the entrance of my mouth. I'd been caught off guard, completely unprepared for his lips to be on mine again. To be reminded how good they felt there. How I could imagine his mouth kissing me other places. I'm pretty sure Barrett St. Clair's lips were made for sin.

Then, he told me it wouldn't happen again. Good. I don't need the distraction.

"Chloe," JoAnna's voice makes me jump, "sorry, I didn't mean to sneak up on you."

"No problem. I was just working on the editorial calendar."

"Perfect. Can you send me your edits on *Sail Away*?"

"Of course." I nod, then turn back to my computer.

With all my editorial assistant duties and the added responsibilities to fill in for Lacey as an assistant editor, along with the Books 4 Kids event tasks, my to do list is overflowing.

I clear my mind of thoughts of Barrett, because thinking about him isn't on it.

I haven't seen Barrett since yesterday morning in the car on the way to work. He texted me that he would be working late last night and this morning he was nowhere to be found. Not that I was looking for him.

I'm settling in at Barrett's place. Last night I ate the dinner Dimitri had prepared by myself, then curled up with a book in front of the fireplace in Barrett's study. Yes, it's June, but I couldn't resist. I wonder if I can add use of his study in the month of December to my list? He said it could be anything as long as it doesn't interfere with his business deal.

Or maybe my good mood is because of the bathroom at Barrett's place, I'm still not adjusted to its size and amenities. The tub and shower jets, dimmable vanity mirrors, and heated toilet seat. It does everything but shave my legs, which I've just finished doing in the bathtub.

I lay my head back on the built-in head rest and enjoy the feeling of my smooth skin as I glide one leg over the other.

I thought I'd be more annoyed with being Barrett's plus one. He didn't exactly ask nicely when he told me we'd be making our first public appearance tonight at the Top Dog Gala. Maybe I would be if I wasn't in love with the gorgeous blue dress that I get to wear tonight. It's backless and makes me feel sexy. And the fact that people will be showing up in half an hour to do my hair and makeup. I didn't even get my hair done for prom. I don't know why Barrett hates going to events. Dressing up is fun.

I pull the plug with my toes, a move I've mastered in less

than forty-eight hours, and lift myself up and out to grab my bathrobe out of the warming drawer. Yes, this bathroom even has a heated drawer to put your towel or bathrobe into so it is toasty perfection when you get out of the bath or shower. Rose showed it to me yesterday and I nearly collapsed on the floor.

In the closet, I pull open the drawer I put my underwear in Thursday night. I move through the colorful array of options, cotton thongs, cotton boy briefs, lots of cotton. My eyes find that gorgeous blue dress again. This isn't going to cut it. I slam it shut and move over to the next drawer. I already know what's in it and when I saw it yesterday, I vowed I'd never touch it because who needs sexy silk and lace underwear when you're fake dating Barrett, the Ice King? My hands move over the slinky material of a silk black thong. I snatch it up quickly, then slam the drawer. It's for the dress. Nothing more.

The underwear aren't the only items in the closet that aren't mine. There are a few new dresses, wide leg trousers and blouse options, flirty skirts and tops, belts, shoes and the most adorable tank and shorts silk lounge set. It's lavender, my favorite color. It's sexy and chic and came with a matching fuzzy long-sleeve cardigan sweater. I stared at it for a good five minutes yesterday. It looks like a cloud and while I'm tempted to put it on now, I slip on the panties instead and retie my robe.

A minute later there's a knock on my bedroom door and I open it up to find two men standing there. One that looks like a teddy bear with a beard and thick wavy brown hair and a thinner man with jet black hair that may be wearing eyeliner.

"Chloe?" they say in unison. "I'm Hans," teddy bear says, "and I'm Franz," the dark-haired man says, "and we're here to primp you up!" they add together in some kind of accent.

"Franz?" I question. "Is that French?"

"No. And I'm Will," Franz says. "That's just a fun little intro we like to do."

"Oh, okay. Well, come on in." I wave them into the bedroom.

"Where should we set up?" Will asks.

"The bathroom, maybe? It's got plenty of room."

He peeks his head in.

"Damn, girl. How many BJs you have to give to get a place like this?"

"Oh, um." I struggle to answer because Barrett is my fake boyfriend but if people think he's my real boyfriend, then I probably give him blow jobs on occasion, which would be fine because he's my boyfriend, but he's not and we don't. What was the question?

"He's kidding," Hans says, unfolding what looks like a director's chair and motioning for me to sit.

"I wasn't really," Will complains, opening the largest makeup case I've ever seen.

"We brought champagne." Hans pulls it out of his bag. I wonder what else he's got in there.

He pops the cork and I laugh, feeling at ease about the whole thing for the first time today.

"You just sit back and relax and we'll work our magic."

An hour later, Hans and Fr—Will are on their way out and I've pulled on the sapphire blue gown that matches my eyes. I love how I look, like me but with more sparkle. I'm excited to go to the event and I'm also a little tipsy from the champagne. But my bubble bursts when I descend the stairs to find Barrett waiting in the foyer, looking gorgeous in a fitted tuxedo, and he barely glances at me.

He's a man of formalities, which I would think includes

telling a woman that she looks nice, but he just stares at me, his jaw working itself over before he reaches for the door.

"Ready?" he asks.

"Mmhmm," I say with pursed lips, because I know he hates when people mumble and don't respond with a definitive yes or no. Which is funny, because I hear him do it all the time.

In the car he's on his phone. I pull mine out, happy that I haven't played today's WordIt yet and have something to occupy the silence between us. I start with C O U N T, one of my starter words but have no luck. Then, I use S H A P E and the E is yellow so I know it's in the word but not the right place. I find an L and a D but struggle to get the word.

"Hmm." My brain is thinking hard out loud.

The car stops, I look out at our destination, a restaurant called Cipriani, located adjacent to the Chrysler Building. The driver door slams shut with Marcus's exit.

"It's ELDER," Barrett announces and it catches me off guard.

"What is?" I ask.

"The WordIt today."

My hands fly to my ears, but I can't unhear it.

"Shh! You can't tell me."

"I just did," he says, his voice void of feeling.

"I didn't ask you," I snap back, my irritation growing at his lack of consideration.

He shrugs. "I don't have time to sit here and wait for you to finish."

"Is that what you say to all the ladies? What a charmer," I say in a huff. "I was almost there. I was going to get it." My desire to be at this event with Barrett is diminishing by the minute and we haven't even gone in yet.

Marcus opens my door and I climb out, tossing my phone and the unfinished WordIt game in my clutch. I'd rather end my one-hundred-ninety-seven-day win streak than use Barrett's tip to finish the game.

Outside the car, Barrett takes my hand. My wrist is limp, barely holding on.

"You are horrible. I can't believe you did that," I bite out as we walk up three elongated, red-carpeted stairs before entering the door of the art deco style building.

"It's a word game." He waves to someone on the red carpet they've set up outside the venue and guides us into the line. "Relax."

"Says the man who is as rigid as a cement block," I retort.

Inside, there's a backdrop with the Top Dog charity logo, along with its top sponsors, where guests are taking photos.

Barrett drops my hand to place his on my lower back and moves us into line. My backless dress makes our contact skin to skin. Surprisingly his touch isn't rigid. It's warm and firm, his palm applying slight pressure into my spine, and I'd give anything to be somewhere I could smack his hand away. But, we're up next, the couple in front of us moving from the X in front of the backdrop so we can proceed.

We smile for the cameras, Barrett's arm around my waist, pulling me in close. The second we make it into the screening tent to check in, I step out of his reach. He doesn't bother to address my rebuff.

A woman checks us in and gives us our silent auction bidding numbers and dining table number, then we move into a side room for cocktails. My heels are new and I'm struggling a bit, the balls of my feet absorbing the pounding of the hard marble floor, but when Barrett offers his arm, I push past him.

"Chloe," he hisses in my ear, grabbing my elbow to keep me in place. "Do I need to remind you why you're here?"

"No." I give him my coolest stare. "I'm aware. But I don't want to spend one more second with you than I have to."

With that, he lets me go. Where I'm going, I'm not sure,

but the room is spacious and I'd like to give myself some space from Barrett. The bar seems like a good idea but I don't even make it that far before a waiter with a tray of champagne offers one to me.

A glass of champagne and a few passed hors-d'oeuvres later and I'm feeling less feisty. I've lost track of Barrett but a chilly breeze from my two o'clock tells me he's not far.

I don't recognize anyone. Why would I? This is Barrett's social circle. I'm a loner chugging her champagne but that's better than being around Barrett's grumpy ass. If he's my lifeline at this event, I'd rather drown.

"There you are," a woman says behind me.

I turn around to find a gorgeous brunette dressed in a pretty bubble gum pink gown. She looks familiar but I'm uncertain why she would be looking for me.

"I'm Emma, Barrett's cousin." She smiles radiantly at me. "We met in passing at one of Aunt Jo's book launches."

"Oh, that's right. I knew you looked familiar." I stick out my hand. "Chloe Anderson."

"I know who you are, silly." She pulls me into a hug. "And what you are."

"What's that?" I ask nervously.

"Barrett's girlfriend. I had to see it with my own eyes."

She looks around, probably expecting Barrett to be nearby. She'll be disappointed I ran him off.

"Oh. Right."

"You are tiny," she says, then her eyes widen with alarm. "Sorry, I hope that's not rude. People always think I'm short. My mother's a runway model, former runway model. She's sixty now so the eye cream campaigns keep her busy. Honestly, she doesn't look a day over forty." Emma pauses, likely retracing the point she's trying to make. I recognize this because I do it a lot, too. "My point being, people wonder why I didn't get her height. I blame my dad. It's the quintessential leggy model falls for short photographer," she waves at herself, "therefore producing less than average height offspring."

She takes a sip of her champagne.

"Sorry. I talk a lot. It's genetic."

"Then you can't be related to Barrett."

That earns me a laugh.

"Our mothers are sisters so it might just be a Smith girl thing."

"Your dress is gorgeous." She looks me over again. "Your ass looks amazing in it."

"Thank you." I smile. Her compliment gives me reassurance. What I didn't get from Barrett.

My mind returns to earlier and Barrett's lack of interest in my appearance. Nothing worse than putting in the effort and nobody bothers to acknowledge it. I could have been wearing a potato sack and he probably wouldn't have noticed. I make a mental note to try that at our next event.

"I was just going to say the same thing about your dress." I recall what JoAnna has told me about her niece. "You're a dress designer, right?"

"Bridal gowns mostly, but I play around with my own cocktail attire, too. The perk of making your own dresses is you can play up your assets," she does a little shimmy of her ass, "and find the most flattering form for what you don't have." She slides a hand under her slight bust.

"Well, you look amazing."

"Thank you." A brilliant smile lifts the corners of her mouth. It's like looking in a mirror. Something tells me that might be the first time she's heard that tonight, too.

"Where is Barrett?" she asks. "I can't imagine he's far. He wouldn't want you to get snapped up by a smooth talking, Golden Retriever lover.

I shrug. "He was going to make the rounds. Business." It's

not really a lie, I imagine that's exactly what he's doing. That's all he seems to do.

"Ugh. That guy works too much. I work too much and I still have time for a social life. Barrett's work ethic is right up there with Ebenezer Scrooge. His mood, too."

I laugh, knowing I've had similar thoughts about him.

"Are you two close?" I ask, curious to get more information about Barrett without having to ask the man himself.

"We're both only children, and with our mothers being sisters, we grew up together. He's always been the older brother I never had."

"I'm the oldest of five and always wished I had an older sibling."

"How old are you?" she asks.

"Twenty-five."

"Well, I'm twenty-nine. So that's done." She threads her arm conspiratorially through mine and starts walking us around the room.

"When I heard Barrett was seriously dating someone, I was shocked. But now I've met you and it all makes sense."

Heat rushes to my cheeks. I appreciate the compliment but I also know there's no truth behind it.

"So, bridal gowns? What made that your design focus?"

"I worked for DVF for a while, but every day wear wasn't my thing. I love romance and what is more romantic than two people falling in love and getting married? I wanted to be part of that. I started Emma Belle Bridal last year and I'm planning to launch my full bridal line in Vegas next year."

"That's amazing."

"Maybe you'll be my first customer." She lifts her dark brows knowingly.

I laugh at the notion that I could be getting married in a year. To Barrett. "I'm not so sure about that."

"I'd love to beat you to it, but my boyfriend, Alec, is dragging his feet."

"How long have you been together?" I ask.

"Two years." She sighs. "He should know by now, right?"

"I'm not the person to ask. I've never even dated a guy seriously." I catch my slip before she notices. "Before Barrett, that is."

"Ladies." A gorgeous, dark-haired man with a wide, sexy smile nods in our direction as he passes us. He tosses me a wink.

"Hunter." Emma returns his nod, matter-of-factly.

He passes, and I turn to follow his form making his way through the groups of people.

"That is Hunter Cartwright. He's a notorious bachelor and an incorrigible flirt. I'd tell you to watch out for him, but you've got Barrett and they're friends, so it won't be necessary."

Emma walks us around, and introduces me to a few of her friends. "Besides the socialites and trust fund babies, it's typically an older crowd at most of these things. Should we peruse the silent auction items?"

We exit the cocktail lounge and walk across the hallway to a smaller room where the silent auction items are.

Most are pet related, an all-expense paid trip to Bark Avenue Grooming, a posh doggy salon and spa, a photoshoot with your pet with renowned fashion photographer T.K. Lopez, and a year supply of top shelf premium dog food. There are other items, vacations, jewelry and even a car. None of it is of interest to me. Until my eyes snag on a poster for the Goldendoodle Foster Program of NYC.

"Aren't they adorable?" Emma says, noticing where my attention is focused.

"And snuggly and lovable," I say, thinking back to my conversation with Barrett yesterday in the car.

Pets aren't allowed in my building, except for Ralph the mouse who has made himself welcome anyways. But Barrett's home? That would be a perfect place for a sandy-colored curly-haired pup. Barrett would never go for it, though.

A chime fills the air. I look at Emma for understanding.

"That's to let us know dinner is being served."

My stomach falls, not because I don't want to eat, but because I really don't want to sit next to Barrett for the next hour. I know, it's silly. WordIt is just a game, but it's a small thing that gives me joy and he ruined it.

Emma and I make our way into the main room and find our table. It appears Barrett bought out a table with his company and we're sitting together. I really like her. I hope she doesn't hate me when Barrett and my fake relationship ends.

At the table, Emma introduces me to Alec, her boyfriend, and the rest of the group. A Wall Street broker, Derek, and his fiancée, Madison, who looks flawless in a red spaghetti strap gown.

"I can't stop staring at her. Do I know her from somewhere?" I whisper to Emma.

"She's a socialite, at the top of New York's elite social circle."

"And I'm eating dinner with her?"

Emma giggles. "There's nothing to be stressed about. You fit right in."

I doubt that, but Emma is at ease, so it puts me at ease. That is, until Barrett arrives. He shakes hands with the other men at the table.

"Emma." He gives her a kiss on the cheek. "You look beautiful."

I gape at the effortlessness with which that compliment fell from his lips. It has now been established that Barrett is in fact capable of giving compliments. If Emma wasn't his cousin I'd be super pissed right now.

"Madison." Barrett plants the same perfunctory kiss on her cheek. "You look lovely as always."

Lovely as always? Lovely as always?! If the woman always looks this good it should not require a mention. What about me? I was primped up by Hans and Frans aka Will, the dynamic duo of all things hair and makeup, and I got nothing. Barely a glance before Barrett was out the door.

Barrett then has the audacity to slide one of his massive hands around my waist. His long fingers grip my hip bone. My brain scowls at his touch, but my body has amassed an entire cheering section and they've all gathered between my legs. They're outfitted in Barrett St. Clair fan club gear.

"Chloe," Barrett draws me out of my head, "this is Carl, he's our in-house counsel at SCM."

I aggressively shake Carl's hand, desperately trying to transfer my pent-up anger to someone or something. An elbow to Barrett's ribs would have been preferable.

"And his girlfriend, Lindsay." Barrett points to the blonde bombshell beside Carl.

I shake Lindsay's hand, a little less aggressively.

"Nice to meet you." She smiles kindly and I'm thankful I didn't crush her hand.

Barrett leans in to give her a half body hug, since he's only got the one arm available, and a kiss on the cheek.

"Did you get your hair cut?" he asks her.

"Yes. I'm surprised you noticed. It was only a quarter inch." She laughs, then pats Carl on the arm. "Carl didn't even know."

"It looks great," Barrett follows up and I think I'm going to lose my mind.

He observes a quarter inch of hair has been removed from a woman's head that he doesn't see every day, yet he can't acknowledge the effort that I put into my appearance tonight? I know this is a fake relationship, but the effort to tape my boobs for the backless dress, ladies and gentlemen, was real.

A simple 'you look nice' or 'that blue dress is pretty' would have sufficed. He picked the dress out. He could have complimented himself with that one. Why is it so hard to say something nice to me?

I'm about to storm out but a waiter places a plate of food in front of me. It's filet mignon and grilled shrimp. I drop into my seat so fast Barrett is startled.

During dinner I focus on eating the delicious food and talking with Emma and ignore Barrett, except when I have to smile at him adoringly, and that one time when I was lovingly patting his thigh but decided to pinch and twist instead.

By dessert, Barrett's arm is resting over part of the back of my chair, which wouldn't be a big deal except my dress is backless and I've now accidentally leaned into his hand twice. Those fucking hands.

When it happens again, I nearly jump out of my seat.

"I'm going to the ladies' room," I announce in monotone. Now who's the robot? I feel like Barrett's charm is wearing off on me.

"Hurry back. They'll be serving dessert soon," Emma says cheerily.

I don't use the ladies' room, but instead wander the hall. I take another lap through the silent auction.

"Anything interesting?" The male voice beside me causes me to look up. It's the handsome man from earlier. Hunter Cartwright, Emma had said.

"Nothing I can afford." I smile.

He laughs. "But it's for the dogs."

I laugh. "Yes, they are cute," I say, looking at the poster for the Goldendoodle dog fostering program.

"Hunter Cartwright." He extends his hand and I take it.

"Chloe Anderson."

"Nice to meet you." He smiles again, his blue eyes sparkling. "That's some dress."

"Yeah?" I say, surprised. "Thank you. My date has yet to comment."

As soon as I say it, I hate that it is what has been bugging me all night. I shouldn't care what Barrett thinks. I don't need his approval. I don't need him to tell me I look nice.

"He's an idiot."

"He's actually a smart businessman." I'm shocked the words fall from my mouth so easily. They're true, of course, but I thought I'd be the last person to defend Barrett tonight.

"Chloe." We both turn to find Barrett entering the room. His dark expression lightens when he sees Hunter.

"St. Clair," Hunter extends his hand and Barrett takes it. They both pull each other in for a half shake, half man hug and pat on the back. "Good to see you."

"I saw Hannah inside, she said you were here. We should grab lunch sometime," Barrett responds.

"Sure. I'll have Jeannie call Bea to set it up," Hunter responds.

They smile at each other. Long lost brothers these two.

"So, you're the idiot," Hunter says.

"What?" Barrett questions.

"Chloe here is with some idiot that doesn't recognize she's the most beautiful woman at the event."

Barrett's stare falls on me and I chuckle, shifting from foot to foot. That's not really what I said, but Hunter seems to be enjoying ribbing Barrett.

A moment of silence passes before Barrett answers, "No one's called me an idiot in a while and gotten away with it. I'll take that out on you on the racquetball court."

Hunter laughs. "Sounds good. I'll see you two. Nice to meet you, Chloe." He pats my arm and gives Barrett a nod before disappearing.

I expect Barrett to acknowledge what Hunter said, maybe say I look nice, even if it's only because Hunter called him out. I guess I shouldn't expect things from Barrett.

"Dinner's over." That's what he says. "I'm going to find Fred before he leaves. Then we'll go."

"Sure," I say, keeping my voice calmer than I feel.

I turn back toward the tables of auction items, and when I glance behind me Barrett is gone.

My eyes catch on that Goldendoodle foster program poster again and I get an idea. A feeling of true giddiness passes through my body for the first time since I walked down the stairs at Barrett's house.

A few minutes later I return to the main room, a glass of champagne in my hand and a smile on my face.

CHAPTER 13
Barrett

I usually avoid events like tonight, The Top Dog Gala, like the plague. But with my sights set on Voltaire, I'm making every effort to show Fred that SCM is the right choice. That effort is me putting on this tuxedo, mingling with people I have no interest in talking to and bidding on silent auction items with highly offensive price tags.

At the bar, I order a scotch while Carl orders a gin martini. I sip my scotch and take in the room. After dinner, the ballroom lights dimmed and several tables were cleared to make room for the dance floor. A jazz quartet is now playing softly while couples dance under a canopy of stars that lowered from the ceiling.

All of this for dogs.

My eyes find Chloe, standing near the dance floor with the group of women from our table.

From the moment she walked down the stairs at my place, I knew I was fucked.

That Chloe at my side wasn't going to be helpful, but a distraction knocking me off my game.

I haven't been able to take my eyes off her all night.

That dress. The one I picked out. The one I had no idea was backless until she did a little spin to show off the dress. It has been taunting me all night. The way the deep blue color makes her eyes sparkle and the fit hugs all her curves. I have no one to blame but myself, but that hasn't stopped me from acting like a complete asshole.

And when I saw her in the auction room with another guy? I had dark thoughts until I realized it was Hunter. He's a bachelor, but he'd never fuck with another man's woman.

Except Chloe isn't mine. It only appears that way and once we're over, once my deal with Fred is secured, I'll have no claim to her.

"From a legal standpoint, it's cut and dry, but we need to press Fred on the timeline. Keep him focused on the benefits of the merger before anyone else can get to him. I dropped off documents yesterday. Have you had a chance to look through them?"

Chloe laughs at something Emma says and my scowl deepens.

"Are you listening to anything I'm saying?"

My attention returns to Carl, but he's already followed my gaze to where I was watching Chloe a moment ago.

"I heard you. I'm working on it."

Carl nods in Chloe's direction. "What about her?"

"What about her?" I say with more bite than necessary.

"Jesus. Someone is testy tonight."

I take another sip. The familiar burn of the scotch at the back of my throat brings up the memory of the last event I attended. Weeks ago, when my mother was determined to set me up with Eileen's daughter and I told Fred I had a girlfriend. Chloe pretending to be my girlfriend was supposed to make my life easier, but it's not. It's more complicated. And far harder.

"She's fine. We're fine."

Carl chuckles. "That's what Lindsay says when she wants to cut my balls off. It actually means the opposite of fine. Surely you know that."

"Fuck off."

Carl's chuckle fades away. "This arrangement you've got going with Chloe, it's not going to interfere with the deal, is it?"

"Nothing is interfering with the deal," I growl.

"You say you've got it under control, but, man," Carl looks me up and down, "you don't look like a man in control of himself."

He takes my silence as permission to keep talking.

"I'm just saying, I can see the tension between you two, feel it. Maybe you guys should fuck it out. You know, get her in your bed to get her out of your head."

I've got a good four inches on Carl. I put my glass on the bar, then lean in, staring him down.

"When I want your opinion on my personal life, I'll ask."

Carl lifts both hands in surrender. "Cool, man. It was only a suggestion."

I straighten my suit jacket, then move through the crowd.

Determined to not let Chloe's alluring presence and her disdain for mine affect me, I set my sights on Fred, who is sitting across the room at a table alone. A rare moment without Frankie. This evening might not be a waste after all.

As I make my way to Fred, I'm stopped countless times, people I don't know or do know but forgot their names pull me into conversation. Finally, I make it to his table.

"Fred." I clap him on the shoulder. "How are you?"

Fred turns, a good-natured smile on his face. "Mr. St. Clair, I wasn't expecting to see you here tonight."

"Dogs are man's best friend, right?" Even I can feel the sincerity of the evening's forced niceties wearing thin.

"Exactly. Take a seat. You need a drink?" He motions for a

waiter. With his suit jacket open, I can see the buttons on his dress shirt straining. A walk to the bar would probably do him some good.

"I'm good." I wave him off. "We didn't have much time to talk at tennis on Thursday and—"

"That was a good time. Except Chloe getting smacked in the head. How's she doing?" He looks around. "Is she here?"

"Yes, and she's fine. The bruise faded quickly."

I should ask about Frankie, but I don't want to talk about the ladies. I want to get to the fucking point about the acquisition deal I'm trying to put together.

"Oh, good. I didn't realize I had that much power behind my back hand."

"It's okay. She's recovered. What I wanted to talk—"

"Is that Chloe dancing?" Fred squints over my shoulder.

"I don't—" I turn in the direction he's looking and see that it is Chloe dancing with a guy. He spins her once and she laughs. I don't want to care. I need to talk to Fred. This is the only chance I've had alone with him all week. But, when the man Chloe's dancing with comes into view, my blood starts to boil.

There are many companies in the pursuit of Voltaire, but the only company, aside from SCM, that could come to the table with a lucrative deal would be Shaw & Graham.

"With Ryan Shaw?" Fred's eyebrows would be lifted to his hairline if he had one.

I fucking hate the vulnerability of this moment. I shouldn't have to worry about what Chloe's doing while I'm talking to Fred. What the fuck is she thinking?

Frankie strides up to the table, placing her hands on Fred's shoulders, her long turquoise nails digging into the fabric of his suit.

"Hi, Barrett, good to see you." She glances around. "Where's Chloe?"

Fred pats her hand. "It's a sensitive subject. She's dancing with Ryan Shaw."

I stand, realizing there is nothing more I can accomplish with Fred tonight.

"It's good to see you both. If you'll excuse me." I do my best not to act affected but if I were a cartoon character, I'd have steam coming out of my ears.

I don't wait for their response; I move with purpose onto the dance floor and next to where Chloe and Ryan are still enjoying their dance together.

"Barrett." Chloe starts when she sees me.

"St. Clair." Ryan eyes me with a smug glance.

"I'd like to dance with my girlfriend."

Ryan lets go of Chloe who stands there staring at me like I'm a monster with three heads, of which none of them think logically when she's around.

"Sure." He shrugs like he's letting me dance with my girl-friend. "See you around," he whispers to Chloe and I fight the urge to put him in a choke hold. I've never put anyone in a choke hold, but I imagine it wouldn't be that difficult in my current state. Adrenaline pumping, blood boiling, fingers itching to squeeze into the flesh of his neck.

The music changes, the upbeat song giving way to a slow ballad. Chloe's staring at me wide-eyed. We look awkward standing here among the dancing couples, so I move closer, placing a hand on her hip and pulling her into me. It's a reach, but she places her hand on my shoulder. My other hand closes over hers.

"I saw you talking to Fred," she says.

I think she's trying to make conversation. She doesn't realize that exact sentence is like poking a hungry bear you just stole a fish from.

"I was talking to Fred until I had to come over here and pry you out of Ryan Shaw's clutches."

"That's a little dramatic, don't you think?" She laughs, which only serves to piss me off more. "I wanted to dance and he asked."

"The fact that I had to leave my conversation with Fred to come over here is the issue." I try to keep my voice calm but it's rising with every protest out of Chloe's pretty little mouth.

My hand on her hip tightens reflexively and my blood boils over just thinking Ryan's hand was here moments ago. "We're leaving."

I drop my hand from her hip and use our joined hands to pull her through the crowd.

We pass by the dessert table, Chloe nearly making a play for a tiramisu bite before I redirect us past the assortment of sweets and out the ballroom doors.

Chloe's silently fuming next to me in the car and the moment Marcus pulls to a stop in front of my house, she flings the door open and hops out.

If she wasn't angry with me before, announcing we were leaving before dessert was served did the trick. I say goodnight to Marcus, then climb the stairs and let myself in. Yes, Chloe locked the door even though she knew I was only moments behind her.

I find her in my study. It's an easy guess, I could hear the wheels of the ladder moving on their railings. I'll need to let Rose know it needs to be oiled.

"What the hell are you doing?" I ask, trying to keep my temper even, but seeing Chloe leaning precariously off the top of the ladder makes every muscle in my body tighten. She's had several glasses of champagne and she's in an evening gown for fuck's sake. At least she had the wherewithal to take off her heels.

"Selecting a new book. Do you have *Manners for Dummies*?" She turns to dangle one leg off the step.

That move right there sends my heart rate through the roof.

"Chloe, put both feet on the ladder and come down. Now." There's a pleading edge to my tone which only pisses me off more. I hate the weakness I feel in situations like this.

"Make me."

My hands grip the ladder, but I know I won't climb it. It's a ten-foot ladder, not the Empire State Building, yet the fear feels the same.

This time when Chloe leans off the ladder, she removes her foot and a hand. The weight shift sends the ladder sliding to the right and catches Chloe off balance.

My heart stops when I see her nearly topple off the side.

"Chloe!"

She hugs the side railing with her arm and manages to grip back onto the step with her toes.

"Jesus Christ." I wipe at my brow, the tension in my body now dripping out of every pore.

"I'm fine. Don't get your panties in a twist."

Fucking hell. I'm going to kill her.

From the top of the ladder, Chloe studies me a moment, her eyes narrowing in on my clenched fists. She must see it written all over my face, the fear, because she slowly makes her way down to the bottom. I move back so she can place her feet on the floor. When she's back on solid ground I grip the ladder railing above her head and push it, sending it screaming down the track until it hits the end with a thud.

"What the hell is wrong with you?" Chloe's eyes widen in the direction I sent the ladder.

"It was safer on the ladder," I say, taking a step closer toward her. I fist my hands in my pockets, hoping that will keep me from touching her. From strangling her for scaring the shit out of me on the ladder, and for making me miss out on an opportunity to talk to Fred tonight.

Her blue eyes widen in shock, and she takes a step backward. "You're mad at me? No, I don't think so." She points a polished red nail toward my chest. "You're the one who's been such an ass tonight."

I step right into her finger. Her short nail doesn't even press past the material of my shirt.

"I spent the majority of the night away from you at your request, then when I was in the middle of talking to Fred, I discover you're dancing with another man. The same man whose company is also trying to acquire Voltaire."

"Right. It's always about business and Voltaire. Never about people and feelings, because they have them you know. Feelings. People. Me. I have feelings." She drops her finger from between us, probably a bad move on her part. My body immediately takes the given space. "I didn't know. I probably shouldn't have danced with him then, but he was nice." Her eyes lift to mine. "And he liked my dress."

"Of course, he did." I move my hands to the shelf above Chloe's head. "He wants anything that's mine."

"You are the worst. You couldn't give me a compliment if you tried."

"That's what this is about? What Hunter said?"

"No." She looks defiant, her features pinched tight. "Yes. Maybe if you weren't doling out compliments left and right to anyone who wasn't me, this wouldn't be an issue."

"You want to know why I told other women they looked nice, or lovely or some other bullshit nicety tonight?"

Her face softens. "It wasn't bullshit. They did look lovely."

A puff of air escapes my nostrils, which is fitting. I'm the bull and Chloe is the red flag waving in the distance, taunting me, teasing me. Except, now she's right here within reach. I lower my face toward hers. The scent of her shampoo mixed with hairspray and her floral perfume wraps its arms around me, pulling me in further.

"You drive me fucking crazy."

"Same," she says, tilting her chin up, giving me access to her full lips.

I don't think before I crush my lips to hers. It's what I've wanted to do since the moment she descended my staircase tonight. Chloe's perfect, pliable lips on mine. She meets me there, hungry just like I am. Or it's the natural reaction to the frustration we're feeling with each other. Pent up anger and lust.

My hands drop to her hips, lifting the skirt of her dress to free her legs. I lift her up, pressing her back into the bookcase. Her legs wrap around my waist, aligning our bodies. Her fingers are in my hair, pulling me closer. It's not possible to get closer. My tongue sweeps against the seam of her lips. She opens wide, letting me dive in to taste her. My hips rock into her, it's a primal instinct to press my hardness into her softness. Chloe moans at the contact, and I nearly come at the sound of her breathy sighs.

Maybe Carl was right. I just need to be inside her, then all the madness will stop.

My fingers trace the inside of her thigh, inching toward her center when my phone buzzes in my pocket. Fuck. I should ignore it, slide my fingers beneath Chloe's panties. That's where I want to be, but habit has me releasing her. My fingers retreat to pull my phone from my pocket.

It's Fred.

"Barrett." His voice booms over the line when I answer. "I saw you and Chloe headed out early. I hope everything is okay."

My eyes find Chloe's. Her hair is wild from my hands, her lips swollen, lipstick smeared. Her breaths are coming out deep and heavy.

"We're good. We wanted to get home early tonight." I try to casually adjust my raging hard on.

I turn away from Chloe, wanting to be fully present for the conversation with Fred I missed out on earlier.

Fred chuckles. "Sorry to interrupt. Frankie wanted me to call right away. We're headed to the Hamptons next weekend for Fourth of July. We'd like you and Chloe to join us if you don't have any plans."

"We'd love to," I answer automatically. There's no schedule to check, if Fred Hinkle is in the Hamptons, that's where I need to be.

"You and I will golf while the ladies shop and Frankie's dying to get out on the boat."

"Sounds like a great time." A perfect time to talk with Fred.

"Great. We look forward to seeing you both next weekend."

We hang up and I turn back to Chloe, except she's no longer there. She must have slipped out while I was talking to Fred. I tell myself it's for the best. Tonight was a fucking mess and I need to not let my dick run this operation. That was never part of the plan. Fred's call is the perfect reminder of why Chloe is here, to help me land this deal with Fred. That's it. I can't let my attraction to her get in the way of acquiring Voltaire Telecom.

CHAPTER 14

Chloe

We're going to the Hamptons this weekend. Barrett informed me of this over a mostly silent dinner on Sunday evening, where he skimmed through work emails on his phone between bites until I requested that he not have his phone at the table. He told me that was what he usually did before I was his house guest, and I retaliated by adding a no phone at meals rule to my list. Barrett's hazel eyes challenged mine before he simply stood up and set his phone on the counter before returning to his seat.

Fifty-one percent of the reason I added it was because I hate when people have their phones at the table while eating a meal, forty-nine percent of the reason was to spite Barrett.

It backfired because then we just sat in silence. I forgot who I'm dealing with. He's a robot with an off switch. This week there have been no signs of the edgy, dare I say expressive Barrett from Saturday night. He's got that guy under lock and key.

Not that I've seen him that much. He's up early and off to work before I come downstairs, and I've been walking to work with the weather being so nice in the mornings.

I have yet to crack the code on the whole ladder thing. He was mad before I went into his study, but me being on the ladder only served to anger him more. In the moment I liked it, I thought it was a game, but there was something in his face that made me realize it was more than him being annoyed that I danced with another guy or cost him a chance to talk with Fred. Like it made him feel out of control.

But that kiss?

If that was my punishment, I'll take another.

We've said zero words about the kiss, but there have been many heated glares and awkward fingers fumbling to pass the pepper. Barrett more of the glares and me the fumbling fingers. Barrett's fingers have no problem gripping pepper shakers.

We've yet to acknowledge that his hands were under my dress with my back pressed up against a bookcase. Those long, firm fingers sliding up the inside of my thigh. I still wonder what would have happened if he didn't answer his phone. I think about it daily. In my bed. In the bathtub. Even once in Barrett's study when I knew he was working late. I've really given it a lot of thought. More than I should.

Yesterday morning, I banged my toe on the sofa by my bed and when I went to the freezer to get some ice, I found one of the shelves stocked full of cookie dough ice cream. I asked Rose about it. She was cleaning the third-floor bathroom and informed me it had been put on the grocery list.

Not wanting to take advantage of Barrett's hospitality, what little there is of it, I didn't add anything to the shopping list. Dimitry is an excellent chef and I have been enjoying the dietary variety his meals provide aka something other than ramen noodles. Now, there's a freezer full of ice cream. I'll have to eat it all before I leave because I know Barrett won't eat it and it will go to waste. Not on my watch.

That's what I'm doing right now. I just got home—

Barrett's home—from work and slipped into something more comfortable—the silk lavender tank and short set with the cozy cardigan sweater—and I'm eating ice cream and reading a book on the couch in the study.

I'm so engrossed in the book and the ice cream that I don't hear Barrett come in. It's a romantic suspense novel and I'm almost at the part where she's going to find out if the man she's been sleeping with is the killer or if it's the other guy, so the slightest creak has me jumping and a glop of ice cream lands smack onto the page.

"Have you eaten dinner?" he asks, staring at the bowl of ice cream in my hands.

I can't decide if he's simply asking or if he's accusing me of having dessert first.

"Not yet," I reply.

"I'll heat up the food," he says simply, then he's gone.

I quickly clean up the glop of ice cream, scooping it off the page with my spoon because there's no need to be wasteful. I'm nervous and excited. It's ridiculous really, but I'm hoping that maybe Barrett's effort to talk to me, acknowledge my presence and speak actual words is a sign we can call a truce. I'm ready to make amends. While we were never friends before, I'd like to at least be amicable. I don't want to be stuck in this weird tension for the next five weeks. Since I know Barrett isn't programmed to manage feelings and emotions, I'll have to be the bigger person and apologize.

I find him in the kitchen already setting our plates on the table.

"I'm sorry about Saturday night." There. I said it. I want to move forward.

"Why are you wearing that?" is his response.

I look down at my clothing. The silk lounge set, and the matching fuzzy cardigan. I put the sweater on because the temperature of the house with the air conditioning on was cool.

"It was in my closet. Was I not supposed to wear it?"

"I know where you found it, I bought it for you."

"Thank you. It's really nice." I rub the soft sleeve of the sweater.

"I didn't intend for you to wear it to dinner," he responds, jaw tight.

"Oh. When am I supposed to wear it?"

"In your room. To bed."

"So, you bought me something this nice, something I can't wear out of the house, but also something you don't want to see me walking around the house in?" I'm so confused. "I saw the price tag on it. I feel like I should wear it every day to get the value out of it."

Barrett rubs his chin. Those fingers are doing that lip tug again.

"Wear it whenever you want," Barrett mutters, but a second later his fork clinks against his plate. "You know what? No. If you're going to make me sit here and have nothing to do but look at you, then that outfit is off limits for dinner. I don't want to be eating my dinner and have to see you looking like...like...that."

My hands grip the back of the chair.

"Like what?" I say, ready for a fight.

Barrett stands and any power I felt standing over him is gone. His tall, broad frame towers over me.

"Like I could eat *you* for dinner," he says.

Holy shit. That is the last thing I expected him to say. That's the issue with Barrett, he is impossible to read. While I'm trying to figure him out, he's like some artificial intelligence that gets smarter and maneuvers around every attempt. His stare is so intense, the green with gold flecks disappearing behind a ring of black. The tension and silence that fills the air is suffocating.

I can't help myself, I start laughing. Not because any of this is remotely funny, but because that's my coping mechanism in this awkward, but highly arousing situation. Do I want Barrett to eat me for dinner? My body does. It's sending out all sorts of signals. My nipples are rock hard against the thin, smooth fabric of my tank and the panties I changed into earlier after a bath...soaking wet. But my brain is a loose cannon, thinking of all the awkward and embarrassing things that could happen if Barrett were to feast on me. So here I am standing in the middle of Barrett's kitchen, aroused and laughing while his face hardens to stone.

"I'm not laughing at you. I'm laughing with you," I explain, sounding like a parent consoling a child, which is disturbing in and of itself. Except Barrett isn't laughing. "That's not what I meant." How can I make Barrett understand that inexperience makes me a little skittish when it comes to sex and all that stuff without telling him how inexperienced I am? I'm not a virgin, but sometimes it feels like I might as well be.

The words *it's not you, it's me* threaten to leave my mouth, but I manage to reel them back. Also, Barrett has already pushed his chair in and left, so it doesn't really matter what I say at this point. After a failed attempt to eat my dinner, which I've already ruined with the ice cream, I go to my bedroom.

The calendar on the writing desk indicates I have a little over four more weeks as Barrett's fake girlfriend. I'm not even halfway through this exhausting agreement, and I don't know how it could get much worse.

That's when it hits me.

We'll be spending the weekend in the Hamptons with Fred and Frankie.

They'll expect us to stay in the same room.

The same bed.

Fuck.

Barrett

When I arrive to dinner, Chloe is already seated at the table. She's typing something out on her phone but when she sees me, she moves to place it on the counter. I immediately take notice of the way her shorts hug the curve of her ass. They're not the skimpy silk ones she wore last night when I made a fool of myself at dinner, so it's determined it doesn't matter what Chloe wears, I'm going to be turned on.

I run my hand through my hair, something I've been doing a lot of lately and drop into my chair.

"Hi." Chloe gives me a small smile.

"Listen, Chloe—"

My words are interrupted by the doorbell.

"I'll get it!" Chloe jumps up excitedly and sprints from the kitchen.

I'm not expecting anyone so I stand and follow her out to the foyer.

Chloe's already there, door open, talking to a woman.

When Chloe turns around, she's got a dog in her arms.

"What—"

"Good evening, Mr. St. Clair." The woman extends her hand out to me. "Jillian Massey from Goldendoodle Foster Program of NYC. Thank you so much for your generous donation at The Top Dog Gala. The proceeds that go to Animal Medical Center also sponsor free vet care for our rescues and the foster program, as you know."

"No." I shake my head, looking at the mass of sandy curls in Chloe's arms. "I didn't know."

"Well, let me tell you about Baxter. He's a neutered, four-year-old, small Standard Goldendoodle. He's been with us for six weeks. He's a bit of a lounger. Not as active as some of the other young dogs, but he will play fetch with a tennis ball. I will warn you, while most dogs get anxious about storms, Baxter gets overly so. He's a cuddler and likes to be near people."

"He's so sweet." Chloe laughs when Baxter licks her mouth.

"Well, I'll let you get acquainted with Baxter here, and I'll go grab the rest of his stuff from the car."

As Jillian descends the steps it dawns on me that this ball of fur intends to stay here. In my house.

"What the hell, Chloe? You adopted a dog?"

"No. I'm fostering a dog." She buries her face into his curly mane. "Don't worry. Baxter's temporary, just like me."

She lifts her eyes to mine and I see the challenge there.

"No. No way. No dogs. We had this conversation last week in the car."

"You said dogs were messy. Baxter is fully house-trained and he's hypoallergenic. No shedding."

"I don't have time for a dog."

"Baxter isn't for you. He's for me. I'll be taking care of him." She nuzzles his nose and a ripple of jealousy settles into my gut. It's ridiculous. I'm not jealous of a dog.

Jillian returns with a bag full of supplies.

"Everything is in here. Even a small supply of food. He prefers a vegan diet, all-natural ingredients made from scratch."

I shoot Chloe a death glare, but she just smiles.

"I'll take care of it." Shifting Baxter to one side, she accepts the bag from Jillian. "Thank you."

"What's the return policy?" I ask. Both women's heads jerk in my direction.

Jillian gives me a small smile. "If this pairing doesn't work out, you're free to bring him back to the rescue shelter, but ideally we'd love for Baxter to stay here until he matches with his forever home."

"And how long will that be?" I ask.

"It could be next week; it could be a few months."

"Thank you, Jillian." Chloe sees her to the door.

When she returns, I stare at the ball of fur in her arms.

"You can keep him for a day," I say.

"What?"

"It'll be like a dog for a day. Then he needs to go back."

"That's silly."

"Chloe, I'm serious," I say, with an edge to my tone.

"I am, too." She doesn't back down. "I'm putting it on my list."

"You can't do that."

"What do you mean? You said anything as long as it doesn't interfere with your business deal or our fake relationship."

Fuck. She's right. A dog, while not anything I want to deal with, fits into the parameters of the agreement I spelled out. And he won't be here permanently. He's temporary, like Chloe.

Chloe notices the moment that I realize this, her face lighting up even brighter than it did when she was snuggling Baxter. I've never seen her smile like that. She's happy. The dog makes her happy. Looking at Chloe my chest feels tight, but I refuse to acknowledge what it could mean.

"Fine," I mutter.

"You say that like you're allowing it, not like you had no choice."

I follow Chloe back into the kitchen where our food is still sitting at the table. She sets the dog on the floor, then opens the bag Jillian gave her with his food in it.

I grab our plates to reheat the food that is now ice cold, thanks to Baxter's arrival.

He moves to follow me, obviously thinking I'm going to feed him.

On my way to the microwave, he gets tangled under my feet and I almost drop the plates on the floor.

"Chloe, why is the dog next to me? There's all this space." I motion to the open concept chef's kitchen around us. "It doesn't need to be right underfoot."

Chloe bites her bottom lip, trying not to laugh. "I think he likes you."

While the food reheats, Baxter sits near my feet, looking up at me and wagging his tail.

"This is not for you." I point toward the food in the microwave. "In fact, none of this is yours," I motion to our surroundings, "so don't get used to it."

He just stares back, mouth open, and with that dopey look on his face.

"Don't let the cranky man scare you, Baxter," Chloe says, coming around the island to set his bowl of food on the floor near the table. "His bark is worse than his bite."

She knows nothing about my bite. If she did, she'd take those words back.

Baxter busies himself with eating the food in his bowl while I set our plates on the table.

While we eat, Chloe's attention wanders to the curly-haired dog slopping food out of his bowl.

"Isn't he cute?" she asks.

"Cute? More like messy."

Chloe laughs. "Do you ever plan to have kids? Because if you think Baxter is messy, you're in for a real treat."

"Kids get older, then they take care of themselves."

"Sure, but there are a lot of messes in there before that happens. You do remember being a kid, don't you?"

"My father was much older than my mother when they married and had me. He liked things to be in their place. Kids were to be seen, not heard."

"He would have hated my house. Five different voices, all trying to talk at once." She pauses a moment to take a bite of the salmon. "How old were you when he died?"

"Fifteen."

"I'm sorry. That must have been tough."

"It was fine. I hardly knew the man. He worked all the time. It was mainly my mother and me, and nannies when my mother was working."

"Still. Losing a parent can't be easy."

My throat tightens, making the bite of food I just chewed difficult to swallow. I don't want to talk about my father. There's nothing to say. I need to shift the focus back onto the task at hand, our upcoming weekend in the Hamptons with Fred and Frankie.

"What are you going to do with the dog when we're in the Hamptons?"

"The dog? His name is Baxter. And we'll bring him with us."

"What? We can't bring him."

"Why not? You said Fred has dogs. I'm sure he wouldn't mind."

"I mind."

Chloe's eyes light up. "Having Baxter there will give you another commonality. Isn't that the whole point of all this? Why you needed a fake girlfriend? And getting a dog is one of the most legitimate couple things."

I scowl, but I see her point.

"Is that why you signed up for the dog fostering program?" I ask. "To be helpful?"

Chloe smiles sweetly. "I just want my fake boyfriend to succeed in his business endeavors so I can break up with him."

I glance at the dog—Baxter—and the mess he's made around his bowl.

This better be worth it.

CHAPTER 15

Barrett

We're just outside of Southampton when I get the text. I read it in disbelief.

"Fuck." My hand clenches around my phone. It's impossible to keep the frustration I feel inside.

Chloe flinches from where she's reading a book beside me in the car. Between us, Baxter sits up, his open mouth turns in my direction and I get a whiff of doggy breath.

After my efforts to make him sit on the floor of the car failed, I gave up. He's had his head in Chloe's lap the entire drive until now. I put my hand out to guide his face away from mine, but he thinks I'm offering to pet him and moves closer.

"What?" Chloe asks.

"Frankie got lip injections and is having a bad reaction so Fred cancelled. They're not coming."

"Oh, no. Is she okay?" Chloe turns in my direction, her eyes wide with concern.

We both look forward as Marcus turns left to pull the SUV through the gate and into the circle drive of Fred's Southampton estate.

Knowing the chance to talk business with Fred this

weekend won't be happening now puts me in a bad mood. That was the whole fucking point of this trip.

"I think so." I shake my head. I didn't ask.

Shit. Now, I feel like I've somehow made my position with Fred worse. How could I forget to ask how his girlfriend was doing? Leave it to Chloe to remind me I'm a self-centered asshole. My first thought when I read his text was my lost opportunity. I didn't think about Frankie and what she might be going through. I didn't know you could have bad reactions to lip injections.

I stare at Chloe, the way she's nervously chewing on her bottom lip.

"What should we do?" she asks, reaching over to offer Baxter the affection that I denied him.

"Fred insisted we stay." I note the direction in Fred's text. He wants us to stay and while my opportunity to discuss our deal is gone, the next best thing to gaining his support would be to honor his request. It will be a reason to follow up with him next week. "They had meals prepared and staff is here."

"Okay," Chloe says simply.

Now, not only am I losing the opportunity to talk with Fred, but I'm stuck in the Hamptons with Chloe. And the dog.

We file out of the car while Marcus pulls our bags from the trunk and Fred's housekeeper, Lucy, shows us inside.

"Here is the room I've prepared for you. I hope you find everything to your liking," she says, leading the way into a large master suite. It's nautical-themed. Paintings of boats. Anchor and rope wall décor. Navy and white bedding. There's even a dog bed on the floor next to the window.

Chloe was right, Fred was elated to hear that we had a dog. I failed to mention that he's temporary, but none of it will matter in the end.

Chloe sets her bag down on the striped bench at the foot of the bed.

"It's lovely. Thank you."

She sets Baxter down and he starts sniffing around the room.

"If you need anything, please let me know. Dinner will be served at seven."

"Thank you." I nod at Lucy on her way out of the room.

"Pretty nice, right?" Chloe opens her suitcase and starts to unpack.

"Sure." I do the same, doing my best not to notice the lace underwear that she accidentally drops on the floor before swooping in like a hawk to grab them. Her cheeks flush with color and my dick twitches.

I already know what the underwear looks like. They were on the emailed invoice I received from the department store that Bea purchased them from, and I looked them up online just to torture myself.

"Do you want top or bottom?" Chloe asks.

My mind immediately flashes with an image of Chloe beneath me. Her fiery red hair spilling over the pillow. Definitely top, although I would love to see her tits bounce while she rides me. It really shouldn't be an either or.

I clear my throat and the image from my head. "Excuse me?"

"Drawers." I turn to find her pointing at the chest of drawers. "Top, right? Since you're taller," she mumbles and that crimson flush reaches her temples.

Also, the sundress that she's wearing is driving me fucking crazy. It accentuates her full breasts and her trim waist. The blue dress with tiny white flowers is far from erotic, but it still manages to stir my dick to life. When Chloe bends over to zip her suitcase, I inwardly groan.

I'd still be in this situation if Fred and Frankie were here, but at least they would be around to create a buffer.

I've been in this room with her for three minutes and my dick is already hard as a rock. We haven't even addressed the fact that there's only one bed here. No couch, not even a chair. Only an overstuffed bench that looks nearly as hard as the erection Chloe is giving me. We're both doing our best to keep up the charade that this isn't the first time we'll be sharing a room. A bed.

I have to get out of here.

"Do you want to go for a walk? Check out some shops?" Chloe asks just as I tell her, "I'm going for a run."

"Oh, sure. That's nice." She nods. "I'll see you at dinner?"

"Yeah. See you at dinner."

I run six miles. Not because I'm a runner or in training for anything, but because that's how far I get before I feel the tension of spending the weekend alone with Chloe subside. Then I think about her in that silk pajama set and I have to spend an extra five minutes in the shower with my dick in my hand.

Ultimately, I arrive at dinner no better than I was before the run.

Chloe, on the other hand, is full of excitement over the bookstore she and Baxter found. I wolf down the petite filet and vegetables Fred's chef has prepared, then take my glass of wine to his office. The only way to make it through this weekend is to avoid Chloe. To not hear the exhilaration in her voice when she tells me about the cute downtown shops she visited. To not bear witness to the brilliant smile that appears on her face when she talks about things she loves. And most of all, to not be present when she slides her enticing body beneath the sheets of our bed.

Last night I worked on my laptop for as long as I could. I checked to make sure Chloe was asleep before brushing my teeth and climbing into bed with her. It's a king-size bed, yet somehow during the night we managed to meet in the middle. By morning, strands of her hair were tickling my chest. Her toes were pressed against my shins and I had the strongest urge to pull her close.

Trying to secure this deal with Fred and therefore being forced to be around Chloe this much is giving me the worst case of blue balls. If I had a signed agreement with Voltaire, then I'd gladly accept this punishment. But with no progress made, I'm starting to wonder if I can make this deal happen. After this weekend, the only thing I'll be closer to is my will power snapping where Chloe is concerned.

I turn to find her softly snoring, blissfully unaware that a raging boner lays only a foot from her.

Fuck. I've never been this hard. I slide my hand into my boxer briefs, giving myself a few strokes. Chloe shifts next to me. The gap in the covers reveals where her t-shirt has slid up her front, exposing the smooth, tempting skin of her belly.

I stare at her bare skin and give myself another stroke.

I recall the moment at dinner this week when she laughed after I told her I wanted to eat her. It was not the reaction I had anticipated. How she disappeared from the study the night of the gala after we kissed, when I was moments away from finding out if her arousal matched mine. I can still feel the softness of her thigh under my palm. It's clear, I'm the only one suffering with the tension between us.

What the hell am I doing? I can't touch myself here with her sleeping beside me no matter how optimal it is for visual stimulation.

With Chloe still softly snoring, I throw back the covers. Another run, that's what I need. To rid myself of this pent-up energy. It's likely the only way I'm going to make it through the weekend. Physical exertion that doesn't involve touching Chloe.

From his spot on the dog bed, Baxter's head pops up, the tags around his collar jingling. I grab a pair of shorts and stalk into the bathroom. When I head down the stairs, Baxter follows.

"You want to go?" I ask.

He wags his tail.

"Okay, but here are the rules. We're running. You have to be able to keep up. No stopping to sniff things every five seconds."

He lets out a bark, which I believe to be a verbal agreement to our contract. I grab his leash off the bench by the front door and we head out.

Gray clouds hang in the sky and the air is muggy. I take the same path as yesterday, down Main Street, running past the shops and bars. Baxter hangs with me for the first few miles, all floppy tongue and bouncing stride, but he gets distracted by the dog treat bowl that is out front of Tate's Bake Shop. It's all downhill from there.

The sky opens up on our way home. We're already going at a snail's pace, so when Baxter all but stops, I scoop him up and carry him the rest of the way.

"You smell like wet dog," I tell him.

He pants in my face, then licks my cheek.

"We had a deal. This was not part of it."

By the time we return to the house, we're soaked.

Lucy greets us with towels and a cup of coffee. She's been busy making breakfast. The amount of food she has prepared is excessive. It's far too much for two people.

"When would you like breakfast?" she asks, fluffing Baxter's wet coat with a towel.

"Soon. I'm going to take a shower first."

She nods. "Coffee for Miss Chloe?"

"Sure."

"How does she take it?"

"Two sugars and cream," I rattle off like an expert boyfriend. The only reason I know that is because I overheard Rose asking Chloe last week so she could make it for her.

Lucy prepares the coffee for Chloe and hands me the mug.

With Baxter still enjoying his pampering from Lucy, I take the coffees and go upstairs.

Chloe's still asleep. I take her in. Her head is the only thing I can see. The rest of her body is burrowed into the covers. Her red hair, wild and loose over the pillow, her long lashes hovering over her lightly freckled cheeks.

I set her mug down on the bedside table. Maybe the aroma will wake her up. The cold water sliding down my back redirects my attention to the shower.

In the bathroom, I strip out of my wet clothes and step into the shower. Any relief I had achieved from the run quickly dissipates as I stand under the water, my dick quickly springing to life again. This is becoming a routine. Run, shower, stroke my dick thinking about coming inside of Chloe. What I had put to an end in bed earlier, I let myself continue this time.

With my throbbing cock in my hands, I imagine Chloe's face clouded with lust at the sight of my erection. Her hands wrapping around its thickness, her sweet, pink lips parting to welcome me into her warm mouth. I imagine bending Chloe over my desk and fucking her hard, my cum sliding down her inner thighs. Marking her as mine.

She's the farthest thing from it. Maybe that's why I want her so bad.

That's why when her image appears in the doorway, through the steam of the shower, I don't break my rhythm.

Chloe's there, her wild red hair and expressive eyes watching me and I meet her stare head on.

Her baggy t-shirt covers her tiny shorts, making it appear like she's got nothing on underneath. Even through the steam I can make out the peaks of her nipples through her shirt. My mouth aches to taste one.

I stroke harder, my hand tightening around my shaft.

Knowing Chloe's eyes are on me, taking in every detail as I stroke myself, only urges me on.

With each pull, I roll my wrist, squeezing the sensitive head. Chloe's mouth is gaping open, a perfect 'o' forming on her lips. I imagine it's her mouth I'm fucking. My spine tingles and I let out a guttural groan of pleasure.

A second later, the hot liquid of my orgasm explodes from the head of my cock, and her name falls from my lips.

My eyes close with the intensity of my release. Fuck. That was insane.

When I finally open my eyes, Chloe is gone.

CHAPTER 16

Chloe

I slam the bathroom door shut and rush to the dresser.

Sweet Jesus. What just happened?

Still half-asleep and needing to pee, I just walked in on Barrett showering.

Naked.

Obviously, that's how people shower.

I glance around, wondering if I've been caught. Of course, I was caught. Barrett saw me.

He saw me through the foggy glass of the shower and still kept stroking himself.

Without much effort, my brain replays the moment back in vivid detail.

Barrett naked in the shower. Steam rising around him. One large hand braced against the tiled wall while the other fists his hard cock, pumping furiously.

When I walked in, his head had been down. I should have left, but I stood there frozen, my legs powerless to move. My eyes unable to look away as the water sluiced over his broad shoulders, down his strong chest and through the tributaries of the V indentations at his hips.

Did I mention the monster cock in his hands?

Yeah, that thing.

It's clear now why Barrett's hands are large. They have to be to manage other large things.

Barrett's hips flexing as he thrust harder, faster, into both fists. The way he stared at me from behind the glass. The potent lust in his eyes and the guttural sound he made when he came. And said my name. Now, it's all seared into my brain.

I hear the water shut off in the bathroom—had I really been oblivious to the sound before?—and it spurs me into action.

I don't even know what I'm putting on, but something other than pajamas so I can go downstairs before Barrett comes out of the bathroom.

I manage to find jean shorts and a t-shirt and throw them on.

If it weren't July I'd probably opt for a sweater, too. Anything to put more layers between my body and the outside world where Barrett will inevitably be. Barrett and his massive cock.

Why is it that walking in on Barrett stroking himself feels more mortifying than when he walked in on me in the bathtub?

Because he saw me and he didn't stop. He looked me straight in the eyes while his dick continued to thrust into his hands. I watched everything, too captivated by what I was witnessing to turn away. And he knows I liked it. I could tell by the way his eye narrowed and his mouth curved into a devilish grin. *Gotcha.*

I comb through my wild hair, then race down the stairs, nearly tripping on the landing and plummeting to my death down the wood staircase.

· · ·

Lucy greets me with Baxter at her feet, who jumps up at me, so I lower down to snuggle him.

His usually fluffy hair is damp.

"How'd you get wet?" I ask him, thankful for the distraction.

"Mr. St. Clair took him out for a run this morning. They both came back soaked," Lucy replies.

Her comment only reminds me of wet Barrett in the shower. Well, it was a good ten seconds without his naked image in my brain.

Lucy has fresh squeezed orange juice, bacon, eggs, pastries and fruit ready to serve.

"Would you like to wait for Mr. St. Clair?" she asks.

"Um," I start, not knowing how long Barrett will be, or if I can ever face him again. I really thought sharing a bed was going to be the issue. I didn't give myself enough credit that I would manage to find other awkward yet sexually arousing situations in which I could embarrass myself. Maybe I'll take my breakfast to go and start the long, yet necessary trek back to the city so I don't have to die of mortification.

"No need to wait. I'm here."

Too late.

I turn to find Barrett standing in the doorway dressed casually in a fitted navy polo and gray slacks. My eyes automatically lower to his crotch and I swear I can see the outline of his dick. What's left of his impressive erection. I can't look at him so I busy myself loading up a plate of food.

"Coffee?" Lucy asks.

"Yes," we say in unison.

"I left you a mug on the bedside table." His deep voice reverberates in my ear.

I keep facing forward even when I feel Barrett move closer, the warmth of his chest near my shoulder and back as he leans in to dish up some eggs.

"Oh?" I say. It's an effort to keep my voice neutral. "I didn't see it." *I was too busy staring at your giant cock in the shower.*

"Cream and sugar?" Lucy offers, completely oblivious to the electricity crackling between me and Barrett.

"Cream, please," Barrett replies.

"Yes," is all I manage to say, but Lucy must be well versed in women who are stunned speechless because she manages to make me the best cup of coffee I've ever had.

We sit in the breakfast nook. I shovel in my food while Lucy informs us of the day's schedule.

"Mr. Hinkle had a boat ride planned but the weather doesn't seem to be cooperating."

For the first time this morning I glance out the window to find gray clouds and rain drops peppering the surface of the swimming pool.

"If there's anything you'd like me to set up, please let me know. It's questionable if the firework show will still happen with the rain. It will likely be a last-minute decision."

"I'm sure we'll find something to do," Barrett replies. I feel his eyes on me, and I can't not look at him. The second I do, I realize it was a horrible idea. Those intense hazel eyes are studying me. His lips turned up in a smirk. I watch those long fingers, the same ones that were wrapped around his erection in the shower, manipulate his spoon as he digs into the juicy flesh of the grapefruit. His mouth closes around the pink flesh and he groans in satisfaction. I nearly topple out of my chair.

My core clenches involuntarily.

Sweet Jesus. I'm in trouble.

∼

Barrett must sense my stress because after breakfast he doesn't make good on his threat of us finding something to do, but instead retreats to Fred's home office to work. For once, I breathe a sigh of relief that all he does is work. That's where I want his energy focused right now, instead of on me.

The rain continues to pour and I spend most of the morning reading a manuscript under a cozy blanket with Baxter curled up next to me. He seems exhausted from the activities of the morning. I can totally relate.

Having put enough time and distance between Barrett's shower, I retreat upstairs to take mine.

I'm in and out in record time. I also lock the door because that seems to be a major factor in this issue we keep having with bathrooms and walking in on each other and self-induced orgasms.

I throw my hair in a top knot and put my t-shirt and shorts back on. Feeling refreshed, I return to the sitting room and my book. But I feel restless, so I peruse the cabinet of books and games. I settle on Scrabble because I've already played WordIt today and it's the next best thing.

I set up the game board, place the tiles face down and mix them around.

I've never played Scrabble by myself before, but I'm sure I'll manage. I'm deciding whether I want to play as two players alternating or just one when Barrett clears his throat behind me.

"What are you doing?" he asks.

I know Barrett well enough by now to know that some-times his questions come out as accusations even when he doesn't mean it that way. Now being a perfect example.

"Playing Scrabble."

"By yourself?"

"Do you want to play?" I ask.

His answer is to sit across from me. I'm surprised that he doesn't ask to move the board so we're sitting in proper chairs. My size is more conducive to this seating arrangement than

Barrett's tall frame. Instead, he folds his long legs under the coffee table and rests his back against the sofa behind him.

"What's with you and word games?" he asks, carefully selecting his tiles. It's a methodic process so intense I wonder if he's using those telekinetic powers of his to read the letters on the tiles. Maybe that's x-ray vision. The concentration of Barrett's stare makes me think he has both.

"I like words."

"I can tell."

I arrange my tiles, moving them around to find out which word option will get me the most points. I think back to last weekend when he ruined my WordIt streak. I've decided I don't want to just beat Barrett. Annihilation would be preferable.

I have a thousand Es which seems annoying at first, but then I discover that I can play the word SQUEEZE using two letters with huge point totals and one happens to land on a double letter score space.

"Thirty-five points! Beat that." I'm ready to declare victory.

Barrett studies his tiles saying nothing. His long fingers manipulate the tiles, thoroughly feeling them out. I should be used to this by now, but come on. Starting off with a thirty-five-point word in Scrabble is huge.

Ironically, that's the word that Barrett plays off my last E. HUGE.

"Congratulations," I say, trying to keep a straight face, "eight points."

I write down our first-round scores using a piece of paper and pen I found in the box. I'm going to frame this score card and hang it in my apartment.

Which reminds me. "I talked to my landlord yesterday," I say, arranging my tiles again, looking for another high point word. "I was supposed to be able to move back in next week but she said there were delays." I lift my eyes toward Barrett. "Do you know anything about that?"

While I'm not entirely anxious to return to the shoe box that is my apartment, especially after living at Barrett's spacious and luxurious brownstone, I do want to make sure the timeline for completion coincides with me being single again. It would be weird if we broke up and I was still living at his place.

"It's not ready yet," he responds. No details, no explanation.

Inspired by Barrett, I play the word HUMDRUM. It earns me a triple letter score and a double word score for a total of thirty-eight points. It also earns me a smile from Barrett.

"Why are you smiling?" I ask. "You're losing."

"Am I?"

"Yes to both." I laugh.

He shrugs.

"You should smile more," I tell him, an idea forming in my brain. "In fact, I'm going to put it on my list."

"That seems like a waste."

"Not at all." I shake my head. "It's a great smile."

"How many times of day would be sufficient?" He's amused now.

"It doesn't matter, as long as it's always directed at me."

My eyes widen reflexively and I want to smack my hand over my mouth. Why did I say that? Am I flirting with Barrett? That seems impossible.

His lips twitch as he rotates a single tile between his thumb and forefinger.

"I don't want to tell you what to do—" he begins, but I start laughing.

"You don't?" I laugh. "I don't think anything can be further from the truth."

He narrows his eyes at me, and I motion for him to continue.

"You're not using your requests very wisely."

"Oh really?"

"With the addition of me smiling more, you only have one request left and still four weeks before your time is up."

"So, I'm maximizing the time I have with the requests I've made."

He hums thoughtfully.

"I'll be curious to see what you come up with for your final request."

"And what would you suggest I add to the list?"

Barrett leans forward to place his tiles on the board. He uses the S from SQUEEZE to spell the word SHOWER. When my eyes lift to find him staring at me, my mouth goes dry. That single word sets off a highlight reel of what I walked in on this morning. The heat in Barrett's eyes is unmistakable. It's a perfect match to the lust-filled stare he pinned me with this morning.

Barrett earns a measly twelve points, his strategy is mediocre at best, yet he looks like he's having the best time. He sits back against the sofa, those graceful fingers of his drumming against the table.

It occurs to me that Barrett isn't actually trying to win this game. He's playing a different game altogether. I think it's called *Make Chloe Squirm* and the objective is to make me squirm. It's an easy game really, and Barrett excels at it.

This is confirmed when he uses his next turn to play MOIST.

My mind returns to the car that first morning after I moved into his place and the WordIt that day was MOIST. So were my panties after he bent down to give me a simple goodbye kiss, which he thought I wanted when in fact I was only trying to give him his coffee.

"Your turn," he says simply, like I'm not fighting every cell in my body to not fling myself over this table and into his capable hands. The seam of my jean shorts is pressing in just the right spot that I can feel the pulse of my clit against the rigid fabric.

I stare at the Scrabble tiles, unable to form anything in front of me into a word.

"I'm sorry to interrupt." Lucy appears in the doorway and I have the urge to run over and hug her.

"Nothing to be sorry about. Come on in. How's it going? Want to play Scrabble?" Should I invite her to sleep over, too? We'll have movie night and share popcorn. Lucy will sit in the middle to chaperone. Sounds like a fun time.

I can feel Barrett's eyes on me. I may have the higher point total but he's the real winner here. *Make Chloe Squirm* was a success.

"No, thank you." She has the decency to respond to my gibberish. "The rain has stopped and I've arranged a wine tasting at a vineyard nearby."

Lucy's right. A glance out the windows confirms the rain has stopped and the sun is peeking out from behind the clouds. Again, the activities inside the house have distracted me from paying attention to anything else.

"They'll have antipasto and charcuterie, and an assortment of snacks. You'll be able to watch the fireworks there as well."

"Sounds great," I say enthusiastically. Surely *Make Chloe Squirm* can't be a public game. I wonder if there are any concerts or largely populated festivals we could attend.

"The driver will pick you up in thirty minutes," Lucy tells us.

"Go ahead and change. I'll put the game away." Barrett doesn't have to tell me twice. I practically run for the stairs, enjoying the cool breeze that my quick pace generates. Holy hell it was hot in that room.

I grab some clothes and use the bathroom to change and freshen up my face. Ten minutes later, I exit the bathroom to find Barrett shirtless and mid-zip on a pair of snug fitting white pants.

"Sorry. I didn't realize you were changing in here."

Barrett smirks. "I'm in a far less compromising position than this morning, aren't I?"

"Right," I reply, while suppressing the urge to fan myself. I don't want to talk about this morning. I'd prefer to bury that conversation with Jimmy Hoffa's body.

I try to avert my eyes, but let's be honest, why should I?

I already discovered Barrett has those Vs of muscle on his sides this morning in the shower. Somehow, they look even more lickable with a pair of pants on. And those pants? Lord have mercy.

They're the gray sweatpants equivalent of Hamptons attire, hugging Barrett's muscular thighs and perfectly high-lighting the bulge between his legs without being indecent. I already know what he's packing. I've seen it in action and yet I'm shocked to see it pressed up against the fabric of his pants.

You'd think after seeing him masturbate in the shower, a simple zipping of his pants wouldn't feel so intimate. But those fingers pressing the button through the hole at the top of his pants is practically porn.

He reaches for the shirt on the bed, a button-down with a striped green and blue pattern that makes his eyes that much more intense. I busy myself with placing items in my clutch but out of the corner of my eye, I watch every single motion as he buttons his shirt.

I'm attempting to put on the delicate chain necklace my parents gave me but my shaky hands make the precision I need to hold the tiny clasp open impossible. Barrett moves in behind me, wordlessly taking the chain's ends from my fumbling fingers and connecting it. He lays it gently against my skin, his fingertips grazing the base of my neck, sending a shiver down my spine.

"Thank you." I smile at him in the mirror.

He nods, those intense hazel eyes boring into mine, telling me everything and nothing at once, before turning toward the door.

I'm not much of a wine drinker but it's clear from the tension between Barrett and me, I'm going to start today.

CHAPTER 17

Barrett

Chloe's wearing tight white jeans and a flirty little tank top that opens in the back. It makes the silk camisole she wore to dinner last week look like a parka. It hugs her breasts in front, giving me an ample view of her cleavage and causing the crotch of my pants to tighten—again.

We're seated at the winery with a tasting flight, but Chloe doesn't appear to be tasting her wine as much as slinging it back.

The hostess brings us a charcuterie board and I'm happy to see Chloe inhaling that as well. At least she's not drinking on an empty stomach.

"What do you think of the Chardonnay?"

"Which one was the Chardonnay?" she asks.

"The one in your glass."

"Oh. It's nice." She bites her lip. "I'm not much of a wine drinker."

"Really? I think you've got it down." I informed her that she doesn't have to finish every tasting, that's what the buckets are for, to pour out anything you don't want to finish, but

Chloe thought that was wasteful and has been drinking every drop that is put in front of her.

"I'm not much of a drinker at all. Didn't party much in high school or college. I read a lot of books, though."

"I've noticed. Tell me about Books 4 Kids," I say, taking a sip of my wine.

"Is this an inquisition on where your donation is going? I thought we covered that when I picked up the check."

"I can tell you're passionate about it and I want to know more about it."

"I volunteered in my hometown library when I was a teen, tutoring kids with reading disabilities and leading story times for the younger kids. I even learned to play the ukulele to do sing-alongs and make it fun."

"The ukulele?"

"I wanted to play the guitar, but my hands were too small," she waves them in front of her, "they still are. The chords were hard to reach on the guitar, so ukulele was a good instrument to learn. You'd have no problem with that, your hands are huge."

"You're going to give me a complex."

"Because of your huge hands?" She laughs. "They're huge compared to mine but they're proportionate to your body."

She doesn't have to say what she means, it's implied. It's convenient I have these large hands to fit around other large parts of my body. Looking up to find Chloe watching me in the shower this morning has been at the forefront of my mind all day.

"I've always loved books and reading. When I found out there was an actual career where I could read books for a living, I majored in English literature and set my sights on New York."

"And you enjoy working at St. Clair Press? With my mother?"

"Your mother, of course. She's amazing. I've learned so much from her." Chloe stares at her glass of wine before returning my gaze. "I wouldn't be doing this if it didn't matter that much to me. It's not just a job. I love reading stories that the author has poured their heart and soul into with the hopes that it will connect with someone. And when I connect with it and pass it along to JoAnna or an assistant editor, then I feel like I get to share in that effort of putting their story out in the world."

I expected Chloe to be passionate about her career, but hearing her talk about it like that makes something inside of me crack open. Yes, Chloe made an error in judgment by hosting that party at my mother's apartment, but I'm the guy who's been holding her feet to the fire. Making her believe that her career aspirations, of being an editor and helping bring amazing stories into the world, could disappear in an instant.

I've been so focused on Fred that I haven't seen it from her perspective. I haven't thought about the hours she might spend worrying about what she'll do if my mother finds out.

I watch Chloe dab at the corner of her eye, then take a sip of wine.

"Favorite book?"

She laughs. "Impossible to choose."

"Fine. What genre do you prefer?"

"You can't make fun of me."

"I will not make fun of you." I make an x over my heart.

"I love a good psychological thriller, but I also enjoy romance."

"Why was that so hard?" I ask.

"I feel like you're judging me."

"How so?"

"You're like oh, look at Chloe, she's super inexperienced so she reads romance novels to help her with guys."

"That is not what I was thinking at all." I pause for a beat. "How inexperienced are we talking?"

She shakes her head. "Forget I said that."

I smile at her. I want to know more. I want to know *everything*. But, I can tell it makes Chloe nervous and I don't want her to retreat.

"Why are you looking at me like that?" she asks.

"You told me I should smile more. You put it on your list."

She purses her lips. Those sweet, kissable lips. "It feels like you're teasing me."

"I'm making conversation."

"Ah, I was confused. That's not your usual approach." She finishes off the Chardonnay in her glass. "You like silence so you can study people and make them squirm. I'm surprised you haven't used that tactic on Fred yet."

"It's a unique situation with Fred. He eventually needs to sell, but he's got enough time and assets to not be forced into anything."

"I don't know how any of this works, but if you close the deal—"

"When I close the deal."

"Okay, *when* you close the deal with Fred, what does that mean? Is your company the best or something?"

"It already is the best."

"So, you don't need Voltaire to make SCM the top media company but you want it anyway because..."

"My Uncle Leo, my dad's brother, ran the company when my dad died. He's a nice guy, charming in fact."

"You two are related?" She lifts her brows.

"Very funny." I smirk. "Uncle Leo's too nice. He wasn't cut out for business and it showed when the company lost millions of dollars under his leadership."

"So, you're in charge now."

I nod. "The last seven years have been about returning the company to where it was when my father died."

"I don't know anything about business, but is there a point when you're happy with it? That you know your father would be proud of where you've taken his company and you don't have to work eighty hours a week?" Chloe asks, elbow on the table, chin in her hand. She's waiting for my answer with interest.

I open my mouth to answer, but I don't know what to say. Under my management, SCM is now the top media company in the country, top five in the world. During my time as CEO, we've acquired hundreds of millions of dollars in assets. My company, the company my father started forty years ago, is now worth billions. Chloe's question strikes a chord. When is it enough? When have I reached my goal? I've been working non-stop for seven years, killing myself to reach a goal that's a moving target. There's no end. Everything has become so much of a habit that I haven't been paying attention to the reason anymore.

I watch Chloe slather a cracker with goat cheese then top it with prosciutto. It's another realization that makes me feel worse about the situation with Chloe. I try to push it out of my mind.

"You like to talk," I say.

"That's not an answer."

"It's an observation. I have them as well."

"What is your observation?"

"That the ping pong table is open and we should play."

"Ping pong." Chloe rolls her eyes. "What is with you and racquet sports?"

"I have excellent hand-eye coordination, agility and endurance."

"You're humble, too." Chloe laughs.

I lead us to the ping pong table on the lawn, across from

the seating area. There are other lawn games, bean bags, horseshoes, bocce ball, and a large chess board with two-foot-high chess pieces.

I lift the wine glass in my hand. "This will be my handicap."

"If that's the case, it's mine, too." She takes a sip of her wine.

"No, I'll hold the glass with one hand. You can put yours down."

"Oh," she says, setting her wine glass on a nearby table. "All right, I'm ready."

I serve. The ball bounces on the opposite side and right past Chloe.

"Maybe they have a puzzle we could do instead? I'm great at puzzles."

"You can do it. You need to keep your eye on the ball," I say.

"Eyes on balls. I should be good at that." Chloe laughs.

I move to her side of the table.

"What are you doing?"

"Helping you with your stroke."

I move behind her, placing my hand over hers on the ping pong paddle. My chest presses into her back. She smells so good. Fuck. This was a bad idea.

"What were you saying about stroking?" she asks, the wine clearly making Chloe more relaxed. My brain immediately returning to this morning when she walked in on me in the shower.

"Get your mind out of the gutter and focus," I growl in her ear, because my mind has been filled with all the filthy things I want to do to her all fucking day. "Okay, slow and steady," I say as I guide her arm back and release the ball. We follow through and it gets over the net.

"I did it!" She jumps up and down.

"Hardly." I hide a smile. She looks so cute celebrating. Come on, Barrett, get it together.

"I'm still going to celebrate." She sticks her tongue out at me.

"Let's see if you can return from an actual serve." I leave her and head to my side of the table—hoping the semi-erection she's given me isn't noticeable.

I serve across the table and Chloe's return hits the corner of the table before bouncing out of my reach and onto the ground.

Chloe celebrates like she's won Wimbledon.

"Beginner's luck."

"I don't think the girl that got smacked in the head with the ball the first time she played tennis has beginner's luck."

I toss the ball over for her serve.

Chloe serves it and I return it, then she barely gets it over the net and it double bounces before I can scoop it up.

The game continues like that.

And that's how with wild, erratic movements and zero grace, Chloe beats me at ping pong.

"Are you sure you were trying?" Chloe asks, laying down her paddle on the table.

"Of course, I was trying. You know how much I like to win," I say, setting my paddle down, too.

Chloe's elated smile lights up the entire vineyard. When she directs it at me, heat radiates through my chest. It suddenly feels like there's nothing I wouldn't do to keep that smile on her face.

CHAPTER 18

Chloe

I'm having the best time with Barrett. I didn't think it was possible. I didn't think Barrett was capable of a good time, let alone having one with me by his side. Wine equals fun with Barrett.

"Let's play a game," I say.

"We've played every lawn game they have here." He motions to the open lawn.

"No, I want to play a game that doesn't involve that giant hand-impenetrable-eye coordination thing you've got going on." I circle my finger in his direction, then lift myself up onto the wooden ledge that surrounds the winery's yard. I'm just tipsy enough to not have a single care about the white pants I've got on or what my ass might look like when I get down from said ledge. "Something I might be good at."

"You won ping pong. And you almost won bocce ball, until that last ball went rogue and decapitated one of the knights on the chess board."

I want to pretend I'm offended, deny Barrett's alleged claims that I am not the world's most underrated bocce ball player, but Barrett is full on smiling now and my argument evaporates.

I like smiling Barrett a lot. So much so, that when he takes a step back, I grab a fistful of his shirt and pull him closer. A moment later he's standing between my spread legs.

"Let's play truth or dare," I announce within inches of Barrett's face.

"That's what you want to play?" His lips twitch.

"'May the odds be ever in your favor,'" I say dramatically.

"How does that apply here?"

"I don't know. I just wanted to say it." I shrug. Let a girl have her moment. "Okay, truth or dare."

"Truth," he says.

"What's up with the ladder?"

"What do you mean?" The material of his shirt grows taut as he retreats.

"You had a reaction to me being on it and while I know you were upset about me dancing with Ryan Shaw, it seemed like more than that."

Barrett takes a deep breath in; his eyes drop to his feet before he meets my gaze again.

"I don't like heights."

"You're afraid of heights?!" My voice rises, mainly due to disbelief.

Barrett narrows his eyes at me.

"Sorry."

I nod for him to continue.

"Even something as simple as a ladder gives me anxiety. I've learned to manage it, avoid things that trigger it."

"Do you fly?"

"With the window closed."

"What about tall buildings?"

"You won't find me with my nose pressed to the window."

"That's fascinating."

"Why?"

"I thought you were the kind of guy that isn't afraid of anything."

"You thought wrong." He studies me for a moment. "My turn."

Ah, yes. I forgot about that part.

"Truth or dare?" he asks.

"Option C. We make out." I lick my lips and Barrett's eyes drop to my mouth. Where's a 'who can kiss their sexy fake boyfriend the longest' contest when you need one? "Fred may have spies in the bushes. We should make it convincing."

We're so close now, we're breathing the same air.

He swerves at the last minute and his lips brush along my jaw.

"You're such a tease," I say.

"You wanted to play this game."

"That was before I realized I'd have to participate," I whine.

"Okay. We don't have to play." Barrett shrugs and I think I've gotten off easy. He places those hands of his, the same ones that were wrapped around his hard length in the shower this morning, on either side of my hips. He must be a mind reader. "Let's talk about this morning."

"Of what are you referring to?" I ask like I haven't been thinking about it all day.

"You watching me in the shower."

I can feel the heat of embarrassment crawling up my spine, but then I remember that Barrett stood full stop in the bathroom watching me get myself off in the bathtub and I didn't give him shit about it.

"That sounds creepy. I didn't have binoculars or anything. Not that I would have needed them to see that monster—" I stop myself short, but that doesn't prevent my eyes from dropping to Barrett's crotch. I finally manage to close my eyes and look away because they're traitorous and I can no longer trust them to behave. "It seems we're even now, wouldn't you say?"

"For me watching you in the bathtub."

I nod.

"Apparently we're just two creeps who don't knock."

"Chloe." Barrett's voice draws my attention back to him. I've never heard him say my name that way before. There's no anger or annoyance, it's more resolve and curiosity with a dash of reverence. I like it and now I can't look anywhere but at him.

"My turn," I say.

"I thought we were done playing."

"It's my game. I make the rules." I have to get this game back on track. It's dangerously close to *Make Chloe Squirm*. Somehow everything Barrett does leads back to that.

I don't even have to think about what I want to ask him. It's been on the tip of my tongue all day and since he brought it up, I have to ask.

"When you were in the shower this morning, you know," I clear my throat, "what were you thinking about?"

Barrett doesn't hesitate either.

"You."

He says it matter of fact, taking a drink of his wine like he didn't just throw a stick of dynamite in my underwear.

"That's interesting. I have so many questions."

Barrett grins. "Back to my question."

"Did you have a question? I don't recall."

He lowers his face closer to mine, puffs of air from his words caress the shell of my ear.

"Did you enjoy the show?"

The air rushes out of me with a heavy sigh.

"Did you like what you saw? Me fucking my hand while I imagined it was your pretty mouth? Filling your sweet cunt with my cock?"

My legs tremble with his words.

"Barrett." I can't help that it comes out almost like a moan.

The sky is dark now. The strings of white lights hung across the seating area and yard provide a warm glow. Soft jazz music plays from the outdoor speakers, interrupted only by the laughter from two couples playing bean bags yards away, when a wild throw lands in the bocce ball area. Meanwhile Barrett's filthy mouth has soaked my panties.

He's waiting for a response. This is the moment in any other interaction with a guy that I would cut and run. But it's not possible to run from Barrett. He's my fake boyfriend for another month. I'll have to see him again. That and he's got me boxed in right now so there is literally no escaping.

"Do you want to know why I laughed at dinner when you said you wanted to eat me?" I ask.

"Yes." His gaze is intent on my face.

"Because I was nervous."

"You thought that I was..." Barrett's expression moves from confusion to concern. "I would never force myself on you. On any woman. Which maybe doesn't ring true with the fact that you are reluctantly pretending to be my girlfriend for a business deal, but I would never physically force myself on you."

"I believe you. That's not what I was nervous about."

"Okay. What was it?" he asks.

"I've never done that before," I admit.

"Had sex?" His deep voice makes his words carry and I glance around in a panic.

"You are so loud right now!"

"You're the one yelling."

"No. Not sex," I whisper. "I'm not a virgin. I've had sex before. The other stuff. It kind of got skipped over."

I wait until it clicks into place.

"Oral sex."

"Stop saying sex."

He nods, studying me for a beat before leaning closer. He almost looks angry. "It sounds like you've been fucking idiots who only cared about getting their dicks wet."

"Two idiots. That's how many I've had sex with."

Barrett nods but doesn't say anything else. I don't know what I expect him to say. I'm dying to know how many women he's slept with but also not because the thought of him with another woman kind of makes me want to throw up. That could also be the wine swirling around in my stomach.

His silence on the subject of my inexperience makes me paranoid. Does he think it's weird?

"The fact that no one has tasted you is a real shame, but it's a mistake I don't plan on making. The thought of it turns me on even more."

My eyes widen at Barrett's statement. It's both thrilling and nerve wracking.

"Really?" I ask.

"Yes."

With one hand cupping my jaw, Barrett presses his lips to mine.

His phone starts ringing the second our lips connect.

He curses, pulling away to take his phone out of his pocket. I want to throw his phone in the bushes and beg him to put his lips back on mine. Maybe I'll put that on my list.

"Hello?" he answers, his tone clipped, but then it softens. "What?" When his gaze returns to me, his eyes are wide. "Okay, we're on our way."

"What's going on?" I ask as Barrett's large hands encircle my waist to lift me off the ledge. He takes my hand and leads me through the winery's yard, around the side and out front.

"Barrett. What's happening?"

"It's Baxter. When Lucy took him outside, fireworks

started going off at a neighbor's house and he got scared. He ran off. She can't find him."

My heart sinks.

"Oh my God. I'm a terrible dog mom. I should have known he would be frightened. He hates storms, of course he's going to hate fireworks. What was I thinking?! Now he's out there somewhere alone and scared. What if he gets hurt? What if we don't find him? What if—"

Barrett pulls me in close.

"We're going to find him." He says it matter-of-factly. "I'll employ a full-time search and rescue team if I have to."

"You'd do that? For Baxter?" I ask with tears in my eyes. Distraught that Baxter is missing, but with Barrett's words, I'm feeling more hopeful that he'll return safely.

"I'd do it for you. Because you love Baxter and I..." He pauses, looking down at me, "well, you're my girlfriend. It only makes sense that I would use any means to make you happy."

Right. It's all about appearances. If we were really together and Barrett truly cared about me, finding Baxter would be top priority. That's what he means. He's got to play his part in this.

The car pulls up as the first whistle of a firework ascends into the night sky and bursts open brilliant red.

"We better hurry." Barrett ushers me in. We keep our eyes out the windows on the drive home, but it's dark and hard to see much.

When we arrive at the house, Lucy opens the door in a panic.

"I'm so sorry!" she says, her face full of guilt. "I took him outside and when the neighbors started setting off fireworks, he ran."

I don't even know where to begin the search, but Barrett already has a plan.

"It's okay, Lucy, we'll find him." She nods, seemingly calmed by Barrett's determination, just like I was. "You stay here in case he shows up. Chloe, you go with Mac in the car. Drive toward town, he might have wandered that way to get away from the sounds. I'm going out back, into the wooded area."

He requests a flashlight from Lucy, who hurries to grab one from the pantry.

"Call me if you find him, and I'll do the same," he tells me before rushing out the back door.

Out front I hop into the car and ask Fred's driver, Mac, to drive toward town. He keeps a slow pace, an easy thing to do with no traffic, it being a holiday and the fireworks display still popping off in the distance. While it comforts me that there aren't many cars on the road, which could pose a threat to a frightened dog running around, it also means there's no one to ask if they've seen Baxter.

Minutes tick by and the hope I felt earlier is slowly being replaced by panic again. Mac drives up and down the streets, but with so many gated homes, there's no way to check every yard.

Guilt gnaws at me. While I've always wanted a dog, I can't help feeling terrible about the reason I signed up to foster Baxter—to drive Barrett insane. I knew he would be displeased about a dog in his space, so, selfishly I used Baxter for my cause. I brought him here for the weekend, and now he's missing and it's all my fault.

When I feel like my chest is about to cave in, my phone starts ringing.

"Barrett!" I answer with my heart in my throat.

"I found him." The second he says the words, the tears in my eyes fall with relief. "We're heading back to the house."

"Okay. I'll see you there."

I tell Mac the good news and we circle back toward Fred's house.

Upon arrival, I find Baxter wrapped in a towel, sitting in Barrett's lap, only his head and wet, muddy paws peeking out. Barrett is rubbing Baxter behind his ears and talking to him in a soothing voice. I stand there for a moment, undetected, while this man I once thought was made of ice comforts an anxious animal.

Unable to stay away any longer, I enter the kitchen.

"Where did you find him?" I ask, moving to cup my hands around Baxter's head, who immediately licks my face.

"He was huddled down under a neighbor's porch. He went through the wooded area behind the house and ended up a few houses down."

When I look up at Barrett, he's smiling down at me. There's a streak of mud on his cheek.

"Thank you." With emotion rising in my throat, it comes out as a whisper.

His hazel eyes intent on mine, he simply nods. With that one look, my stomach cartwheels.

"He's going to need a bath."

Barrett stands, and for the first time I realize how dirty he is. The dirt on his face is nothing compared to the mud on his shirt. And his white pants...they're gray now. I don't know if they can come back from this. It's a pity, his butt looked great in those pants.

"You're going to need one, too," I say.

Our discussion at the winery about him in the shower this morning pops into my head. Even though I'm his fake girlfriend, I have to admit that him confessing his thoughts about me while he stroked himself this morning made everything between us feel very real. And now this perfectly kempt man, who doesn't like a hair out of place, is covered in mud from trudging through a wet forest to rescue Baxter? My heart and my panties can't take it.

I peel my gaze away from Barrett's muddy appearance, because if there's anything more attractive than a man getting wet and dirty while rescuing a scared animal, I'd be hard pressed to find evidence.

"I'll give him a bath while you clean up. I mean, not in the same bathroom." Again, my mind goes back to watching Barrett naked in the shower, so I laugh to keep from turning beet red. It doesn't stave off the embarrassment so I gather Baxter in my arms. "I'll have Lucy help me. Okay, bye."

I leave Barrett standing in the kitchen, amused with my awkward departure, I'm sure.

Lucy helps me draw a bath and keep Baxter relaxed while I suds him up. Once he's clean, I dry him with a towel, but he manages to escape and shake, sending water all over us.

We return to our bedroom, Baxter clean and dry, while I am now muddy and smell like wet dog from wrangling him in the tub.

Barrett's not there.

The shower is empty. I knocked at least fifty times before I opened the door. So, after settling Baxter onto his dog bed, I gather some pajamas and take a shower myself.

We've been in the Hamptons one day, yet it feels like so much has happened. My body is exhausted, and my head has a slight ache from all the wine I consumed earlier. The buzz I had at the winery is long gone, chased out by the adrenaline and panic I felt when Baxter was missing. I long for the loose-tongued Chloe that told Barrett about her sexual inexperience. Now, I'm just a ball of nerves wondering if Barrett will deliver on his promise to right that huge injustice.

When I exit the bathroom, the bedside lamps are on and I find a shirtless Barrett on his laptop, the computer screen casting a glow on his chiseled torso and arms. In the middle of the bed, curled up next to him, is Baxter. Apparently, the no dogs on beds rule has been broken, at least for tonight.

Barrett looks up from his laptop.

"Hey." I wave.

"Hi," he says, his eyes lingering at the chest of my t-shirt a moment longer before they drop back to his computer.

On the bedside table I find a glass of water and two ibuprofen.

My eyes dart to Barrett. "Thank you."

"Of course," he replies, eyes focused on his computer. The energy between us at the winery is a distant memory.

I take the pills and climb into bed. Baxter shifts, pressing his head under my hand.

"Is the light bothering you?" Barrett asks. "I can go downstairs."

"No, it's fine," I say, enjoying his presence. The tapping of his fingers against the keys.

While part of me is confused that Barrett is showing no interest in me or any of the things he said earlier, the other part of me is relieved.

Even though I'm attracted to him, more so after this weekend, getting involved with Barrett would only complicate things.

I'm supposed to be focused on my career. Proving to JoAnna that I can handle my current duties while covering for Lacey. And the Books 4 Kids event is this coming Friday. I need everything this week to go well and the event to go off without a hitch.

Beneath the glow of Barrett's laptop, with Baxter's wet nose nuzzled into my hand, I fall asleep.

CHAPTER 19

Barrett

We're back in the city by three.

After breakfast, Lucy insisted on making Baxter gourmet dog food to take with us. She felt horrible about his disappearance yesterday and wanted to do something to spoil him. I think it was a bit much, but I didn't want to refuse her generous offer. She'd likely be relaying to Fred how the weekend went and I wanted to leave the best impression with her.

While we waited, Chloe lounged by the pool reading her book and I worked on my laptop, my eyes frequently wandering from the screen to Chloe in her pink bikini.

At home, we went our separate ways, but a few minutes ago, Chloe entered my study with Baxter on her heels.

"Are you okay if I read in here?" she asks.

"Sure." I motion to the sitting area.

Chloe sits down on the sofa, and settles in. She's quiet for a moment, and I think she's going to read but then she calls out to me.

"Frankie texted me."

"Really?" Maybe I shouldn't be surprised. I know Frankie

likes Chloe but it never occurred to me that they would spend time together outside of our couples' activities.

"She reports that her lips are less swollen and she should be sucking Fred's dick by tomorrow at the latest."

I clear my throat. I don't want to imagine any intimate acts between Frankie and Fred but the words 'sucking' and 'dick' out of Chloe's mouth have sent all my blood rushing south.

"That was word for word," she says.

"Glad to hear she's feeling better," I say.

"And she invited me to get my nails done. She wants me to try out her press-on nail line."

"What did you tell her?" I ask.

"I said yes. I thought it would be helpful for you with Fred. You know, a little good will between the girlfriends."

I nod. "Thank you."

She turns back to the manuscript she's reading. "Especially since this weekend was a bust."

"What do you mean?"

She looks up again. "Oh, just that you didn't get any time with Fred. I can tell you were frustrated on Friday when he didn't show up."

She's right. I had been livid that Fred would cancel last minute, leaving Chloe and me in the Hamptons with no hope to make progress on my deal with Voltaire. But then I spent yesterday with Chloe and I forgot about Fred and the deal. It wasn't on my mind when I was playing Scrabble with her or pointing out the various cheeses on the charcuterie board, and memorizing her facial expressions as she tasted each one. And it definitely wasn't on my mind when she looked me in the eyes and told me no one has ever gone down on her before.

I watch her for a moment, her wild ponytail and baggy t-shirt make her look effortlessly sexy. Damn. I want her. Badly. But I want her to want me just as bad. This weekend was a step in that direction, but she's not there yet.

Case in point when a minute later she flips a page, then looks over at me.

"Oh, and can we just forget everything I said this weekend?"

"What do you mean?"

"You know, the truth or dare sharing. It was a bit of an overshare on my part. I'd like to rescind that information. Extract it out of your brain."

I almost laugh. There's no fucking way I'll be forgetting that conversation anytime soon. Or the way it felt to kiss her, not because we had to put on a show, but because we wanted to. Thinking about it only makes me want to do it again.

"No," I growl.

"What? Why not?"

"It was the first thing on my mind this morning and it will be the last thing on my mind tonight when I fall asleep across the hall from you."

Chloe's eyes widen at my confession. I can see her cheeks turn rosy from across the room.

I stand and move toward her. When I'm at the back of the sofa looking over her, Chloe has to lean back to look up at me. I've found in my business dealings that patience is the key. Waiting for the right deal. Not getting ahead of yourself. Keep the upper hand by not appearing too eager.

None of that seems to be working in my situation with Chloe.

"I'm also going to think about you when I fuck my hand later," I say.

Her breath catches and her mouth drops open. The sound already has me hard. Yes, I'm definitely going to be thinking about her later.

I lean down and kiss her on the top of the head. It's a chaste gesture compared to what I want to do to her.

"Goodnight, Chloe."

I leave her there on the sofa, pleased that it takes her a good ten seconds to call out goodnight behind me.

I'm in a meeting with Carl when Bea buzzes to tell me that Chloe is here. My day has been insane, moving from meeting to meeting, business lunch to conference calls, but any spare second I've had to myself, I've thought about Chloe. The silver lining to Fred and Frankie not being able to make the trip to the Hamptons was getting to hang out with Chloe, just us. Now, we understand each other better. I've made my intentions clear that I want her, but I'm waiting for her to be more comfortable with a physical relationship.

Chloe walks through the door of my office, her hair piled high on her head, a bright blue skirt that sways around her legs when she walks and a delicate blouse pulled snug against her breasts. A breakfast meeting had me out the door early, and I find myself annoyed that this is the first time I'm seeing her today.

Carl stands.

"Chloe, nice to see you," he says.

"Carl." She nods and I immediately pick up on her curt tone.

Carl shoots me a look.

"We'll finish this discussion later," I tell him.

He nods and gathers his things. In typical Carl fashion, he mouths something behind her back as he leaves. I think it was 'you're fucked.' He thinks things between Chloe and me are still tense because I haven't told him otherwise.

"Hi," I say, moving toward Chloe. I'm aware that she's usually the one making an effort while I hold back, but I want to change that. "To what do I owe the pleasure of this visit?"

"I just came from Frankie's." She sniffs like she's about to cry.

My gaze drops to her hands, where they're covered in black leather.

"Are you wearing gloves? In July? I thought you were getting your nails done?"

"Yes, I did. It was awful. My nails are awful. I came here because I don't know what to do," she cries.

I don't like seeing Chloe upset, but my chest swells with pleasure that she's seeking me out.

"They can't be that bad." I hold one arm and pull off the glove. Oh shit.

Words escape me as I take in Chloe's manicure. Having seen Frankie's nails, I knew how she liked to wear hers, but I had no idea that she would pick out something similar for Chloe. The nails are at least three inches long and Chloe's hands are petite so the three inches of nail off the end just looks wrong. Not only is the length too much, but the nail shape is round at the nail bed, then sharpens to a point, making it look like a set of cat claws. The color is a neon yellow and there are some black spots which I think are supposed to be some kind of animal pattern.

"They're not that bad." My attempt at reassuring Chloe does not go well.

"Not that bad? Not that bad?!" Chloe yanks off the other glove and lifts both hands in front of my face. Ten claw-like highlighter yellow nails coming at me is enough to make my balls draw up. I instinctively step back.

"I can't open a soda, Barrett." She pulls out a can of seltzer water out of her purse and tosses it at me. I catch it with one hand.

"I'll help you open it." I pop it open easily. I think that only makes her madder.

"I could hardly button my skirt when I went to the bathroom."

"I can help with that, too," I offer. It'd be my pleasure.

She pins me with a glare.

"I can't have you following me into bathrooms. And that's not the point. Frankie wants me to keep them on until Friday. She's got a photoshoot for her nail line and she loooves how cute my little hands are," Chloe makes air quote marks around little and I nearly lose an eye, "so she told me to keep them on so she can put me in her sales book."

I don't know what to say but it doesn't matter because Chloe keeps going.

"I was trying to read in the car and I ripped the page. I already scratched my leg, who knows what condition I'll be in by Friday? It's like Edward Scissorhands over here." She clinks the nails together. It does make an eerie sound. "How am I going to do anything?" She sighs, her voice going quiet. "Like how am I going to touch myself? I'll shred my labia trying to rub my clit." She drops her head into her hands and cries, defeated.

My dick jumps at the thought of Chloe touching herself, but I force those thoughts to take a backseat to what is obviously a traumatic experience for her.

Cautiously, I step forward and gather her in my arms.

"I'd never let that happen," I say, rubbing a hand over her back.

She presses her nose into my chest.

"We'll figure it out," I tell her.

"We?" She sniffles.

"Do you want to put that on your list?" Please put it on your list, my dick chimes in.

"You giving me orgasms because I'm Edward Scissorhands and I can't do it myself?"

"Sure." Any excuse for Chloe to let me touch her would

suffice. "Orgasms? Now you're getting ahead of yourself," I tease.

Chloe snort laughs into my dress shirt and when she pulls away it's covered in tears and probably snot. I don't even care. Having this moment of levity with her, even if it's because she got the world's most bizarre manicure, is nice. She lifts her hands to wipe the tears from under her eyes but she can't get them without poking herself in the eye.

"I can't even..." Chloe's words trail off when I press my thumbs under her eyes and wipe the wetness away. She blinks, her wet lashes tickling my thumbs.

"Thank you," she says.

"You bet," I say, my hands still cupping her cheeks.

She takes in a shuddering breath and lifts her gaze to mine. We stand there for what feels like forever, neither of us wanting to move from the moment. We're so close, it feels like there's nothing left to do but lower my head one more inch and claim her mouth.

I gently press my lips to hers, wanting it to be a reassuring kiss, but it turns deep and hungry in an instant.

My hands move down Chloe's sides, grazing her breasts, sliding over her hips before making their way to grip her ass. Her soft moan nearly undoes me. I'm envisioning Chloe on my desk with her legs spread wide when Bea's voice fills the room.

"Fred Hinkle is on the line." For the first time since this whole thing started, Fred is the last person I want to talk to right now.

I reluctantly release Chloe. "I've got to take his call."

"Yeah." She nods with a dazed look on her face.

"You going to make it home okay?" Neither of us address the fact that I've called my brownstone home. It is Chloe's home currently, but this is the first time I've referred to it as that. The satisfaction of knowing she'll be there when I get home is startling.

"I'll be fine." She gives me a small smile.

"I'll have Marcus pick you up."

"Okay." She nods. I place a kiss on her forehead, then quietly close the door behind her before picking up Fred's call.

"Fred," I answer, my thoughts still on Chloe.

"Barrett," Fred's voice booms into my ear, "how was the weekend?"

"It was great. Thank you for your hospitality."

"We're sorry we didn't make it, Frankie was upset about her appearance, you know how women can be."

"Yes," having just witnessed Chloe's meltdown about her nails, "I understand."

"I just heard from Frankie. She loved how Chloe's nails turned out and is excited for her to be featured in her company's first look book."

"Yes, Chloe told me the exciting news," I force out, feeling guilty that Chloe is upset because of a situation I've put her in.

"You know, I'm really enjoying how well the ladies get along. I didn't think we had much in common before, but getting to know you and Chloe has made me realize I was wrong."

"We've enjoyed getting to know you both as well." It's not exactly a lie, our time with Fred and Frankie has been entertaining to say the least.

"I'll get to the point. I've given my people the go ahead to set up a meeting with your folks."

I sit up in my chair. This is the moment I've been waiting for. The reason I've been playing happy couple with Chloe, going on dates with Fred and Frankie, trying to get my deal in front of Fred.

"That would be great, Fred." I keep my tone even, not

wanting to show the enthusiasm I'm feeling that this deal—THE DEAL—is finally moving forward.

"I've seen the initial timeline documents and I think we can get this closed fairly quick."

"I'll let my legal team know," I say.

"Let's do dinner next week."

"I look forward to it."

"I'll be in touch."

I hang up the receiver. That familiar thrill of an impending deal sends a jolt of gratification through my body. It's the feeling I chase from one deal to the next.

I reach for the receiver to call Carl.

He answers on the first ring. "You're still alive."

"Yes. Why wouldn't I be?"

"Chloe looked pissed."

"She got a bad manicure from Frankie. She'll be okay."

"I just got an email from legal at Voltaire. They're setting up a meeting."

"That's why I called. Fred called me. He's moving forward with the deal."

"That's the best fucking news I've heard all week."

"It's Monday."

"Still. We need to celebrate. McNally's at seven?"

"Can't. I told Chloe I'd be home after work."

I can't wait to tell Chloe, to let her know that her efforts with Frankie were not in vain.

"Ah. The old ball and chain. In your case it's more of a zip tie situation," Carl says.

"What are you talking about zip ties?"

"Not permanent. An easy out. Also, Lindsay is going through a bondage thing lately so I just picked some up from the hardware store. She wants to get kinky. I'm into it."

"I don't want to know." I groan.

He's only reminding me of my own words on the topic,

but Carl's assessment of my relationship with Chloe doesn't sit well. While this is the outcome I wanted, for SCM to acquire Voltaire Telecom, as far as my relationship with Chloe and the timeline we discussed, it's no longer satisfactory to me. Luckily, I'm a persuasive businessman who knows how to get what he wants. And one thing is for sure, I want Chloe.

CHAPTER 20

Chloe

After a soak in the tub, which unfortunately did not take off my nails—Frankie's Faux Nails glue is legit—I pull on leggings and a t-shirt, no bra. That is the extent of my effort to get ready for dinner.

After the stress of this weekend's fireworks fiasco, Baxter is glad to be home.

Even though Barrett was initially opposed to Baxter's presence, I think they bonded Saturday night. Barrett seems less annoyed with having Baxter here now. He might even be enjoying him a little. Like a moment ago when I walked into the kitchen and found Barrett throwing the tennis ball for him.

Barrett's already got dinner served, peppercorn steak with broccolini and mushroom risotto. When I struggle to cut the steak up, he does it for me.

After dinner, I settle into the couch in the study. Baxter normally sits next to me, but I can tell the nails are freaking him out. Me, too, buddy.

I expect Barrett to move toward his desk, but instead he joins me on the couch with a glass of wine in his hand.

A few minutes go by and I have to close my book, my hands are cramping from holding my fingers awkwardly. I close my eyes and sigh.

"The nails are because of me and the deal with Fred and our arrangement. How can I make you feel better?"

"Build a time machine and take us to Friday."

He smirks. "Time travel isn't my specialty. Anything else?"

The way he says it, followed by the heated look he gives me reminds me of what I said in his office earlier when I was under duress.

"I'm not putting orgasms on my list," I say.

"Why not?" Barrett asks.

"Because I'm not going to force you to pleasure me. That would be weird." My face is already heating at the thought.

"Chloe, you wouldn't be forcing anything. I want to fuck you with my fingers."

My gaze moves to where Barrett is slowly rotating his wine glass on the arm of the couch. His fingers pinching the stem, twisting it slowly.

"And my tongue," he adds.

I'm speechless.

"Maybe I'll put it on my list," he says.

"You don't have a list," I argue.

"Maybe I'll make one." He stands and walks over to his desk.

"You can't do that."

"Eating Chloe's pussy whenever I want." He pulls a piece of paper out of his desk and starts writing with a pen.

I don't know whether to laugh or melt into a puddle on the floor. I'm so turned on right now, but also completely intimidated thinking about doing anything sexual with Barrett. Do I want it? Yes. Could Barrett think I'm the most awkward, inexperienced woman he's ever been with? Absolutely. And that freaks me out.

A minute later he hands me the paper with his writing on it.

I shake my head. Resistance appears to be my kink. Hearing Barrett tell me what he wants to do to me is hot, and teasing us both only serves to turn me on more. "I'm not signing that."

Barrett nods, but I can tell he's frustrated. Trust me. I am, too. I'm basically cock blocking myself. Suddenly, he shoots to his feet to grab his phone off the coffee table.

"Have you played WordIt today?" he asks.

I lift my hands up. "I can barely hold onto my phone. No, I haven't played."

"We'll play for it. First person to solve today's WordIt gets to decide."

"Decide what?" I ask.

"If I get to put my mouth on you." He says it so casually, like he's offering to open a door for me.

I laugh. I'm amazing at WordIt. There's no way in hell Barrett will win.

"Are you good with the rules?" he asks. "Whichever way this goes, you're good?"

I bite my lip, thinking. Do I want Barrett to put his head between my thighs? Yes. Do I like that he'd have to earn it by beating me at a game that I kick ass at? Double yes.

"Yes." I nod, then clicking my fingers together nervously, I remember why we're doing this in the first place. "How am I supposed to play?"

Barrett grabs an iPad off his desk that has a stylus. It's better than me trying to tap the phone with my nails.

"First person to solve today's word gets to decide." I can feel the waves of excitement rolling off Barrett. Either he's excited to compete or he's excited about the prize. Me. I gulp. No, this is fine. I'm going to win so I don't even need to think about it.

"In the event of a time tie, person with the fewest guesses wins."

"Fine," I say, determined the winner will be me. I pull up the website for the game. Barrett does it, too.

We share one last glance and I can see it there in Barrett's eyes. Determination. My stomach flips with nervous anticipation. I want to win, but part of me wants Barrett to win, too.

"Ready. Go," he says.

"You didn't say set." I argue, but Barrett is already typing away on his phone. Shit. I think of a word that uses common letters.

SPEAK

The letters flip and everything is gray, meaning I didn't get any letters right.

I pick another word, making sure to not use any of the previous letters.

CLOTH

I hit the jackpot. O is yellow indicating it's in the word but not in the right place, and T and H are green meaning they're correctly placed. My eyes lift from the screen to find Barrett studying his phone intently. He must feel my gaze on him, because he lifts his eyes. Those hazel pools stare back at me and for a moment I think he looks defeated. Unsure. I almost feel bad. Maybe I should let him win? Give him a few extra seconds to think about the puzzle before I continue. But I don't even have to give Barrett more time. A split second later the corner of his lip lifts in a sexy smirk. He types something out and before I can even look back at my screen, he's showing me his phone. There, highlighted all in green, indicating he guessed the correct word...MOUTH.

Barrett's eyes are lit with something else now. He looks like the cat who ate the canary, or in this case, the man who is going to eat *me*.

"Wait," I say, even though Barrett hasn't moved an inch. I

feel like the kid on the diving board who is about to get pushed off but wants to stand there just a little bit longer to overanalyze and freak themselves out. I hated that part of swimming lessons. I get why I needed to learn to swim, but if I found myself randomly on the end of a diving board, I could simply walk back to the ladder. I didn't have to learn to dive.

"Chloe, I'm about to drill a hole through my pants just thinking about tasting you. I want it that bad."

My gaze drops to Barrett's lap. He's not lying. Beneath the denim fabric, I can see the large bulge there.

"Yeah?"

He nods.

"Stand up, Chloe."

In the past an order like that from Barrett would warrant a mouthy comeback and an eyeroll, but right now I like bossy Barrett. His authority on this particular matter is comforting, and it gives me the courage to stand, albeit on shaky legs. Barrett's hands move to my hips. The heat from his palms sear through the fabric of my leggings as he cups my ass. His thumbs stroke my hip bones and he pulls me closer to him. Those magnificent fingers of his edge into my waist band, pulling it down an inch to expose my stomach. Barrett leans forward, placing his lips on the skin above my waistband. My stomach quivers. He lifts his eyes to mine and I'm dead. Even if he were to stop right now, it would be the most satisfying sexual encounter of my life. That's a little depressing, but the fact that he's going to keep going, that there's more, is beyond thrilling. My legs are jelly, I can't move, yet I think I'm going to fall. There needs to be a warning. Do not operate heavy machinery (aka my legs) while under the influence of Barrett St. Clair's touch. Barrett senses my distress and shifts me to stand by the couch. In one swift movement, he's slipping my leggings and underwear off yet he also manages to lay me on the couch. Or I might have collapsed. Either way I'm better now that I'm horizontal. Except Barrett is staring between my legs and it makes me feel naked. Because I am, but also, I'm feeling vulnerable.

"I'm going to collect my winnings now." He says it so enthusiastically, like eating me out is going to be the highlight of his day.

Barrett's dropping between my thighs and I'm that kid on the diving board again, nervous to take that leap. I'm about to take the chicken exit—back to the ladder I go—when Barrett's hot mouth descends on me. Maybe he knew anymore lead up would only make me more jittery, or maybe he's just fucking starving, but I don't have time to analyze because the moment his mouth is on me my hips jerk and my core clamps down tight.

I can't see his mouth but if I had to clock its movements it would go something like this.

Swirl.

Lick.

Suck.

Teeth graze.

Suck harder.

Repeat.

With that punishing rhythm it's not going to take long for me to come.

Another sensation I had no idea would feel this good... Barrett's late day stubble scraping along my inner thigh. His hands are pressing my legs open, but I have the urge to wrap my legs around his head and ride his face. Why had I been so intimidated by this before? The lack of enthusiasm from guys I've dated in the past was a major factor, but with every gratifying lick, Barrett is quickly putting my insecurity to rest.

"Do you know how gorgeous your pussy is?" he asks, as he uses his fingers to spread me open. Oh, Jesus.

"Hmm?" I'm barely lucid.

"I'm the only man who has tasted it." It's a fact that Barrett seems to take great pride in as he worships me with his tongue.

He licks the length of me.

"And it's so fucking sweet." He looks up from between my thighs and our eyes connect. His lips glistening with my arousal. Just when I think I can't possibly be more turned on, he grins like the devil and says, "It's mine now."

He's a kid with an ice cream cone that refuses to share. Barrett's possessive talk only coils the tension in my belly tighter. I can feel my orgasm climbing. A rollercoaster climbing to the top. He slides one long finger inside me and I'm done.

"Oh, God. Barrett. Yes," I say breathless. "I'm coming."

I cry out as my hips jerk off the couch and my legs clamp around Barrett's head. He's going to die, I'm going to strangle him with my legs, but I can't stop. It's too good.

When I can breathe again and my heart isn't going to leave my chest, I open my eyes to find Barrett still between my legs, gently prying them open.

"Oh, no. Did I suffocate you?"

"I'm fine. But it wouldn't have been a bad way to go." He grins.

He emphasizes this by sucking his finger into his mouth. The one that was inside me and is now covered in my juices. Sweet Jesus.

I want to be embarrassed, but Barrett's unabashed desire to taste me and the aftereffects of my orgasm leave me craving more. That and I can see his erection pressing against the zipper of his pants.

"Take this off." I claw with my nails at his shirt. The post orgasmic brain-altering chemicals floating around my body have taken over. "I want you naked. I want your cock in my mouth." Who am I right now?

Barrett shakes his head, and moves out of my reach. His lips are wet from me and it's the hottest thing I've ever seen. He wipes his mouth with the back of his hand and I stand corrected. *That* is the hottest thing I've ever seen.

"If you want to call the shots, you'll have to win next time."

He's talking about WordIt.

"There's only one word a day. I'll have to wait until tomorrow!" I whine. Now that I've had a taste (or in this case Barrett has had a taste), I want more. The bulge in Barrett's pants is screaming for relief, yet he seems determined to leave it be. I'd say I was a sore loser if I hadn't been the one riding Barrett's face to orgasmic pleasure a moment ago.

Barrett stands and adjusts himself, then places a kiss on my forehead before retreating.

"Goodnight, Chloe."

~

But it wasn't a good night. While my body was sated by Barrett's tongue, my mind was restless. And my nails felt like a new appendage that I wasn't sure what to do with. I tried a thousand positions. Hands resting on my chest like Sleeping Beauty. One hand tucked under my pillow, the other resting on top. Both hands overhead, but then my arms fell asleep.

Once I finally got comfortable, my mind drifted to Barrett. Thinking of him across the hall and wondering if he'd taken care of himself. Regardless of the rules of the game we'd played, I couldn't help but feel a sting of rejection when he pulled away.

Thoughts of Barrett and what more might happen between us kept me up and I ended up oversleeping, somehow tapping the dismiss button on my alarm instead of snooze. Then there was the complication of what to wear. After spending ten minutes trying to button a blouse, I gave up and threw on a tank dress and heels.

At work, as I anticipated, everything has been taking longer with these nails than it normally would, typing especially. With the additional workload I've taken on in Lacey's absence, going slower is not going to cut it.

I spent fifteen minutes trying to scan a signed contract, but kept messing up the email address I was inputting. Then, I accidentally deleted a week out of the editorial calendar, so I spent half an hour recreating it, and double checking that I hadn't left off any important deadlines.

At this pace, there won't be enough hours in the day to get everything done.

Not to mention, JoAnna left for London last night for meetings with our UK office, and in her absence, I have to finalize everything for the Books 4 Kids launch event on Friday.

With the added challenges, my mind should be focused on work, but I find myself thinking about last night with Barrett.

Mostly about his tongue and his fingers and the way his hazel eyes looked staring up at me from between my thighs.

I'm in mid-thought when Jules appears and sets a brown bag onto my desk. She'd asked if I wanted to go to lunch, but with the setbacks I had earlier, I hadn't been able to take a break.

"Chicken salad sandwich," she announces before dropping into the chair across from my desk. "And a chocolate chip cookie."

"You're the best!" I open the bag and tear into the sandwich wrapper, an easy thing to do with my claw-like nails.

"I couldn't let you starve. You'll need your energy later." She wiggles her eyebrows.

I told her about WordIt and Barrett's skilled tongue.

"It was probably a one-time thing. You know, because he feels bad that my nails are hideous."

"No, he'll want it again. No man tells you your pussy is his and then doesn't come back for more."

Maybe I shared too much. I take a bite of my sandwich and try not to blush. I had to confide in Jules. I'm out of my depth here with Barrett and his expert mouth.

My phone buzzes with a text. My heart skips a beat wondering if it's from Barrett.

But, it's not. It's from Lauren asking if I got my bridesmaid dress.

After several attempts to text and autocorrect failing me every time, I give up and do a voice message instead.

"I got my dress. Love the lavender, it's so pretty. Will take to the seamstress tomorrow."

I set my phone down and turn to Jules.

While I was messaging Lauren, she was breaking off a bite of the cookie she got me.

"What do you think it means?" I ask.

"That I should have gotten two cookies." She hums around a bite.

I shake my head, but realize I gave her no context to my question.

"About Barrett and last night."

There's a celery string stuck between my molars but it's impossible to grasp with my nails. I give up trying to pinch it and take another bite.

"I think it means you're the luckiest girl in the world. And you should plan to lose at WordIt every night."

"No. I mean was it weird that he didn't want me to reciprocate?"

"Maybe he wanted it to be all about you. You are going above and beyond as a fake girlfriend with this nail thing."

"Yeah," I say on a sigh.

"Hold on." Jules' eyes narrow. "Did you want to reciprocate?"

"Um, I guess I thought it was the polite thing to do." And the outline of his dick had made my mouth water.

"Wait a second. Do you have a thing for Barrett?" she asks.

"What?"

"I thought this was a fun game. Like he's trapped you in this fake relationship, so you're happy to receive orgasms in return. A bonus for putting up with Barrett's cranky ass. Is there more to it?" She's eyeing me closely. "Do you have actual feelings for him?"

I slowly shake my head, but all I can think is—do I? Everything feels different after this weekend. But maybe I'm just mistaking feelings for physical attraction and chemistry. Lust. There's definitely plenty of that between me and Barrett. But in the Hamptons, it felt like more.

"Good." Jules takes another bite of the cookie, then pushes the rest toward me. "I don't want you to get hurt. And while I have no doubt he enjoyed giving you an orgasm, Barrett seems like the kind of guy that can easily walk away when he's done getting what he wants."

I consider her words while I swallow a bite of sandwich.

Jules is right.

Barrett and I are fake dating so he can get close to Fred. We have an expiration date and I can't let an orgasm, no matter how mind blowing it was, let me forget it.

I glance at the screen of Barrett's phone, my mouth hanging open in disbelief.

"How is that possible?"

"I must be a superior WordIt player." He grins.

"You didn't even know what WordIt was," I say, exasperated at the outcome of the game. "I told you about WordIt. You can't beat me at the game I told you about." I sigh. "Again."

Fresh out of the shower, I'm wearing a t-shirt and sleep shorts, my wet hair is pulled up into a knot on top on my head. I met Barrett at the racquet club after work. My nails the perfect excuse to not play tennis, I had planned to listen to my audio book in a cozy nook of the club's lounge, but after being entranced watching a sweaty Barrett play his Wednesday evening match, my priorities changed. I'm not even sure how that is possible, but it is. Hearing Barrett grunt with effort to return a serve had to be the hottest thing I've ever heard. I had no idea tennis was so erotic.

Thinking about it makes my eye twitch. I rub my eye and end up scratching my eyelid.

"Ow. You'd think I'd be used to these by now."

Barrett pulls me to standing and kisses the spot where my eyelid hurts.

"Come with me," he says.

"That's what I've been doing. For the past two nights," I mutter. It's not really a hardship but I am starting to get frustrated with my 0-3 losing streak.

I follow him upstairs and into my bedroom. The past two nights when Barrett has won our WordIt competition, he's immediately lowered me to the couch in the study and feasted on his prize. It's still bizarre to me that he wins and I get an orgasm. I guess we're both winners.

That being said, I'm getting frustrated. I want to reciprocate. I'm dying to reciprocate, especially since every time he's pulled away I've seen the impressive bulge in his pants. I know what's in there. I've seen it in the shower, and I want it badly.

I tell myself it has nothing to do with feelings, like Jules and I discussed, but a mere curiosity. Like how quickly could I make Barrett come with my mouth?

"I thought we'd change it up tonight."

"Yeah?" My eyes can't help but drop to the bulge in his pants.

He adjusts his erection. "Not that."

"Oh." I pout.

He tips my chin up with his fingers. "I want you to sit on my face."

My body's reaction to Barrett's request is to send a fresh wave of arousal between my legs. It's gearing up for what is to come. Literally. My brain, on the other hand, is two steps behind.

"How does that work? Won't I suffocate you?" I already thought I cut off his air supply the first time he had his head between my thighs.

His hands slip beneath the hem of my shirt, his seeking fingers skim along my ribcage. His thumbs circle the peaks of my nipples. "I'll be fine. Better than fine." He smiles wickedly. "I want to look up and see your gorgeous tits above me while I fuck your sweet cunt with my tongue."

That'll do it. I'm convinced Barrett's dirty talk could make me do anything. I'm already considering anal and we haven't even had sex yet.

I practically rip my shirt off. My shorts and panties quickly follow. I'm an eager beaver until I realize I have no idea what to do.

Barrett pulls his shirt over his head, then me onto the bed to straddle him. This is new. I like the feel of his hardness beneath me. I rock my hips and press into him. I imagine how good his bare cock would feel against me. His pants are ruining everything.

He reaches up to cup my face, then tugs me down to him. His kiss is firm and hungry. Our tongues lap each other up. When he breaks the kiss, I've nearly forgotten what we're doing.

Barrett's hand reaches between us, skimming over my wet, sensitive flesh.

"Mmm," he growls. "You're so wet for me right now."

I rock my hips against his hand, wanting his fingers inside me, but he pulls his hand away. Gripping my hips, he encourages me to move up his body.

"Hold onto the headboard," he instructs.

I shift my body forward, moving my knees past his chest, then his shoulders. Barrett lifts me the rest of the way. My knees are now spread on either side of his head. I'm hovering above Barrett's face. There's no doubt he can see *everything*.

"Are you sure I'm doing this right? I feel like my ass is on top of your mouth."

"You're doing it exactly right," Barrett's rumbles from beneath me, his hands gripping my ass now to hold me in place. "You're fucking gorgeous sitting there. I can't imagine a better view."

"You'll tell me if you can't breathe?" I ask. "Wait, how are you going to tell me if you can't breathe? If you can't breathe you won't be able to talk."

Also, my quads are on fire. Barrett must realize this.

"Chloe, stop hovering." He presses on the tops of my thighs. "Sit on my face and let me take care of you."

He makes it sound so simple. So, I do what he says.

Any insecurity I had about this position is quickly erased with the first swirl of Barrett's tongue on my clit. Sweet baby Jesus, that feels amazing. It's the same as before, yet totally different with me on top. I manage to find a balance between a thigh workout and being a complete dead weight.

"I love knowing this pretty pussy is mine." Barrett sucks hard on my clit.

We find a rhythm, his tongue, my hips, and I think I've got it all figured out, my orgasm is on the horizon, until I shift my hips too far forward and his tongue licks me *there*.

The sensation, foreign yet scintillating, sends me shooting up like a rocket.

"Oh my God, you just licked my asshole."

I can feel Barrett chuckle beneath me.

"I know. That was the plan."

"Oh. I thought maybe I messed up."

"Did you like it?" he asks.

I think about it for half a second.

"Yes."

He licks me again, rimming me with his tongue, and this time I embrace the sensation. Liquid heat pools in my low belly. My skin dampens with the desire that is overwhelming my body. I'm dizzy with pleasure.

He shifts me down, his mouth now capturing my clit.

From behind, I feel his finger sweep wetness from my pussy to the puckered bud of my ass. He swirls it there, causing the ache in my core to build. I don't know what it will feel like, I've never had anyone put anything in my ass before, but something tells me it's going to be good and the urge to press against his finger is strong.

"I bet no one has been in this tight little ass of yours."

My response is muddled in my brain because all I can focus on is the way he's fucking me with his tongue, rocking my hips so his nose presses into my clit.

"Do you want my finger in your ass, Chloe?"

"Yes." The word is out of my mouth before my brain can object.

He gently presses in and I can already tell it's going to be the most intense orgasm of my life, which is saying something, because the past two nights have already taken the top spots.

I'm not even moving, yet my body feels like it's about to spin off in every direction. My hands grip the headboard, holding on for dear life.

He uses his free hand to grip my ass and all the sensation

together—his tongue and his finger and the pressure on my clit—has me exploding into a million pieces.

I'm still gripping the headboard and panting when Barrett eases me back to straddle his hips. My attention is immediately drawn to the rock-hard bulge beneath me. I press my hips down against him. My clit is sensitive after my orgasm, but I can't help myself.

"Easy," Barrett says, lifting me off him and onto my back. He switches places, straddling me now.

"What are you going to do about that?" I'm hoping I can entice him into letting me touch him, but as usual Barrett is a stickler for the rules.

"I'll take care of it later." He hovers above me, his arms flexing as he lowers to press a kiss to my jaw.

"Or you can take care of it now?" I say, my eyes glued to where his erection is strained against his zipper. "That would be okay."

"You want to watch?" He grins wickedly.

I nod eagerly. I should be in complete dismay of where all this sexual confidence is coming from, but I'm too excited about a front row seat to Barrett pleasuring himself.

Barrett unzips his pants and frees his hard length from his boxer briefs. The dark hair at the base of his dick is neatly trimmed. I saw him in the shower in the Hamptons, but up close is completely different.

Barrett licks his hand, then slides that hand down the length of his cock. Another lick and he begins to stroke both hands up and down in unison while also rotating his wrists. He's not gentle with himself, as his hands squeeze his steely flesh and his forearms flex with each stroke. His breathing is heavy, his eyebrows drawn down in concentration. I'm intent on what he's doing, but then I can feel him watching me. He looks so serious that I'm completely caught off guard when he looks up and winks at me.

"Cup your breasts," he says and I do. My hands knead and squeeze. I circle a thumb around my nipple, relishing the hunger I see in Barrett's eyes and recognizing the ache that is starting to build again between my thighs.

"Just like that." He groans, his hips flexing with every stroke. He drops his gaze between my thighs. "Fuck. Look at how wet you are. You're dripping wet. Do you like seeing me fuck my hand, Chloe? Imagining I'm deep inside your tight little cunt?"

His words are too much. I snake a hand from my breast to my clit and start a demanding rhythm of my own. I guess I was never in any real danger of shredding my labia. I hope that doesn't mean our nightly WordIt game is over.

"Do you know how gorgeous you look right now?" His words come out with a pant.

I want to see Barrett finish but my own orgasm is threatening my eyes to close and to throw my head back. Barrett leans forward, his erection pressing into my belly, and whispers in my ear.

"I'm going to come all over your perfect tits."

That sentence sends me over the edge.

"Oh, God. Barrett. *Yes.*"

My back arches up and a million sparks of pleasure explode from my core and radiate throughout my body. I recover just in time to open my eyes and see Barrett kneeling over me, his hands wringing out pleasure, sending the hot liquid of his orgasm across my chest.

I lay still, wondering what I should do, what the protocol is for this moment. The evidence of an insanely hot hookup with my sexy fake boyfriend slowly drying on my chest.

"Don't move," Barrett says. He climbs off the bed and walks into the bathroom.

With Barrett gone, I give into the urge to run my fingers through his cum, smear it across my chest. Then another thought occurs to me. I haven't tasted him. Curious, I put my finger in my mouth.

It's tangy and slightly salty, with a sweet, milky texture. I like it. I go for another taste.

At that moment, Barrett strides into the room with a wet washcloth in his hand.

"Jesus, Chloe."

"What?!" I say, alarmed by his sudden appearance. Also feeling embarrassed and maybe a bit guilty, of what I'm not sure. Curiosity?

"Are you licking my cum off your chest?"

"Um, yeah. Is that okay?"

"Yes. It's insanely arousing." He walks to the bed and climbs over me. "Did you get enough?"

I nod and he begins to clean himself off of me.

It's a good question, but I'm starting to wonder if I can ever get enough of him.

When he starts to move away, I grab his arm, careful not to claw at his skin with my nails.

"Stay."

CHAPTER 21

Barrett

Chloe stares up at me with those big blue eyes.

"Yeah. Okay. But put this on." I hand her the robe hanging on the bathroom door. She pulls it on and ties it around her waist. With her gloriously naked body no longer on display, I can focus.

She pulls back the covers and slides in, patting the space beside her, but a picture frame on the bedside table draws my attention.

It's a family picture. I immediately pick out Chloe. She's the oldest child, yet her petite frame places her toward the front of the picture.

"You've told me how loud and busy your childhood was. What's it like having that many siblings?" I ask, holding the picture up so she can see. "Are you close with everyone?"

Chloe leans back into her pillow. "Chaotic." She laughs. "But seriously, you're never lonely. There was always someone to play with growing up. As a teenager that became annoying because there was always someone around. It was hard to get alone time. I shared a bedroom with my sister, Lila. The boys shared and then Penelope, the baby, got her own room."

I'm realizing that while I view Chloe's tiny apartment as inadequate, she sees it as a milestone. Her own space. I feel like a jerk for being critical of it, but in my defense, there were repairs that needed to happen.

"Lila and I are three years apart, which at times felt much further, but we've been close since high school. Levi and Hudson are five years younger and Penelope is seven years younger. She just graduated from high school.

"The downside was we didn't travel much or take vacations. That's what books were for. Escapism in its cheapest form." She slides her hand under her head. "I'm sure you traveled a lot as a kid."

"My dad worked all the time, but my mother took me places. Paris, London, Venice. There's a photo of me in my mother's office when I was three or four eating gelato outside the Colosseum."

"You do like ice cream! I knew it!"

"I was four and it was gelato."

She smiles. "That's definitely on my bucket list."

"Gelato?"

"No. Traveling out of the country. A stamp in my passport. I have one. I got it when I turned eighteen thinking I was an adult and I was going to see the world. I haven't made it that far."

"You moved to New York. That's impressive."

"Yeah. I guess it is. I love being here. I can't imagine living anywhere else."

We're quiet for a moment, my hand slowly tracing up and down her back. It's impossible to be near her and not touch her.

"What was your dad like?" she asks.

"He was older when he and my mother married and then she had me later in life. If he were alive, he'd be eighty-six."

"I didn't realize he was that much older than your mom."

"He was a bachelor, married to his work before my mother convinced him to settle down. Except marriage and a child didn't really change his work habits. With my father absent all the time, I imagined a different life for myself. Traveling, having a family and being young enough to see my kids graduate and get married or have kids of their own. One where I would be there for my children. Not an empty chair at the dinner table. I wanted to do things differently. Ironically, now business is the only thing I care about."

"That's not true." Chloe shakes her head. "You care about your mother."

"When her opinions aren't suffocating me."

"And surely your friendships, like with Carl."

"I can take him or leave him," I joke, but Chloe doesn't laugh. "I'm an island that no one wants to get stuck on."

"Not true. I'm here and I like it."

"That's because I've plied you with orgasms." *And black-mailed you to be my fake girlfriend.*

Chloe's quiet and I wonder if she's thinking the same thing.

"Two more days until these nails come off." She lifts her hand off my chest to wave her fingers.

"You must be excited."

I press the palm of my hand to hers, then our fingers interlace.

"Beyond." She bends her fingers, tickling the underside of my fingers. "I have gotten more used to them. I can probably do most tasks now without injuring myself or others."

As if to prove it, she circles her nail around my nipple.

"How long is this game going to go on?" she asks.

"How long do you want to play?"

"I'm determined to win. I still can't believe you're that good at WordIt."

"It must be beginner's luck," I say. Knowing full well luck

has nothing to do with it.

We fall asleep like that. Chloe's head on my chest and my heart beating steady under the palm of her hand.

"You're in a good mood," Carl comments.

"I'm in a fucking great mood," I say, spinning my racquet before wiping the sweat from my brow, then tossing the towel onto the bench. Sleeping with Chloe in my arms last night, I was the most content I've ever been.

When I woke up this morning with Chloe tucked in beside me, I thought about how I could get used to that. Her beautiful, smiling face greeting me every morning. Me pressing her hands over her head so that I can kiss her even though she insists that she needs to brush her teeth first. The desire to have her building to an immeasurable level.

"You know, I have to hand it to you. I wasn't sure we'd get Fred to come around, but you did it." Carl takes a drink of water. "We're still waiting to hear back from Voltaire's legal team, but I think the deal is well on its way."

Right. Another reason to be in a fantastic mood.

"Good," I say, albeit distracted by thoughts of Chloe.

Carl laughs. "Good? That's all? You've only been obsessed with landing this deal for the past few months."

"And we'll close the deal, so we're good."

"And then what?"

"What do you mean?"

"What's next? You always have a deal on the back burner. The next target."

"I don't know." I shrug. Carl's right, I'm always after what's next, never content in the present. It's different now with Chloe in my life. What's next is figuring out how to keep her.

It must be written on my face.

"Wait a minute. I know that look. It's the look of a man who's wrapped around a woman's finger. This is about Chloe. You really like her."

My eyes narrow.

"Go ahead. Try to deny it," he says.

I can't. I don't want to, but that doesn't mean I'm going to gab with Carl about my feelings for her.

"Should I remind you of all the advice you've given me? Minimize distractions, don't make it personal, eye on the prize? Sound familiar?"

Those are my words repeated back but they sound foreign to me now. Chloe's not a distraction, she's the main attraction and I want to make it personal.

My eyes are on the prize and it's making Chloe mine.

"Don't worry. I've got it handled."

While Carl opts to stop for a beer in the men's lounge, I head for the locker room, eager to get showered and get home.

On my way down the hall, I hear a familiar laugh. I turn around but no one is there.

The woman laughs again, then I hear whispering.

I wouldn't bother with further investigation, but I could have sworn it was Frankie's laugh. I wonder if she and Fred are here.

I back track, but there's only the door to the stairwell leading down to the lower two levels. Deciding to not give it any more thought, I start moving back down the hallway. The laugh registers again. It's bugging the hell out of me now. I either need to find out what's going on or give it up and go shower.

Determination to uncover the mystery of Frankie's soundalike laugh has me moving back to the stairwell door and looking through the window.

What I find there has me wishing I would have kept moving.

The woman is in fact Frankie, but the man who has her pinned to the wall isn't Fred. It's Vance, one of the tennis pros at the club.

I hear their murmurings as they echo off the cement walls. They're kissing, which is evidence enough, but from the thrusting motion of Vance's hips, I can tell they're doing far more than that.

My guts twists and I back away from the stairwell door.

Fuck. Chloe's instincts about Frankie had been right. I'd had my suspicions, a woman like that with a much older man like Fred is your typical gold digger stereotype. I'd hoped I was wrong. For Fred's sake.

Now, I've seen it with my own eyes.

My mind immediately goes to the deal with Fred. I can't begin to know what his response would be if I told him about Frankie's infidelity. He'd be hurt, maybe embarrassed. And I'd be the messenger of that pain. No matter how good my intentions would be, saving Fred from further heartache and financial loss, he might not see it that way. Fred is prideful, he's already making me earn this acquisition. I've been jumping through hoops to get this deal closed. He could walk away with Voltaire, give Ryan Shaw the chance to swoop in and take it out from under me.

No. I can't let that happen. I can't do anything to jeopardize the deal with Voltaire moving forward.

We're a month out from signing. Surely, not much harm can be done in four weeks.

Besides, it's not my place to tell Fred something so personal. We don't have that kind of relationship. It's just business.

I head for the men's locker room, determined to forget what I saw in that stairwell.

CHAPTER 22

Chloe

"So, when do the cat claws come off?" Jules asks, reaching for another bag to fill with books.

We're spread out in the conference room at St. Clair Press. The table is covered with books and other supplies to assemble the takeaway bags for the Books 4 Kids event.

"The photoshoot is at ten. Then I'm going straight to the nail salon to have them removed." I glance at the clock. I've got forty-five minutes before the photoshoot.

"I don't know how you've managed all week."

I press the sticky part of a sticky note onto the stack of bookmarks. When I lift it, the bookmark comes with it, then I detach the bookmark and place it into the bag.

"It's called getting creative." I smile.

Jules laughs at my system for putting bookmarks into the bags, but seriously it works. That's how this week has been. Finding work arounds for tasks that having these long nails make difficult. Using a quarter under the tab of a soda can to open it, wearing elastic waist skirts, and while I love holding a book when I read, I've discovered a new appreciation for audio books.

"Is that what's happening between you and Barrett?" She wiggles her eyebrows. "You're 'getting creative'?"

I can't help but blush at the memory of the last four nights. Barrett's mouth on me, those proficient fingers of his thrusting inside me. The orgasms I've received softening the blow that Barrett has beat me at WordIt four days in a row. I've still gotten the word correct, but Barrett has been faster.

I'm counting down the minutes until my nails are a reasonable length, but I also have to wonder what will happen between Barrett and me once they come off? And there's also the frustration that I still haven't touched him yet. I didn't think it would be that frustrating, but after everything we've done and I have yet to hold his cock in my hand or put it in my mouth, I'm starting to go insane.

"Did you get any action last night?"

"He ate me out on his desk. Two orgasms," I say, trying not to pout.

"So, no," Jules makes a motion with her hand and places her tongue into her cheek.

"No. I don't know how much longer I can take it. I'm an excellent WordIt player, how does he keep beating me?"

"What about your list?" she asks.

"What about it?"

"Don't you still have one more request?" She wiggles her eyebrows.

"Yes."

I think about our agreement and the request list that Barrett set up at our lunch meeting weeks ago. How he said I wasn't using my requests wisely.

"So, request to suck his dick."

A strangled laugh escapes me. "Oh my God. I cannot do that."

"Why not? That's how you started this whole WordIt

thing, because he was desperate to have you. You said he's rock hard every time you fool around. Maybe he doesn't want to rush you. He's waiting for you to be ready to suck his monster cock."

"Jesus, Jules." My eyes dart to the door. The conference room is all glass. We're in a fishbowl. I just hope no one passing by can read lips.

"No one can hear us."

With Barrett's nightly WordIt victories this week, I've gotten over the anxiety I was feeling about hooking up with him, feeling awkward about his mouth between my thighs. We've done things I never even considered, let alone thought I would like.

It's because I trust Barrett. I like giving him control of my body, knowing he will make it good while also pushing me out of my comfort zone. I can't imagine feeling that way with someone else. These thoughts stray way outside of the 'we're just hooking up because we're fake dating' boundary that I've assured Jules I'm staying inside of.

When Lauren texted me earlier and asked if I had a plus one to her wedding—she's trying to decide if she wants a head table with all the wedding party or a sweetheart table for just her and Jeff—I only fantasized about Barrett spinning me around the dance floor in his tux for ten minutes before I responded that I would be dateless.

Barrett and I will be broken up then. The six-week time-line for our agreement will be expired. While we've hooked up, Barrett hasn't indicated that anything has changed. We're still getting what we both want, but now I'm getting orgasms.

I grab another bag from the stack and go through the motions of filling it. Jules continues to work, her focus no longer on Barrett's monster cock, but telling me a story about the date she went on last night. The guy asked if they could have sex before they went to dinner because he doesn't perform well on a full stomach.

As Jules continues her story, I think about the blank space I have left on my list. Jules is right. I don't want to wait any longer to put my mouth on Barrett.

CHAPTER 23

Barrett

I'm drafting an email when Chloe bursts through my office door. I'd be surprised if I wasn't so fucking happy to see her there.

Every night this week we've played WordIt to determine who gets the pleasure of making the other one come. Every night this week I've won and fucked Chloe with my fingers and tongue. It's been a measure in restraint not giving in when she reaches for my belt. Pulling away from her warm, sweet body every night. But it's been necessary. I'm dying to be inside her, but I want Chloe to be comfortable before we move on to the next step, because I know when that happens, I won't be able to hold anything back.

She's breathing hard, like she ran here in her red high heels, the same color as her lips again today.

"Hi," she says, still working to catch her breath.

"Hi," I say, standing from my desk chair.

She turns to lock the door before striding over to move between me and my desk. Needing to be closer, I slide my hand to her hip and pull her to me.

"This is a nice surprise." I smile down at her.

"Do you have lunch plans?" she asks, grinning from ear to ear.

I glance at my watch with my free hand. "In twenty minutes. Should I cancel?"

"No, that should be enough time."

"Enough time for what?" I ask, curious to find out what has her bursting into my office.

Her hands grip my arms and I immediately notice the absence of Frankie's Faux Nails. Chloe's nails have been transformed to their usual, much shorter, state and covered in a soft pink polish.

"I like your nails," I say, taking one hand and examining them more closely. "The color will look nice against my sheets when I pin your hands above your head later."

Chloe's eyes go wide, a momentary falter before she regains her focus.

"We'll see about that," she says playfully. "By the way, I think you're cheating at WordIt."

My lips quirk at her accusation. I will neither confirm nor deny it.

"The last four nights have demonstrated I'm a superior WordIt player. I'm determined to win. The prize," I slide my hand under her skirt, "is, after all, very motivating. Did you want to play now?"

"No." She moves out of my grip to pull a piece of paper from her purse. I recognize it as her list. "I don't know how you've managed to beat me every night but I can't take it anymore." She sets it on my desk and points to her writing. "I've added giving you a blow job to the list. I didn't want it to come to this, but it's a necessity at this point. I can't focus on anything else. I've got the Books 4 Kids event tonight. I'll be distracted at best, deranged at worst. I won't be able to form coherent sentences with you next to me while I think about the weight of you in my hand. And I can't be wondering what your dick might feel like in my mouth while I'm handing out books to children. It wouldn't be right."

She uses our joined hands to pull me around my desk and over to the sofa on the far wall.

I want to laugh at how serious Chloe is about giving me a blow job. My dick is already pressed against my zipper, having become fully alert the moment she walked into my office.

"Sit." She pushes on my chest, indicating her request. It's barely enough momentum to move me an inch, but I do what she says and take a seat on the sofa. Chloe kneels between my legs, placing her hands on my thighs.

"I've always wondered what your lips would look like stretched around my cock." I reach forward to cup her cheek, placing my thumb pad on her lower lip and giving it a tug.

"You have?" She welcomes my thumb into her mouth and swirls the tip of it with her tongue.

"Every damn day since I met you."

"You're joking. You barely said a word to me when your mother introduced us."

"That's because I knew you were trouble," I confess.

I trace my thumb around her lips, letting the wetness from her mouth coat her there.

Chloe grips my wrist and places my hand by my side.

"Speaking of trouble, those hands of yours don't exactly play fair, so keep them to yourself right now."

I do as I'm told, while Chloe reaches forward and unbuckles my belt. Those soft pink fingernails work their magic on my button and zipper, then she's yanking down my boxer briefs and releasing my rigid length.

She wraps a hand around me, and her eyes go wide when she can't connect her fingers to her thumb. Me, I'm in fucking heaven watching this fantasy unfold.

"I guess that's why your hands are so big. It would be hard to jerk off with small hands."

I rock into her touch. "I like seeing your hands wrapped around me. They're perfect," I grind out. The contact with her soft, warm hand is undoing me quickly.

I continue to watch her examining my dick. It has to be the hottest thing I've ever seen. I think if there wasn't a time constriction, Chloe would spend hours getting acquainted, stroking and playing, tracing every vein with her polished finger before teasing me by tracing them with the tip of her tongue.

After another minute of exploration, Chloe's mouth closes around my head. The warmth, the wetness, fuck, the swirl of her tongue.

My exhale comes out ragged.

Maybe it's because Chloe charging into my office demanding to give me a blow job was completely unexpected, or because I've been anticipating this moment all week, but one lick of her tongue and I'm a fucking goner.

My eyelids close. The amount of pleasure that builds from a single swipe of her tongue is confounding.

She takes more of me in, then wraps her hands around the base to fist the length she can't fit in her mouth. Against the mounting pleasure, I force my eyes open to see the reality of what I've been fantasizing about, Chloe's lush, red lips wrapped around my cock. Her cheeks are hollowed out as she sucks me farther back into her throat. She peers up at me from under her long lashes, those blue eyes filled with lust and satisfaction and wonder.

Of course, it was going to be good. How can it not be? Watching the woman you're crazy about find pleasure in making you feel good.

She's found a rhythm and it's driving me insane. My balls draw up tight.

"Chloe, I'm going to come."

She hums against me, somehow managing to pull me in farther.

Fuck. The sensation is too much.

With Chloe's eyes on me, I spill my pleasure down the back of her throat. A moment later, I withdraw from her mouth. Her lipstick perfectly in place, no one will ever be able to tell she had my cock in her mouth. That lipstick company should be commended.

I reach for her, pulling her up and onto my lap. I want to touch Chloe. My fingers ache to slide under her skirt and feel how wet she is. How much sucking me off turns her on.

She steadies herself with one hand on my shoulder while the other hand wipes the corners of her mouth.

"Not too bad, huh? Even with my small hands." She laughs, and I can hear her nerves returning.

I shake my head. "I'm going to get nothing done the rest of the day. All I'll be able to think about is how fucking good it feels with your perfect mouth wrapped around me."

My hands move to her thighs, gliding along the smooth skin there before disappearing under the hem of her skirt. I grip her hips and press her against my still hard cock.

Chloe gasps but still manages to squeak out words.

"I should go," she says, shifting to move off me, but I hold her hips in place, loving the feel of her hot pussy against my erection.

I lean forward and press my lips to her jaw.

"You're not going anywhere until you come."

"That's not how it works," she protests. "I put it on my list."

"Fuck your list. I need to feel you. How wet you are right now. How much you liked having my cock in your mouth."

I rock into her center again and she moans. My smile is wicked. I know I've won.

I don't give her a chance to protest again. My fingers dive

underneath her panties and I'm greeted by Chloe's swollen, wet pussy. She rocks her hips again, this time two fingers slide inside her, filling her up.

"Maybe I did cheat at WordIt. Maybe after I tasted this sweet little cunt, I knew I had to win. I had to have you again and again," I thrust my fingers in and out, harder. "Would you blame me?"

Her arms wrap around my neck, her breasts crushed to my chest as I fuck her with my fingers.

I hook my fingers inside of her and kiss her neck. She's already so close. Sucking my dick has put her on the edge of the cliff and her orgasm is building quickly.

"Oh, God. *Barrett.*" Chloe's eyelids flutter shut. Her lips part on a breathy sigh. Damn. Watching her come is a fucking privilege.

"Let go, Chloe. Show me how much that sweet pussy likes to come on my fingers."

Her walls clench down around my fingers, squeezing me tight, then a rush of wetness slides down my hand. Fuck, yes. I wish it was my head between her thighs, lapping up her sweet juices.

My erection swells between us, but I know there's no way I'm going to take this any further right now.

I kiss her lips gently, letting her bask in the post orgasm glow before helping her to her feet and setting her clothes right.

"That was unexpected." Chloe sways on her feet as she adjusts her skirt. "I didn't come here for that. I was going to give you the best blow job you've ever had then walk out leaving you wanting more."

I finish tucking in my shirt and buckle my pants, then reach for her.

"Mission accomplished," I say, placing a kiss on her lips

that turns hungry in a second. Bea buzzes through on my speakerphone.

"Mr. St. Clair, Marcus is downstairs to take you to lunch," she announces.

"I've got to go." I reluctantly pull away. "Do you want a ride?"

"I'm headed home—err, to your place. I've got to change, then get over to the Books 4 Kids event to help set up."

Chloe's mention of my place being home for her, regardless of the fact that it was a slip that she quickly corrected, makes my chest expand. I have to admit that even before our relationship was physical, I liked having her there. Even when she was driving me crazy, wearing that tiny silk lounge set and fostering dogs without my approval, I wanted her there.

I kiss her again. "I'll see you there later."

"Sounds good."

She smiles and pulls out of my arms.

I've got the strongest urge to cancel the rest of my day and leave with her. Get ready for the event with her, help her with whatever she needs. Anything to be by her side.

I watch Chloe reapply her lipstick. Velvety red coating her lips that surrounded my cock minutes ago. I've never had this conflict before. In the past if it was between business and a woman, ten times out of ten I would choose to pursue a deal. I worked at all hours, missed dates, didn't prioritize anyone over my business.

Chloe is a game changer. I want to put in the effort with her. And I will.

But I've got a lunch meeting with Fred.

"Fred's signing the intent to sell letter today. The first official step in SCM acquiring Voltaire Telecom."

"Congratulations!" Chloe reaches up to plant a quick kiss on my mouth. "We'll have to celebrate tonight."

"Tonight is about Books 4 Kids and all your hard work."

"We can celebrate both." She smiles, then presses her lips to mine one last time before sailing out of my office.

I finish dressing, then move to my desk to grab my wallet.

Chloe's list is still sitting on top of my desk. It's complete now. The last item filled out in purple ink—BJ for Barrett—written in Chloe's feminine handwriting, with a smiley face next to it.

I fold the paper up and put it in my desk drawer.

In the car on the way to lunch, I should be thinking about Fred and the Voltaire acquisition, but my mind is with Chloe and counting down the minutes until I see her again.

The only thing I know for sure about the Books 4 Kids event is that myself, along with other—and far more prestigious—volunteers, will be recording a read aloud that will be featured on the Books 4 Kids website and used to promote the Read With Kids YouTube channel that St. Clair Press has started to help promote early childhood literacy.

Upon arrival, I am checked in by a man at a table and given the book I will be reading.

It's titled *Grumpy Monkey*.

My lips quirk as I flip through the book, admittedly knowing why Chloe chose this one for me to read.

"You're here." I turn to find my mother approaching.

"Yes. And ready to read a book about a monkey having a bad day."

It's not relatable at all. I'm having a great day.

I got a blow job from Chloe, then Fred signed off on the letter of intent to sell Voltaire to SCM.

She smiles and takes the book from me.

"I'd say Chloe knows you well. But then I'm not certain if

this book fits you as of late." She hands it back to me. "Something's different about you."

The implication is I've changed since dating Chloe. Fake dating her. My mother doesn't know that it's not real.

"Oh? I don't think so."

"Chloe's good for you. She softens your edges." She smiles.

I nod, and start flipping through the pages of the book. There's no use trying to deny it. She's right. Spending time with Chloe has made me realize what I've been missing out on and think about the man I want to be. Whether it's taking time to understand each other, or not letting work take over my life. By getting to know Chloe, and seeing her perspective, I have discovered I can do better. I want to do better.

I'm never going to be easygoing, but that's not what Chloe needs. She needs someone to challenge her, encourage her, push her to be even more amazing than she already is. I want to be that guy. But is that what she wants?

Before Chloe, I was fine with working every second of the day, but I want other things now. With her.

She's across the room, helping set up the story time for L J Bowan, a famous children's fantasy book author that my mother introduced me to earlier.

The room is packed full of kids and their parents.

I have no issues with public speaking. I've done it so many times in my life that it's second nature. Business meetings, award galas, keynote addresses, but reading a children's book in this intimate setting is suddenly making me sweat.

It's not the kids or the camera that have me worked up. It's that I want to impress Chloe. If the entire crowd clears out when I get up there, I'll feel like an idiot.

"I'm a lucky man," I finally respond, ignoring the knots in my stomach.

She nods. "And how's everything going with Fred?" Our

eyes connect and her eyebrows lift. She's never asked about deals before, but then again none have been this important to me.

"It's almost done." I think back to earlier this week and Chloe's nail debacle. While seeing Chloe naked and making her come have been the benefits of her manicure from Frankie, those nails were ridiculous and they're something we'll be laughing about for years to come.

Years to come. My brain is on a runaway train with thoughts and images of life with Chloe.

I swallow hard.

"I'm happy for you, Barrett." My mother squeezes my arm. "And proud. I know that's what you've been working hard for."

"Thank you."

"And I know your father would have been proud, too."

I nod. That means a lot. It's the reason why I've been working so hard all these years to put SCM on top. To honor my father's legacy. I'm realizing that I want a legacy of my own. It has nothing to do with business and everything to do with Chloe.

CHAPTER 24

Chloe

The only thing sexier than a man reading a book is a man reading a book to a child. A sweet little redhead toddled up to Barrett and plopped herself down in his lap during his story time reading. He glanced down at her for a moment, shifted the book to keep it in the camera frame and continued on. How the hell am I supposed to resist that? It's not possible. I don't even want to try.

I'm so entranced with Barrett's story time delivery that I barely notice Emma approach.

"He must have a thing for redheads," she says, her gaze on Barrett and the little girl.

"I really like him," I gush. I'm a cartoon character with hearts for eyes. "Like a lot."

She laughs. "He's your boyfriend, that's normal."

"Right." I nod, because while Barrett and I have been getting to know each other the past few weeks, to the outside world we're already a done deal. Feelings revealed, everything sorted, when in fact nothing is obvious, except for the fact that if we don't have sex soon, I'm going to spontaneously combust.

My underwear is already wet thinking about our hook up in his office this afternoon. I still can't believe I burst into his office in the middle of the day and demanded to suck his dick. Who does that? Fake girlfriends who are dying to suck their fake boyfriend's dick, I guess.

And then he wouldn't let me leave without feeling me come on his fingers first. My clit throbs recalling his demanding words. While I'm not usually a fan of him telling me what to do, bossy bedroom Barrett is my favorite.

Oh God, now I'm thinking about his hard length pressed between us. Wondering what it would feel like if he pressed his thick crown against me. If I slid down onto his length.

"I'm dying to know more details about that look on your face," Emma smiles mischievously, then scrunches her nose, "but also not because Barrett's like my brother." She looks around. "Is it too late for you to date someone else? Someone we can gossip about without me feeling weird? I can introduce you to other successful, workaholic businessmen if that's what you're into."

I laugh quietly, making sure I'm not disrupting Barrett's reading.

"It might be too late," I say. It's definitely too late for me to reconsider having sex with Barrett. While not executed yet, that decision has been made. It's happening.

I quickly tamp down my lustful thoughts when JoAnna walks over.

"Everything turned out wonderful, Chloe," she says, giving me an air kiss on both cheeks. "I really appreciate all you've done with the Books 4 Kids launch. I know it wasn't easy with you also taking on Lacey's workload."

I smile, but it wasn't easy. This week was overwhelming, but helping me through it was Barrett. The orgasms were amazing, but also how attentive and sweet he was. Helping me with the Books 4 Kids bags and taking Baxter for walks when I was working late. It made me wonder if that's how he would be as a partner, if we were really together.

The three of us watch Barrett continue to read the book.

JoAnna leans in and whispers to me, "I'd ask how you got him to do this, but I already know."

"You do?" I ask, wondering exactly what it is that she knows.

"It's obvious." She smiles at me, then turns to watch Barrett. "The only reason a man does something for a woman that he wouldn't normally do is because he's in love."

My heart skips a beat at JoAnna's statement. And I have to restrain the nervous laughter that wants to bubble out of my throat. Barrett in love? *With me?*

For a moment, I let JoAnna's wild assertion fester in my brain. What would it be like to be Barrett's, for real? To be by his side because he wants me there, not because he needs a fake girlfriend for a business deal. Weeks ago, I would have laughed at the thought. Now, it doesn't seem as absurd.

I can see it clearly. Time together spent cuddling on the couch, weekends strolling the city with Baxter and of course, lots of hot, passionate sex.

Sex with Barrett. That's a fantasy I've spent a lot of time thinking about the past few days. I'd like to make that fantasy a reality as soon as possible.

But, as much as I've gotten to know Barrett, I still have to wonder what is real and what is part of our arrangement. He's still focused on his deal with Fred and our relationship is a part of that. We're not a real couple. Yes, we're hooking up now, but orgasms don't equal love.

While JoAnna's words are tempting to consider, I remember the real reason Barrett is here. I put it on my list. JoAnna thinks it's because we're together and all I had to do was ask. That's the furthest from the truth. Maybe his reluctance to make this appearance has eased since we've been hooking up, but I doubt he would be here if I didn't make it one of my conditions to continuing this fake relationship with him.

He's given me no indication that this is anything more than a business arrangement with benefits.

Now that my nails have returned to their normal length, I have to consider that everything might go back to the way it was before Frankie's Faux Nails wreaked havoc on my life. There have been no conversations about what would happen when the nails came off. My obnoxious manicure had been the entire reason we started playing WordIt and Barrett was able to prove how skilled his tongue and fingers really are.

Now I'm wondering if I should have put sex on my list. Crap.

I watch as Barrett closes the book and like the other readers before him, he gives a final remark directing viewers to the Books 4 Kids website. When he's done, the little redheaded girl jumps up and gives him a hug.

With her in his arms, our eyes connect and he winks.

Sweet Jesus. I don't know how I'm going to do it, but I've got to find a way to have sex with that man before the night is over.

I've meeted and greeted. I even waited until all the children left with their bags of books in hand. Now, in this room full of adults sipping wine and cocktails and nibbling on passed hors d'oeuvres, I can't take it any longer.

"I need to speak to you in private about an urgent matter," I whisper in Barrett's ear. His concerned look tells me that came out far less sexy than I had planned. I sound like an accountant finding a discrepancy in someone's bookkeeping. I'm trying here. I really am.

I take his hand and he follows me through the crowd, I keep a sweet smile on my face as I walk past the director of Books 4 Kids and the group of authors and celebrity readers she's talking with. Nothing to see here, folks. Just a woman trying to seduce her fake boyfriend at a children's fundraising event.

Outside the event room, I walk us down the hallway and upstairs.

A benefit of organizing this event is that I know the building well, and I know of a place I can take Barrett to be alone.

We reach the top landing and I turn right down the hallway. Finally, I open the door to the room I was looking for and pull Barrett in behind me.

"Where are we—"

It's the library's prop room. Inside, we're welcomed by an assortment of old furniture pushed along the walls, costume racks shoved into one corner, and a variety of boxes, stacked haphazardly throughout the room. Musical instruments, letter charts and boxes of toys that they use for the little toy library once a week.

Barrett glances around the room before his gaze lands on me.

"You wanted to talk?" His lips quirk with intrigue. "Here?"

I'm realizing maybe this isn't the best location for seduction, but I can't back out now. We're already here.

"Um, yes."

He moves closer, and with every step his shoes strike the linoleum floor, my heartbeat ratchets up a notch.

"And what was the urgent matter, Chloe?" he says softly, like he doesn't know how turned on I am right now. Like he can't see what he does to me.

I don't get to answer, because his hands lift to my face. His fingers curve along my jaw and into my hair, the pads of them applying just enough pressure to my neck to angle my face upwards. The brush of his thumbs against my cheeks has my mouth opening to him before our lips even meet.

When his warm lips brush mine, I melt into his mouth.

Barrett's kiss is sweet, yet hungry. Gentle, yet demanding.

I think I'm the only one who feels the urgency of desire, but when I press my hands into his stomach and grip his shirt, our kiss turns white hot. It's like someone turned up the flame on a gas stove and it feels like we're going to boil over.

"I don't think I can wait to have you." Barrett's voice is hoarse with need. His hand reaches beneath my dress. *God, yes.* His fingers hook into the waistband of my thong as he yanks the garment down my legs, then easily lifts me up. He pins me against the wall with his thigh between my legs, the hard muscle there applying pressure in just the right place. "Tell me to wait, Chloe."

I want to laugh. He wants me to be the one to shut this down? Has he looked in the mirror? Does he realize I just saw him reading stories to children? And smiling. At the same time. And that wink he delivered at the end of his reading? He had to know it would come to this.

I want him too badly to stop.

The need that's been building inside me all week. It's a necessity at this point. I won't make it much longer without knowing what it feels like to have him inside me.

"I can't wait," I say. I slide my hand down the front of his pants to cup his hard length and he groans into my mouth.

His lips fall to my neck while my hands move inside his suit jacket. His tie dangles between us, tickling my cleavage. One could argue we've got too many clothes on for this, that I should wait until I can feast on his naked body, but there's only one thing I really need right now. I hurriedly reach for his belt. Barrett must be thinking the same thing.

Our hands collide, both trying to move fast, but only managing to get tangled in the process. Finally, we work together, me unbuckling his belt, while he makes quick work of his zipper. I reach inside his briefs, stroking his silky length, while Barrett lifts the skirt of my dress over my hips, exposing me to him.

His fingers press into me. He's checking to see if I'm ready for him. I'm not even embarrassed about how wet I am. I've seen his dick and my body knows what it needs to prepare me for this. I'm beyond ready. I wrap my arms around his neck as he lifts me up into his arms, our lips crash into each other, licking and biting until we're breathless.

"Barrett. Now," I say.

He holds me over him, slowly lowering me. Inch by inch, I take him in. I'm so wet that I can practically hear the suction as he presses inside me.

Barrett sinks into me, and my hips flex in response. The pressure of him inside me is overwhelming and so satisfying.

"Are you on birth control?" he asks, his cock already seated deep inside me. I guess better late than never. "I'm clean. Shit. We should have talked about—fuck—you're tight."

"Yes. Birth control," I choke out, my breath leaving my body as I adjust to his size. "I'm clean. There's been no one since college."

Barrett grips my ass, holding me steady as he slides out, then back in. His cock fills me up so good, the moment he withdraws I feel hollow.

"Chloe, you feel so fucking good." His warm breath tickles my neck. "It's unreal."

He slowly eases in again, nearly splitting me in two.

"You're gripping me so tight." His breath comes out in puffs. It's clearly an effort to go slow. "Is this okay?"

"God, yes. Don't stop."

I squeeze my legs around his waist, sending him deeper

and his rhythm picks up.

Maybe I am a virgin. It's never felt this good. I'm clearly unacquainted with sex where your partner wants it to be as good for you as it is for him.

The head of Barrett's cock finds the perfect spot inside me. The continuous pressure there ignites a fire deep in my core.

He kisses me deep and slow as he fucks me hard against the wall, his hips setting off an unrelenting rhythm.

My head falls back as I arch into him, meeting his thrusts eagerly. I'm acutely aware of the brick wall scraping into my back, Barrett's fingers gripping my flesh to hold me to him. It's nothing compared to the pleasure building between my legs. Also, Barrett's dick is absolute magic. I've clearly blocked out every other sensation.

"Oh, God. Yes!" I urge him on.

"That's not your library voice, Chloe." Barrett's voice is low and seductive in my ear. "Someone will hear us. Someone will know you're getting fucked good and hard up here."

"So good." I sigh. I can feel the tension in my lower belly. Everything coiling tight.

Another thrust, and Barrett's lips against my jaw has me pulsing around him. It's nearly painful how hard I'm coming, clamping down around his thick cock. Barrett shudders. A moment later I can feel him pulsing inside me, the sensation followed by his hot seed spilling deep inside me. Another first for me.

We stay joined together, Barrett's grip lightens but he doesn't let me go. He holds me close and kisses me gently.

There's a calmness now to the frenzied desperation we felt a moment ago.

Barrett pulls back to look at me.

"That was..."

"Insane," I finish for him.

"You okay?" he asks. "I didn't hurt you, did I?"

"If by hurt you mean pleasured thoroughly, then yes."

He chuckles, then carries me over to the desk where he grabs a few tissues from the box there. Slowly, he pulls out, the friction in that movement threatening to put me back at square one. Needy and desperate to have him.

He sets me down and hands me a tissue. He tucks himself back in his pants and buckles his belt while I address the situation between my thighs. A wet, rushing sensation takes me by surprise. I quickly shove a tissue there.

I look up to Barrett, concerned.

"Is that normal? Does it fall out after?"

"My cum," he says, stepping forward to place a hand between my thighs. He hooks a finger inside me and groans. I have to steady myself against the desk. "Feeling my cum inside you...fuck...we have to go now before I bend you over this desk."

When my underwear is back in place, Barrett takes my hand and leads me out to the room.

We join the party just as the dessert trays are coming out, but Barrett steers us toward the exit. I look longingly at the mini macarons and bite-sized cheesecakes I picked out.

"We can stay if you want," Barrett says. "Or we can go home, and you can eat cookie dough ice cream while I lick *you*."

Okay. Easiest decision ever.

We do have to say goodbye to JoAnna and Emma, who I feel bad that we're leaving because she's alone. Alec had something come up with work last minute and he couldn't make it.

"Let's do lunch next week," she says.

"I'd love that," I say as Barrett leads me away.

At home, we're barely in the door before Barrett pulls me close and kisses me breathless. He's reaching for the zipper of my dress, when Baxter appears. He nudges at our legs and whines. He needs to go out.

I pull back and drop to my knees to pet him.

"How's my boy? I missed you." He licks my face, his tongue inches from where Barrett's used to be. "Do you need to go out?"

"I'll take him," Barrett volunteers. He pulls me to him again, his hand sliding under my dress to squeeze my ass. "I'll meet you upstairs. Bonus orgasms if you're naked when I get there."

A few minutes later, I'm in my closet taking off my dress when I hear Barrett enter my room.

"That was fast. I'm not even undressed."

He smirks. "Baxter and I have an understanding. I'm taking him for a long walk in the morning in exchange for his promptness tonight."

He stalks toward me, lowering his suit jacket down his arms as he moves. I'm still in my bra and underwear. I wonder if the bonus orgasms are off the table.

Without preamble he reaches behind me to unhook my bra, while my fingers dive for the buttons on his shirt. Shirtless, he lowers down, taking a hardened nipple into his mouth. His warmth sucks me in and my knees go weak. My hands grip the warm, muscular flesh of his shoulders to steady myself.

Those long fingers of his curl under the waistband of my thong before he tugs it down my legs. In one swift motion, Barrett pulls me to him and stands.

Our mouths tease together as he walks us across the hall and into his room. He lowers me to the bed.

"I want to go slow, but already knowing what it feels like to be buried inside you makes me eager to feel it again," he says, moving up the length of me, planting kisses on my belly, my breasts, my jaw, until he reaches my lips again.

"Don't go slow," I tell him, wrapping my legs around his hips until I can feel him there at my entrance.

And he doesn't, at least not that time.

CHAPTER 25

Barrett

I slide onto the leather seat then loosen my tie. Marcus closes the door behind me.

Tonight, sitting across from Fred Hinkle and his lawyer, Carl at my side, talking concessions and allowances, weeks from finalizing the deal I haven't been able to stop thinking about the past three months, my mind was elsewhere. Chloe.

How good things have been the last few weeks. How quickly everything has shifted between us. How I couldn't wait to get out of that meeting and see her.

That's how it has been every day this week. I've been working late nights, crawling into bed to find Chloe's sleep warm body. Fucking her gently until her soft cries fill my bedroom, then we curl into each other for another few hours of sleep.

She deserves more than that. I want to give her more. I want to take her on a real date. Something that doesn't involve a hair and makeup team and a ballroom full of people vying for my attention.

Just the two of us.

I come home to find most of the lights off, only a warm

glow coming from my study. At the sound of my footsteps, Baxter appears. The soft clinking of the tags on his collar let me know he's approaching. I drop my wallet and phone on the table by the door, then bend down to rub behind his ears. He nudges his wet nose into my palm, and I scratch his chin.

"Where's our girl?" I ask, knowing that Chloe's in one of two places.

When I stand again, Baxter moves toward the study.

I push the cracked door open to find Chloe tucked under a blanket on the couch, sleeping. Baxter immediately settles himself into his bed near the fireplace. My footsteps on the wood floor creak, causing her to startle. Rubbing sleep from her eyes, she sits up, her wavy red hair loose and wild around her shoulders. She's wearing the silk camisole from the lounge set that drives me crazy, one side's tiny strap has fallen off her shoulder exposing more skin.

"Hey," she says, stretching her arms overhead as I approach. "What time is it?"

"Late," I say. If the hunger in my voice isn't evidence of my building need for her, my dick swells when I pull the blanket back to find her in lace panties.

"How did the meeting go?" she asks.

"We're getting close. Two weeks out."

She smiles. "Are you excited?"

"It's not a done deal until the ink is dry on the documents."

"It's okay to be excited. To take a breath and realize you're getting what you wanted."

With her tank top askew, it allows me better access. I lean down and kiss along her collarbone.

"What is it that I want?" I ask against her skin. "Hmm?"

"Voltaire Telecom," she whispers.

I've got plans that didn't involve touching her, but I can't help myself. I slide my hand between her thighs and cup her. I can already feel the wet heat soaking through the crotch of her panties.

"Guess again."

"Mmm," she moans, then rocks into my hand.

Do I crave Chloe's body? Yes. Do I love pleasuring her and taking pleasure from her? Most definitely. But I also want to spend time with her outside the bedroom. And I know with my work schedule, we haven't spent much time together outside of social events since the weekend in the Hamptons.

I pull my hand back.

"Chloe, I—"

She leans forward and silences me with a kiss. Her arms wrap around my neck, pulling me closer as she climbs into my lap. Her smooth thighs bracket my hips as she presses her center against my erection and the words die on my tongue.

"Did you play WordIt today?" she asks. Her skin is sleep warm and feels amazing underneath my palms.

"I haven't had a chance."

"Spoiler alert. It was FUCKME," she says, unbuckling my belt.

"That's two words and six letters," I argue, guiding her tank top over her head.

"You're quite the wordsmith," she says, pulling her thong to the side before slowly lowering herself onto my cock. She gasps.

"Jesus, Chloe." Her slick pussy grips me so fucking tight.

I hold her hips, needing a minute before I can move.

"I've been waiting for you to walk through that door and fill me up. I already touched myself thinking about it."

My dick swells with her confession, and I pull her to me for a kiss.

I think back to a few weeks ago, and how timid Chloe had been about sex. Now, she's got no issue telling me when and where she wants me to fuck her. It's the biggest turn on. Right now, even if it means we're late, there's no way I'm going to deny her.

I cup her breasts; I'll never get over how good the weight of her feels in my hands. My mouth captures a nipple, tracing its hard peak with my tongue, then sucking it deep and making her muscles clamp down even harder around my cock.

I grip her ass as I slam up into her hard, matching her rhythm over and over. My index finger teases under the scrap of lace between her cheeks. I move down until I can feel her wetness, where I'm sliding in and out of her, then back up to rim the tight, puckered bud there.

With the next thrust of my cock, my finger presses inside her back entrance.

"Oh. God." Chloe moans.

Her head falls back. I can tell she's close from the flush of her skin and the breathy sounds she's making.

When Chloe's orgasm hits, her pussy squeezes my cock so tight it's almost painful. Her muscles pulse over and over, milking me good. One more thrust. That's all it takes and I'm spilling deep inside her.

She collapses with a satisfied sigh into my chest, and I wrap my arms around her.

"That was..." I can't even get the words out. I'm completely spent.

"Yup." Chloe nuzzles my neck. "No words."

I press my lips to her jaw, and let my hands tangle in her hair for a moment before I lift her head to look at her.

"I'd love to stay in this position all night, but we've got somewhere to be."

"What?" She looks down between us, where I'm still hard inside her. "You're kidding, right?"

"I was about to tell you, but you distracted me." I flex inside of her and she bites her lip. Maybe we shouldn't go. I could stay here, buried inside her all night.

"Ugh, what could we possibly be doing at ten o'clock at night?" Her pout is adorable. And now that the brain fog from my orgasm is subsiding, I remember the plan.

"We're going on a date."

"Now?" She lifts herself off me, stands, then waddles to the tissue box on the side table with the grace of a newborn foal.

"I could grab those for you," I say, not even trying to hide my smile.

"This works. Gravity is part of the process." She shimmies out of her thong, then shoves a wad of tissues between her thighs. "You could have told me before, now I'm a mess."

I love that this woman can be incredibly sexy one minute, and adorably awkward the next. It's by far one of my favorite things about her.

I stand to zip up my pants.

As a means to distract myself from the visual of Chloe completely naked, my cum leaking out of her, I check my watch. "Marcus will be here in a few minutes."

"Barrett! Seriously?!"

"Rose packed your bag. All you need to do is get dressed. Something comfortable." I can't take my eyes off her full breasts. "And easily removable."

"Wait, what? Where are we going?" She pulls her underwear and tank top back on.

"You're getting a stamp in your passport."

Her eyes widen with excitement.

"Ahh." She gasps, one hand gripping her chest. "Are we going to Canada?"

"No."

Her lips twitch. "Then, how are we going to leave the country and still get back for work tomorrow?"

I'm full-on grinning now. Chloe's eyes narrow.

"Did you seriously call your mom and tell her I won't be at work tomorrow?"

I walk over and lift her into my arms. She feels so good there.

"Do you trust me? To get on a plane with me and not know where it's going until we get there?"

She studies my face for a moment before nodding.

"Good. Then get dressed." I place a final kiss on her lips before lowering her to the ground.

"Oh!" She turns back before she reaches the door. "What about Baxter?"

His head lifts from where he's been snoozing. Had I forgotten he was here? Should we have had sex with him lying right there? I decide we'll need to think about that in the future.

The future that is me and Chloe and Baxter all living here. The thought easily surfaces.

"Barrett?" Chloe interrupts my thoughts.

"I'll take him out now. Rose will be here with him this weekend."

Chloe smiles. "Okay. I'll be back shortly."

When she's gone, I whistle to get Baxter's attention. He stands and stretches, then follows me to the front door where I grab his leash.

We take a lap around the block. Baxter does his business and when we get back to our stoop, Marcus is there loading our bags in the car.

After Baxter is settled into his kennel for the night, we leave for the airport.

On the drive, Chloe lays her head on my shoulder, and I wrap my arm around her. She's been working as hard as I have, putting in extra hours for the assistant editor position she's filling in for along with being my mother's assistant. I know she's working hard to prove herself in her job and the publishing industry itself, and I hate that I had once threatened to take it all away.

When we arrive on the tarmac, I gently wake Chloe.

Marcus unloads our bags and we ascend the stairs to the plane. Inside the cabin, I introduce Chloe to Libby, the flight attendant, and the pilots, Kip and Cory. They're all part of my usual crew.

Libby pours me a scotch and offers Chloe a drink before letting us know we'll be taking off in ten minutes.

I walk Chloe to the back of the plane.

"This is insane!" Chloe squeals with delight. "I can't believe you have your own plane."

"Actually, the plane's not mine. It's chartered. It's not fiscally responsible to own a plane. Maintenance costs are brutal."

She laughs. "Says the man with billions of dollars."

"And I don't fly much," I add.

"Oh God, that's right. You don't like to fly."

"I'll be fine." I take a long pull of my scotch, letting it smooth out the edginess I feel. With Chloe here, it's different. Her excitement and enthusiasm calm my nerves.

"What's back there?" she asks, pointing to a closed door.

"The bedroom."

"This plane has a bedroom?" Her mouth gapes open.

"How else am I going to fuck you at ten thousand feet?"

"Oh my God. We cannot. People will know." She looks around.

"Libby? The one other person in the cabin?"

"Yes."

"Then you'll need to work on being quiet."

"Maybe you need to work on not making me scream." She lifts her eyebrows in a haughty expression.

I shake my head.

"You should take the window," I suggest, dropping into the aisle seat. I close my eyes and exhale a deep breath.

Chloe reaches for my hand. "Is there anything I can do? To distract you?"

I turn toward her and open my eyes.

"You being beside me is the best distraction."

The engines roar as we pick up speed down the runway. Chloe pushes the window shut and squeezes my hand.

"We didn't fly as a family. Too expensive for seven people. We took road trips instead."

She starts telling me about the time her family went on a road trip to South Dakota. The music her parents made them listen to and how packed it was with seven people and how you could barely move. How her youngest sister got left at a rest stop and how the van smelled like farts and fast food.

"So, the next time you're flying around in your private chartered plane, remember you could be stuck in a smelly van."

I chuckle at that. A minute later we're airborne, my anxiety about this flight eased by Chloe's entertaining story. She finishes her story while I finish my scotch. Then, somewhere over the Atlantic, we make good use of the plane's bedroom.

CHAPTER 26

Chloe

We're in Paris.

The city of lights. And love.

That's where Barrett has taken me. On *a date*. This man is unreal.

I barely slept on the plane, Barrett's roaming hands and mouth keeping me up half the flight, but it doesn't matter. After a shot of espresso and a flaky croissant that tasted of butter and sin, I've got the energy level of a five-year-old at Disney.

The hotel is extravagant. Marble floors, gold-plated ceilings, French blue walls with intricate gold-painted details, and crystal chandeliers. That's just the lobby.

We're staying in the penthouse. The first thing my eyes connect with when the door opens is the Eiffel Tower right outside the window. French doors open to a balconet, I can't help but step out to get a better look.

"Barrett! You have to see this."

I turn to find him in the middle of the room, his hands shoved into his pockets, watching me with a smile on his face.

"The view is good from here."

"Right." I nod in understanding. Looking out at the famous landmark, I wonder what Barrett has planned. Will we sight-see? Check out museums? Eat delicious French food until we're stuffed? I've already determined I could sustain myself on croissants if necessary.

"What's the plan?" I move to wrap my arms around his waist, my temple resting at the center of his chest. I'm in Paris, with Barrett. It's surreal, yet it feels natural. As if I could be anywhere right now, it would be here. And if I could have anyone by my side, it would be him. I wouldn't have said that a month ago. I can't believe how quickly my feelings about him have changed. "Louvre? Musée d'Orsay? Walk along the Seine?"

"I thought we'd take a tour of this bed here."

I turn my head to look up at him. "You brought me to Paris to have sex?"

"Among other things." He grins down at me. His fingers slide into my hair and he kisses me sweetly.

The kiss turns burning hot in seconds and I'm considering forgetting all about the enchanting city out the window in favor of spending all day in bed with Barrett, but he pulls away and gives my ass a sharp smack.

"All right. Let's go or we'll never leave this room."

We both know he's right.

Out on the street, there's a car waiting for us. Valentin, our driver, takes us through the city. While I can't always understand what he's saying due to English being his second language, Barrett is a diligent guide, pointing out shops and restaurants and sharing facts about history and architecture.

The day goes by in a blur.

A private tour at Louvre, lunch on the patio at Le Servan where I don't bother to look at the menu but everything that is put in front of me is delicious—mussels, sardines on brioche toast and black pudding. And Bordeaux wine which Barrett explains the history of. I love how excited he gets talking about it all. I've never been a history buff, so it's fun to hear all the random facts he's got stored in his brain.

After lunch we opt to walk and bid Valentin farewell. We spend the afternoon touring Notre-Dame, then make our way over to Ile St. Louis. Even though I'm still full from lunch, I can't pass up ice cream at world famous Glacier Berthillon.

I select tiramisu flavor while Barrett opts for the wild strawberry sorbet.

"This is ruining Ben & Jerry's for me," I tell him between licks.

With his arm around my back, he pulls me in close.

"This is making me think of your mouth around my cock," he whispers against my ear. I nearly choke on my ice cream.

We take our ice cream to go and walk along the Seine. It's a warm afternoon, and having gotten a double scoop, I have to work hard to eat it before it melts.

Just when I think the day can't get better, Barrett leads me to where a boat is docked at the riverside. A private boat tour along the Seine. And there's champagne.

"You're really raising the stakes for future dates," I say, immediately regretting it. Barrett never indicated that there would be other dates. This could all be for show. An elaborate date to prove that we travel like any legitimate couple would.

Barrett pulls me into his lap, his hair sexy and windblown from the boat ride.

"I'm up for the challenge," he says, taking my face in his hands. He tastes like strawberries and champagne. And forever.

I'm torn because I want to pay attention to the tour that Michelé, the boat captain, is giving us, but I also want to curl up in Barrett's arms and fall asleep. The travel and exciting day of sightseeing is catching up with me.

I yawn.

"Close your eyes. It's okay."

With the warm evening breeze in my hair, and Barrett's strong arms around me, I decide to take a quick nap and let my eyes fall closed.

∼

When I wake, we're still on the boat, but it's dark now. Barrett's eyes are closed, his lips parted slightly, his chest rising and falling evenly under my palm.

I look up to find we are moving down the river toward the Eiffel Tower which is now lit up in warm yellow lights against the night sky.

Michelé steers the boat toward a nearby ramp. We have to be close to our hotel now.

"Hey." Barrett shifts under me to look around.

"Hi. We both fell asleep."

He laughs, rubbing his face.

Michelé says something in French that Barrett must understand. He shakes his hand, then tips his head at me.

"Bonjour," I say, excited to use one of the few French words I know.

We walk over the bridge to get to the other side of the river.

"Are you hungry?"

"I don't think I'll ever be hungry again." I press a hand to my stomach where eating for a day in Paris has made the waistband of my shorts tighter. "But walking feels good."

He nods, and we walk in a contented silence. Our path uncertain, but directed by the warm glow of the city's greatest landmark.

My feet are exhausted from exploring the city today, but as the sky has darkened, there's a new feel in the air. Nighttime in

Paris is a whole other experience, and I don't want to miss a minute of it. The people gathered on patios, eating and drinking, the fluidity of their spoken words while foreign is hypnotizing. And there's music. A woman's soft, yet captivating voice reaches us from afar.

As we walk through the Jardin du Champs de Mars, the source of the music becomes apparent. On one side of the green space, a small band is performing. It's an informal concert, with many couples and groups stretched out on blankets enjoying the performance.

"What about dancing?" Barrett asks.

"I thought you weren't a fan of dancing."

Wordlessly, he wraps his left arm around my back, then takes my hand in the other. I put my free hand on his shoulder. He pulls me close and leans down, his lips brushing against my jaw before he whispers, "There are many things I wasn't a fan of before."

He doesn't elaborate on what those things are or what he means by 'before.' He doesn't have to. I know the feeling.

There, in the city of lights, wrapped in Barrett's arms, I realize this fake relationship is quickly starting to feel very real.

CHAPTER 27
Barrett

Watching Chloe take in Paris is doing funny things to me.

I've been here countless times, but I've never experienced the city before like I am with Chloe. She wants to see everything, try everything. Her constant wide-eyed stare as she takes it all in is intoxicating.

Not to mention the way she looks right now, her hair wild from sleep, spilling over her shoulders as she rides me.

Last night, we'd fallen into bed, our bodies exhausted from jet lag and a day of sightseeing. We found our pleasure quickly before drifting off to sleep, our limbs tangled in the sheets.

Due to a perfectly placed mirror on the back of the bathroom door, not only do I get the pleasure of watching Chloe's breasts bounce with each thrust, but I can also see my cock sliding through her wet folds.

"Fuck. You have to see this."

Chloe's startled when I grab her hips and lift her off of me. Turning her so that her back is to my chest, I hold the base of my dick and slide back inside.

"Oh, God," she gasps. I watch as Chloe's hooded gaze falls to where we're joined. The visual is even better now.

Her head falls back against my shoulder. I kiss along her neck and the shell of her ear.

"See how perfect you look taking my cock? How much your sweet pussy loves swallowing me up?"

I know we're both close. I drop my hand from where it's cupping her breast to her clit, and apply pressure there.

"Oh, Barrett. Yes. Please," she moans.

I love taking care of her like this. Touching every inch of her body, hearing her moans, and feeling her pulse around me as she comes. I never want it to end.

I rock up into her over and over, loving the sight of her slick and greedy, taking me in. Chloe reaches back, thrusting her fingers into my hair. The sharp tug on my scalp only spurs me on.

With our eyes locked in the mirror, we come apart together.

After a shower, we had breakfast at Café de Flore, a coffeehouse known for attracting famous writers and philosophers. We perused the book stalls along the Seine. Even though they were in French, Chloe purchased three books because the covers were pretty.

Now, we're finishing lunch on the patio at a bistro near our hotel. Just like yesterday, she had me order and was excited to try everything the waiter brought. That's one of the things I admire about her. She isn't afraid to try new things. To get out of her comfort zone. I know because I've been pushing her out of it since we started this whole fake dating arrangement.

There's nothing fake about it now. Nothing fake about how I feel about her.

She's wearing a white sundress with ties at the shoulders.

Her hair is pulled up on top of her head. With no makeup on her face, I can see the light smattering of freckles on her nose.

She catches me staring.

"What?" She looks behind her, oblivious to the idea that in a place like Paris where everywhere you look, the architecture and sights are breathtaking, it's her I can't keep my eyes off.

"Are you ready to go?" I ask.

"Oh. Sure." She stands and positions her small purse across her body. "Where to now?"

I take her hand and we start walking along Rue du Maréchal Harispe.

I know she wants to see the Eiffel Tower. She hasn't asked about it. I know she's let me take the lead on showing her the city, defaulting to my expertise, but there's no way I can let her leave without seeing the view from it.

I have no desire to do it, but that shouldn't stop Chloe from experiencing it.

As we walk, Chloe talks about how much fun she had yesterday and how she still can't believe that we came to Paris for the weekend.

"Oh, I should grab something for Jules. She's going to freak out. And my family. Maybe an ornament? Or shirts? What do you think?"

"We'll hit the souvenir shop after."

"After what?" she asks.

I nod in the direction we're headed.

Chloe's eyes light up. "The Eiffel Tower?"

My answer is to take her hand and lead her to a small building on the side.

"Isn't the line over there?" she asks.

"I had Bea arrange this," I tell her after I check in with the security guard.

"You both going up?" he asks when he returns.

"No, just her," I say, dropping her hand so she can follow him to the entrance. "I'll wait here."

Chloe grabs my hand. I look from where our hands are joined up to her face.

"Come with me."

I want to share everything with her, but I can't do this. I shake my head. "I can't."

She lifts up on her toes and takes my face in her hands.

"Barrett, do you trust me?"

I hold onto her wrists.

"Of course. It's not about that."

"Isn't it? I got on a plane not knowing where I was going, because I knew if I was with you, it would be okay." She looks around. "And it's better than okay. I get it. You're scared, and you might freak out, but if you trust me then you know that you'll be okay because I'll be with you."

I look into Chloe's eyes and I know that I'm falling for her. Now I'm not sure if the fear twisting in my gut is from thinking about being nearly a thousand feet off the ground or fear that she doesn't feel the same way. And if she does, can we make this work? There's a reason I needed a fake girlfriend. Business has always come first.

I decide to not focus on the latter right now, and be in this moment with Chloe.

The confident look in her eyes is what does it for me.

"Okay," I say. Chloe jumps into my arms and presses her lips to mine. "You can return the favor later."

Her eyes go wide, then she presses her lips together, fighting a smile. "Looking forward to it."

The guard leads us to the east side entrance and we take a lift from the esplanade to the second floor. There we're greeted by another guard who is working the private lift that will take us to the top. Inside the lift, Chloe reaches for my hand. It's sweaty. Fear is oozing out of my pores now and I can feel the dizzying sensation with every inch this lift goes up.

The glass lift moves through the impressive architecture of the tower, giving a view of the intricate work of the inner side of the wrought iron structure. But with every inch we climb, my fear does, too. I close my eyes and focus on my breath. When I open them again, Chloe is there in front of me.

"I should have stayed down," I say, closing my eyes again. "You're missing it."

"I'm exactly where I want to be," she says. "Can you open your eyes and look at me?"

I open them again.

"Just focus on me. I know you can do this."

I take a deep breath and focus on Chloe's face. I start counting the freckles on her nose, and before I finish my tally, the lift stops at the observation deck.

"Enjoy," the lift operator says as we depart.

"Right." I swallow hard, but Chloe takes my hand and leads me to the platform.

"Wow," she says, taking in the view. I focus on her and once my breathing has normalized somewhat, I shift my gaze to the horizon. On one side is the city, building and roads, bridges crossing over the Seine, while on the back side is the Jardin du Champs de Mars where we danced last night.

I find that if I look out and not down, I can control my breathing and it's not as overwhelming.

While Chloe steps onto the clear platform, I keep a distance and take deep breaths. Again, her wonder and curiosity capture my full attention. In situations where my fear of heights is triggered, it helps to have something other than the fear to focus on. Right now, Chloe is that something for me.

She motions to a woman with her phone, asking if she'll take a photo of us. We stay for a few more minutes, then board the lift back down. This time, I keep my eyes open and focused on Chloe's smiling face. She stares back and squeezes my hand.

When we're safely on the ground, she wraps her arms around my neck and kisses me.

"You did it."

"Thank you." I kiss her again. "For being patient with me."

She pulls back, but I keep her body pressed to me.

"Well, you, sir, have earned a favor of your choosing." She wiggles her eyebrows. "Feel free to make it sexual."

I chuckle. Goofy Chloe is the sexiest. My dick immediately twitches against my zipper.

There's no way around it, I need Chloe.

My need is more than my body's physical response to hers pressed against mine. It's more than having someone to comfort me during a moment of stress.

I want to laugh with her and listen to how her day went.

I want impromptu lunch dates and to be each other's plus ones.

I want a wife and family of my own someday. Hell, I'm starting to think I want that dog she tricked me into fostering.

I want everything with Chloe, but I've never done this before. I've never had to balance running a company and being in a relationship. I want to put in the effort with Chloe. I just hope I don't screw it up.

CHAPTER 28

Chloe

I'm on my way back to Barrett's place after work when I get a call from the seamstress who is altering my dress for Lauren's wedding. There was a mix up and although I had asked them to switch the delivery address to Barrett's, it was accidentally delivered to my apartment.

I tell her it's no big deal and reroute the driver toward 116th Street. I haven't been to my apartment since I left nearly a month ago and it would be a good idea to check out the progress on the fix ups.

Outside the building I find a shiny new intercom system that allows residents to buzz guests in. And to my surprise, the door and handle have been changed also. I've got my key in my hand, but there's nowhere to insert it. I stand back to verify that I am at the correct address. It's only been a month but with all the sex Barrett and I are having, I might have orgasmed my old address right out of my brain.

It's the right address. What the hell has happened here?

I'm standing there wondering what to do when a familiar face opens the door from inside. It's my neighbor Todd and he's dressed for work in black scrubs and a backpack over his shoulders.

"Hey, Chloe, good to see you."

He holds the door open for me.

"You, too, Todd." I smile. He's a big burly guy with a reddish-brown beard and bald head.

"Are you moving back in?" he asks.

"Um, I was stopping by to pick something up." I can already see the garment bag hanging from a hook under the mailboxes. Someone must have let the delivery person in.

"Make sure you don't lose your key fob." He lifts his key ring to show me a small card hooked to one of the rings. "Fifty bucks for a replacement, so I would keep good tabs on it if I were you."

"Okay." I nod, noting to make sure I don't lose my key fob once I actually receive it. I'm wondering if it was sent to Barrett's place.

Todd departs and I take in the small entryway. It's freshly painted and has new hand railings on the stairs. There's also a heavy-duty all-weather rug and a plant in a yellow pot in the corner by the mailboxes. I throw the garment bag over my arm and head for the stairs.

Upstairs, the changes continue. New paint, floors refinished, updated light fixtures overhead. When I get to my apartment door, I have to check the number because the doors are all freshly painted and the tiny heart engraving below the peep hole isn't there anymore. The black doors are modern and nice, but I do miss seeing that heart engraving.

I look around again before using my apartment key that by some miracle still works. I thought my landlord was going to get rid of the mice, not redo the entire building. The key works, but the lock is firm now, no jiggling in a precise way required.

On the other side of the door, I find more changes. My

belongings are there, but they've been rearranged, likely due to the fact that the floors and wall paint are new in here, too. The brick wall looks less crumbly, I'm not sure what has been done to remedy that. The light fixture overhead is new...it has a ceiling fan now. The most startling change is the tiny window in the front isn't tiny anymore. It's large and takes up the upper half of the wall. It also seems quieter; did they add more insulation? Or maybe that's the result of a window that is properly sealed. There's no sign of Ralph, either.

I'm in shock. The place looks great. But more surprising is that according to Todd, it's been complete for weeks, yet I've heard nothing from my landlord or from Barrett.

I pull up her number and hit the call button.

"Hello?"

"Hi, this is Chloe Anderson in apartment 2B on 116th Street."

"Hi, Chloe. How are you? How is everything with the apartment?" She sounds eager to please.

"Good. I was wondering where my key fob was sent. I never got notice that the apartment was ready."

"Oh, I'm so sorry about that. I was certain I sent everything to you. I double checked multiple times."

"Okay. Can you verify where it was delivered?" I ask.

"Yes, let's see. It was delivered on July 10th to the temporary address on file."

"Was it signed for?" I ask, wondering if maybe it got lost in transit. I really don't want to pay fifty dollars for a new key fob.

"Yes, by B. St. Clair," she confirms. "Did you not receive it? I can send out another one free of charge. They normally cost fifty dollars, but I can make an exception this time."

"No," I tell her, "that's not necessary. I'm sure I'll be able to locate it."

I end the call and lock up my apartment. Garment bag in

hand, I start the walk toward the subway, and wonder the whole time why Barrett would keep this from me.

❦

I find Barrett in the kitchen. The sight of him, blue dress shirt with sleeves rolled up, his strong hands working the cork out of a bottle of wine, nearly knocks me over. Also, he's having what seems like an intense conversation with Baxter.

"I think we should tell her."

"Tell me what?" I ask.

Before I can inquire further, Barrett greets me with a passionate kiss and a moment later I'm on the kitchen counter, my legs wrapped around his waist. My hands are in his hair and his are working their way up my thighs, and underneath my skirt.

It's only when our intense make-out session knocks the garment bag off the stool that I remember my annoyance with him.

I push on his chest to get some space and hop off the counter to retrieve the now slumped over garment bag.

"What's in the bag?" he asks.

"My dress for Lauren's wedding."

"Ah. Lauren of the bachelorette party." His tone goes serious as he remembers why we're in this situation. A situation in which I'm not sure what's happening anymore. His deal with Fred will be signed next week and then what? There's been no discussion about what would happen after the deal closes now that we've been hooking up.

We're supposed to break up, but that was before I started falling for him.

"It was at my apartment," I say, then wait for his reaction. When his response is to reach for his glass and hand me the other, I continue. "Do you know what else I found there?"

"What?" He's the picture of innocence.

"A completely redone apartment." I flap my arms around, the incredulousness I felt earlier returning.

"You're upset about your apartment being updated?" he asks.

"No. It's not the new paint or the new light fixtures or the entryway plant or the fancy intercom system that I'm upset about."

"So, what's the problem?" He looks nonplussed and it only serves to frustrate me more.

"It's done!" I gesture wildly. "And I had no idea. That's the issue."

"Okay." His face is giving nothing away.

"My neighbor said everything was completed weeks ago. A key fob was sent to this address and signed for by you, yet I've never seen it. Can you explain that?"

Barrett's hand lifts to his forehead, his fingers rub back and forth there. Those long, firm fingers that gripped my tits this morning when he fucked me in the shower.

I can't let Barrett's fingers distract me. Or soften the irritation I feel that he's been keeping this from me.

"You're right. I signed for the package."

"And?" I prompt him to keep going.

"And I put it in my desk."

The image of Barrett spreading me wide on his desk comes to the forefront of my mind. *Focus, Chloe.*

I shake my head to dispel the image. Clearly Barrett's fingers and mouth and dick have made it hard to be annoyed with him.

"When were you going to tell me?" I ask.

He sets his wine glass down on the counter, and I do the same when he moves his hands to my hips and pulls me closer to him. My hands grip his forearms, the skin there is warm, the muscles beneath taut, both reminding me how nice it feels to be wrapped in his arms.

"Never." He says it so earnestly my nervous reflex is to laugh.

"You're kidding, right?"

His gaze is piercing, unwavering. But then his mouth breaks into a grin and he shrugs.

"Eventually. When the kids ask about your first place in the city and it reminds you that you used to live somewhere else."

"We have kids? If you're trying to not freak me out about living with you, talking about our future children isn't the way to go. You haven't even asked me to move in. We're not even a real couple. Are we? I mean things have obviously changed between us, but we haven't discussed anything official."

"I thought that was implied. You know, by not telling you your apartment is ready."

"I can't move in with you. It's too soon." It's too soon for a lot of things. Mostly the way I feel about him.

"You're already here."

"Only because Ralph skittered across the floor and freaked me out. Although he was kind of cute." I think about that little gray mouse and wonder where he is now. Hopefully relocated to a nice farm he can roam around. "I just didn't like the surprise of him being there. But that situation is resolved now."

"Is it? How do you know for sure?" Barrett asks, his eyebrows lifting with feigned skepticism.

I don't know what's happening right now. Barrett wants me to live here with him, yet he's said nothing to me about changing our previous arrangement. We're set to break up next week and he's talking about kids? What the hell is going on? Did I miss something? The confusion must be all over my face.

Barrett leans down and kisses me gently on the lips. A reassuring kiss.

"Chloe. I want you here with me. I want our arrangement to end and us to be together because we want to. Keep your apartment. It'll be there if you want it. But if you want to be here, I want you here. Sleeping in my arms. Waking up every morning together."

As Barrett says the words, I let out a shaky breath. More than moving in with him permanently, the reassurance that he wants to make our relationship real makes my stomach fluttery and my heart pound happily against my ribcage.

But that doesn't mean I'm not going to negotiate.

"Access to the study?"

"Unlimited."

"Rose would continue to stock the fridge with cookie dough ice cream?"

"Yes."

"I'd get half of your closet?"

He shakes his head.

"There's a second closet identical to mine."

I tap an index finger on my lips in consideration.

"How much tennis will I have to play?"

"Only when you want to, but the outfit is required bedroom attire."

"I was thinking I would take lessons. Frankie said there's an excellent tennis pro."

Barrett shakes his head. "I'll teach you."

I shrug. "Okay."

"Sex?" I question. As if it's going to be an issue. We can't keep our hands off each other.

"Lots." He backs me against the counter, his hands cupping my ass. "Are those your only demands?"

"I'm easy to please," I shrug, "ice cream and orgasms."

I wrap my hands around his neck and pull him to me. Our kiss turns me hot and needy in five seconds. My fingers are zoning in on Barrett's belt, but he reaches for his phone. Heck of a time for a work call.

I bite my lip, waiting as patiently as I can while he taps on his phone.

"Here," he says, turning the screen toward me. I recognize it as the security camera footage from JoAnna's apartment the night of Lauren's party. "Delete it."

My eyes lift from the phone to meet his.

"Go ahead." He hands me the phone.

I press the delete button on the screen and confirm it when it asks if I want to permanently delete the video. Barrett removes the phone from my hands and sets it aside.

His hands resume their position on my thighs, inching underneath my skirt. His lips trace along my jaw, the feath-erlight kisses making my clit throb.

"Now tell me you're mine because you want to be." His voice is low, a hoarse whisper that sends my pulse skyrocketing.

Without that video there's no evidence of the party. Barrett's telling me I could walk away, if that's what I want.

"Chloe?" I hear the vulnerability in his voice. The uncer-tainty that comes with showing your cards and waiting for the other person to do the same.

I don't want to be anywhere but here. With him.

"I'm yours," I whisper.

Barrett's lips part in a sexy smile before his hands move to my cheeks and he kisses me breathless.

I press into him, letting my hands wreak havoc on his perfect hair. He pulls away again and I nearly let out a frus-trated groan.

"Hold on. Is there something you'd like to ask me?"

"Can we have sex now?" I ask.

Baxter barks to get Barrett's attention. He puts the ball in Barrett's hand and leans back on his hind legs, ready for the next toss.

"No."

He tosses the ball and Baxter goes racing out of the kitchen to retrieve it.

"No to sex or no that's not it?"

"Chloe." He shakes his head, but he's grinning at me.

I wrack my brain. I really thought it was the sex thing. Barrett leans down to pick my bridesmaid dress up off the floor.

"Oh! Do you want to be my date to Lauren's wedding?" I ask. "As my non-fake boyfriend?"

"Yes." He punctuates his answer with a kiss, then he scoops me up off the counter and carries me to the dining room. I guess sex is back on the table. Literally.

CHAPTER 29

Barrett

"Everything looks good," Chloe says, turning over her menu. "How am I going to decide?"

"Who says we have to? Let's get it all," I say.

My phone buzzes in my pocket with an incoming call. I reach in to silence it, not bothering to check who's calling.

We're tucked into a booth at the back of a trendy brunch spot in Tribeca across from the independent bookstore we stopped in earlier. The large bag of books we purchased nestled next to Chloe on the booth bench.

"That would be crazy. But I guess we already had sex this morning, so it doesn't matter how full I get."

"You realize that means nothing. After watching you devour a plate of blueberry lemon ricotta pancakes with powdered sugar on top, I'm going to want to fuck you again."

Chloe's eyes widen.

"Barrett," she whisper-hisses while squirming in her seat. "You can't say stuff like that in public."

I shrug. "You mean I shouldn't say that I want to fuck you all the time?" I place my hand over hers on the table and rub my thumb over her knuckles. "Don't worry. If you're too full for sex, I'll gladly spend an hour with my head buried between your thighs."

"You're ridiculous." She shakes her head.

My phone starts buzzing again.

"Do you need to answer that?" Chloe nods toward the buzzing sound.

"No. It's fine."

"Barrett. You can answer the phone. It might be an emergency."

"I don't want to answer the phone." But, when I take it out of my pocket and see Carl's name on the screen, I give in.

"What?" It's not the most welcoming answer because I'm not in the most welcoming mood. This is the second weekend that I've spent Sundays with Chloe, no work, no interruptions, and I want to keep it that way.

"Hey, man. Where are you?" he says.

"Getting brunch with Chloe. What do you need?"

"I'm in the office. I thought we'd be going over the final contracts today."

"No. That's what Monday is for."

"Really? That's never how you've wanted to handle a deal like this before."

"That was before." I glance over at Chloe studying the menu with deep concentration. I don't know why she's bothering; I was serious about getting everything. I was also serious about eating her for dessert.

"So, do you want me to go over it and mark notes for our meeting tomorrow?"

"No, I want you to leave the office now and do something with your Sunday other than work."

Carl sighs.

"This is a big fucking deal, Barrett. I didn't want to say

anything, but it feels like the last few weeks your head hasn't been in the game. Until these papers are signed, Fred can walk."

"He's not going to. There's no reason for him to." I say it with confidence, though I know Carl is right, there's always a chance something could change his mind.

"Fine. I'll see you at seven tomorrow," Carl says.

"I'll be in late. Make it nine."

"Wait, are you serious?"

"Goodbye, Carl." I end the call and turn my phone on silent.

"Everything okay?" Chloe asks.

"You bet."

The waitress walks over to take our order.

"We'll take one of everything."

"Excuse me?" She looks panicked.

"He's kidding."

"No, I'm not. She can't decide, so we're going to try everything."

"That's a waste of food. We won't be able to eat it all," Chloe argues.

"Fine. We'll take one of each from every section. Chef's recommendation."

The waitress looks between us and smiles, then jots it down on her notepad. "Sure thing." She gathers the menus and leaves.

"What do you have going on this wee—" I begin, but Chloe's attention is on the front windows of the restaurant, her eyes narrowing as she stares intently.

"Oh my God. Is that Frankie?"

I turn around to follow Chloe's stare.

Outside the window, on the sidewalk, is a woman in a tight mini dress and heels with a man's arms wrapped around her waist while they both lean over the menu posted by the door. It is Frankie. And Vance from the club.

Fuck.

I turn my attention back to Chloe, but her eyes are still on Frankie and her sidepiece.

Our booth is quiet as she takes in the scene behind me.

"That is definitely Frankie! Oh my God, Barrett! They're making out. She's cheating on Fred." Chloe's eyes widen, her nostrils flaring in outrage. "Can you believe this?"

I struggle to find the words. "It's awful. I feel for the guy. He adores Frankie," I say.

"You're going to tell him, right?" Chloe asks.

"What?"

"That you saw Frankie kissing another guy. You have to tell Fred."

I lean into the backrest of the booth. I've seen them doing way more than kissing.

Chloe shifts her gaze back to me. It's clear the moment that she realizes I'm not as surprised by this discovery as she is.

"Wait. Did you already know this?" she asks.

While not telling Chloe that I saw Frankie and Vance together was an omission, I can't outright lie to her face.

"Yes. I saw them together. At the club. A few weeks ago. He's a tennis pro there."

"What?! Why didn't you tell me?"

I pause, wondering what the issue is. "Why would you need to know?"

That question doesn't go over well.

"Um, because their relationship is the reason we've been fake dating."

"That was before. We're together now."

"Are we? Because this seems like information that you would share with someone you're dating."

"It doesn't affect you. Or us," I argue.

"It doesn't affect me? What if Frankie calls and wants to hang out? What if we see them out at an event? Am I supposed to pretend that I don't know what is going on?" Chloe shakes her head. "You have to tell Fred."

"No. I can't tell Fred. There's too much at stake."

Chloe laughs humorously. "Your deal? That's why you haven't said anything?"

"I'll tell him. After we've signed."

Chloe gapes at me, the color in her cheeks darkening. "You're going to let Fred sign away his company to you, a man he trusts, and *then* tell him you knew his girlfriend is cheating on him?"

I take a sip of coffee, trying to get a handle on the situation. I have to make Chloe understand how this could fuck up everything I've been working for. How important this deal is for me. Carl is right. The deal isn't done until it's signed. If I tell Fred about Frankie, there's no telling how he will react.

Chloe thinks we would be doing him a favor, but Fred is content with Frankie. The whole thing could blow up in my face. Blow up the deal I've been working months to secure.

"I've been busting my ass to make this deal happen. I'm not going to throw it away because Fred's girlfriend is using him. It's not personal—"

"It's business. Right. Of course, this makes perfect sense."

"What do you mean by that?" My jaw clenches.

"I guess I forgot who I was dealing with. I forgot you were the man who blackmailed me into this entire charade. That you'll do anything to get what you want."

"You weren't complaining when I fucked you in the shower this morning." I let my emotions get the best of me and I can see the hurt on Chloe's face. I lean closer, reaching for her hand. "Shit. I didn't mean— Can we—"

"I know exactly what you meant. I was a part of this with you, deceiving Fred and Frankie by letting them think we were together so you could close a deal. I guess the joke's on me, because I was starting to think you weren't the cold, calculating businessman I once thought you were."

"And you're perfect? Need I remind you that you're here because you didn't want to tell my mother about the party at her apartment to save your job. Isn't that the same thing? Withholding the truth to get what you want?"

"Not at the expense of people's feelings!"

We stare at each other, neither of us willing to budge.

"Barrett. You have to tell him," she says, her voice barely above a whisper.

"I can't do it. I've worked too hard to get to this point. Voltaire is the final deal that will put SCM at the top. Where it was when my father was CEO. It's all I've been working for. You have to understand that."

"I don't think your father was the type of man who would want you to get it this way."

"You don't know what type of man my father was," I counter. I barely knew the man, but I'm certain he wouldn't have let his emotions get in the way of a business deal.

"I guess I don't know you, either." She stands and gathers her things.

Panic rises in me. I don't want her to leave like this.

"Chloe." I grab her hand as she moves past me. "Please. This isn't about us. I need you to see that."

She turns to look down at me, her blue eyes glassy, lined with unshed tears.

"It's about your priorities, Barrett. And I can't be with someone who doesn't understand that."

She pulls away and I let her go. I've made an effort to change my lifestyle for this relationship, but I'm not going to budge on this. I need her to understand that this isn't negotiable. I will move forward with the Voltaire Telecom deal.

The waitress appears with a large tray full of food. "I hope you're hungry."

I've lost my appetite and deep in the pit of my stomach I know I've lost Chloe.

CHAPTER 30

Chloe

Everything around me blurs as I quickly make my way down the street. It's the same warm, beautiful Sunday it was when I went in the restaurant with Barrett, but everything has changed.

The faster I walk, the harder it is to keep the tears at bay. I swipe at my cheek while turning a corner and end up nearly running into a woman.

While I'd had my suspicions about Frankie's intentions with Fred, seeing Frankie with another guy was a complete shock. But nothing could have been more surprising than Barrett's reaction to the situation. The fact that he already knew, and had no plans to tell Fred is unbelievable.

How could Barrett value the acquisition deal with Voltaire over Fred's feelings? It makes me think I don't know him at all.

My mind is a jumbled mess of thoughts so I keep walking, trying to make sense of what just happened. I end up walking the two miles to my apartment.

Inside, I collapse onto my bed. The fresh paint smell still hangs in the air. I haven't been back here since the day I picked my bridesmaid dress up and discovered the apartment building had been redone. Another thing Barrett chose to keep from me.

I lie there and cry until my head hurts. Until my eyes can't produce any more tears and the searing pain in my chest has become a dull ache. I fall asleep, hoping that eventually I'll wake up from this bad dream.

The next morning, my eyes are red and puffy and no amount of coffee can keep them open. I call JoAnna to tell her I'm not feeling well. I doubt that Barrett would have told her what happened between us. He'll want to keep everything quiet until his deal is signed.

I text Rose about packing up my things. She responds right away and with no questions asked, has Marcus deliver my personal items from Barrett's place in an hour. I'm grateful because while I don't mind wallowing in self-pity right now, I'd like to do that with breath that isn't repugnant. Also, my tears have been replenished and I can't stop crying long enough to leave my apartment to purchase a new toothbrush.

At some point the tears have to stop, right? I'm praying for dehydration.

Barrett calls and I let it go to voicemail. I stop myself from listening to his message.

I can't hear the sound of his voice or I'll start crying again. Start asking myself how I fell so hard for a man that doesn't believe people are more important than adding more money to his company's portfolio.

I force myself to go to work on Tuesday. I have to tell JoAnna about Lauren's party. My fake relationship with Barrett. Everything. It won't make what I've done right, but at least she'll have all the facts and can decide for herself.

I know I'm potentially blowing up my career, but I realize

I'll always be worried that she could find out. If I'm going to advance in my career, I want to do it with a clear conscience.

JoAnna knows there's something wrong the moment she sees me in the doorway to her office.

"Chloe, come in. Are you okay?"

"Um." I falter with how to start the conversation.

"If you're still not feeling well, you should've stayed home."

Maybe I could take the easy way out? Buy myself another day? It's tempting, but I know I need to clear this up.

I take a breath and tell her everything. The party. The arrangement with Barrett. How I developed real feelings for him and how we were dating for real until Sunday when we broke up. I think we broke up. I'm a thousand percent certain that the ache in my chest is from a broken heart.

JoAnna pats my hand, a kind smile on her face. "I know."

"What do you mean?" I ask.

"Not about the party, but now it makes sense. I thought it was interesting that you and Barrett were dating out of the blue and the kiss you shared the morning you told me—if I've ever seen a first kiss, that's what one looks like. Hesitant. Unsure. Captivated. I wasn't sure what was going on between you two but I wanted it to play out. Honestly, I liked the idea of you two together. I still do."

"Sorry to disappoint you."

"You did the right thing taking a stand for what is right. Barrett is a hard man to stand up to. Like his father before him, he's got great ambition and sometimes—most times—he can't see past it. But I know he was different with you. He wants to be different."

I nod. It's all I can do. Talking about Barrett sends a fresh wave of emotion over me. The tears are threatening again.

"I'm so sorry about the party. I was afraid to tell you. I didn't plan it. I needed a place for my friend's party when I failed to confirm my reservation at Le Pavillon and they gave the booking to another group. Then you called and asked me to go to your apartment to bring up the misdelivered books and I just stayed. I didn't think you would find out. I know that sounds bad. I love my job. I love that you've given me the opportunity take on Lacey's assistant editor position so early in my career. I want to be an assistant editor. I know I've got more to prove. I just hope I haven't screwed up my chance to do that here at St. Clair Press."

JoAnna leans back in her chair, her gaze unreadable. It reminds me of Barrett's. I have to hold in a hiccup.

"You're right. You have much more to prove here," she says pursing her lips. "So don't let this happen again."

I slowly let out the breath that my lungs were holding onto.

"Definitely not." I shake my head.

"Good." She nods, and I stand.

I'm about to exit her office when she calls out.

"And Chloe? I know it's between the two of you, but don't give up on him. I know he loves you. He just needs time to figure out what's important."

I nod, biting my lip so I don't cry. I want that to be true, but Barrett told me from the beginning that his business is the most important thing. I should have known that when it came down to it, he would make this choice. But it doesn't make it hurt any less.

On my lunch break I call the Goldendoodle Foster Program to check on what to do about Baxter. I can't keep him at my apartment and while I think Barrett was starting to tolerate him, I doubt he wants to keep him permanently.

The receptionist informs me that Jillian is not available, but she's happy to look into Baxter's file for information.

"It shows here that he's been adopted."

"When? To whom?" I ask.

"I'm not allowed to disclose that information."

"It's been one day," I say, shocked that in my absence Barrett would get rid of Baxter that quickly.

"But here at the Goldendoodle Foster Program we're always happy when our animals find their forever home."

She's right. I should be happy that Baxter has been adopted. For obvious reasons, I couldn't keep him, but it breaks my heart that I didn't get to say goodbye.

"Okay. Thanks."

"You have a wonderful day now," she says cheerily. The moment I end the call, I burst into tears.

The next few days pass in a blur. I work, I go home, eat ice cream for dinner and cry. On Thursday morning, I wake up with resolve. I cannot be a blubbering mess at Lauren's wedding. I have to put my heartbreak on pause, if only for a few days. I pack my suitcase, grab the garment bag with my bridesmaid dress in it and vow to not think about Barrett all weekend.

CHAPTER 31

Barrett

I stare at the piece of paper. Chloe's list.

1. Barrett attends Books 4 Kids event
2. Chloe gets to use Barrett's study for reading
3. No phones at the dinner table (ahem, Barrett)
4. Foster Baxter
5. Barrett smile more (at me)
6. BJ for Barrett

It reminds me of the last six weeks with her. The frustration, the fights, the understanding, and the way she finally trusted me with her body and her heart. And I fucked it all up.

Half the items on this list are about me. She could have asked for anything, but she asked that I smile more. At her.

"Mr. Hinkle and Mr. Lancaster are here," Bea notifies me over the intercom.

"I'll be right there," I say. I push my hands through my hair, then slowly stand. I move toward my office door. I purposely divert my gaze away from the sofa. I spent half of yesterday staring at it, thinking of Chloe's impromptu visit a few weeks ago. Remembering her there makes my body ache.

I miss her touch, her taste. The adorable way she rambles about nothing, her never ending books to be read stacked up on my bedside table. The way she looks incredible in both a baggy t-shirt or a sexy silk nightie.

I've tried to call her but she doesn't answer. I hate not knowing if she's okay. Of course, she's not okay. I broke her heart.

I've spent five nights in my bed alone and every moment has been agony. I need her pressed up against me, her wild hair tickling my face. Her soft breathing had become the sound-track to my most restful night's sleep.

Carl must have been notified already. He's approaching my office as I exit.

"Let's get this deal done," he says, holding out his fist to me. I blank stare and he eventually drops his arm. "You still in a shitty mood?"

"What do you think?" I level him with a glare.

I was supposed to be in Vail with Chloe, her friend's wedding is tonight. I had thought about showing up to surprise her, hoping she'd forgive me, but when the closing with Voltaire got moved to today, I had Bea cancel my ticket. She doesn't want me there anyway.

We walk down the hallway to the conference room where the Voltaire group is waiting for us. Fred's shiny bald head peeks over the top of one of the leather chairs at the table.

I've felt nauseous all morning. I've never felt this way before closing a deal. The usual rush of excitement and thrill of victory is nonexistent.

Carl and I enter the room and shake hands with the Voltaire group. Fred's meaty hand palms my shoulder when he tells the others about how he beat me at tennis two days ago. My smile is forced, not because I give a fuck about our tennis match, but because in this moment I don't give a fuck about anything. Except Chloe.

While Carl talks to Fred's legal team, and verifies that the independent notary has everything she needs for the signing, Fred motions me over to the side of the room.

"I've got to show you what I picked up at the jeweler's earlier."

Fred pulls out a small velvet box from inside his suit coat pocket. My heart lurches in my chest and I plead for there to be a set of earrings inside that box. When Fred opens it, the nausea I felt earlier returns, tenfold.

Inside Fred's box is a huge diamond ring.

"Fred, I—" I can't believe he is planning to propose to Frankie.

"I'm ready for the next chapter of my life," Fred says. "I'm going to ask Frankie to marry me tonight. It has been fun getting to know you and Chloe, so I wanted to share the news with you."

"Isn't it a bit early for that?"

Fred shrugs. "I have no doubt that she'll say yes."

Fred's right. There's no doubt Frankie will say yes. This is clearly what she wants, to marry Fred, gain access to his money and have an affair on the side. Fuck.

"No, I mean in your relationship," I say.

"When you know, you know."

Except Fred doesn't know anything. He doesn't know that Frankie is cheating on him and therefore likely using him for his money and status. Fred is too territorial about Frankie for him to know about her disloyalty and not care.

"Just tell me you're happy for me and we'll get this deal done."

I clear my throat. "I'm happy for you, Fred."

Fred must take my struggle to congratulate him as jealousy.

ERIN HAWKINS

"It's not a competition. You'll get there with Chloe soon enough."

He has no idea that Chloe left me.

We take a seat and Carl starts to go over the documents. I don't hear a single word he's saying. All I can think about is Chloe. Our time together and what I'd started to envision for our future.

What I've been working for, this deal with Voltaire, means nothing without her.

SCM is at the top. I've refused to acknowledge that I've already reached the goal I set when I took over the company seven years ago because I was too afraid of what to do next. What would my life look like without another deal to chase after, another business victory under my belt? Chloe changed that. For the first time since I took over SCM, I had a vision for myself that didn't involve working eighty hours a week, dinners alone and an empty home.

Chloe was right. People mean more than business and if I would have realized that before, I would never have put this deal with Fred and Voltaire ahead of my relationship with her. I would have had the decency to meet with Fred and tell him what I saw weeks ago. It wouldn't have mattered what the outcome was, because I would have known that I was doing the right thing. It took losing Chloe to understand that.

Carl points to where the 'sign here' flag is placed by the line for Fred to sign. Fred picks up the pen and leans forward, pressing the tip to the paper.

"Wait."

Carl, Fred, and everyone else turns toward me.

"Fred, I have to talk to you."

Fred rests the pen on the table.

"Not here. Outside." I motion for us to leave the room.

"What are you doing, Barrett?" Carl grabs my arm before I can follow Fred out of the conference room. "Can this wait?"

"No." I shake my head and shrug him off.

I indicate for Fred to follow me back to my office, then shut the door behind us.

"What's this about?" Fred shoves his hands in his pant pockets. "We're good to go. I'm ready to sign."

"Frankie is cheating on you," I say.

"What?" His face drops into a somber expression.

"I saw her a few weeks ago with another man."

"It was probably her assistant. They're together all the time."

"They were kissing." I shake my head. "Chloe and I saw them again last weekend. We were eating brunch at Harold's and they were on the sidewalk holding hands. We saw them kiss. You can ask Chloe. She was there."

"No. That's not right. Frankie was out of town visiting her mom."

"I saw what I saw Fred. I wanted you to know." I take a breath, knowing if I want to make this right, I have to come clean about everything. "And Chloe and I were not dating."

"What?" Fred's eyes bulge with anger.

"I told you I had a girlfriend to build a relationship with you so I could negotiate this deal. I'm not proud of it. I did it because I was desperate to close the deal, but I did fall in love with Chloe in the process. She wanted me to tell you about Frankie and I wouldn't. I wanted this deal more than I cared about your feelings or hers.

"I was wrong. I'm sorry I abused your trust and misled you and Frankie about Chloe and me. I'm sure it's hard to believe me now, but I do have the best intentions by telling you about Frankie."

My chest is a million pounds lighter, but my heart still aches. I need to find Chloe. I need to tell her I was wrong and beg her to forgive me.

Fred is silent for a moment, then he starts shaking his head.

"I hope Chloe forgives you because there's no way in hell I'm signing those papers now."

I nod. That was expected.

Fred storms out of my office and down the hallway.

I don't waste any time striding out to Bea's desk.

"I need a plane to Vail. Can you get my flight back on the books?"

She smiles. "I didn't bother to cancel the first one."

I glance at my watch. If I can leave in the next hour, I might be able to make it to the reception.

Carl appears a moment later. "What the fuck, man? Fred just stormed out of the signing. He was not happy. What did you say to him?"

"The truth."

He follows me back into my office where I'm hurriedly collecting my wallet and phone.

"Which is?"

"I found out Frankie was cheating on him."

"Shit." Carl rubs his hand along his jaw. "I want to be surprised, but I'm not."

"Chloe found out that Frankie was cheating and when I refused to tell Fred, she walked."

"That's why you've been cranky as fuck this week. I had no idea you two broke up."

"I've fucked this whole thing up, but my head's on straight now. No deal is worth losing Chloe. I have to get her back."

"Fuck yeah." Carl pumps his fist in the air. "Um, how are you going to do that?"

"I don't know, but I've got a long plane ride to think about it."

I don't bother packing a suitcase, I'll worry about clothes when I get there. But I do stop by my place to grab Baxter.

He's sleeping in his dog bed in my study, so I pick the whole thing up and load it into the car.

"We're going on a trip," I tell him. I'm that guy who talks to his dog now. "We're getting Chloe back."

I know honesty is the best policy, but I'm thinking reinforcements never hurt. I'm hoping Baxter's cuddly, lovable face will help persuade Chloe to give me another chance.

After a six-hour flight, Baxter and I land at Eagle-Vail airport. A forty-minute drive takes us to Lionshead Village at the base of Vail. The two whiskeys I had to get me through the plane ride have worn off, leaving me with a dull ache in my head. Baxter nudges at my hand.

"Don't worry, buddy. We'll get her back." I'm staying strong for Baxter. I have no idea what Chloe will say when she sees us.

My late flight time means I've missed most if not all of the ceremony.

I guide Baxter as I follow the signs indicating Lauren and Jeff's wedding until they lead me to the base of the mountain.

"I need to get to Lauren and Jeff's wedding," I tell the guy leaning against the small operation booth.

"You're in the right place." He nods.

"Great. Where is it?" I ask.

He points his finger upwards. "Up top."

For the first time I look up at the mountainside in front of me. It's late July, so the only snow visible is at the top peak. The rest of the mountain is covered in grass and rocks. The ski runs can only be defined by the pine trees gathered on each side of the trail. There's a dirt path that mountain bikers are currently traversing down.

"What?" I pull my attention from the mountain to look back at the man.

"That's where the best views are."

Of course, they are.

"How am I supposed to get there?"

He motions behind me. "Chair lift will take you."

I watch the chairs swing from the belt as they move up the mountain. There's no window to shut. Only open air and a thirty-foot drop. My stomach immediately twists, and my palms start to sweat. I can feel the fear taking over. I shake my head. No fucking way.

Beside me, Baxter watches the chairs moving, his tail wagging with excitement. I can tell he's dying to go for a ride.

"They're coming down, right?" I ask. I can always wait to talk to Chloe after the ceremony.

He looks at his clipboard. "Reception goes until eleven thirty."

I glance at my watch. It's seven. Fucking hell. I'm going to have to ride this chair lift if I want to see Chloe. Or wait four hours.

I watch a young family board the lift. Surely those parents wouldn't be taking their children on that if it were a death trap. The logic is there, but where heights are concerned, my brain doesn't do logic.

I think of Chloe at the Eiffel Tower. How she encouraged me to face the fear. She held my hand and helped me focus on my breathing. I felt like I could do it when she was with me. But now she's at the top of this mountain and I don't even know if she'll see me if I happen to make it up there.

Baxter licks my hand, then moves toward the lift. Without hesitation, he jumps on the chair that is swinging around. The lift operator presses the button to halt the chair's progress.

"Dude, are you getting on?" he calls. "Your dog can't ride alone."

Trying to steady my shaking hands, I ball them into fists and take a breath.

I want to see Chloe. I need to see Chloe. I have to get on this lift.

That's my mantra right now.

Baxter barks.

"Yeah, yeah. I'm coming."

The entire ride up, I'm sweating. I want to puke but I keep my gaze up. Baxter is sitting calmly beside me and I am unreasonably mad at him. How can he be so calm so high up?

I hold onto Baxter with one hand but my grip is still firmly on the chair lift.

"Sir, you're going to need to put the bar up," the attendant says to me as we get closer. My legs are shaky and I'm not even standing yet.

"I know," I say a bit breathless.

Another beat passes. My eyes are closed tight.

"Sir? The chair lift is going to go around."

I can't do it. I'm willing my hands to move to lift up the bar but I can't. There are alarms going off now and I'm not sure if it's in my head or really happening.

The sounds are still going as I realize we've stopped. The attendant is pulling the bar from my hands and there's a group of people ahead staring at me. I stand but stumble back a bit before putting Baxter on the ground. I move out of the way just enough for the chair lift to continue and I lean over, trying to take deep breaths. I need my heart rate to slow down.

"Barrett?" I hear Chloe behind me. I want to be excited to see her, but my vision hasn't returned yet. "Oh my God, are you okay?" I hear her rushing toward me.

I open my eyes and find her there, kneeling in front of me in a lavender dress. Her red hair is pinned back with a few loose strands framing her face. Her blue eyes wide with concern. It seems impossible that she looks more beautiful than the last time I saw her.

"Oh my God! Baxter!!" She laughs as he runs and jumps into her arms, no longer in fear of the alarm I set off. I watch as Chloe massages his ears and rubs her face against his. I was counting on him to help me, not steal the show. "How did you get him back?"

"He never left," I say, my breathing finally evening out.

Her brows crease with confusion. "He was adopted. I called the foster program."

"I adopted him." I clear my throat. "I mean, we adopted him."

With a final pat to Baxter's head, Chloe stands.

My hands move to her cheeks. I pull her closer, my forehead presses to hers. Damn. It feels so good to touch her again.

"We were taking pictures. The bridal party. And we heard the lift alarm and I saw you."

Her hands wrap around my wrists. Initially, I think it's so she can touch me, too, but she pulls my hands away from her face and steps back.

"I'm glad you're okay, but I can't do this."

Seeing her. Feeling her. I'd forgotten what I wanted to tell her.

"Chloe, wait." I reach for her hand. "I need to explain. I'm sorry. I messed up. With you. With us."

She pulls her hand away and crosses her arms against her chest, but she doesn't make a move to leave. Hope blooms inside my chest. As long as she's willing to listen, I know I can make it right between us. I have to. I love this woman so much; I don't know what I'll do if she walks away again.

I step forward, needing to be closer to her.

"I told Fred about Frankie," I say.

Chloe's eyes lift to mine.

"What did he say?"

"That I was wrong. He didn't want to believe it."

Chloe nods. "Sometimes you don't want to believe the worst about the person you love."

Her statement hurts. I know she's talking about me. But she also said that she loves me. I hope it's still true.

"He called off the deal."

Chloe's deep inhale is audible.

"I thought he'd understand." She bites her lip. "Appreciate your honesty."

I know she thinks I'm devastated about the deal falling through. I shake my head.

"I don't care about the deal, Chloe. I care about you." I slide my hand around to her lower back and pull her in close to me. "Yes, the deal was my sole focus. I was determined to convince Fred that I was the man he should sell his company to. I was so determined that I didn't care that I was using you to get what I wanted. I know I should regret forcing you into a fake relationship, but I can't. Just being near you makes me a better man. You made me realize I was missing out on life. I've fallen for you, Chloe. Hard. I love you and I need you to forgive me for being an ass. For risking what we have for a business deal."

A tear falls down Chloe's cheek, but I'm quick to wipe it away.

"Don't cry."

"They're happy tears." She smiles, then laughs. "I can't believe you adopted Baxter."

I smile down at her before running a hand through my hair. "You heard the other stuff, too, right?"

"Hmm?" Her brows rise and her lips quirk to one side. She's messing with me.

My hands grip her waist, pulling her in closer.

"Please forgive me, Chloe. I messed up, but I want you to

be mine. No, I need you to say you're mine. Because I am yours with no ulterior motives. I love you, Chloe."

"I forgive you." Chloe's face breaks out into a huge smile. "And I love you, too."

I lower my lips to hers and do what I've been dying to do since I made it to the top of this mountain. Her lips are soft and warm. She opens up to me and I'm quickly lost in the feel of her. My hands grip her waist, lifting her up to me. Her arms wrap around my neck and I deepen the kiss.

I want to stay here in this moment with her, but I have another confession to make.

This is a fresh start and I need to be honest with Chloe.

I pull back, my thumb tracing over her lips where mine used to be.

"There's something I need to confess."

She sniffs. "What is it?"

"I cheated."

CHAPTER 32

Chloe

"What?!" My heart drops out of my chest. I can't believe what Barrett is telling me.

His eyes widen. "Oh, shit. No. Not like *that*. I cheated at WordIt."

It takes me a moment to let his words sink in, but when my body has recovered from the emotional rollercoaster ride it just took, I find my gaze narrowing at Barrett.

"I knew it." I point a finger at him. I want to be annoyed at his confession, but I'm curious more than anything. "How did you do it?"

"I bought WordIt."

That's not what I was expecting him to say.

"What? When?" I ask, confused.

"After that day in the car."

"The first day we rode to work together? When I told you about it?"

"Yeah."

Color has returned to his once ashen face, and then some.

"I don't understand."

"SCM purchased the app from the original creator. When

319

we played the game, I knew what the words were." He smiles wickedly. "I even picked one of them out."

"Why would you do that?" I ask.

Barrett smirks. "Why do you think?"

"I am so mad at you right now." My hands push at his chest, but he continues to hold me close. "You made me think I was losing. I was so frustrated I couldn't win. That you were better at WordIt than me. And I couldn't touch you."

I can't believe he bought the app.

"How much?" I ask. Deciding now when Barrett is groveling is the time to get all the facts.

"How much what?"

"Did the app cost?"

He sighs, looking sheepish again. Not something I'm used to on Barrett. "Two million dollars."

"You paid two million dollars so you could win WordIt and go down on me?"

"I didn't buy it with that intention, but it did come in handy."

"That is not good business sense."

"I think it makes perfect sense." Barrett's lips lower to my ear. "Tasting you, knowing your sweet pussy was mine, was worth every penny."

Later, when the bridal party is finished taking photos and dinner has been served and Barrett has charmed my mom and dad, I pull him out onto the dance floor.

"Your parents are great," he says.

I turn to find Baxter in my dad's lap as he talks with my mom and other guests at their table. While no dog is completely hypoallergenic, Baxter doesn't seem to bother my mom's allergies.

I smile. Barrett holds me to him as we move to the slow, romantic ballad. I know we reconciled outside but there's still more I need to say to him.

"I told your mom about the party. And about us," I say.

"What did she say?"

"To never host a party at her apartment without her permission again."

"Understandable." He brushes a loose hair from my cheek. "And about us?"

"She was on to us from the start, but she liked the idea so much she didn't say anything."

"Smart woman." He grins.

"I want to make sure we're on the same page with this fresh start."

"Okay." He nods for me to continue.

"If we're going to work, I need you to stop keeping things from me. You not telling me about Frankie to protect your deal is one thing, but not telling me about my apartment being finished and buying WordIt and adopting Baxter...I like surprises but not when they involve major decisions in my life. I want to be involved in those."

He takes a moment to answer, which makes me feel like he's really considering it.

"I get it and I can do that. But I know at some point I'll probably screw up again, it's inevitable, and I need you to stay and work through it with me. Deal?"

"Deal," I say.

Barrett lifts me up in his arms for a kiss that takes my breath away and the rest of the night is pure magic.

The next morning, Barrett's deep inside me when his phone starts ringing on the bedside table.

"Your phone is ringing." I gasp when he hits just the right spot.

"Don't give a fuck," he says, one hand palming my ass to

leverage his thrusts while the heel of his other hand presses into my lower abdomen, creating the most delicious pressure. His gaze is between my thighs, where we're joined. His brow is furrowed with concentration, a bead of sweat slides from his hairline down his temple. I'll never get over how gorgeous he is. The way his top lip curls up when he's really focused on something. That something being my orgasm right now.

Finally, the ringing stops and I can focus on the way Barrett's thumb is now circling my clit.

"You look so beautiful taking my cock." His words are dirty, but his eyes are reverent when they meet mine. "Come with me, Chloe." He grips my ass, changing the angle and this time when he slides in, I shatter around him.

"Oh God. Yes." I sigh as I pulse around him, milking his cock. The intensity of my orgasm sends Barrett over the edge. He shudders and I feel him pulse inside me.

A moment later he collapses on top of me, peppering me with kisses before rolling so I'm on top of him.

"Any bridesmaid duties today?" he asks, stroking my back with his fingertips.

"There's a brunch and then the rest of the weekend is ours to explore." I bite my lip, trying to hide my smile. "We could ride the Alpine Coaster."

His brows lift in disbelief. "That death trap on wheels I saw on the side of the mountain yesterday?"

I laugh as he flips me over and pins my hands above my head.

"You're trouble."

"You love me."

"I do." He kisses my nose before pressing his lips to mine.

Six weeks ago, I couldn't have dreamed up this scenario. I didn't want to be Barrett's fake girlfriend, but somewhere between the biting words and the heated glares, I fell for him. Now, I couldn't imagine not being his real girlfriend.

I'm in love with Barrett, I'm making strides at work to become an assistant editor and we have a dog, who if we're not careful my dad might try to dognap. And to top it all off, today's WordIt was HAPPY. With SCM's ownership of WordIt coming to light, I realize that might have been arranged by Barrett but the feeling is the same. We're happy, and that's all that matters.

Epilogue

FOUR MONTHS LATER

CHLOE

Snow falls in big flakes around me and a sweater-clad Baxter as we walk down the street. Barrett had questioned the sweater I put on him this morning, but now I'm glad he's got protection from the elements. Baxter knows when we're close to home, because he's familiar with our route, but it could also be because it's currently lit up like the Empire State Building.

The vision I'd had for decorating Barrett's—ours now—brownstone windows with lit up wreaths for the holidays has been executed. We spent the weekend before Thanksgiving hanging them. Barrett didn't understand why we couldn't hire someone to do it and I had to explain to him that it was half the fun to do it yourself. He finally got into the spirit and I rewarded him with a stellar blow job, our newly lit Christmas tree twinkling in the background.

The large main floor window contains the nine-foot Douglas Fir covered in enough lights to be a fire hazard. It looks perfectly magical.

I should be used to the sight by now, the Christmas decorations have been up since before Thanksgiving. Since the weekend before we flew back to Colorado to celebrate the holiday with my family. My parents had met Barrett at Lauren's wedding, and they've been a fan of his since the beginning, but it was fun to see him with my siblings. I think not taking work and himself so seriously has given him the capacity to open up to people more easily. He fit right in with my family. Helping my mom prepare dinner. Throwing a football around with my brothers and dad while I ogled him from the sidelines. Talking with Lila about the business classes she's taking this semester. She seemed to care less about Barrett's take on business strategy and ethics than she did having his attention on her. When he wasn't looking, she started fanning herself.

Inside, I hang up the garment bag in my hands, then my coat. After Baxter shakes the dusting of snow off himself, I take off his damp sweater and hang it up, too.

Baxter moves toward the study and I follow him. Inside we find Barrett sitting at his desk. Baxter saunters over to Barrett for some affection before settling into his bed near the fireplace. When I push the door the rest of the way open, his eyes find me in the doorway.

"Hey," he says, his voice deep and raspy. Just that one syllable makes my stomach flutter.

"Hey," I say, taking in the scene. His computer is off, no cell phone in sight, just a glass of scotch sitting on his desk. I glance over at my desk. Since I officially moved in, Barrett rearranged his office to fit a desk for me. I insisted I'd use it for work, but I've yet to sit at it. Instead, it's piled high with manuscripts and trade paperbacks that I've found at the used bookstore we frequent on weekends.

I edge in between him and the desk, his hands move to squeeze my hips.

"Sorry I'm late. Shopping with Emma is fun, but time consuming."

"It's fine," he says, pressing his lips softly to mine. The taste of him, a mix of scotch and spice and maleness that is distinctly Barrett, melts in my mouth.

MARRY

The WordIt word today flashes behind my closed eyes. Thinking about it again sends a rush of excitement through my body.

I had been surprised. At first, I thought it was MERRY for the upcoming holiday, but one incorrect letter had proven me wrong.

MARRY

I've been reminding myself all day that while Barrett's company owns WordIt now, he's not directly in charge of the words. And, since he confessed to purchasing the app and using it for his benefit where I was concerned, he has refrained from interfering with my favorite word game.

We've talked about it. Marriage, that is. But it's always been something we've said would be further in the future. Not four months after we officially started dating.

Barrett wraps his arms around me and I feel content.

With the snow falling outside and the fireplace casting a warm glow against every surface of the room, I'm struggling to be excited about going out tonight. I could stay here in this cozy space kissing Barrett, among other things, all night. But JoAnna is having a holiday party and it would be frowned upon if we didn't attend.

Barrett smiles. "I'm glad you had fun. Did you buy anything?"

"I found a dress for the SCM holiday party."

"I can't wait to see it."

"It's backless." I smile wickedly as Barrett narrows his gaze.

"Of course, it is," he says, kissing my neck. I give into the feel of his warm mouth for a minute, then sigh when I force myself to pull away.

"We're going to be late. I still have to change."

"You look beautiful. Don't change a thing," he says, looking up at me with adoration that I'll never get tired of.

"I'm wearing jeans. JoAnna St. Clair doesn't do jeans, you know this."

He rotates me until my ass is facing him.

"Hmm. I think she'd agree these jeans are special. Your ass looks insane." He grips me through the denim and while I'd love to stay in this moment with him, I know where it leads. Me bent over this desk. Then I'll need a shower in addition to a new outfit. There's no time for it.

I shimmy away and run for the door.

"Give me ten minutes." I rush upstairs to change.

In the car, Barrett opens a bottle of champagne.

"A holiday gift from Fred and Helen," he says, passing me a glass.

"That was sweet," I say, taking a sip of the bubbles.

Even amidst the cheating accusations, Fred did propose to Frankie. A few weeks later, he discovered for himself that she was unfaithful and took back the ring. After he and Frankie broke up, Fred ended up getting back together with his ex-wife, Helen, who he realized he was still very much in love with. Then he approached Barrett about resurrecting the deal for SCM to acquire Voltaire Telecom. They signed the deal a few months ago. Barrett asked Fred to stay on as CEO but he was all too happy to retire. He and Helen have been traveling and are expecting their first grandchild in May.

"How was your day?" I ask, trying to find a topic that doesn't involve me asking him about the WordIt word today.

"It was good. Work is slowing down. We finished wrapping up the year-end analysis. There are a few deals still in the works that we'll push until the first of the year so that everyone can take off the next two weeks."

"That's great."

"And I got my Christmas shopping done already."

"With Bea's help?"

He shakes his head. "No, I did it myself. I went to the stores and everything."

"Cheers to you doing your own Christmas shopping."

"And cheers again to your promotion." Barrett clinks my glass and smiles at me. "It was well deserved."

"Thank you."

The last few months, I've been working hard to prove myself to JoAnna, and build back her trust after Lauren's party. Last week, I officially earned the promotion to assistant editor. We celebrated with dinner at Gallagher's.

"There's so much to celebrate."

The bubbles are making me giddy.

"Like today's WordIt," I say, unable to contain it.

"What was today's WordIt?"

"When I first got some of the letters, I thought it was going to be MERRY with an E for the holidays, but it was MARRY with an A..."

"That's interesting." Barrett nods, his eyes filled with humor.

Oh God. I am reading way too much into it.

"Not that I think we're celebrating because of that. It's just a word on a game. It's not about us or anything. I'm definitely not expecting that. Maybe the programmers messed it up and it was supposed to be MERRY. It is a homophone and those can be tricky for people." I swallow back the last sip in my glass. "Forget I said that."

At that moment, we pull up to our destination. The Pierre Hotel.

Snow is still lightly falling, so Marcus walks us to the door with an umbrella.

We enter the lobby, which is quiet, and ride the elevator to JoAnna's penthouse apartment. We're not that late so it's odd there aren't other party guests arriving. When the doors open, I'm even more confused when Barrett leads me into an empty foyer, through the empty living room, and straight into the kitchen pantry.

"There's no one here. Did we get the time wrong?"

He shuts the door behind us.

"What are we doing in here?" I ask.

"This is where I do my best negotiating," he says.

"In your mother's pantry?" It's funny how the memory from six months ago of being in here with him seems foreign now. Where I once thought he was cold and dismissive, I have discovered warmth and kindness. And the disdain I had for him before? Now, I only feel love.

"Yes." He nods.

Barrett gathers my hands in his.

"Chloe Elizabeth Anderson, I've got a proposition for you."

"What is it?" I feel my eyes widen, because I'm not sure what's happening. Unless...

"I need a date." He pulls out a small velvet box from his jacket pocket and takes a knee in front of me. "For the rest of my life."

Oh my God. I can feel the tears immediately press against my lower lids. Barrett takes my shaking left hand, the other is pressed against my mouth, stifling a sob that's threatening to escape.

"You make me a better man just by knowing you. Loving you has changed me. For the better. I love you, Chloe. I want us to spend the rest of our lives together." His hazel eyes look up at me in earnest. "Will you marry me?"

I can barely get the words out, but I know my head is nodding yes, because Barrett smiles and slides the diamond onto my finger. I can't think right now. I'm overwhelmed by emotion, and the weight of the most stunning ring.

Barrett gathers me in his arms and presses his lips to mine.

"You're it for me, Chloe. I'll go at whatever pace you want. We can get married tomorrow or be engaged for two years. The only thing I care about is that you're mine and I'm yours. That's all I need."

"Tomorrow seems a little rushed. It won't give Emma much time to make a dress."

"Okay, not tomorrow." He deepens our kiss; his hands slide into my hair and I feel that delicious tug in my core building.

"I love you," I manage to tell him between kisses. "Should we go home now? I don't think I can handle having sex in your mom's pantry."

Barrett groans, running a hand through his hair. "I didn't really think this through."

"It's okay, we can be in bed in fifteen minutes."

He chuckles, takes my hand and leads me out of the pantry. This time when we enter the living room, it is filled with people. I'm beginning to understand his frustration.

"She said yes!" he announces, lifting my hand with the huge diamond ring on it while smiling down at me. Everyone cheers.

JoAnna approaches and wraps her arms around me.

"Congratulations," she says, giving me a warm hug.

Then there's Jules nearly toppling into me with excitement.

"That diamond is ginormous!" she says.

Emma, Carl, Lindsay. Colleagues from work. Bea and her husband, she introduces as Stan. My parents. Wait. *My parents.*

"I can't believe you flew to New York for this," I say, laughing through happy tears.

"Barrett is very convincing." My dad chuckles. "Especially when he picks you up in a private plane. Makes it hard to say no."

My mom rolls her eyes at him. "We wouldn't have missed it, even if we had to fly ourselves," my mom says with tears in her eyes. "We love you so much."

We greet the rest of the guests and sip on champagne.

Once everyone is mingling, Barrett and I find a quiet corner and he pulls me into his arms. My fingers stroke his midnight blue tie.

"I was wrong," he says. "I can't wait two years to marry you."

"I can't wait two years either." I press my lips to his jaw. "One year."

"Four months."

I laugh. "Six."

"Done."

There in JoAnna's penthouse apartment, where our fake dating scheme began, we celebrate our very real engagement with family and friends.

THE END

Thank You

Dear Reader,

Thank you for taking the time to read my book. I know there are a gazillion books to choose from, so readers like you who take a chance on an indie author are so appreciated. THANK YOU!

Thank you to my husband, Eric, and our kids for supporting me in my passion for writing. I couldn't do this without your love and support.

To my family, Mom, Dad, and Jenny, John and Linda, Adam and Debbie, Jill and Paul: Thank you for your continued love and support. It means the world to me!

Thank you to my friends who have supported me on this journey; asking how writing is going, buying my books and spreading the word. Thank you for your friendship and love: Amanda, Ashley, Courtney, Erica, Hadley, Kate, Sam, and Sara. Special thanks to Amanda for sharing photos of her naughty bachelorette cake that inspired the one Chloe got for Lauren's party.

About the Author

Erin Hawkins lives in Colorado with her husband and three young children. She enjoys reading, running, spending time in the mountains, reality TV and brunch that lasts all day.

Made in the USA
Thornton, CO
08/14/24 18:39:52